THE BOOK OF IZZY

BY
BEN GONSHOR

AOS Publishing, 2024

Copyright © 2024

Ben Gonshor

All rights reserved under International
and Pan-American copyright conventions

ISBN:978-1-990496-46-2

Cover Design: Jessica James

Visit AOS Publishing's website:
www.aospublishing.com

For My Family

"Pain is sitting by the desk,
writing a long letter.
The tears in its eyes,
are true and profound.

Fate, my fate..."

Itzik Manger -
Unter di khurves fun poyln
"Beneath the ruins of Poland"

1

I hate these fucking meetings.

"There are to be no photos of me from the left. It's my bad side," Mrs. Fischer admonished me.

And I'm gonna be late.

"You'll be sure to remind the photographer that my sister-in-law is never to be placed next to me or the bride. She smells something awful. Never mind, I'll tell him. She'll ruin the wedding gown if she stands anywhere near her."

The Fischer wedding. Mrs. Fischer's daughter, but you know how it is. She's been the bane of my existence for months; driving me bonkers with all matter of minutiae for a wedding she's probably been planning since the bride exited her vagina. Meetings like this make me wonder if anyone's paid a visit there since.

"Now, as soon as the ceremony finishes," she continued, "the doors to the garden are to open immediately..."

"... and the wait staff are to be ready with the crab we imported from Alaska exclusively for this event at one hundred dollars apiece," I interjected. "I've got it all written down."

"Where?! I don't see you taking notes."

"I've committed it to memory. Trust me, I sleep, breathe, and eat this gig," I lied to her. I've got a memory like a hamster.

"This what?" she asked.

"Gig. You know...wedding, event, show. Synonyms, Mrs. F."

"Young man, I've told you repeatedly not to refer to me as Mrs. F. And you will not refer to my wedding as a gig, show, event, or whatever other term that comes into your head. Where is Manny?"

Her phone rang before I could answer her.

"Yes, dear," she yammered into her phone. "I'm in a meeting about the event, what is it?"

Mrs. Meredith Fischer, real estate broker extraordinaire. Or so she would have you believe. Actually it's Mr. Fischer's father and then Mr. F. who built the real estate empire that bears the family name. The missus runs the residential arm which, if you believe my uncle, is one missed daily dose of Mrs. F.'s benzos from going to shit.

I turned to her daughter for some levity. Felicity Fallon Fischer —
yes, you read that right — had been immersed in her phone something
fierce for the last hour.

"Another shelf break off the Antarctic, triple F?" I asked, referring
to her by the nickname I'd given her.

"Huh?"

Mrs. F.'s *tsatske* daughter is one of those nauseating "umm-like-
you-know-ers," manglers of the English language whose every thought
can be communicated with just those words. It's simply a matter of the
order in which they're used. I've wanted to warn Jared, the husband-to-
be, that I think I saw her online leading the say-no-to-the-swallow
movement that I believe started trending. I've reconsidered.

"I'm sure you're getting really excited," I said to her. "We're
turning the golf club into something magical for the out-of-towners'
dinner."

"I don't golf," she replied dismissively.

"Do you pool?"

I lost track of the answer somewhere amidst the rat-tat-tat of the
above-mentioned catch-alls, all the while checking the time on my
phone.

Shit. I'm so late.

"Young man, where were we?" Mrs. Fischer chimed back in after
her call.

"Somewhere in the garden with Alaskan crab," I said, as my cousin
Manny walked in.

"Manny, lovely you could join us, dear," Mrs. Fischer said, using a
term of endearment that out of her mouth sounds more like derision.

"Sorry I'm late, Meredith. Where do things stand?"

"We've got crabs," I said to him, which elicited a chuckle from the
tsatske.

"That's fine, dear. Delighted you're here," Mrs. F. continued.
"Now, when the newlyweds enter the ballroom, there will be none of that
Jewish music."

"Come again?" I said.

"The music that's played at Jewish affairs when the bride and
groom enter," she replied. I forgot to tell you, she's a *shikse* — never
converted.

"You mean a hora?"

"If that's the Jewish music, then there will be none of that. This is a classy event."

"Yeah, you're right," I said and stood up from the table where we were meeting. "Welcoming the newlyweds into the hall for the first time as husband-and-wife to a prophetic Biblical passage, extolling the new bride and groom as harbingers of a better tomorrow, is classless. But the pig on a spit you're having placed in the center of the room for dinner is the height of refinement. I'm done here."

I then exited the room to the sounds of crickets and my cousin Manny chasing after me.

"Dude, what the hell?" he barked, pulling me back by the arm.

"What, *what the hell?* I'm sick of this."

"That's a million-dollar gig in there. Get unsick of it. Go back in and apologize."

"For what?"

"For being you."

"Go fuck yourself."

"I'm not kidding."

"I have to go. I'm late for a funeral."

"Whose?"

"Artur Knekht. You should come; he was *zaide*'s friend."

"You kidding me? You just pulled that stunt 'cause you have to rush to this guy's funeral?"

"He's the last, Manny."

"You're doing it again."

"Doing what?"

"That thing that happens with you when you go off your meds. You lose it."

"I'm not losing it, you asshole. And I'm not off my meds."

He just looked at me with the smug assuredness of catching someone in a gotcha.

"Sort of," I offered. "I'm testing the waters."

"We discussed this with my dad," he replied dismissively. "Because of your condition, you're not supposed to do that without our permission."

"First of all, you're not my doctors. Secondly, it's not a 'condition,' it's fucking depression. And lastly, I just told you I'm not going off my meds."

"Then why are you playing with them again? This gig is next week."

"Lisa left me. "

"Who?"

"Don't do that, you prick. You know who she is."

"The wedding weirdo?" he retorted, referencing her online infamy for having posted photos of her ceremony...while it was happening. The marriage lasted six months, but apparently, her profile says they're still friends, so by definition that means it worked out okay.

"Yes, her."

"When?"

"Last week. It's the fucking meds. I couldn't get it up."

"I doubt she left because you couldn't get a hard-on. Besides, you're the rock of Gibraltar, baby!"

He inherited that condescending term of endearment from my uncle. I fucking hate it. And he was referring to an erstwhile version of myself, a period during which an affected co-ed philosophy major was so taken that she felt the need to reference the great wonders of the world to describe...it. It really was a great time. One could say it was my classical period. Beginning in my late teens and reaching its apogee in my early twenties, it was a series of hits and very few misses, culminating in a torrid affair with a female professor of the Catholic persuasion who, upon first coital, felt the need to confess, as it were, that it was as if she was fucking Jesus. Which on the face of it is truly high praise, but admittedly that first encounter didn't rise to the level of a religious experience for me at least, as my mind kept racing, picturing how *he* might have, all the while wondering if the next day our secret dalliance would come undone by this latter-day Mary Magdalene beginning to spread the "Good News."

"These days, it's more like the Banana of Panama," I replied to Manny, who could appreciate the metaphor, what with his years-long regimen of hair-regrowth treatments. Drip, drip.

He may be my uncle's son, but he's actually a good kid, Manny. I wouldn't want that pressure. My uncle's an asshole. Sure, a *makher* in the music business, the biggest this side of the Mississippi, but he's not a *mentsch,* though my mother begs to differ. So, what does it all matter? We've never discussed it, but I don't think Manny ever really wanted to follow my uncle into the business. He's got eczema; I'm sure it's a sign. But he's good at it, a real entrepreneur. Something I'm not. When we were in high school, Manny, who is a few years older than me, insisted that I let him be the tour manager of the band I started. Of course, touring in those days meant nothing more than deciding whose basement the next rehearsal would be in. But Manny had ambitions, if not necessarily the thorough research skills required for the job. I'm reminded of when he came to one of our rehearsals to proudly announce that he had booked us our first gig at the finish line of a charity marathon. Manny was so proud that he got us a midday slot, one he figured was prime for audience attendance at the show. That he didn't bother to read the fine print, specifically that the race was in support of kids with ADHD who had, shockingly, all finished the marathon in record time, hours before we arrived to set up, was what you would call a slight oversight. No matter, Manny didn't sweat the small stuff.

When he went away to college at one of those Big Ten party schools, where he majored in frat with a minor in hash, he saw it not so much as an opportunity to grow as a person as much as one to evolve as a businessman. And he did. To this day, he is revered as the finest party promoter in the annals of Big Ten history, which, if you've read your Big Ten history, is truly saying something. And that's where he met Veronica, his dimwitted, *shikse* wife, with whom he has two beautiful children whose names I can never remember — they're named after natural things, like rain or river or some related *narishkeit*.

He was right, in a way, to dismiss Lisa. We hadn't been together long, and even that, being together, stretches the bounds of credulity. Life hasn't been easy since Her. I'm not saying she's the one that caused all this. My therapist says it's giving her too much credit for the demons of my own making. Paid a week's salary for that nugget, thank you very much. We've agreed to settle on Her being the straw that broke the camel's back and that, in looking back at my life, I was a wreck waiting to happen. My words, of course, though my doc being a chain-smoking hardass from Bed-Sty, she wouldn't have said it much differently. You can't blame her, what with her career making turn as the chief therapist at Attica, post-riots. My honor, I suppose. Anyway, it's been three years since Her, bouncing from one pill to the next as each one fizzles out, and the rush is on to get the next one into the system before the bad shit kicks in again. Sometimes I feel like I'm doing all this for somebody else's benefit. Manny, my uncle, even my doc. "You're fine. You're right where you need to be," is what one of my tree-hugging friends on the West Coast always tells me. My therapist's retort when she initially heard this was, "if talking you off your balcony every six months is where 'you need to be,' then let *him* be your doctor and see how that goes."

She exaggerates; it's not that bad. Or maybe it is, and I don't know anymore. These fucking meds. As far as I'm concerned, once they've got them in you, you're doomed. Penis killers, I call them. You know what I'm talking about. The first time after Her was a nightmare. And it's been a desultory series of shooting crap in the dark ever since. "I'll prescribe a pill for that," my doc said, the appointment after that first aforementioned unsuccessful attempt. "You won't believe how many men your age I've got taking them," she continued, leading me to believe that we're all just pawns in some sick and twisted game of theirs - whereby the winner of most hard-on medications prescribed wins a trip to Mars, to which I hear the inventor of the pills already has dibs on renaming rights.

"You know what she said to me when she left?" I said to Manny, speaking of Her. "'You're not what I need.'"

"I know, Izzy. I know."

"I still have the ring."

"It'll take time, however long. But you can't go off your medication. My father won't allow it. And to tell you the truth, I can't either. You just can't keep doing this."

"I have to get to the funeral."

"I can't let you leave until you go back in there and apologize to Mrs. Fischer and her daughter."

"Fine," I said, and we walked back into the room where Meredith and Fallon were each engrossed in their phones. I then approached Mrs. Fischer and sat next to her at the table.

"Mrs. Fischer," I said in a dulcet, contrite tone. "Please accept my sincere apologies for my outburst. It was disrespectful, rude, and simply unacceptable. I'm truly, truly sorry."

Which went nowhere.

"Manny, this imbecile has serious mental problems and I refuse to have him working on my wedding."

"That's it," I said, slamming my palm on the table and then headed for the door when Triple F stopped me.

"Wait, umm, like, stay, you know," she said.

"Thanks, Fallon," I replied, "but I have a *levayeh* to attend."

"A what?!" Mrs. Fischer shot back.

"It's Yiddish for funeral. I look forward to attending yours soon."

Looking at Manny as I left, I knew there was another conversation to be had with him in the not-too-distant future.

2

It always struck me as totally douchey that the first thing you see when you enter the foyer of Mendelman's funeral home is a life-sized portrait of the *pater familias*, Lou. It's got that Rembrandt feel to it, apparently by design, as the commission stated explicitly that the artist should make liberal use of *chiaroscuro*. The old man believed it served to evoke a sense of doom and gloom that was good for business. And make no mistake, the death business has been good to the Mendelmans. Mind you, not that I completely begrudge them the success. *You* go and find someone who would choose to be in that line of work. But the Ferrari he drives around town, I think, is a little much. Every time I see it, I want to key his car and leave a note to the effect that he should remember that he'd made millions on the backs of the community's mourners. I tried it once, but when I was told, by the gentleman who had the same idea I did, that the Mendelmans increased their annual pledge by a considerable sum, I reconsidered; if only for the sake of the indigent who benefited. Anyway, the Italian social hall that is Mendelman's funeral home is a big, cold venue with many rooms to cry in; each one is named appropriately enough after one of Jacob's sons. And the sign listing the day's funerals as I walked in said that Artur Knekht's was in the smallest one, the Benjamin.

As it turns out, I arrived early. Don't tell Manny. But still, it pisses me off that I was the only one in the room other than the token quorum of men scattered about, mumbling verses of Psalms to themselves. Another sign of the times. For this, Knekht got to live to the ripe old age of ninety-nine? To die alone with no one in the room who had any idea who he was or what he stood for? I'm sure had he known this is what he had to look forward to, he would have told them at seventy-five to keep the triple bypass and chosen instead to die then and there. At least then he would have been surrounded by his comrades from the Jewish socialist movement, a.k.a. the Bund, who would have sent him off with a proper funeral, complete with poetry and song and tributes from those who would have given meaning to the occasion. That's how I remember them, the funerals for my *zaide* and his friends. They would be filled to the rafters with the men and women whose lives were forever changed by Hitler, but who nevertheless found the strength to persevere and

8

immigrate to this country with nothing but the shirts on their backs, to build a new life based on the values and ideals inculcated in them by the Bund. Without the blood relatives who didn't make it, friends became family. And when it came time for each of them to leave this world, they did so with peace of mind. Their "family" would see to it that they received the send-off that befitted an individual who had come through the ashes, yet somehow continued striving to build a world based on equality, social justice, and *mentshlekhkayt*. But instead, we're left with what, an empty room but for a bunch of alcoholic *schnorers* living off the Mendelman teat? *Az och un vey*, it just bites.

Chirp.

"I can't believe it's so empty," Faygen said as he entered the pew and sat down beside me.

"I know, I was just thinking the same thing."

"*Az och un vey.*"

"Yup."

" *Vus hert zikh?*" he asked.

"I've been better," I replied.

"Work?"

"Work, life, everything...I dunno. My book got rejected again."

"I'm sorry to hear that."

"Whatever."

"Did they give a reason?"

"Yeah, too 'Holocaust-y.'"

"They didn't say that. You're exaggerating."

"Actually, they kinda did. I was on speaker in my agent's office, listening in on her conversation with some *tzatzke* assistant, and that's kind of how she put it."

"I'm sure it's disappointing."

"You think?" I said, my voice dripping.

"Have you talked to any of your friends in Los Angeles about it?"

"It's a novel, not a screenplay."

"I know, but you did well there. Maybe someone can help."

I said nothing, as I'd been down this road a zillion times regarding my time in L.A. Yes, I did well, but I fucking hated it. And rightfully so, as far as I'm concerned. From the moment I got up to ask a question at the end of our first seminar in film school, I was branded as "that weird guy." In case you're wondering, I deigned to ask a top studio executive whether William Goldman was right when he said that "nobody knows anything" in Hollywood. From the looks I got from my classmates, you'd think I'd asked the Pope whether he wears underwear under the costume. But following the "you'll never eat lunch in this town again" dressing down I got the next morning from the aforementioned studio tool, I knew La La Land wouldn't be the place for me. Not to say that I didn't make good use of my time there. Over the course of that first year, I'd made friends with a fellow malcontent in the program, who decided to make better use of his time and money by converting his summer internship into a full-time desk gig with one of the hotshot MP Lit agents over at ICM. Maybe it was UTA. Or another agency with a *farkakte* name. I dunno, it doesn't matter. Suffice it to say, he saw where the money was printed, if not where the bodies were buried, and that was on Wilshire Boulevard. I had other ideas, as me getting up every morning at the crack of dawn to put on a pin-striped Brooks Brothers, only to spend the next fourteen hours taking it up the ass from some *putz* with a small one, struck me as way more Wall Street than Sunset. For some reason, he got off knowing he was inches away from a guy who, as it turns out, is serving three life sentences today for nothing having to do with agenting. That privilege wasn't why I was there. Truth be told, looking back on it, I don't know why I was there. Wait, that's wrong. I do. I had an important story I wanted to tell, which I soon learned nobody was interested in. Not "high concept" enough, which to the uninitiated, is Hollywood shorthand for "no superheroes, no dice." Regardless, we made a good team, him and me. I could write, and he needed to build a roster. Within six months, he was off the desk, got poached by a rival who gave him one of his own, and I sold my first spec to a shingle with a housekeeping deal at Paramount. I won't lie; there's something to be said for six figures, lattes, and flip-flops. But at the end of the day, I wasn't telling the story I came to tell. He knew it. With every paint-by-numbers assignment he landed me, I thanked him by complaining that it was all grist towards the fall of civilization. And it didn't help that I expressed as much in the meetings I took, which I should tell you, culminated in a particularly awkward *rendez-vous* he scheduled for me with a D-girl over at Warners. Admittedly, I was hungover and the traffic through Laurel made me particularly ornery that morning. But when she decided to act smarter than she had any right to be by suggesting I reference the latest binge sensation in the next draft, I just lost it on her: "No, I'm not gonna make it more *Breaking Bad!"* I yelled at her. "It's a fucking cartoon, you dimwit!" The long and the short of it: My erstwhile buddy's now a *macher* agent in Hollywood who doesn't take my calls, I plan weddings for my cousin, and my book is never getting published.

"I spoke with your mother yesterday," Faygen continued, changing the subject. "She says you're not getting along with Manny again. Are you okay?"

You notice he said "mother," not "mom." He's formal like that, Faygen is. You'd expect that from a guy who wears ascots, bowties, and socks with sandals.

"Yeah, I'm fine," I replied. "It is what it is. Nothing's gonna change."

"It saddens me that you're unhappy," he said before a light bulb went off."It just occurred to me."

"What?"

"I might have something for you if you're looking for a change. I've got a big case I'm working on."

I should pause here to tell you a bit about Abraham Faygen, because he's like a dad to me and one of the few people I'm close to. Yes, he's a lawyer. Labor. Which makes sense as, like my mom, he's a child of the Bund and has dedicated his life to the Left. Although, he even admits that these days the Left isn't what it was, and he's finding it harder to find his place there. Regardless, he's all about fighting the good fight and never letting bad people get away with doing bad things. That's something in today's world. I don't say this in front of him because I don't like blowing smoke up people's asses, but between you and me, he's a fucking genius. I'm serious, like MENSA smart. I know that to be true because any kid who can recite Peretz's *Monish* by heart at the age of five is either wicked smart or has serious psychological issues. In his case, I think it's a little from both columns. I never knew his father as he died quite young, years before I was born. He was a Ph.D. in Economics, which for a dude from the Polish town of Chelm, is saying something. But that meant little to the gang at the *Arbeter Ring*, the Workmen's Circle, where his real clout was chairing the Zyglboim branch and the august Labour Relations *komitet*. If that wasn't enough to make the ladies in the auxiliary wet, the fact that he was the only one with a car for grocery runs is what really made him a stud. As for Mrs. Faygenbaum, she survived Auschwitz, but only after having the privilege of having her first child ripped from her arms and thrown out a third-story balcony window during the roundup moments before she and her first husband, Mendl, got herded onto the train. Mercifully, as these things go, he succumbed to starvation before arrival at the death camp. So, I guess she could be forgiven for not having her shit together when raising *Avreml* as an only child after the war. I don't know what happened to her there, but she ended up with an oral hygiene obsession and a myriad of other neurotic, compulsive tics and tendencies that she unwittingly passed onto her son. Maybe that's why he's single. I dunno, I'm guessing because despite the genteel, confident intellectual exterior, he's actually a completely insecure, nervous wreck. I sometimes think he'd rather spend his free time kicking back with a fine single malt and getting off on the latest issue of the *New Yorker* than figuring out how to get off. I don't delve. We've all got our *pekl*. Actually, I always thought he and my mom should hook up. They've been close friends since they were kids, both having grown up in the Bundist world of ideas, culture, and politics, which in their cases, amounted to living out their adult lives carrying a torch for a lost world and living with the complex of knowing that they'll never measure up. It's essential to have things in common, right? Anyway, it's a real shame where Faygen's concerned because I've been told that watching him litigate is high art, even when you allow for his neurotic habit of flossing in public when he gets nervous and excited.

CHIRP.

"No thanks, Faygen," I said to him and began to look around to see where the noise was coming from.

CHIRP.

"I didn't even tell you what the case is yet."

"Do you hear that?" I asked as the sound continued getting louder.

"Hear what?"

CHIRP. CHIRP.

"You don't hear it? It's like there's a bird in here somewhere."

"I don't."

"It's getting louder! You don't hear it?!"

"Izzy, I don't hear anything. Maybe outside?"

"No, it's like it's right here!"

CHIRP! CHIRP! CHIRP!

"WHAT THE FUCK!" I shouted as I turned towards the window at the far side of the room and jumped out of my seat at the sight of its massive shadow hovering above the ledge outside.

The *schnorers* in the room all raised their heads from their holy books and looked at me with gazes of derision as I'd caused them to lose their place, which meant they had to start reading Psalms over from the beginning. It's true. It's written.

"What's wrong?" Faygen said and looked at me with deep concern.

CHIRP! CHIRP! CHIRP!

"Look! Don't you see it?" I said, pointing at the window.

"What? See what? There's nothing there, Izzy."

"Are you fucking blind?" I yelled back at him.

"Izzy, there's nothing in the window."

He was right. There wasn't...

...It was gone.

And so, too, was the noise.

"Never mind," I said calmly as I sat back down.

"My god, Izzy. You're shaking. What did you see?"

"Nothing," I replied, knowing better than to say anything more. I've been here before...seeing things.

But this time, it was different.

"I'm fine. I'm sorry," I said to him, which I repeated loudly for the *schnorers'* benefit as well.

"Don't apologize. But you're not fine."

"I am. I really am. It's the meds. That's all it is. Just the fucking meds." We sat in awkward silence for a minute or so as there was nothing more to say other than I'd freaked him out.

"Izzy," Faygen eventually began again as he removed his warm blanket from his breast pocket and began to floss his teeth. "I'm worried," he continued. "What can I do to help?"

"Nothing, I'm in a rut. I'll come out of it. I always do."

"You don't deserve to suffer like this. You need something in your life that makes you happy."

"We all do."

"Do you think you'd be interested in getting involved in theatre again?"

"Why do you ask?"

"I've been asked to participate in the Yiddish Theatre's new production."

"They're still around?"

"Believe it or not."

"I had no idea."

"It's The *Dybbuk*."

"Great choice."

"They need a good Khonen," he said as he looked at me earnestly, referencing the main character in the play.

"I haven't been on stage since I was a kid."

"You're a natural. I already told Luba I'd talk to you."

"Haven't heard that name in ages. She's still breathing?"

"Yes. She remembers you well."

"Not my thing, but thanks for asking."

"Say you'll think about it."

"No."

Before he could reply, the *schnorers* stood as a sign of respect for Knekht, whose modest casket was now being wheeled into the room by another one of their ilk. He placed it at the front of the little stage that normally would be the place for invited speakers, who would now begin to eulogize the deceased. But seeing as how there were no next of kin nor comrades to speak for him and certainly no rabbi or cantor, an awkward silence fell upon the room as, one by one, the *schnorers* began to turn their gaze in mine and Faygen's direction as if looking for guidance on what to do.

"This is awful," I said to Faygen.

"It is."

"Should we sing *Di Shvue*?"

"It would be the appropriate thing to do," he replied.

And so to honour Knekht, the last of my *zaide*'s generation, the likes of whom we'll never fucking see again, me and Faygen stood up and proudly sang the anthem of the Jewish Labour Bund, *Di Shvue,* "The Oath." When we finished, the *schnorers* continued looking at us for what to do next.

"That's it, guys," I said. "We're done; you can wheel him out."

The *schnorers* heeded my instruction and began to escort Knekht towards the exit as Faygen and I fell in line behind them.

"Do you know where he's being buried?" I asked Faygen.

"In the *Arbeter Ring* section," he answered.

"Good. I'm glad."

"Are you coming to the cemetery?" Faygen asked me as the door to the parking lot opened, and the *schnorers* began to place Knekht's casket into a waiting hearse.

"You know the answer to that question," I told him.

"Figured I'd ask," he replied. We stood silent for a moment, watching as the hearse pulled away.

"That's it, Faygen. The last of 'em," I finally said, doing my best not to let the finality of the moment get to me, which frankly it was. "It hurts."

"It certainly does," he replied, putting his hand on my shoulder. "I'll call you later to see how you're doing, okay?"

"Yeah, sure, thanks. But I'm fine, really."

"No, you're not. But you will be."

And as we parted ways, I headed towards the parking lot, where I could see a flock of birds resting quietly atop a beautiful old oak tree, yet the one I saw was nowhere to be found.

3

I arrived at my mother's place a little early to help out with last-minute preparations for the Passover *seder* when Soffy, her longtime Filipina housekeeper who pronounces it *so*-fee, greeted me at the door excitedly.

"Hi, sweetie," she exclaimed and gave me a hug. "Yumtum."

"*Gut yontef* to you too, Soffy," I said, referencing the Yiddish greeting for the Jewish holidays she'd somewhat added to her vocabulary.

"No suit?!" she asked and looked me over disapprovingly. "Oh, your mom gonna be pissed," she continued as we entered and made our way towards the kitchen, where I could already smell the sweet signs of Passover. I long ago stopped complaining about her running commentary on my life, figuring anyone who wiped before I could was entitled to an opinion. And for the most part, she tended to be correct. Like now.

"What's wrong?" my mother asked soon after Soffy and I entered the kitchen, where my mother was finishing the evening's menu.

"What I say?" Soffy winked and began making her way toward the dining room with a tray of bowls filled with salt water.

"Nothing," I replied to my mother and gave her a kiss. "Smells awesome."

"Come taste the soup; I can't tell," she said. "You ok?"

"Yeah, fine."

"I don't think so."

"Why?" I asked.

"You're wearing jeans for *yontef*?"

"With a fucking tie, thank you for noticing," I replied, nonplussed.

She gave me that look she'd developed exclusively for me over the years to avoid having to say what she didn't want to have to, but always did anyway."

"Already you're fucking?"

We have that kind of relationship, you should know. She calls me on my shit, me on hers. My mother, my friend. Truth, I'm lucky to have her.

"Just tell me what you need help with, please," I said by way of moving on.

"The eggs have to be sliced and put into bowls, *matzah*'s on the table, and the *haggadah*'s as usual in the dining room," she shorthanded while waving her arm around to orchestrate for effect. Meanwhile, Soffy had returned to the kitchen.

"When I come clean?" she asked, remembering my sty of an apartment and handed me an egg slicer.

"I'll let you know."

"I'm sure it's filthy," my mother chimed in and lifted a ladle of soup to her lips. "Taste," she said and gestured it in my direction. "More salt, what?" she asked, knowing full-well I know nothing from these things and that it didn't really matter anyway.

"It's fine," I said.

"The soup or the apartment?" she asked, then added more salt.

"Both."

Ever the democrat, she took another ladleful and brought it over to her diminutive sidekick for an equal opportunity *shmeck*.

"Perfect, sweetie," Soffy said.

"So, do you want to tell me what's wrong?" my mother asked me.

"Nothing, I just didn't feel like a suit," was my pathetic attempt at a reply.

It was a bullshit answer. *Yontef* has always been special to me, and she knew it. Here she was, regally *farpitzed* for the occasion— as she always is, truth be told, even with an apron on—and I couldn't get my shit together for the first night of Passover. She gets it from her mother, that instinct—a gift, really—of knowing how to make *yontef* well, *yontefdik*. She passed when I was young, my *bubbe*, so I didn't have the privilege of knowing her in the way those who did felt privileged. The one thing I do remember were her dying words to me: "Be a *mentsch*," she said when they brought me to visit her in the hospital a few short hours before she passed. To this day, I don't know what the fuck it means other than feeling a deep pit of guilt in my stomach knowing full well that jeans for *yontef* don't cut it. The fact that I managed a tie is a small victory, as far as I'm concerned. It's been rough going since the funeral.

"Have you seen Dr. G. lately?" my mother asked, knowing that the last few days' events deserved a visit to my shrink.

And, of course, she knew what had happened without me having to tell her.

"No offense, Ma, but I'm not paying her three hundred bucks to talk about a stupid breakup," I said and began cutting the eggs a little faster.

"You know I'll pay."

I gave her that look I'd developed exclusively for her over the years to avoid having to say what I didn't want to have to, but always did anyway.

"Fuck off, Ma," I said, but in the totally loving way that she appreciates.

"Manny called me," she continued, letting my *mishegas* go.

"Of course he did," I said, not slightly annoyed that we were going there.

"He's worried."

"No, he's not."

I began cutting even faster.

"Hank, too," she said referring to my uncle, Manny's dad and technically my boss.

"I definitely know *he's* not."

"Stop it. He loves you and cares about you very much."

"No, he doesn't," I said while Soffy nudged me aside if only to relieve the eggs. "He only cares about himself and his fucking business."

"That's not true. He told me he has something important he wants to talk to you about."

"Whatever," I replied, moving on to my next official task and started opening boxes of *matzah.*

"You didn't tell me you're dating," my mother said, and went to the turkey in the oven with a baster in hand.

"I'm not anymore."

"Manny said you were quite upset about it," she said, and gave the roasting bird a good *shpritz.*

"Not about this one," I replied, and she knew what I meant.

"I don't want to talk about Her. It's *yontef.*"

"You're the one who brought it up."

"So that's why you're wearing jeans?"

"No. Maybe. I dunno."

She came over to me and squeezed my face in her hands together with the baster pressing against my cheek.

"You are an incredible young man...," she said, and kissed me "...deserving of love...," kissing me again, "...and you will find someone who recognizes what a gift you are to the world," and again. "Like Jessica," she said, smiling, and trying one more kiss before I ended it.

"And...we're done," I said, extricating myself from the emasculation and took a few of the *matzah* boxes in hand.

"You know I'm right," my mother called out as I headed for the dining room.

"Yeah, yeah."

My entire life, I've refused to give her the satisfaction of admitting that, in hindsight, she was right that the best that ever entered my life was a ninth-grade crush who got me better than any other woman that I've crossed paths with since. Not that anyone really has, mind you. Not since I built walls and started running from myself. Yes, ladies, that's correct. A man just wrote that last sentence. Cost me *way* more than three hundred bucks, you should know, I don't admit it much — actually, ever. The walls and the running, I mean. There have been others that I thought knew me, like Her. But at a time when my world was shattered, and I felt no one could possibly comprehend the loss, somehow Jessica, the girl with the braces and the bottle curls, got it. Ninth grade, go figure.

My thoughts turned to him, my *zaide*, as I entered the dining room, where I placed the *matzahs* on the *seder* table that was set just as it always has been: My *bubbe*'s fine china and crystal that my mother uses only for special occasions; the floral centerpiece signifying spring; the horseradish; the celery sticks; *Haroset*; the egg; the shank...*yontef*. While nibbling on a piece of celery, I took the *hagaddah's* out from my mother's antique cupboard and began walking around the table, putting them down at every place setting, each one bringing back a memory of people and a time that has long since passed. As it does every year, melancholy came calling when my hands touched the suede cover of the *haggadah* from my youth — my *zaide*'s gift to me when I stood on the chair next to his at the head of the table to sing my first "How is This Night Different?" At that moment, I could swear I felt the table beginning to shake, like it always did when the clock ticked somewhere between the morning hours of two and three on *seder* night, and Faygen and my mother started tapping out a hypnotic, rhythmic beat. "*Iztikl,* are you ready?" my *zaide* would shout excitedly as he lifted me up onto his lap and began bouncing me on his knee to the rhythm. Of course I was, as this was when he concluded our *seder* by singing his signature song of the night, "Who Knows One?"

"*Zaide?*" I said to him a little while later as he tucked me into bed.

"Yes," he replied and sat down next to me.

"Why do you sing 'Who Knows One'?"

"What do you mean?"

"It's about God, and you don't believe in Him."

"That's right, I don't."

"So why do you sing it?"

"Well, what do we sing about in the song?" he answered, beginning our frequent Socratic bedtime ritual.

"The *Sabbath* and the *Mishnah.*"

"And what else?"

"The *Torah.*"

"And?"

"Abraham, Isaac, and Jacob.'

"And the matriarchs, too," he added.

"Yeah. The mammas."

"And what else?"

"The tablets."

"And what's written on the tablets?"

"The ten commandments."

"That's right," he said.

"And then we sing about God, who created them."

"Maybe."

"Yudl believes he did," I said, referring to his in-law, who was a believer.

"He does."

"But you don't. I don't understand." He smiled and caressed my forehead as he began his reply.

"You're right, Yudl believes that the things we sing about in the song came to us directly from God, and I don't. I believe they're part of a great story that people wrote a long time ago that describes how the Jewish people came to be. But we both believe all these things are very important."

"Is that okay?"

"Is what okay?"

"That you don't believe what he believes?"

"I think so."

"It's okay because you're both Jews?"

"That's right," he smiled. "We're one people. I respect him, and he respects me."

"But why do you make me sit with you when he reads through the parts of the *haggadah* fast like it's hard to understand. Nobody else pays attention."

"That doesn't mean you shouldn't either. It's important to him. And because it's important to him, it should be important to you too."

"Why?"

"Because it's *kedusheh*."

"What does that mean?"

"What does it mean?" he chuckled softly in a way that suggested that although what he was about to say was plain and simple, it nevertheless carried the weight of all Jewish history in its message. And I could tell because his eyes began to well up as he spoke: "It means, Itzikl...*az a yid darf visn*. No matter what you do in life, you can separate yourself from belief, but not from knowledge and not from the Jewish people. You understand?"

"I think so," I said and wiped the moisture that fell from his eyes onto my cheek. "I like when you sing the song. It makes everyone happy."

"And the sound of happy song and salvation are in the tents of the righteous," he replied.

"What does that mean?"

"What did I just teach you?"

"That a Jew must know."

"Good. That's what it means," he said before pausing for a moment. "You really want to know why I sing the song?" he asked.

"Yeah."

"Because it reminds me of my mother, and she made me really happy," he said. "She learned it from my *bubbe*, and now you sing it too. And that makes me happy. And one day, I hope you'll sing to your children also."

"*Di goldene keyt*," I answered, which elicited a wide grin and more tears.

"Who told you about that?"

"You did. It's the golden chain of Jewish history that ties every generation together."

"That's right. It is," he replied with a big smile and kissed me goodnight.

It felt like I stared at the suede *haggadah* for an eternity before I finally set it down on my plate and headed back to the kitchen.

"Faygen called me after the *levayeh*," my mother said regarding Knekht's funeral.

Although she had by now finished her prep, she was still wearing her apron while leaning against the stove, smoking a cigarette and sipping a glass of Chianti while Soffy washed dishes.

"Of course he did," I replied with not a little bit of sarcasm. "I know," I continued before she could, "he's worried too. Everybody's worried."

"Would it be enough if it was just me?"

I avoided going there.

"You gonna drink the bottle yourself?" I chided her regarding the wine and went to take a glass from the cupboard.

"I didn't think you should be drinking."

"Talk about the pot calling the kettle black," I quipped and poured myself a glass.

"Izzy, stop it. This isn't about me."

"And I told you I'm fine," I replied, and joined her for a smoke.

"He said you were hallucinating."

"He doesn't know what he's talking about," I lied.

"I'm worried about you."

"I wasn't hallucinating!" I jumped down her throat irrationally. "Nobody was at the fucking funeral...the last one...and it pissed me off, so I vented loudly about it. That's it. Fuck!"

Soffy stopped washing and stared at me. "Sorry," I said to her. "I know Jesus wouldn't have said 'fuck.'"

She rolled her eyes, crossed herself, and returned to the dishes.

"Izzy," my mother said, and looked at me like parents do when their child's pain hits them where it hurts, and they know there's nothing they can do about it.

The doorbell rang.

"I'll get it," my mother said to Soffy. "I don't want to let this go," she said to me while putting out her cigarette. "We need to talk about what's going on. I'm not judging."

"Thank you."

"By the way," she said while removing her apron, "Faygen told me it was your idea to sing *Di Shvue*."

"It was."

"That's my boy," she said with a smile. "He would be so proud," she continued, referencing my *zaide*, then planting an infantilizing kiss on my lips before exiting the kitchen to get the door.

My heart started beating a little faster when she returned a few minutes later with my uncle Hank in tow.

Shit.

He looked like he just got off his Gulfstream from god-knows-where, all tanned and dressed sharp as usual in a bespoke blue pin-stripe with matching silk red necktie, pocket square, shoes from an Italian house he owns, and those gaudy gold-plated HF-initialed links he always wears that you can barf from.

"*Gut yontef!*" he said, announcing his presence like a show was about to start and apparently, we're all in for a treat.

He walked over to greet Soffy, who was by now drying dishes.

"Yumtum, sweetie," she said to him. "Where's Fayge?" she asked about my aunt.

"She's coming soon with Manny and the kids."

Hank then came over to me and gave me a perfunctory hug.

"Good to see you, kid," he said, and I was polite in return.

Though Hank doesn't drink, he does enjoy an occasional *l'khaim* so my mother had meanwhile fetched the McCallan 18 he keeps her stocked with and poured him two fingers before refilling her glass of wine and lighting up another cigarette.

They clinked, wished each other well, and then he got down to business.

"You doing okay?" he asked me rhetorically. "I heard what happened with the Fischers."

Of course, he did, and I really wasn't getting into it with him now either, if I didn't have to.

"Who are the Fischers?" my mother asked, blowing out a puff of smoke.

"Remember Mendl Fischer?" my uncle said to her.

"The little Lodzer with the candies?" my mother answered in that typical form of East European Jewish geography, particularly common among survivors.

"Yeah, his grandkid's getting married," Hank replied. "We're doing the gig."

That's right. My uncle, one of the biggest *knackers* in showbiz, still keeps track of the weddings and bar mitzvahs he has Manny running via his Kool Katz Entertainment shingle back home. And if you think I'm kidding when I tell you he knows everything that's happening, down to the last detail, at the business that launched his empire, you don't know my uncle Hank.

"So what happened with the Fischers?" my mother asked.

"They don't want a *hora*," Hank said.

See what I mean?

"It's a Jewish wedding?" she asked again.

"It is," he answered.

"Then I don't get it."

Hank looked at me and then called me to the principal's office.

"Do you want to explain to your mother what happened?"

"Seriously, Hank?" I replied and looked at him, hoping against hope he could sense that I just couldn't and that he'd drop it.

"Dead serious, kid."

What did Einstein say about insanity? Now my palms were sweating too. Shit, it's starting.

"Fine," I said. "I told Mrs. F. I thought not having a *hora* at a Jewish wedding is a bad idea."

"And then you told her to drop dead," Hank clarified.

"You didn't," my mother said in shock.

"Not exactly. Sort of. Yeah, I guess I did," I said, wiping my jeans with the sweat from my palms.

"Oh, Izzy!" she said in that tone that makes you feel like you'll never do anything right.

"For Christ's sake!" I pushed back. "A Jewish wedding without a *hora*. What the fuck is that?"

"A client," Hank said, using the first of his standard teaching moments.

"Then why come to us?" I shouted. "That's who we are, Hank. It's what we do. You, of all people, know that!"

"You're right, Iz. But that's not your call," he replied, using his second more quickly than I anticipated.

"It's bullshit!" I fumed. I was now observing my hands running up and down my thighs and that weak feeling in my knees started to appear. Shit. Shit.

"Is that what you came early tonight to talk to Izzy about?" my mother said to Hank with concern.

"Yes and no."

"So what, you here to fire me?" I asked, fighting to stay in the moment.

"Would the two of you just calm down," he said. "I came here early to talk to you, Izzy, because I'm worried."

"Of course, everybody's worried," I replied sarcastically, which caused my mother to give me a look of displeasure.

"You're a talented kid with a ton of potential," he continued. "I told your mother I have big plans for you with the company, a great future..."

There's a but coming for sure.

"...but we had a deal."

Yup...and "the deal," which, of course, means...

"Oh, Izzy! You didn't stop taking your medication, did you?" my mother asked, girding herself for the answer she didn't want to hear.

I didn't reply, as the unwanted intervention now had me almost totally focused on my HPA axis and wondering how soon before my mind took me to places I didn't want to be.

So, Hank did it for me.

"It's okay, Manny told me," he said.

"Told you what?" my mother asked.

"Izzy's having problems."

Fuck me. Is he really going there?

"He's fine, Hank," my mother said, coming to my defense. "He broke up with his girlfriend. That's not a problem."

Hank looked at me and then, *mano a mano*...

"It's okay," he said, pointing at my crotch. "There are pills for that, and they're great. I use them all the time. But if you want to continue to have a job with me," he said to me now as my boss, "you're going back on your medication. You got that?"

"Izzy," my mother said wistfully and gazed at me as if wanting to reach out to help but not knowing how to because, well, you know.

If I was in my right mind, I probably would have taken a moment to sit with the embarrassment and come up with a witty deflection. But at times like this, when you've got no bandwidth...kaboom.

"I didn't stop taking the meds because I can't get it up!" I lied, yelling at both of them. "I stopped because they're fucking with my head, and I can't fucking write, okay!"

"You can't what?" Hank asked, oblivious to my irrational outburst.

"Don't pretend like you didn't hear me, Hank."

"What are you talking about?"

"He's writing a book," my mother said, and I could sense that she got that I was looking for a lifeline.

"You're writing a book," he said to me, patronizingly.

"He is, Hank," my mother said. "It's about Daddy."

"By the way," I said to my mother, "it got rejected, again."

"Oh, Izzy," she said and I could see her eyes starting to well up.

"Why are you writing a book about my father?" Hank said in a tone that came off accusatory.

"Because somebody needs to give a shit about him," I said derisively.

"Watch it, kid," Hank admonished me.

"It's beautiful," my mother said, tears streaking down her cheeks. "He's been working on it for years and is very passionate about it."

"Is that right," my uncle said coldly and then added with a derisive chuckle, "Go figure, just like your old man."

"Hank, how dare you!" my mother shot back at him and began weeping openly in response to his referencing the man I never knew, the individual who left him high-and-dry back in the day when they had a *simkhe* band together to pursue other interests which, as it happened, also didn't include my mother or me.

"Well, I hope you're not romanticizing my father into the person your mother would have you believe he was," Hank said, ice cold.

"Hank, that's enough," my mother wept. "It's *yontef*."

"It's okay, Ma," I said and turned to my uncle.

"I know you resent me, Hank," I said to him, my mouth now completely dry and hands trembling.

"Izzy," my mother said, trying to stop me.

"No, Ma, let me finish."

And I continued, my voice rising. "You resent me because I look like your father and remind you of my own. As far as I'm concerned, I turned out like the right one and I'm glad I did. I don't need my mother to paint a romanticized version of *zaide*, because I knew him and loved him. And I know that if he were here today, he'd tell you that he doesn't give a shit how fucking rich and powerful you are, but that you should show a little compassion to your own flesh and blood who are hurting, and be a fucking *mentsch*, you asshole."

My mother sobbed at the sight of the tears flowing down my cheeks as I finished.

"I'm sorry, Ma. I can't," I said to her and went to leave.

"Izzy, wait!" she exclaimed and then to Hank, "Why did you do that to him?!"

"Anna, I didn't, I was just..." he answered and likewise called to me. "Izzy!"

I didn't turn back. I left the kitchen and headed for the door, wiping the tears from my eyes.

"Izzy!" I heard my mother's calling again. "He was at Artur Knekht's funeral this week," she told Hank. "Faygen said something terrible happened to him there."

"I didn't know," he said to her. "I wouldn't have said anything to him tonight."

"Izzy!" They both called to me one last time before I walked out and slammed the door behind me.

4

I flushed the toilet, then washed my face and brushed my teeth for what I think was the third time since I arrived at the Savoy Hotel earlier that afternoon to coordinate the Fischer wedding. I know there are all kinds of clever aphorisms for how perfectly normal it is to be nervous before a show, but the way my uncle Hank put it to me was much more prosaic: "Nobody will deal with an event planner with the smell of puke on their breath," he said. "Have a toothbrush with you at all times and keep your shit together." This was typical of him because his bravado was a total sham, belying the fact that back in the day he suffered from a similar debilitation and, according to my mother, would expectorate his dinner before the first set of every gig he and my dad ever played. So, there you have it, nervous puking is a genetic abnormality. I'm sure you can look it up.

Truth be told, that sick feeling in the pit of the stomach that is neither a manifestation of a disease nor a sign of anything going on in your gut—what the professionals refer to as "anticipatory anxiety"—is more than just a minor nuisance I have to deal with every time I feel like somebody's *simkhe* is riding on my ability, to quote my dear uncle, *to keep my shit together.* Not to put too fine a point on it, but the stark reality is that it's a brutally painful reflection of how wrong the road of life has turned, where it seems like there's nothing at the end but a cliff and a wide, untraversable chasm, leading to certain death that you're powerless to avoid. So the professionals, with all due respect, can go fuck themselves. Now, with all that said, I like my cousin Manny, and this Fischer wedding is really important to him. Besides, I think my mother would fall to pieces if she found out I bailed. Not during the same week when she learned that my book's not getting published; that according to Faygen I lost my marbles at Knekht's funeral; and then wrapped it all up in a nice little wacko bow by crapping out on Passover, which according to Faygen, cast a pall over the whole *seder* and left her inconsolable. So, I was determined to make this night a success, if only for my flesh and blood.

I was really on the clock, as the limited attendance ceremony in the boardroom on the second floor was about done, guests had already begun arriving, and I was still missing the camels. I say 'ceremony' merely as a reference point, as it was anything but. As soon as she got wind of the fact that her dimwitted daughter insisted that she would settle for nothing less than exchanging her own vows with, Jared, Mrs. F. made sure the ceremony was going to be quick and to the point — no one in the room but key witnesses and Shoksi, Triple F's yogi who was serving as justice of the peace to certify the surefire embarrassment.

During a break from rehearsal earlier in the week, I asked Jared what he thought about it all, to which he replied quite openly that he was already *shtupping* his ex, but that "Mendel's got a ton of cash, which I need, so I'll make it work." I kept his vow to myself, and although I wasn't in the boardroom, I can only assume he did too. Not that he was wrong, mind you. From the moment he stepped foot off the boat after surviving the war, Mendel Fischer, the little Lodzer whose family owned a tiny laundromat in the old country and knew a thing or two about how money worked, set about investing every hard-earned penny in real estate. Specifically, buying up land in the post-war suburbs where all the newly-paved roads were headed and where he would honor the family legacy by building a network of "Fischer Fresh" laundromats that would eventually stretch coast to coast and set the foundation for the Fischer family fortune. One, I should add, that could afford camels at a wedding.

And they hadn't arrived.

"Zey aren't bringing zem," Phillipe, the French *chef d'evenements* at the Savoy Hotel, said to me with a look of horror on his face as he caught up with me making my way through the lobby towards the garden adjacent to the ballroom to check on Mrs. F's Alaskan crab that was soon to be served. A pastry chef from across the pond with a flair for the dramatic, he'd earned the overwrought title as promotion after gaining a reputation for parading his one-of-a-kind buttery confections through the ballroom on special occasions. When it came to zoo animals, however, he was a long way from *Le Cordon Bleu*.

"What do you mean, the zoo's not bringing them?!" I barked at him. "The *tzatzke* insisted on the camels. It's her favorite part!"

The idea was all Triple F's, an homage, as it were, to the Christmas Spectacular at Radio City Music Hall, which was an annual rite of hers and Mrs. F. The highlight being the nativity scene complete with shepherds who arrive with, you guessed it, live camels.

"Besides," I continued as we weaved our way past a gaggle of Chinese tourists who were checking in and having it explained to them that the foul stench of the farm wafting in from the ballroom was only a temporary nuisance, "Mrs. F.'s supposed to be riding in on one of them!"

I neglected to mention and this is totally to Mendel's credit, that there's no way he was attending his granddaughter's wedding, let alone paying for it, if he was walking into the middle of a picturesque staging of the birth of little baby Jesus. The compromise, as it turned out, was to split the difference on religions. They'd settle on an *Arabian Nights*-themed *simkhe* fit for a sultan, one in which Mrs. F. could still have her wish fulfilled of riding in on an animal that would be somewhat location appropriate. So the camels were still in play.

"Fuck!" I yelled out, causing some in the Chinese delegation to wonder at the neurotic Jewish animal among them.

"*Monsieur* Izzy, are you okay?" Phillipe asked.

"Yeah, fine. My head's just spinning a little," I replied truthfully, as I really wasn't feeling right. And it wasn't the nerves. "Probably just the animal stench," I lied.

"Perhaps she can zit on ze donkey?" Phillipe offered in all sincerity, getting back to the issue of Mrs. F.'s entrance into the ballroom after the crabs.

"Sure, you tell her that," I answered, which caused him to turn his deflated gaze downward. "Don't worry, we'll work it out," I said, and pushed him in the direction of the ballroom. "Maybe they brought a tiger," I joked with a wink before I headed into the garden to check on the crabs.

It's a little-known fact that, like much work of great art, the garden at the Savoy was the result of the serendipitous confluence of a great mind, bags of money, and copious amounts of booze. In this case, it was a legendary landscape architect who, as it happened, was a hotel guest while in town working on a commission going horribly wrong. Having returned from a particularly frustrating meeting with the town elders, who had just scrapped his plan for an expansive reservoir at the heart of his commission, he retreated to the spacious smoking room adjacent to the ballroom, where he sat 'till the wee hours of the morning with the Lord of Savoy himself. It was after finishing a third bottle of bourbon that he proceeded to whip out his ding-dong and pissing into one of the emptied bottles of booze, exclaimed that the room needed vegetation, and perhaps pissed, as it were, that the elders had rejected his plan for a large reservoir, a miniature version at its center. I think about that every time I walk into the serenity of the garden and see the little ducks fluttering peacefully around the pond and passing under the fountain of water emanating from the little stone schlong of the pissing boy statue at its center, which, when you think of it, seems wholly appropriate.

The serenity of the garden didn't last long. As soon as I entered, I was accosted by Moti, the Israeli photographer, who pulled me aside and looked around to make sure no one was in earshot before whispering into my ear: "We've got a real problem," he said to me earnestly in that way people who've served in the military have the habit of doing when conflating the mundane with the potentially really serious. He wasn't long out of his mandatory service in the Israeli Defense Forces, where he served in a "classified intelligence" unit. It instilled so much pride in him that he often forgot the meaning of the two terms, such that I typically had to remind him that what he shared with me was probably the kind of stuff that either I'd be killed for knowing, he'd be killed for sharing, or some combination thereof. Regardless, he's a good kid. Our families go way back, as my uncle Hank worked for years with Moti's grandfather Berl, a photographer whose legend, I believe, stems from having captured the iconic shot of the burning *Altalena* before it sank, but don't quote me on that. Berl ended up setting up the family business here not long after he descended and to this day, they're our go-to photographers. He's loyal like that, Hank is.

"Please tell me it has nothing to do with the animals," I said to Moti as we huddled in the corner of the garden.

"What? No. Wait, what are you talking about?" he answered incredulously.

"Never mind," I said. "What's the problem?"

"I got kicked out of the ceremony. The mother of the bride said her sister-in-law smells."

"Wait 'till she gets down here," I quipped, and nodded in the direction of the guests who were attempting to munch on the grade-A, hundred-dollar-a-piece, Alaskan crab I had imported special, but likely not tasting a thing on account of a plangent gust of some orangutan's rectal effluvium that had just wafted in from the ballroom and smelling something awful.

"They kicked me out of the ceremony, and now there's no proof of the wedding," he continued by overstating the relative importance of his role in the whole thing.

"I'm sure Shoksi's got the paperwork," I replied.

"You okay?" he asked me.

"Yeah, why?" I answered self-consciously.

"You keep looking around the room like something bad is about to happen."

"You never know," I deflected. "Just make sure you guys are set for the procession into the ballroom, okay? It's happening any minute," I continued and slapped him on the shoulder, "I have to go check on the pig."

"Isn't this a Jewish wedding?" he asked me as I started to walk away.

I didn't respond but instead turned back towards him, shrugged my shoulders, and lifted my hands. I then snapped up a piece of crab off the tray of a passing waiter, popped it in my mouth, and continued on to what was surely the next fire that needed to be put out.

The hundred-dollar-a-piece Alaskan crab—that turned out to be a bust on account of the unforeseen zoo stench, which had by now completely enveloped the hotel—was a drop in the proverbial bucket compared to what was in store for the guests when they entered the ballroom for dinner, dancing, and the pig roast. Admittedly, my breath was taken away when I walked into the ballroom earlier that day and saw how it had been turned into an eye-popping rendition of the grandest sultan's palace. It was replete with a kaleidoscope of floor-to-ceiling mulberry silk drapes with bespoke geometric patterns; arabesques that formed an ornate canopy, underneath which stood a dozen thirty-foot tall palm trees imported from Casablanca. There were wall-to-wall Turkish kilim rugs and sofas with cushions embroidered with the bride and grooms' initials, as well as a one-of-a-kind, solid gold hookah pipe, imported straight from the grand souk in Marrakech, placed on each table

It was all the work of one Paul de Camarel, the event's French-Canadian designer who, when I told him the budget for the gig was unlimited and to spare no expense, took no time going to town and whipping it into a veritable Hollywood spectacular. It tickled him pink, as it had been years since he'd had the opportunity to step out for an extravagant event. Even more since his glory years in La La Land, running Vincente Minelli's art department, where the famed director had taken a liking to him on account of his own matrilineal French-Canadian roots. Nevertheless, like many a Hollywood tale, this one ended in a haze of booze, boys, and all sorts of bad one night in the Hollywood Hills, which in no time would see the uber-talented artist returning home, penniless and broken. That he's still around today is due solely to my uncle Hank who, having appreciated de Camarel's earlier work dressing strippers, so to speak, had mercy. He tasked him with starting the art department of his fledgling entertainment business — specifically, jazzing up the weddings and bar mitzvahs that would form the bedrock of his success. It was a job he was grateful to have and one he's kept to this day which, if you didn't know any better, you'd think he loathed. Like now.

"Iz, where's my damn camel?" Paul shouted at me as soon as I entered the ballroom, where he and two dozen members of his team were putting the finishing touches on his *Arabian Nights* masterpiece.

"That's what I'm here to find out," I muttered under my breath. I began weaving my way towards the dancefloor at the center of the room, where he was standing with Phillipe and Nguyen, the hotel's diminutive Vietnamese master chef, whose specialty happens to be in roast pig.

"So, status reports?" I asked as I joined them for a last-minute conclave before the rabble arrived. "I've got to open the room in ten."

"Ze parade of pigs is ready," Phillipe said, giggling like a little schoolgirl in anticipation of the moment when he would literally be leading a parade of twenty pigs through the ballroom that his Saigon Sancho had roasted for the occasion. Paul, in a pot calling the kettle black moment, thought the idea completely over the top when Phillipe brought it up in one of our early production meetings and insisted that it didn't match his vision for the design he was building for the event. When I explained that every true artist had a signature—in Phillipe's case, his food parades—and that Paul should view it from a theatrical perspective, imagining it as if the subjects were bringing burnt offerings to the sultan, he got on board with the vision and actually helped Phillipe and the wait staff with their choreography. Which I should add, was very well appreciated.

"Good to know," I said while looking over at the bandstand, where I could see that the playboy musical director and band leader, Ricky de

Sachon, was getting a hard-on rehearsing a Middle-Eastern number at his keyboard with one of the belly dancers, whose sheer harem pants left nothing to the imagination. We shared a brief, knowing glance with one another as he waved his phone in my direction before turning back to his muse.

"You all right, kid?" Paul asked me.

"Why does everyone keep asking me that?" I replied.

"Because you're sweating," he replied, and started dabbing at my forehead with a napkin before I swatted it away.

"I'm fine. Just got really dizzy when I walked in the room, is all."

"It's ze *merde* of ze animals," Phillipe chimed in. "I'll bring you some water," he added, and walked off with Nguyen toward their kitchen.

"Speaking of which," Paul said just as Gus, the zookeeper, entered the room.

"What the fuck, Gus? Where's the camel I ordered?" I asked him as soon as he moseyed on up to join us on the dancefloor.

"I told you it was gonna be touch and go, dude," he replied nonchalantly.

"What the hell does that mean?" Paul snapped at him.

"Don't blame me," he shot back. "You're the one who wanted the albino camel, and when you couldn't decide, the supplier decided to eat it." Paul looked at me, gobsmacked.

"You shitting me?" I said to Gus. "He ate the fucking camel?!"

"Apparently they taste better," he replied in all seriousness. I laughed at the absurdity, although Paul found no humour in the moment.

"Oh, god!" Paul shouted and began weeping uncontrollably while beginning to pace back and forth on the dancefloor, all the while exclaiming, "*Ishtar!*"

"What's he saying?" Gus asked and looked at me nonplussed. "It's a Hollywood picture that went off the rails." I started to explain. "Apparently they wanted a rare blue-eyed camel and couldn't settle on a price and by the time they came back for it, the trader had eaten it."

"I've got a mule," Gus said in all sincerity.

"I will not have the bride's mother riding in on a fucking donkey!" Paul shot back over his shoulder while completing a lap towards the far end of the dancefloor. "*Ishtar!*"

"It's not fucking *Ishtar*, Paul!" I yelled at him. "Get back here."

"What about a zebra?" Gus offered.

"Wait!" Paul said as he gracefully pirouetted at the far corner of the dancefloor and turned back towards us, suddenly excited. "She's wearing black accents in her Yves St-Laurent chiffon dress. Yes! I can work with that. It's even more dramatic!"

"He means the zebra, right?" Gus whispered to me as Paul hurried to our side.

"You've got a saddle for it?" I asked him. "I don't think Mrs. F. is gonna bareback it."

"Hermie's never worn one, but I think I can make it work," he replied.

"You mean the zebra, right?" I asked with a wink.

"Yeah, his name's Herman. We call him Hermie."

"Lovely," I deadpanned. "Please go introduce him to Paul, and let's make this work. I have to open the doors now."

"You gonna be okay?" Paul asked me with genuine concern as I ushered them off the dancefloor.

"For fuck's sake, I'm gonna be fine!" I snapped at him. "Now, go make the pageant happen."

"If you say so," he replied, shaking his head like he knew better. "But you don't look so hot."

I said nothing, just pointing my finger toward the zebra he needed to inspect before turning in the other direction, towards the doors that I was now going to open for the waiting guests.

A little while later, once the five hundred-plus guests were seated at their tables under the sultan's canopy, I took up my position at the sound and lighting table located to the side of the bandstand and gave the signal to the operator, Jean-Guy, for the pageant to commence. As the lights dimmed, the sound of timpanis began to swell over the P.A. system. The spotlights on the ceiling focused the guests' attention on the grand entrance to the ballroom where Paul stood, dressed in full Arab garb, flanked by two hotel wait staff in tuxedos. Then, like Moses parting the Red Sea, he raised both his arms dramatically in the air while the two penguins opened the doors. Moments later, as the sound of timpanis gave way to the familiar theme of Maurice Jarre's music to the film *Lawrence of Arabia*, he thrust his arms down. Taking that as their cue, a dozen men on horseback, dressed appropriately in flowing white robes with swords drawn across their shoulders and each carrying a lit torch, began entering enter the ballroom, heralding the imminent arrival of the bride and groom.

"Izzy?" a diminutive Jewish man shouted at me over the music. Looking about ninety and dressed in a rumpled tuxedo he probably hadn't worn since his wedding, he had walked over from a nearby table to where I was stationed just as the pageant began. "Remember me?" he continued as the music grew louder.

I didn't, and I kept my gaze fixed on the ballroom's doors, hoping he'd walk away. No dice. He just stood there, waiting for an answer.

"I don't mean to be rude, sir," I finally yelled back over the music. "Now's not a good time."

"Finkelman! Avrom Finkelman!" he shouted again. Great, I thought. A million-dollar gig with everything riding on my shoulders for the next two minutes, and I'm having to deal with someone who decided to pay me a visit and head down memory lane.

"Of course!" I finally offered by way of trying to brush him off.

"I knew it!" he exclaimed and waved to the nearby table where he came from with a big smile on his face like he was making good on a bet he'd just won. "They didn't believe me, but I said it must be. You look just like your *zaide*!"

Meanwhile, I was signaling Jean-Guy to transition the music away from Maurice Jarre to "Paid in Full," Eric B and Rakim's hip hop classic, which trumpeted the arrival of the next group in the wedding party, the in-laws, escorted by a harem of belly dancers. If you ask me, the choice of music was rather inspired. I'd suggested the remix version of the well-known eighties jam during one of our tense production meetings when, for a change, Mrs. F. was getting on my nerves and I felt everyone was losing sight of the fact that this was a wedding after all, and it needed some meaning beyond all the window dressing we were discussing. When I played it in the room it was actually well received by the witch, on account of what she dubbed "that Arab part," which she believed lent an air of authenticity. Of course, the joke's on her as "that Arab part" is, in fact, taken from the song *Im Ninalu*, a Hebrew poem by the seventeenth-century Yemenite, Rabbi Shalem Shabazi. It was made famous in the last quarter of the twentieth-century by Israeli pop diva Ofra Haza, whose chorus is roughly translated as "if the doors of the wealthy are locked, the doors of Heaven will never be." If no one else in the ballroom appreciated the nuanced 'fuck you' to the Mrs. as her in-laws entered the room, at the very least, it made me chuckle.

"Mine was the first *simkhe*, you know!" Mr. Finkelman continued shouting at me.

"Not now, I'm busy!" I yelled back in a way that I totally acknowledged was absolutely rude of me. But in the moment, it felt necessary.

Didn't seem to matter.

"It was my daughter's wedding, the first your father and uncle ever played!" he said. "Oy! Could they make things festive!" he exclaimed, clapping his hands together for emphasis.

"The good old days," I then offered, trying to focus my attention in two directions at once.

"Not this *nariskhkeit*!" he replied and waved his arms around the room dismissively at Paul's masterpiece. I wanted to nod in agreement but kept it to myself.

"Seeing you, it makes me feel like they're here!" he said. "You're too young to remember, but this is where they made the magic happen. In this room."

I'd heard, though he didn't mention the fact that this is where it all went to shit, too.

"There's an energy in the room tonight," he said. "It's like ghosts I'm feeling, you know what I mean?" he said and looked at me, waiting for an answer.

I didn't oblige as I had to give the go-ahead on the next phase of the pageant: the burnt offering to the sultan, a.k.a Phillipe's parade of pigs, set to the music of "Be Our Guest" from the soundtrack to *Beauty and the Beast*. Although Paul rightfully indicated to Phillipe during our production meeting, albeit rather indelicately, that his choice of music bore no connection to the theme of the event and was a piece of garbage besides, the song stuck as it was the only way I would convince the tightly-wound Frenchman to return to the table following a tantrum that saw him leave the room in tears, swearing never to return. Ultimately, he did and was now basking in the adulation of five hundred-plus know-nothings, dazzled by him and his team's swine dance throughout the ballroom.

"You okay?" Finkelman asked me.

I said nothing as something suddenly caught my attention.

"Do you see that?" I asked him and pointed toward a corner of the room where, while tracking Phillipe pirouetting with a platter of pork, I happened to spot...Her.

"See what?" he replied.

"There!" I said as I grabbed him and pointed toward where I was looking. "The woman in the black, strapless dress standing with her back against the wall, in the corner, staring right at us?"

"Izzy," Finkelman replied earnestly. "I admit, I don't see so good anymore, but there's nobody there."

"There! There! Are you fucking blind?" I snapped at him while thrusting my arm in the direction of where nobody was standing. "Why can't you see her?" I shouted, causing heads from nearby tables to turn in our direction.

"Maybe you really are seeing ghosts," Finkelman replied with a look of concern. "You don't look so good, *boychik*" he added. "You're sweating. Maybe you should go to the hospital."

"I'm fine," I lied, and wiped away a layer of moisture from my forehead.

I wasn't going to tell him that I hadn't been feeling right from the moment I walked into the hotel earlier that day and certainly wasn't about to argue as to the metaphysical merits that it was on account of the spirit of Hank and my father's *simkhe* band haunting the ballroom. The fact of the matter was that the belly dancers had finished their bit, Phillipe and his pals were done their pig parade, and now Jean-Guy was looking at me, anxiously awaiting the signal to go on the entrance music for the crucial penultimate step in the pageant: The arrival of Mrs. F. on Hermie the zebra, which was right when my cousin Manny decided to make an appearance.

"Everything okay here?" he asked, and looked at me disapprovingly as he arrived at where I was standing with Mr. Finkelman; an attractive, tall, blonde woman dressed in a business suit in tow, who was not his wife, stood beside him.

I briefly acknowledged his presence before I gave Jean-Guy the thumbs-up to go with the next cue. Seconds later, five hundred-plus people got up from their seats and began applauding as the doors to the ballroom opened and the mother of the bride now entered the room astride the back of an exotic animal, to the sounds of the disquieting opening theme of Rimsky-Korsakov's, *Sheherazade*. It seemed oddly appropriate as I clocked Mr. F. and his dad Mendel looking on disapprovingly from their seats at the head table, which they had taken long before the whole *mishegas* of the pageant had begun, I assume to avoid the embarrassment of what everyone was now witnessing.

"What's the yelling all about?" Manny asked me. "I could hear you from halfway across the room."

"I'm calling cues," I lied.

He then turned to Mr. Finkelman and asked who he was.

"This is Avrom Finkelman," I answered for the old man. "He was *zaide*'s friend."

"Are you okay, sir?" Manny asked him earnestly. "I apologize if he touched you inappropriately," he continued and pointed at me.

"What the fuck?" I snapped at him.

"I'm fine. Izzy's the one I'm concerned about," Mr. Finkelman replied and stared at my cousin momentarily. "You're Henryk's, I can see the resemblance!"

"Yeah, Hank's my dad," Manny answered him, and looked at me again. "What the hell's going on?"

"Nothing," I deflected and threw a derisive look at the woman he arrived with. "Who's she?"

"My name's Anne-Marie," she said politely in French-Canadian-accented English, and extended a hand.

"He's hallucinating," Mr. Finkelman chimed in, and pointed at me.

"You're what?" Manny said, and looked at me sideways.

"He's seeing things," Mr. Finkelman continued.

"Okay, Mr. Finkelman," I said, and nudged him toward his table. "We're done here."

"I'm serious. You should go to a hospital," he replied, and looked at Manny. "You work together?"

"Kind of," Manny answered him.

"The next generation, how wonderful!" Mr. Finkelman exclaimed, and then looked at both me and Manny earnestly. "Take care of each other. Family's the only thing that matters," he said as he gave us both a playful slap on the cheek before he turned and finally headed back to his table.

Manny gave me a puzzled look.

"Not now," I replied, and pointed in the direction of Hermie the zebra, who was parading Mrs. F. around the ballroom.

"Why were you shaking him?" he insisted.

"I'm sorry, who are you?" I said to Anne-Marie, refusing to engage with my cousin.

She repeated her name politely, then nodded toward my phone that was lighting up on the table.

"You're buzzing."

"And you're here, why?" I asked, and put the phone away in my pocket.

She didn't answer but looked instead at Manny.

"She's training," he said.

"For what?"

"Iz, why did that man say you were hallucinating? What happened?"

"Nothing. I asked him if he recognized someone who's here."

"Who?"

"No one," I lied.

"What do you mean, no one?"

"Forget it."

"Your mom told me what happened at her house."

"What are you talking about?"

"And at the funeral."

"So?"

"Something's wrong."

"Yeah, something's wrong!" I shouted at him. "You have me running a wedding with that *yente* riding around on the back of a fucking zebra," I said, and pointed in the direction of the head table, where Mrs. F. had now arrived and was being helped down from Hermie by Gus and his team of animal wranglers.

"With you," Manny said. "Something's wrong with *you*. You need to take a break and get help."

"What are you saying? You're firing me... *now*?"

"Of course not!"

"Is that why she's here?" I said, calling his bluff and pointing at Anne-Marie. "She's here to replace me?"

"Anne-Marie is here to observe how to run a Jewish wedding," he said, "my dad's fully on board with the decision."

"Well, that's just fucking perfect!" I yelled at him and then I was somewhere else, gone, as the sudden rush of panic and accompanying wave of one irrational thought after another began to race through my head uncontrollably. You know what I mean. It was in the same instant that I began conflating what I felt I'd done to my mother with a deep-seated pang of unbearable guilt at the loss of Knekht and a generation I felt I was letting down for what, I didn't know. It was compounded by the construct of my own making, the haunting Her, who merited not an iota of any of it but was always there, hammering home my sense of utter worthlessness for everything I'd failed to accomplish and all that I never would. It was in that moment that Jean-Guy tapped me on the shoulder and pointed in the direction of the bandstand, where I could see Ricky de Sachon waving his phone in my direction frantically, awaiting my signal. As my mind now raced with the thought of Mr. Finkelman and the ghosts of my father and my uncle, whose fateful night took place in this room years earlier, I sealed my own fate with what I did next.

"You can tell Hank to go fuck himself," I said to Manny and then, with a sense of confidence that arrived as quickly as the fear and self-loathing vanished, I told Jean-Guy to hold the next cue before turning to the bandstand and yelling out to Ricky: "Do it! Do it!"

"What are you doing?" Manny said to me as a look of horror came over his face, unsure of what was about to happen.

I stared at my cousin and said nothing, not wanting to tell him what I'd been planning from the moment we started working on this *farshtunkene* farce of a Jewish wedding. I began to walk away instead, letting Ricky de Sachon answer for me in a way I never could as he called out to his bandmates: "Okay boys, lez go!" A few seconds later, at the same time that Paul opened the doors to the ballroom for the entrance of Triple F and her new hubby, Jared, I could swear I saw Mrs. F.faint as Ricky and les boys ripped into the hottest rendition of *Khosn Kale Mazel Tov* you've ever heard, Moti all the while snapping away capturing the moment for all eternity. Making my way to the exit, I nodded toward Mr. F., and his dad Mendel, who I could see were on cloud nine as a throng of five hundred-plus were now gathering on the dance floor for a *hora*.

Then again, I'm not sure. I may have been hallucinating.

5

There should be a clause in whatever tome governs the affairs of lawyers everywhere, stipulating that billable hours are wholly contingent upon the attorney keeping up-to-date with their monthly magazine subscriptions, the ones kept for their client in the waiting room of their offices. I would argue, moreover, that in such cases where the legal representative is found to be delinquent in the maintenance of the aforementioned subscription, the fee charged by such legal representative to the client shall be prorated perforce, to that which adhered at the time when the subscription was left to lapse and the legal representative, who is the subject of said clause, shall be obliged, specifically waving the benefit of division and discussion, to agree to the terms as set forth therein. Or something to that effect. That's what came to mind as I sat in the waiting area of the law firm of Manley, Manley, and Faygenbaum, reading a ten-year-old issue of *The Nation* while waiting for my meeting with Faygen, when his sassy secretary, Antonella, arrived to usher me in.

"Mr. Faygen will see you now. Please follow me," she said quite breathily, and I quickly fell in line as she sashayed me down the runway of the office, past hers and a half dozen other of the paralegal desks, to the end of the hallway where Faygen was waiting to greet me at the door to his corner office.

"Can I get you gentlemen anything?" she asked as we entered.

"Tea, please," Faygen answered her quickly.

She then turned to me and asked if I wanted anything, in that tone of voice of hers that was just superb. As I contemplated an answer, I could sense that Faygen was anticipating the worst, but I rose to the occasion: "Yeah, no, I'm good with nothing, nothing at all. Happy to just hear the words coming out of your mouth," I said, causing Faygen to roll his eyes and shake his head from side to side, which I assume meant I was wrong and delivered as he expected.

"You sure?" she asked me again eagerly, ignoring my idiocy. "We've got great bottled water."

"Yes, you can bring him a bottle of water, Ms. Napolitano," Faygen said in that overly-formal way he often does when addressing even those nearest to him. "That will be all, thank you."

"Yeah, thanks," I said as she turned to exit with a catwalk-worthy spin so perfect that I felt it merited applause.

Faygen then gestured for me to sit opposite him at his desk, which was overflowing with file folders that suggested he was either in the midst of a case of massive importance or equally as behind on the paperwork for dozens of others. In fact, his entire office was an unholy mess of documents and assorted leather-bounds that, to the untrained eye, would suggest he was not doing his job. Knowing Faygen as I do, however, he probably could make perfect sense of it all.

"I didn't think you'd come," he said as he sat across the desk opposite me. "I'm glad you did. How are you?"

"I'm good, ready to start fresh," I replied in an 'acting-as-if' moment that would have done my therapist proud, but which was a total crock of shit, as I didn't really know where I was, not after what I'd done just a few nights before at the Fischer gig.

I don't mind sharing. Fact is, I should have known that the phenomenal rush of adrenaline masquerading as confidence that I experienced upon leaving the wedding would wear off only a few short hours later, to the point where I woke my mother up in the middle of the night with the kind of phone call she never explicitly said she hated getting from me, but I can only assume was obviously the case. Put yourself in her shoes: What would you do if, in the middle of the night, you were suddenly awoken by a phone call where the voice on the other end was your own flesh and blood, sobbing uncontrollably and pleading for help, as the will to live, while miraculously strong, was nevertheless being seriously compromised in such moments by a pull towards a jump off a balcony that was growing more tempting by the minute? And what if this time was when it actually happened? That's how it was, is, and always has been, living this thing I call my life.

"Go, get out, run!" the voice inside my head, or maybe it was hers, I don't remember, was what got me out of the apartment just in time, landing me curled up on the bench in the park across the street. My mother picked me up a little while later and took me home to hers where I spent the night, not for the first time. Over breakfast the next morning, we both knew better than to address the points that were obvious because we'd been there before, individually and together. I knew it; she knew it. I wasn't going to let my tears wet her perfectly executed plate of French toast over my reluctance to accept that it wasn't just the withdrawal from meds, which I should, by all rights, not have stopped taking. And she wasn't going to replace coffee for Chianti to summon the courage to push me harder than she wanted to so as to get the point across that, although she's always blamed herself for all of it, she wouldn't know what to do with herself if the next middle-of-the-night phone call came from someone other than me. By the way, contrary to what all the high-priced, so-called experts in the white coats and fancy offices will tell you, that is what it all boils down to: Will you enjoy your French toast soggy with wine, or golden and fluffy with a kickass cup of freshly ground, dark roast Sumatra coffee?

You can't use that last nugget, I'm already in the process of copyrighting it. Anyway, we'd been there enough times together to know that despite it all, we were living the lives we were, we wouldn't worry about what Manny, Hank, or anybody else thought about what I'd done, nor the ramifications. No matter what, we had each other. So, as I then washed and she dried, we pacted that I wasn't going to wallow in my misery interminably but that I would be proactive for a change, and regardless of whether I knew what the future had in store, I would get up in the morning and do something, anything. This is how I found myself sitting across from Faygen a few days later, taking him up on his offer to come work for him without any idea of what I was doing and how I would do it.

It didn't take more than a moment or two into Faygen's attempt at explaining his rationale for asking me to his office, before his fabulous Italian *tsatske* entered with bottles of water, followed shortly thereafter by a tall, silver-haired man in a crisp, blue pinstripe who appeared at the door in a mood something unpleasant.

"Faygen, my office, now!" he said gruffly, and turned away.

"Who's that?" I asked Faygen.

"The senior partner," he replied, and got up from his chair.

"Seems like a complete asshole," I offered unsolicited.

"Mr. Manley is a very nice man," Antonella then scolded me.

"Yeah, totally got that impression," I replied, then turned to Fagyen, who had already taken his roll of dental floss from his desk drawer and began flossing, which meant something was wrong. "What did you do?"

"About to find out."

"He's upset you took the case *pro bono*," Antonella told him matter-of-factly.

"The one you were just starting to tell me about?" I asked.

"Yes," he said and then turned to her. "I haven't even told him anything about it yet," he said, nonplussed.

"I did," she answered him, and then added, somewhat sheepishly, "he knows I haven't been paid in a month."

"Oh, Ms. Napolitano," Faygen said in a voice that was at once deflated and disappointed, which made me suddenly feel like I was in the middle of something personal that I shouldn't be. "Sorry, Iz, this was unexpected. But I have to attend to this," Faygen said as he tossed his used piece of floss in the garbage, and then addressed his assistant as he began making his way out of the office. "Ms. Napolitano," he said to her, now in a confident tone of voice like massaging his gingiva had somehow given him a sudden jolt of self-assuredness. "This case will set everything right. Trust me, it's big," he said, and left the office.

Judging from her facial expression, it seemed she'd heard this line of argument not a few too many times before from Faygen and didn't seem all that convinced. Nevertheless, although he hadn't yet told me anything about what he wanted from me by way of help where the case was concerned, I'd known Faygen long enough to be confident of the fact that if he had just taken on a case *pro bono,* he'd done so after considered thought that it was either going to be a huge payout if he nailed it, which was never really what floated his boat, or it had huge implications from a social justice standpoint that, although near to his heart, sometimes clouded his judgment when it came to the ability to pay the bills. Knowing him as I do, I assumed it was the latter and hoped to God he would make enough money to pay his secretary's salary.

"Mr. Faygen, wait!" Antonella shouted once Faygen had left, which caused him to pop his head back into the office momentarily. "This piece of paper you left on my desk for Mr. Fishman..." she said, waving a little sticky note in her hand.

"Oh, yes. I completely forgot!" he said and then looked at me. "Iz, I need you to do some research. Please visit the address written on that piece of paper and call me later to talk about it."

"That's it, no details?" I asked incredulously.

"For now," he said with a wink, and then, taking a moment to say nothing at all other than to look at me in a way that expressed his genuine concern for my well-being, he gave me a thumbs up and turned to leave.

"Here you go," Antonella said as she handed me the piece of paper, and we both began to leave the office.Looking down at it as I made my way back down the hallway of paralegals toward the exit, I began to chuckle because the address Faygen had written down was one that hadn't entered my mind in years, but it immediately began conjuring fond memories of a time long ago. It was clear to me at that moment why Faygen had winked at me as he left, as the research he was asking me to do likely had absolutely nothing to do with the important case he would have to tell me about some other time.

A little while later, I found myself walking through the bowels of the Jewish Community Centre where the noise was deafening and the air thick with sawdust. I passed by two burly men pushing a large piece of plywood through a table-mounted saw in the production shop, a space I once knew as the legendary rehearsal room number twelve, *en route* to the non-descript black door with no handle at the far end of the room, otherwise known as the entrance to Luba's office. A knock likely to be unheard above the din, I pushed the door open gently and swept myself in on a carpet of dust and wood chips into the small ante room. It is there that I found Jackie, Luba's secretary for over half a century, sitting at a desk devoid of anything resembling work, which she may have actually done once upon a time. She was, as I remembered her, busily filing her nails and chewing gum while yelling into her phone something to someone about matters non-theatre-related. She smiled as I entered and took a moment away from her chat to whisper to me, "She's been expecting you," then gestured towards the door just to the side of her desk, whose jamb was noticeably smaller than average, yet somehow the perfect fit for the giant of Yiddish theatre on the other side.

The familiar bright orange poster for *Tevye*, her first production, still hung on the wall directly opposite the door as I entered. The room was much smaller than I remembered, but I guess that's to be expected when you haven't visited in over twenty years and puberty had intervened in the interim. To describe it as an office would be overstating the case for what amounted to not much more than a large closet. Its walls were decorated floor-to-ceiling with framed posters from each of the over one hundred productions she'd directed, as well as framed awards from the myriad she'd received from across the globe over the course of her illustrious career. Each one rightfully honoring the doyenne of Yiddish theatre who had devoted a lifetime to promoting and preserving it after what should have been its death following Hitler. The passage of time had done little to alter the hallowed space, where every inch of what little shelving she'd been given was used to preserve the collected works of Mendele, Peretz, and Sholem Aleichem, the holy trinity, as it were, of Yiddish literature, along with those of other literary giants of Yiddishland. It was also used to store the dozens of *maquettes*, each a piece of art in its own right, from some of her most celebrated productions, most notably those for *Gimpel the Fool, The Unseen, In My Father's Court,* and the rest of Bashevis' oeuvre that she'd charmed the notorious curmudgeon into granting her the exclusive right to adapt for her theatre company. The room was permeated by a heavy, stale mixture of greasy French fries and cigarette smoke that I could recall from my days attending after school Yiddish theatre classes for kids. They were led by the diminutive, round woman with the oversized, thick-rimmed glasses half the size of her face, who I found sitting behind the little table tucked into the far corner of the room -itself a vestige from one of the early productions - and smiling from ear to ear as I walked in.

"*Itzikl!*" she greeted me excitedly in that delicate voice of hers, which pitched uniquely childlike, using the diminutive of my name reserved for use by only my nearest and dearest. "French fries!" she then exclaimed with her charming little giggle that was at once disarming and inviting. I closed the door behind me and crossed to the desk where she sat, a half-eaten hamburger and French fries sitting on a torn, greasy paper bag to one side of her, a lit cigarette resting on an ashtray on the other, and, in between, her century-old Remington Yiddish typewriter that she never gave up in spite of the digital age, the sight of which brought a smile to my face.

"Hi, Luba, it's good to see you again," I said, and instinctively gave her a gentle kiss on the head like she was family, which is how we always treated each other, before putting a piece of greasy potato in my mouth and taking a seat opposite her.

"*Itzikl,*" she said my name again, but this time in a tone that resonated with a sense of urgency as if to suggest we were dispensing with pleasantries and getting straight to the matter at hand; it's the kind of thing that would be off-putting to most, but typical of artists deeply immersed in their craft that those who know it learn not to take offense. She then took a deep drag of her cigarette before snuffing the butt out in the ashtray. As she exhaled dramatically through both nose and mouth, she lifted her chin into that stylized position ready for monologue delivery, as if it was held up just enough so that an orange could fit between it and her throat. She then tossed her hair over her opposite shoulder with an equal amount of flair, all of which suggesting an air of confidence that actually belied a deep-seated nervousness. I just assumed that was the case because when I walked into the building, it wasn't hard to miss the giant poster advertising her landmark production of S. Anksy's *The Dybbuk* that was starting rehearsals in less than a week, and she hadn't yet cast the leading male role, which I just knew from the moment Faygen brought it up at Knekht's funeral was going to result in my being summoned.

The words that then flowed from her mouth as she began to speak consisted of a series of random thoughts about the play, its history, the writer, and the repertory company that performed the original production, the vaunted Vilna Troupe. The aforementioned was coupled with non-sequiturs about her life; the importance of maintaining Yiddish theatre; producing the play; and how vital my implication in it was thrown in for good measure. To the uninitiated, it all would have sounded like nothing more than the ramblings of someone suffering from an acute case of dyslexia or some kind of childish gobbledygook. But for those of us born into the world of Yiddish-speaking immigrants, for whom English was likely a third or fourth language they only acquired later in life, their disjointed, meandering discombobulations begging for a properly-placed adjective, required no Rosetta Stone to decipher. Truth be told, whatever Luba couldn't express in a language far from her mother tongue could be conveyed through hand gestures and various bodily gesticulations, or even a cup of coffee tossed at your head to get a point across that she couldn't otherwise find the appropriate words for. An actor's actor, as they say.

"I'm flattered," I answered her, and insisted that my time as a thespian came and went with her youth theatre.

"You're a natural. There's nobody else who can play this part," she retorted, and gestured for me to keep eating the deep-fried kryptonite on her desk. "Anyway," she continued, "I already told everyone you'll do it."

And here we go.

"I'm sorry, Luba," I replied, and found myself immediately shifting uncomfortably in my chair. Given that I had just wiped the slate of my life clean and there was nothing but an open highway ahead of me, I had no good reason to refuse her other than my own fear of leaving a comfort zone, which if you're still reading at this point, we both recognize is no comfort zone at all. Why she hadn't chosen to direct the greatest play in the Yiddish theatre canon, our *Lear* or *Hamlet*, I should point out, wasn't for me to ask. The fact remained that here she was, at the end of a remarkable career that defied all the odds, choosing to finally do it, and if, at the eleventh hour, she was bereft of an actor she felt could take on the lead male role, turning to me to help fulfill her lifelong dream, who was I to refuse her?

Nevertheless, even though I could see she was feeling no less uneasy than I was, I demurred: "I just...I can't," I fumbled, with not a little amount of shame in my voice and with the discomfort growing, I stood up to leave.

"Wait!" she said, and waved for me to sit back down in my chair. "Give me a minute, for two seconds," she said in that inimitable way that was uniquely hers. She then turned slightly and pointed toward the baroque mirror hanging on the wall behind her desk, a memento of her award-winning turn directing herself in *Mirele Efros*. "What do you see?" she asked me in all seriousness, then a second later, couldn't help but let the grin appear on her face, followed by that little, disarming giggle. Looking at my reflection, I too started to smile, and realized that she was doing it again — that thing she always did at the last minute, when the chips were down and she needed to pull a rabbit out of a hat to make magic happen.

I needn't have said anything because we both knew the answer to the question, which itself derived from one of the iconic lines from the play, *The Dybbuk*, when The Messenger pulls Reb Sender aside and recites a parable that goes as follows: Once, a wealthy man came to see the *Rebbe*, who looked him in the eyes and immediately discerned he was a miser. The *Rebbe* pulled the man over to the window and asked him, "Tell me, what do you see?" The rich man looked out the window and said, "I see people." The *Rebbe* then took him over to a mirror and asked the question again, "What do you see?" The rich man answered that he saw himself. "You see," the *Rebbe* said to him, "the window is made of glass and the mirror is made of glass, but the mirror has a little bit of silver in it, and as soon as the glass is slightly silvered, we only see ourselves."

It was the first thing we learned as kids in her youth theatre. For Luba, the parable held deep meaning, which came from having lived it personally, starting from her earliest experience on the stage, when a two-line performance with the Yiddish theatre in her hometown of Zhitomir garnered the best reviews for the play. There are no stars here, she would tell us always, only an ensemble. She would quote the parable to us often, reverently reminding us that it had been transmitted to her by her teacher, the legendary, larger-than-life director of the Moscow State Yiddish Theatre-GOSET, Shloyme Mikhoels. The way she flat-out floored him at her first audition, thereby gaining entry into his iconic, world-renowned theatre company and very quickly becoming his star pupil, was the stuff of legend. It was through Luba that we, the kids who came to spend time with her twice a week after school for French fries and immersion in theatre training, as well as Yiddish literature and music, could trace our lineage directly to the greatest figures of the modern theatre — namely Stanislavksi and Meyherold, who were Mikhoels' own teachers and from whom he evolved his unique method for the GOSET. For the sake of brevity, it's like this: It's not enough for an actor to learn how to artfully, gracefully, and dramatically lift a piece of tissue paper—Meyerhold's symbolism—the actor must strive to become one with the piece of Kleenex itself, ruminate over where it came from, ask whether it suffered along its journey to your face and, if it did, play the truth of the moment by asking whether you're worthy of being in the enviable position to be standing here now, holding it your hands about to blow your *shnartz* in it—Stanislavsky's realism. I may have bungled that a bit, but you get the picture.

Luba was truly a sight to behold. I remember it like yesterday how, in the dead of winter, she walked into our after-school sessions with her coat slung over her shoulders, never actually worn, because it was the more dramatic way of making an entrance. When in her presence, you felt like every time she finished speaking, regardless of how mundane the matter at hand, you didn't know whether to applaud or stand for an ovation. She had it, the vision thing, knowing exactly what she wanted and stopping at nothing to get it.

"*Itzik?*" Luba said, and snapped her fingers to get my attention. "Where are you?"

"Sorry," I replied, and returned my gaze to her. "I was just lost in thought."

"*Nu*, so tell me. What do you see in the mirror?"

"Memories," I said softly. "I see memories."

She giggled and clapped her hands near her face, like a bet she made was about to pay off. "So, you'll do it?" she asked earnestly.

"I don't know," I demurred. "I just...I know you need an answer, but I just can't give it to you. I'm not ready."

For a moment, she said nothing and there was a pregnant silence between us before she pushed herself away from her desk to open the drawer, from where she pulled out a plastic folder that contained a stack of yellowed, weathered paper barely held together with pieces of desiccated masking tape.

"Take it," she said, presenting me with the ancient artifact in the same gentle, delicate manner one would a newborn child or even a sacred scroll.

"Is this....?" I began to ask as my eyes widened when I saw what was written on the first page.

"Yes," she said, and smiled as if relieved that she'd successfully unburdened herself of a heavy responsibility that had been given to her long ago.

She didn't have to say anything more. It had become the stuff of legend around her over the years that before Mikhoels left for his trip with Fefer to America in '43, to drum up support for the war on the Eastern Front against the Nazis, he called Luba to his office and gave her something he swore her to protect in the event he should not return. Rumor had it that he had given her a copy of the script to a well-known play. Whether the next part is apocryphal, who knows, but it wasn't just any copy of any script. What Mikhoels handed Luba that fateful day before he left, was the script used for the first-ever production of the play that would become the greatest in all of the Yiddish theatre: *The Dybbuk*, which the renowned Vilna Troupe premiered in Warsaw in 1920. But that's not all: The script that was handed down to Mikhoels from the play's director Dovid Herman was considered to be the only surviving Yiddish manuscript written by the hand of the playwright himself, S. An-sky.

"So, it's true?" I asked and began to gently graze my fingers over the faded ink letters on the first page where the writer had written the play's title.

"Yes," she answered proudly, cocking her head again to the side as if to lend the moment the dignity it deserved. "Mikhoels knew Stalin would never let him produce it, and when he came back from America, it was too late," she said, referencing the fact that things changed drastically for the Jews in Soviet Russia at war's end and with both the Nazis defeated and Stalin's purge back in full force, the writing was on the wall: The cultural institutions were shuttered, including the GOSET and artists, writers, scientists, as well as other leading intellectual lights began to disappear such that by '48, Mikhoels was found face-down in the mud on a side street in Minsk, dead from an apparent car accident that everyone knew was murder. One ordered by Stalin himself.

The words simply wouldn't come as I looked down at the worn, tattered piece of history in my hands. I could only imagine the lengths she must have gone to protect the artifact, starting with that harrowing day when she and the citizens of Moscow were hurriedly boarded onto trains and shipped East, just as Hitler's tanks could be heard rumbling at the city's gates. It was there, in Uzbekistan to be exact, that she would spend the remainder of the war. Did she really manage to hold on to the manuscript when, at the war's end, she returned to the Ukraine to find nothing had remained of her home and family but death, destruction, and desolation; only to then find herself bouncing from one displaced-persons camp after another in Germany, before finally boarding a ship to cross an ocean to an unknown place, halfway across the world? I don't know why the questioning thoughts even entered my mind when I knew full well that from the moment she got off the refugee boat, she had only one goal: To mend the torn curtain of her beloved Yiddish theatre...which she achieved.

"I don't know what to say," I finally managed, pathetically.

"Don't say anything yet," she answered, and smiled at me lovingly like she knew she could finally release herself from what must have felt like the equivalent of schlepping the Jewish exile, for the burden was now successfully transferred onto someone she felt could carry it forward. "Just promise me you'll read it."

"I promise," I said as she handed me the manuscript's plastic folder.

"Now, come..." she said, and slapped her hands on the desk as she jumped up with a sudden burst of excitement. "There's somebody you have to meet!"

It was dusk when Luba and I arrived a little later at a formerly industrial part of town that I never knew existed. For that matter, neither did our cab driver, whose GPS on this occasion happened to be Luba, who had no problem directing us to our destination: A derelict, three-story building at the end of a cul-de-sac with no address, no name, nor any other defining characteristic to distinguish it, save for a small neon sign above the entrance that I believe was in the shape of a woman's genitals. The sea of body art and tuque-topped bearded boys that greeted us when we walked in suggested we'd arrived somewhere in millennial hipsterdom, a hunch quickly confirmed by the Native American land acknowledgment hanging on the wall at the entrance to a place called the Bushy Pussy. Maybe it was the Fuzzy Vagina. Whatever, I can't remember; it's not important. It was some clever millennialism that explained the *farkakte* sign out front.

As it happened, there was a reservation for two by the foot of the bandstand where what passed for music that night was offered courtesy of a waifish twenty-something showing a cowbell no mercy while a similarly aged piece of androgyny flailed at a guitar just flat enough out of tune that I just assumed it was on purpose. Mercifully, they finished up their contrivance as we arrived at our table, and actually came and greeted Luba warmly as they hopped off the stage *en route* to the bar. They were followed shortly thereafter by several of the wait staff who were equally delighted to see her, not the least of whom being a sexy ball of fire in hip-hugging jeans and a tight black tank top, who came flying in from across the room shouting Luba's name and immediately wrapped herself around her in a loving embrace upon arrival at our table. As she did, the busboy trailing behind her dutifully placed a bottle of vodka, shot glasses, and a loaf of freshly-baked Russian bread on the table, which, I should point out, just happened to be a Luba staple.

"Hi, I'm Sue-Ann," the twenty-something waitress said to me, extending a hand forthrightly and, with the other, lifted a shot glass, clinked it with Luba's, and downed it with a *L'khaim* that made you pay attention.

"Doubtful," I thought to myself, and immediately began calculating that the combination of brown bottle curls and olive skin, combined with breasts and hips that curved in a way my *bubbe* would have approved of, didn't add up to Sue-Ann. Then again, the piercing blue eyes and nose that would have survived a Gestapo roundup suggested I could have been dead wrong. I wasn't.

"Sue-Ann, *shmuann*!" Luba admonished her, then looked at me while pouring herself another shot. "Her name's Soreh," she said while nodding insistently to her new friend, then drank, ripped a piece of bread from the loaf, tossed it in her mouth, and proceeded to introduce me.

"I'm sorry, I didn't get that?" Sue-Ann said in regard to re Luba's unintelligible attempt to say my name in mid-chew.

"I'm Isaiah," I introduced myself. "Friends call me Izzy."

"*Itzikl*," Luba offered with a giggle.

"Adorable!" Sue-Ann said in that patronizing way, common among dog lovers when inquiring about a breed they've never seen around the run. "And so Jewish...I like that," she purred, then knowingly struck a pose that emphasized her personalities, while simultaneously resting her right palm on the flesh of its adjoining hip that now introduced itself into the conversation, teasing a hint of color that I imagined made for something interesting further below. She then capped it off with a smile that revealed two perfectly-formed dimples on either side, the kind so charming as to inspire a Rumshinksy tune.

"You didn't drink your shot," she reproached me playfully, pointing at the offending glass on the table that I knew better than to touch. "How about a beer?" she proudly suggested. "We brew in-house."

"Sure," I answered, still somewhat sensory-overloaded. "But nothing too hoppy. I'm not into drinking flowers."

"Double IPA coming right up!" she said, clocking my *narishkeit,* then brushed her hand expertly on my shoulder as she turned to leave. "You're right. He's cute," she said to Luba, then winked in my direction before heading off toward the bar.

"Let me guess," I began to ask Luba, who looked at me with a Cheshire grin on her face that told me everything I needed to know.

"She's Leah," I said, referencing the lead female character in *The Dybbuk.*

Her giggle this time was more of an outburst of joy as she clapped her hands near her face and rocked back and forth happily, like another bet she made was about to pay off.

"Where'd you find her?" I asked, gazing toward the bar where Sue-Ann and her pals were huddled and looking right back at us.

"I didn't; she found me," Luba answered and waved in their direction. "I like her. We've been spending a lot of time together."

"Clearly," I said, and returned my attention back to the table. "She's an actress?"

"Nope."

"So why is she playing Leah?" I asked somewhat incredulously. Mind you, not that it was any of my business but knowing full-well the chops required for the part, it seemed a fair question.

"She read for me. She feels the character deeply."

"She speaks Yiddish?"

"Nope," Luba answered again, with not an iota of concern in her voice.

"I don't get it," I said, and continued, "You want me to play opposite someone who doesn't speak Yiddish, and on top of that, you don't even know if she can act?"

"I don't know if she can act?" she guffawed, repeating my question aloud as if to make me hear how dumb it sounded. "What she just did naturally in that moment," she continued, now more earnestly while gesturing with her finger in a circular motion, "is more than some actors learn to do with a lifetime of training."

"What do you mean?" She didn't answer but cocked her head to the side instead and threw me a look like, again, I should have thought before I spoke.

"What?" I said incredulously, and could feel my cheeks starting to flush.

"She had you mesmerized," she answered with a smile, then drank another shot and tossed a piece of bread in her mouth.

"No, she didn't," I lied.

Luba said nothing as Sue-Ann now returned with my beer, a basket of gluten-free tortilla chips, and an assortment of cheeses, each of which she proceeded to describe as an award-winning artisanal creation sourced from her friends at farms nearby, without specifying whether the pals she was referring to were the farmers or their animals, 'cause these days, you know, it could go either way. Regardless, as she side-straddled a chair that she'd pulled in from a nearby table and invited us to dig in, I thought better than to comment on the fact that without a quality goat on the cutting board, which admittedly was artfully presented along with an assortment of dried fruit and a delightfully-sweet onion *tartinade*, what she put on the table was a whole lot of lactose intolerance.

"So, you're my *bashert*" Sue-Ann said assertively, I assumed in reference to the male lead in the play to whom Leah is predestined.

CHIRP.

"Not quite," I replied, choosing to ignore her Yiddish grammar mishap, and began to look around the room for the window where I thought the sound I'd just heard was coming from. But there was none, just four walls that began feeling closer than they were.

Shit.

"You should do it," she continued cheerfully, "it'll be so much fun."

"Have you read the play?" I asked her, and I could feel my mood turning too fast. "Fun is hardly the word I'd use to describe it."

"Okay, grouch," she said playfully in return, thankfully oblivious to what I knew was coming. "I meant the process of doing it," she continued, then looked to Luba for confirmation. "You said it'll be fun, right?"

Luba likely knew better than to confirm the neophyte's question, given her awareness of the rigors the play would demand. However, she chose instead to give her leading lady a kiss on the forehead that I suppose was to suffice as a reply.

CHIRP.

Fuck.

"You're doing the play in Yiddish, right?" I asked Luba, my voice matter-of-fact now, which came out that way in an attempt to stay in the moment.

"Of course," she replied, and threw me a look of concern like she knew something wasn't right at my end of the table.

"That's what I thought," I said, then turned to Sue-Ann and began my inquisition: "You don't speak Yiddish?"

"I don't."

"Do you read it?"

"A *bisl*," she said and offered a smile that under different circumstances would be adorable, but on this occasion, with my bandwidth shrinking rapidly by the second, it caused me to roll my eyes and shake my head from side to side disapprovingly.

"*Zi farshteyt zeyer gut,*" Luba said to me in Yiddish, as if certifying that Sue-Ann's rudimentary comprehension made any difference for what she knew full well was a legitimate question, although maybe not at the moment.

"That means I understand, right?" Sue-Ann asked Luba cheerfully.

"Yes, *meydele*," she answered, lovingly clutching Sue-Ann's right hand. "*Farshtey* in Yiddish means understand."

"I took a course last summer," Sue-Ann said proudly, and added, "I'm so into Yiddish now."

CHIRP!

I bit my tongue to keep from answering something that I knew would be along the line of "are you fucking shitting me." Particularly as she began to describe the three weeks she'd recently spent at one of those summer intensives. The ones where, by some miracle, those who are lost find themselves through a *leck* of poetry penned by a radical lesbian *Inzikhistke* and a *shmeck* of a song about the plight of the working masses that, when combined with other wholly-misinterpreted revivalist-like *narishkeit,* cause them to totally lose their shit at how cool, modern, progressive and easily-appropriated Yiddish culture is.

Fucking millennials.

"Excuse me?" Sue-Ann snapped at me, the smile replaced with a look of pure venom like she was about to take the glass of beer I hadn't touched and empty it over my head.

"Shit, that was supposed to be my internal monologue," I answered. "How much of that was said out loud?"

"Is he normal?" she turned to Luba and asked forthrightly. At first, Luba said nothing, looking at me instead with furrowed brow, which I took to mean that she agreed with my assessment but was more concerned with what might be going on with me that would make me stupid enough to share it. "Children," she eventually offered and looked at us both as the adult in the conversation, "everything will be fine."

Which, at the moment, for me at least, wasn't true.

CHIRP! CHIRP!

It was time to go.

"Wait!" Sue-Ann pleaded as I stood up from the table. "I didn't mean..."

"It's okay," I interrupted her. "I really need to get out of here," I said without further explanation, and walked around to Luba, whispered an apology in her ear, then gave her a kiss on the head before starting to leave.

"But you didn't touch your drink," Sue-Ann said, grabbing my arm to keep me from leaving.

"You served me flowers in a cup," I quipped about the hoppy pint that I had no intention of bringing to my lips. "Besides," I said, and pulled myself away from her gently. "I'm sure one of the fucking millennials in here will appreciate a free one," I offered, managing a wink and a smile before heading for the exit.

CHIRP! CHIRP! CHIRP!

The sound grew louder as I exited the bar into the night, exposing the futility of my frantic attempt to find where *it* was. But within moments, my breath grew shorter and my heart began to pound against my chest even more quickly as there, in the small pool of light from the neon vagina that reflected in a puddle on the street in front of the bar, its immense shadow appeared and, in an instant, everything turned pitch black. The sound became so deafening as it hovered directly overhead that I soon lost all inhibition and, in a moment recalling my darkest days, I roared out something primal that caused me to fall to my knees, where I began to weep uncontrollably and shout for help to make it stop. But there was no one and nothing there, for as quickly as it appeared it departed just the same, leaving me alone in front of the non-descriptbuilding at the end of a cul-de-sac, with no address, no name, nor any other defining characteristic to distinguish it, drowning in what felt like an ocean of tears. I allowed myself to stay on my knees long enough to let some semblance of calm return and to start feeling my legs beneath me so that I could at least get back up.

Eventually, I did, and as I began making my way home, I turned my head and gazed up at the sky, less in an effort to find where it had flown off to but more in wonder as to why it had entered my life at all and fearful of not knowing when and where it would return. An exercise in futility, I suppose. Picking up my pace, I kicked a nonexistent stone on the sidewalk in front of me out of frustration and in full recognition of the fact that, whether I liked it or not, the fateful choice I made when I threw the meds off my balcony only days earlier, was going to be taking me on one hell of a fucking journey.

I knew better than to expect that I would be getting any sleep that night. Actually, if you've been there, you know what I'm talking about when I say that you're never quite sure if you'll ever sleep again. Like a rudderless ship drifting helplessly from starboard to portside, I lost count of the times I tossed and turned, each time flipping the pillow over for some relief from the cooler side, staring in frustration as the clock kept turning. All the while observing the damn hamster in my brain, who wouldn't stop to take a break. Pride had gotten the better of me hours earlier, keeping me from returning any of my mother's admittedly innocuous checking-in messages on my voicemail. Regardless, even though the true answer to her question wouldn't be what she wanted to hear, I figured a 3 a.m. "how are you?" to lie about it, would do more harm than good. I also knew better than to call my doc, whose away message I had long ago committed to memory, and I just didn't feel like schlepping myself to the E.R, where I knew I didn't have the bandwidth to explain to the new kid in admissions that I was fine, but not quite presently. So, like the *farkakte* new-agers like to say, I "sat with it," glancing longingly every second or so at the empty roll of toilet paper I'd flung to the floor by my bedside, wishing I'd paced myself a little better over the preceding hours, but nevertheless getting some relief from the fact that I'd gotten it to work again, and stared at the ceiling hoping that the inevitable crash would come sooner rather than later.

Don't ask, because I don't know the answer, and while we're at it, I ascribe nothing poetic to the fact that when it finally did, it was just as morning dawned and the first light of day cracked its way into my bedroom, shining a golden hour spotlight directly on my bedside table. More precisely, right on the spot where I had placed the script to the play Luba had given me to read, *The Dybbuk*. All right, fine, cue the heavenly fucking choir — it caught my attention, which caused me to reach over and take the script in hand. I will admit this to you: As I gently removed the fragile manuscript from its protective plastic folder, taking great care as I turned the title page, I began feeling calm. No, that's not it. That's a bullshit description. Honestly, I don't know how to describe it. I want to say relief, like I was finally gonna get some sleep. But that wasn't it, either. Fuck, I can't believe I'm sharing this, but it was like the feeling I got as a kid when my *zaide* would tuck me in tight to the pull-out bed he prepared when I'd sometimes stay over on Friday nights. It had really cozy flannel sheets. Sorry, that's the best I've got. Whatever, you get the picture. It was this feeling of warmth and protection that for some reason started to grow inside me as I began reading the iconic names that An-sky, the playwright, listed in his *dramatis personae*, the characters who I knew well because, for fuck's sake, it's *The Dybbuk*: Khonen and Leah, Reb Sender and Fradeh, Reb Azriel the "*Miropoler Rebbe*," the *meshulakh* a.k.a. the Messenger, et al., followed of course, by the *makhmes vos*; the haunting prologue that precedes the curtain rising on the town of Brinnitz, the place where the action to the greatest play in all of Yiddish theatre takes place:

Wherefore, Oh Wherefore
Has the soul fallen
From exalted heights,
To profoundest depths.
Within itself, the fall
Contains the ascension

I could feel my eyes growing heavy as I turned the page and began to read the first words of the play, which take place in the synagogue on Sabbath eve, during which time the town's poor, benighted *batlonim* attempt to outdo each other with tales regaling the wondrous miracles apparently performed by the Talner, Kaminker, Anipoler, and various other Hasidic *rebbeyim* they'd never met in their lives, including one so expert in the Kabbalah that he could use it to resurrect the dead, summon demons, even the devil. The script began slipping from my hands and my chin collapsed to my chest before I could read on to hear Khonen, the protagonist, inquire earnestly about where he could find such a miracle man and the subsequent whispers amongst the *batlonim* about the curious phenom of a scholar in their midst who was asking the question. That's as far as I would get, for although the sun continued to rise and my room grew brighter with the light of day shining through, the crash had finally come. But it would be a little while longer before sleep set in as the hamster in my head was completing a final lap. It was only when he gave me the thumbs-up that he was done that the answer to the question that had nagged me throughout the night finally came to me:

The bar with the *farkakte* vagina sign out front is called The Vulgar Vulva.

Fucking millennials.

6

They call it the "meet-and-greet": The first day of rehearsal in the world
of theatre, when thespians gather to celebrate their self-importance and
to get excited about a journey they're about to embark upon that the
outside world, frankly, couldn't care less about. The morning after I'd
left her drinking with her newfound hipster friends, I'd received an email
from Luba's secretary, Jackie, that the meet-and-greet for *The Dybbuk*
was called for one o'clock sharp the following Sunday in the theatre at
the JCC. Although I arrived on time, I entered the theatre space and
found I was the only one there. My mind immediately flooded with
recollections of how time was a relative thing in Luba's Yiddish theatre. I
recalled that as kids in her youth theatre, when we sometimes had the
opportunity to participate in the productions of what we called the "adult
group," rare was a rehearsal when those who were called actually showed
up, and if they did, you never quite knew when. It was probably best that
I was the first one there that Sunday, as I had gotten up only a few hours
earlier, and to say that I was ready and looking forward to it, would be a
lie.

"Just go and see what happens," my mother said soon after she
woke me up with a phone call, "if at the end of it, you feel overwhelmed,
then, well...." She didn't finish the thought. She was thrilled about the
idea of me doing the play from the moment Faygen told her that Luba
wanted me for the part of Khonen. And although she'd known about it
long before I did, she kept her thoughts to herself until I told her about
my meeting with Luba earlier in the week. At that point, she wasn't shy
about expressing her enthusiasm that it was the kind of out-of-the-box
change of pace that was probably just what I needed. So, I don't wanna
say that there was a lot riding on this meet-and-greet, but believe you me,
the thought of hearing an "Oh, Izzy" come out of her mouth if and when
I told her I'd reneged and decided not to do it, had my stomach in knots.

Aside from the janitor, who now walked in and set up a table to the
side of the stage along with a percolator for coffee, I took the few
moments I had to myself to breathe in one-two-three, then out the same,
as I walked along the perfectly-painted black stage, where colored gaffer's
tape had been laid to outline the space that would eventually become the
set. I had this feeling as I took it all in, just like the one I had when I

entered Luba's office after what seemed like a lifetime away, that the theatre seemed infinitely smaller than the one I recalled from my childhood. That's not a criticism. Its few hundred seats, divided almost evenly in front of and to the sides of a stage that was pretty close to being in-the-round, created an environment that was charming, intimate and, for the moment, serene. That is, until people finally decided to show up, which killed the quaint.

It began with a gaggle of Luba's old-timers, a cohort of men and women in their mid-to-late seventies, meandering their way in carrying bags and boxes full of food that they began to lay out on the table. The faces looked familiar as the actors I once shared the stage with as a child but the names, for the life of me...Not that it mattered, because mine they remembered shockingly well.

"Look, it's Izzy!" the woman leading them in shouted when she saw me. Carrying two bags of bagels with cream cheese and lox, she appeared to be the youngest and most spry in the bunch. The others whispered to each other as they approached in that way *alte kakers* do with each other, like they're pooling their combined shrinking neurons to come up with some kind of shared memory that results in the delayed "Oh, right, *that* kid" or, in the case of the ones that are too far gone, the side-to-side headshake coupled with the shoulder shrug of resignation. The woman with the bagels and lox introduced herself as Nancy, a delightfully jovial personality who you can imagine might have drawn a spotlight or two in her day, one which had long since passed. "Welcome back to the group," she said while giving me a big hug and then, with a playful "shame on you for taking so long" slap on the cheek, handed me the bags of food and immediately put me to work laying them out on the table for the arriving guests.

"*Itzikl*, you remember me?" a beaming, diminutive pot-bellied man said as we stood at the table where he had made himself a plate impressively quick. Mercifully, I needn't have worried about coming up with an answer, as he was already heading down memory lane, recalling a moment from a play thirty years earlier that, judging by his excitement, could easily have been yesterday. "You used to run from the stage, up the stairs to the top of the audience where I stood with a half-broken bathtub to sell to your *zaide*!" he said as bits of bagel and *shmeer* flew from his mouth like little projectiles of delight. It's interesting, if you think about it, how some people so internalize life experiences that had a great impact on them that even a contrived, small moment in the theatre can somehow, with the passage of time, be conflated as a profoundly personal real-life experience.

"Of course, I remember," I replied with a smile, making sure to repeat the details back to him so, at the very least, to help mitigate the awkwardness. Actually, it was less for him than for me, as the reference to my *zaide* made no sense. It was only in repeating his words that I was able to catch up with him and remember that he was referring to a play I did, where my on-stage *zaide* was an actor playing a peddler and the kid was me, who would accompany him on his wagon, collecting used-stuff to sell. "It was wonderful what you and your *zaide* used to shout from the wagon together..." Mercifully, a woman with a walker, who I assumed was his wife—Khaveh was her name—stopped him in mid-sentence before he could continue and while leading him away, gave me a wink and said with all sincerity, "you were a superstar."

The stage continued filling up as a steady flow of people entered the theatre, including Faygen, who took it upon himself to introduce me to the motley group. Aside from the geriatrics, who it seemed to me were just happy to be there for the buffet, there was the group of doctors; accountants; lawyers; electricians; teachers; and other working professionals whose involvement with Luba's theatre amounted to nothing more complicated than having a reason not to go home at the end of the day. Then there was a French-Canadian guy named Guy, an erstwhile ballet dancer looking for boys; a recently-made-wealthy divorcee apparently looking for the same; a twenty something, pasty-looking lapsed Hasid with Coke-bottle glasses; and another young man who kept pacing back and forth across the back of the stage, who I assumed was some kind of autistic.

"You shitting me?" was my response to Faygen when he told me that none of them were actors as we stood at the food table after we'd finished with the glad-handing.

"You'll see," he said self-assuredly while taking a bite of his bagel and lox, "Luba will weave her magic. She always does."

When I asked him where the actors were who were playing the other lead roles beside me, he shrugged like he had no idea.

"Lovely," I said, and grimaced.

"Relax, eat something," he said, noticing my look of concern. "You should put some food in your mouth. I spoke to your mother this morning, and she said you're anxious."

"I am."

"You don't look it."

"Fuck off."

The look of displeasure he threw me was less a concern at the moment than the complete shock on the faces of the old man with the half-broken bathtub and his walker-wife, who were still huddled at the table and, it seemed to me, started having trouble chewing their food.

"Shit. That was for him," I said to them sincerely, and pointed at Faygen. They turned away and slowly headed in the other direction.

"Should I go over and apologize?" I asked Faygen.

He waved his hand at me as if to suggest I should forget it because, at that moment, Luba was making her entrance trailed by a phalanx of artists dressed in *de rigueur* theatre black, each one carrying an item or two under their arms that, when taken all together, gave the feeling that the professionals had just walked into the room. After exchanging a few pleasantries with the assembled, Luba—who seemed anxious to get the show on the road—called for everyone to gather around at the center of the stage, where the play's creative team was set to make their presentations.

It began with the internationally-renowned set designer, Robbie Mackenzie III, presenting his *maquette* for the play, a work of art in and of itself that showcased the care given by its creator to detail. Sweating of the smallest of stuff made this blue-blooded gentile a legend, with an award-winning career that spanned the world's most renowned stages. But Mack, as Luba would end up calling him, would be the first to say that he held a special place in his heart and always made room in his professional calendar for Luba and her Yiddish theatre that gave him his first break.

As the story goes, it was during his summer internship on one of Luba's productions when, in the middle of the night just days before opening night, she found Mack painting a bookcase on the set over and over until it looked as authentic as can be. The wee hours would turn into morning and all the while, Luba, who not only had a keen eye for talent but understood the passion that drove them, sat on a chair on stage and kept him company, sharing vodka and black bread she'd brought up from her desk drawer until the work was done. By the following summer's production, Mack graduated as Luba's chief set designer. On this day, as he showcased his set for *The Dybbuk*, Mack spoke passionately about how his inspiration came from Luba herself, who, over their many years working together, regaled him with details of the *avant-garde*, expressionistic style that was a hallmark of the productions directed by her teacher, Mikhoels, for the Moscow State Yiddish Theatre-GOSET. His presentation rightfully elicited ooh's and ahh's from the assembled, particularly for the two nifty little figurines of the play's male and female leads, me and Sue-Ann, who, along with the other lead actors, happened to be a no-show.

Chantal Choquette, the play's hard-drinking, chain-smoking hot mess of a costume designer, was an altogether different story. If Mack had the pedigree, she was the miracle; a god-forsaken, drug-addicted street urchin salvaged by Luba from child services years earlier and given a job as a seamstress in her costume shop. Her decision, it seems, was based solely on some scribbling the grand dame of the theatre caught the young Chantal doing out of the corner of her eye during the interview with the teenager's exasperated handlers, who were looking for a place where she could spend her days. Despite the overdoses, multiple breakdowns, and countless harrowing nights chasing ambulances carrying the tortured soul to the hospital, Luba stuck with her. If you want to believe it, the explanation lies in that fateful interview years earlier, when Luba didn't simply clock the young Chantal's sketch, which happened to be of an actor with a fedora and a cape. More importantly, it was the unmistakable twinkle in the young artist's eye, a clear signal to Luba that the soul of an artist was suffocating within and clearly needed a place to call home, which she would gladly provide. That, in a nutshell, is Luba. Anyway, in spite of her profound shyness and fear of presentation of any kind, Chantal nevertheless proceeded to unveil her sketches for the play's costumes, explaining that she took as her main source of inspiration the title of the play itself, which is actually *Between Two Worlds (The Dybbuk)*. The costumes would therefore be evocative of both the traditional European Jewish world and the modern one that supplanted it. As she pointed with her signature unlit cigarette dangling from her trembling hands at the various sketches she'd placed on large pieces of bristle board mounted on easels, my eyes turned to Luba, who, despite her own anxiety at what was about to commence, was smiling ear-to-ear with pride.

That said, next up was the misanthropic French-Canadian lighting designer Luba introduced as Fred, which I'm sure was wrong. I eventually learned that he was new to the team, an eleventh-hour find who likely did his best work alone in the dark, judging by the fact that when called upon to present nothing but a few mumbled words came out of his mouth in incredibly broken English, which amounted to, "I hang the lights, I focus the lights, I take them down when the play's finished." Knowing better than to let the buzzkill moment hang in the air longer than necessary, Luba looked where I was standing with Faygen and gestured to him with her hand that things had to hurry along.

"What are you doing?" I whispered to him as he began fumbling for something in his pants pocket just as everyone's attention began to turn in our direction.

"She wants me to speak," he replied, and I could see he was about to pull out a roll of dental floss.

"About what?" I asked, and caught his hand before he could pull it from his pocket.

"The play."

"So, speak."

"I can't. I'm too nervous."

"What, to the supreme court, you can plead," I said to him nonplussed, "but these *nokhshleppers* make you shit your pants?"

"You do it," he implored me.

"Faygen, I'm not really in good shape either," I answered, and began to feel a pit in my stomach, which made me glad I hadn't put anything in my mouth at that point. "I don't even know what I'm doing here."

If the curt "Avrom!" she sent in his direction wasn't obvious enough, Luba's patience was growing short.

"Just tell them what the play's about," he said, and began nudging me forward a little into what felt like a spotlight I didn't ask to have shined on me. "They haven't read it."

"You're fucking with me, right?"

He didn't do me the courtesy of answering. Rather, he kept pushing me a little further into the abyss, where I now found myself standing before two dozen or so people with cups of coffee and Danishes in hand, looking at me and expecting, well, I don't fucking know what they were expecting. So, I did what Faygen asked: I told them that the Dybbuk is the story of Khonen and Leah—he, a penniless, brilliant, young, newly-minted rabbi; and she, the daughter of the wealthiest man in town—who are drawn to each other in that beautiful, innocent way young lovers can be. But he can't have her because, despite tradition, her father, Sender, isn't looking for the sharpest Torah mind to take his daughter's hand in marriage. No, he wants money to marry money. And although Khonen turns to the Kabbalah—Jewish mysticism—for otherworldly guidance, he is powerless to stop Sender, who returns to town one day to announce that he's found a match for his daughter. Upon hearing the news, Khonen faints and dies, but not before revealing that he's found his answer and that "he's won!" What, we don't know. In short order, a wedding celebration is underway. But when a crestfallen Leah is led to the canopy, she refuses the betrothal, and begins speaking in a male voice, who says that he's returned and will not leave. Fearing she's been possessed by a "dybbuk" —the dislocated soul of a dead person who has yet to find eternal rest—everyone scurries, and bedlam ensues. Soon, Sender visits Reb Azriel, the great *Miropoler Rebbe*, to seek help. When he is initially unsuccessful in banishing the dybbuk, Reb Azriel resorts to the extreme measure of ex-communication. Prior to doing so, however, he is visited by Reb Shimson, the head of the community of Miropol, who reveals to him that a man named Nisn Ben Rivkes came to him in a dream to say that the dybbuk is his son, Khonen, and that Sender is guilty for his death because he reneged on a promise they made to each other long ago and demands that Sender be called to a trial. Reb Azriel says that it sounds serious, but first, he has to excommunicate the dybbuk before any such trial can take place. Eventually, he convinces the dead spirit to leave Leah's body and gives it a few hours to do so.

In the meantime, the trial takes place where it is revealed that as boys in their yeshiva days, Nisn Ben Rivkes and Sender made a pact: That when they got married, if one's wife was to bear a son and the other a daughter, they would be betrothed to each other. Nisn accuses his old friend of breaking his promise because after Nisn died, when it came time for his son to find a wife, he naturally found his way to Sender's home, where Sender would surely have noticed how strikingly similar he looked to his old friend. But instead of asking Khonen who he was and whether he was Nisn's son, he turned away and chose greed instead. Reb Azriel, serving as chief judge at the trial, determines that Sender is not guilty of the promises made before the young lovers were even born. But as penance for the pain he caused, he must say the Mourner's Prayer for Nisn and Khonen every day for the rest of his life. He is also to give half his fortune to charity. Ominously, when Nisn is asked whether he accepts the judgment, there is no response. The trial ends on this note, with a sense of urgency so that the wedding can occur. The dybbuk does indeed leave Leah's body in the time given by Reb Azriel, and everyone rushes to meet the bridegroom and his family. While alone and waiting, Leah is visited by Khonen whose soul has left her body. At that moment, they pledge to be together, if not in this world, then in the one to come. When everyone returns to lead Leah again to the wedding canopy, it is too late: She has died to be with the one she was always predestined to be with.

After I finished, people began turning to one another and started whispering. Although I couldn't make out what they were saying, judging by the look on their faces, it was no doubt something along the lines of, "wow, that's a really cool story, but how good is this Danish?"

"Thank you," Faygen said, giving me a pat on the back as I stepped back to join him again. "There was supposed to be a table read, but with the leads not here today, it was a last-minute thing Luba wanted me to do."

"Whatever," I said to him dismissively, "it's done."

Apparently not, it seemed, because Luba threw me and Faygen another look and again motioned with her hand to keep going.

"What does she want now?" I asked him.

"I told her I'd give some historical background too. She felt it's important for them to know about how special the play is."

"And you seriously can't get your shit together for this?"

"You're doing a great job."

"Fuck off," I said, now totally exasperated. "Honestly, how the hell are you going to be in this play?"

"Please, just do it."

"No," I insisted in a tone that I knew right away was coming from that place inside where the urge to run was starting to grow, and I didn't want to have to start fighting it in public, surrounded by people I didn't know. "Besides," I added, "they're not listening and they don't care."

Well, that is except for the lapsed Hasid, who for some reason, was feverishly taking notes. Before Faygen could respond however, the ball of fire from the bar earlier in the week decided to show up.

"Hey, everyone, *soooo* sorry I'm late," Sue-Ann said cheerfully as she joined us on stage, where Luba proceeded to introduce her to the group, all of whom seemed immediately smitten.

"What'd I miss?" she asked Luba as they wrapped their arms around one another's waists.

"Nothing, *meydele*," Luba answered her in a pleasant tone resonating with boundless patience that, for some reason, totally pissed me off. "*Itzikl* is telling us about the play."

"Oh, how sweet!" Sue-Ann said as she turned in my direction and stared at me Susanna Hoffs-like, which caused me to immediately avert my gaze—that's right, Susanna Hoffs, look her up.

"Izzy, you okay?" Faygen whispered in my ear when the silence in the room lasted longer than it should have.

"Yeah, fine. Why?"

"You're staring at your feet."

I was, and it was because a woman's look in my direction, the kind I hadn't experienced in what seemed like forever, made me feel exposed. And it was fucking embarrassing.

"Go on, tell them about the play," he said, and tried to push me forward again, but I resisted.

"Faygen," I whispered to him while still staring at my feet and beginning to feel helpless like a child. "I have to go. I don't know if I can handle this much longer."

"Yes, you can, you absolutely can," he said by way of encouragement, which didn't do much, to tell the truth. "Please, do me this favor, I promised Luba."

"Fine," I answered him petulantly, if not a little bit pissed off, and began to deliver a perfunctory history of the play to fulfill a responsibility nobody asked me if I'd wanted to take on. "For some reason, people always quibble about when An-sky wrote *The Dybbuk* and in what language," I said. "Honestly, who gives a shit?" I continued, which elicited not a few gasps and looks of displeasure from the Danish mafia, who decided they'd already heard enough and started to talk amongst themselves while retreating to the buffet table for more. "He wrote it around 1914," I continued, speaking more quickly now as I could feel that I wouldn't be able to sustain my composure much longer. "He was inspired by real-life stories he recorded as part of an ethnographic expedition he led before World War I, to preserve a vanishing Jewish world that he felt was too important to let pass into the dustbin of history. It was probably written in Russian first, then in Yiddish. But again, who cares, because he didn't live to see it produced. He died in 1920."

"See, they don't give a shit," I said to Faygen about the pigs at the trough as I stepped back to join him and again looked to the floor, probably out of shame. Yeah, it was shame. "Can I go now, please?" I pleaded with him.

Trust me when I tell you that Faygen isn't someone to whom you'd ascribe quality bedside manner. But at that moment, as nervous as he was himself, he cradled my head in his arm and gently pressed his forehead against mine. "If you go, I won't judge you, and your mother won't either," he whispered as we both looked down at the floor and not at each other. "I see what you're doing. You're thinking about him, and taking this step is also making you feel things you don't want to, so you're protecting yourself," he continued, which caused us both to lift our heads and look one another in the eye. "I know what this means to you and that you want to share it. Tell me if I'm wrong."

I didn't.

"Speak. Trust me, they'll listen," he said as he caressed my head and let me go.

I didn't say anything right away. Being there was hard enough without Faygen bringing up my *zaide*. But he did and now I needed a moment to sit with that before I could open my mouth because I wasn't sure what would come out and, if anything did, how coherent it would be. One thing I was damn sure about was that I didn't know if I could keep myself from crying. A moot point because my eyes started to well up as I continued staring down at the floor, and I was powerless to stop it. Fucking Faygen. When I finally looked up, what I saw through the moisture was a blur but my thoughts were clear.

"This isn't just a play. It's a mission statement," I began softly. "Ansky, like many Jewish intellectuals in Eastern Europe in his time, was struggling with a profound crisis: How could they bring about the hoped-for revolution that would normalize Jews by bringing them into the modern world when they were powerless to do so? They had no territory to call their own and no army to defend it. There was only one weapon at their disposal...their art. And that's the context within which we have to understand *The Dybbuk*; because everything about it is suffused with An-sky's deep-seated desire to have Jewish art and culture viewed on-par with the greatest of the societies in which they lived."

"This isn't just a play. It's a mission statement," I repeated and wiping the wetness from my eyes, I could now clearly see Luba starting in my direction. She wore a serious look on her face and her head was lifted in that way of hers when delivering a powerful speech, which sort of made me feel like I was channeling what she herself would have said had she had the vocabulary in English to do so.

"At the time An-sky wrote the play," I went on, "revolutionaries such as himself were grappling with two major concepts: National self-determination, and the role of the individual in society. It's impossible to read *The Dybbuk* and not see how An-sky used them as the foundational themes in his story. As we know, he sets the play within the context of the traditional Jewish world, but specifically in the arcane world of the Hasidim. That's nothing less than An-sky planting a flag so that the surrounding cultures, who at the time were expounding the virtues of their own folkways and the salt-of-the-earth people who created them, could see that Jews were no different. And what is the love story between Khonen and Leah if not the apotheosis of anti-establishment, individual free will, which at the time was an incredibly revolutionary act of self-expression?"

Judging by how feverishly the lapsed Hasid standing directly opposite me was taking notes, it looked like he was about to have his own moment of self-expression. Even the coffee and Danish gang started paying attention. I didn't look in the direction of the eyes that I had to turn away from moments earlier, but I felt them staring at me anyway.

"The isn't just a play. It's a mission statement," I again said, and began to wrap up. "An-sky, like his contemporaries, strove for their work to be nothing short of high art. And that's why he wrote a deeply serious and profound play, with layer upon layer of meaning, because of the exceptional role those artists gave to theatre as a means of expressing national identity. It explains why he submitted the play to the Moscow Art Theatre, where Stanislavsky himself had a serious interest in producing it and it is apparently based on the great theatre master's advice that An-sky revised the play to include the part of the *meshulakh*,

The Messenger. But the Revolution and its aftermath would prevent An-sky from seeing his play produced in his lifetime."

I don't know why it was in that moment specifically, but that last bit I said about An-sky dying before he could see the play produced stopped me cold. I then began to experience a surge of emotion that I had kept dormant for too long, instantly recognizing that it was about my book that wasn't getting published. Everything blurred again as my eyes started to well up even more than before, and my voice began to quiver as I tried to go on.

"He was between two worlds," I said about An-sky, referencing, of course, the title of the play, but at the same time revealing something about myself that I hadn't intended to and the hurt that I had been sublimating was real. "On the one hand," I said, "the rapidly changing modern one he was so passionately engaged in building, and on the other, the traditional one he was desperately afraid of seeing disappear."

"When he died," I said, my voice beginning to trail off, "the famed Vilna Troupe pledged to premiere the play on the *shloyshim* in Warsaw. And they did." At that moment, I could feel an arm wrapping around my waist. It was Faygen who came to stand beside me, almost like he knew what I was about to say. "This isn't just a play and it's more than a mission statement; it's our legacy," I said as I closed my eyes and for the life of me, I don't know why, but I suddenly began to sway, as if in deep meditation, even prayer. "It is the remarkable words written down by a modern-day, secular prophet and as invaluable to us as a people as the holiest book..." It was pin-drop silent when I opened my eyes and I could see that the collective gaze in the room was fixed in my direction, waiting for me to finish my thought. I turned to look at Faygen, who understood and then to Luba, whose hands were clasped together over her face like she knew even more than he did. At that moment, in front of all of them, I couldn't hold it in anymore, and whether I was conscious of it or not, I gave myself permission to let go. The tears erupted now and as my shoulders began to heave, I did my best to finish my thought: "This play..it's... it's...*hadras koydesh*," I managed to say before I turned and ran out of the theatre.

Whether you're a believer or not, you've got to hand it to the man for giving us crying as our primary method of auto-catharsis. Actually, I'd include jerking off also, so make that two methods. Amen, selah. But if you've been there, you know like I do, that relief through auto-catharsis is annoyingly fleeting. It does fuck all to protect you from the guilt, the shame, the self-loathing, and the incessant ruminating that invariably arrives once the tears have stopped flowing and you've long since shot your wad. So, I'm sure I don't have to explain myself to you for having gone from speech to tears, to running while feeling like you're the biggest fuck up on the planet, all in what was in the span of like...that. And I know we agree that the meds are just a mask for what invariably bubbles up to the surface in some way, somehow, so I don't have to go there either. "They're protecting you," my doc always says, "we know how much worse you are without them." Not the most delicate way of phrasing it, to be sure. But I wasn't about to call and give her the satisfaction of telling her she was right, not at the moment when I found myself racing out of the JCC, my mind filled with thoughts of everything negative about myself, where the only thing I was thinking about was getting home and to my bed, which was the one place that I knew was safe.

"Hey!" a voice called out to me as I left the building and quickly descended the staircase that fronts it.

It was Sue-Ann.

"What's going on?" she shouted again after I didn't acknowledge, and started after me.

"None of your business!" I yelled back, and kept walking.

"Would you stop for a second?" she said as she caught up to me on the sidewalk, grabbed my shoulder, and spun me around to face her. "Don't be such a jerk. Tell me why you're leaving."

"Because I am."

"That's not an answer."

"I don't owe you one," I said, and tried to continue with my departure.

"Yes, you do," she said and pulled me back, which caused people to turn their heads toward us as they walked past. "This is the second time you're just up and leaving without an explanation. What's wrong?"

"Nothing. I never should have come," I said, releasing myself from her grasp, and started walking away.

"I find that really hard to believe," she said incredulously. "Not after everything you just said in there."

"Leave me alone," I answered without turning back, hoping that was the end of it.

It wasn't. I was nearly halfway down the block when I heard her voice again.

"*Hadras koydesh!*" she yelled, which caused me and not a few other people nearby to stop and look in her direction. "Faygen told me what it means!"

The crowd of about a dozen people who'd stopped to witness the show were now staring at me as well, like they were also curious to know and were waiting for me to respond.

"It's the most beautiful thing I've ever heard anyone say," Sue-Ann said.

If you were in my place, in that moment, out there on the street feeling as vulnerable as can be with what felt like all the world staring at you, would you have said anything? Of course, you wouldn't.

Neither did I.

Meanwhile, a voice called out to Sue-Ann from the entrance to the JCC, to which she responded to hold on a second while she made one last effort in my direction. "If you can say that and walk away, then you're not just hurting yourself," she said. "You know that, right?" she asked rhetorically, then turned back and ran up the stairs to the entrance of the JCC.

When people say things like that to those of us who are on the susceptible spectrum, I don't think they realize the impact it has. That stuff I said just a bit ago about auto-catharsis moving swiftly into self-loathing and the feeling like nothing else could possibly exist in the world other than the thoughts that turn you inward on yourself? Yeah, that pendulum can swing back pretty quick. My thoughts now began to race, not so much about how quickly I could get to my safe space, but to what the consequences of taking that action would mean. I believe the douchebags in the white coats call it "cyclothymia," but I'm not sure. You can look it up. Regardless, I don't know that Faygen was right when he said he wouldn't judge, nor would my mother. Sure, they would, and I wouldn't believe them if they feigned otherwise. Not to mention all these other people who I'd just met and who didn't matter, including her, but who all of a sudden now did.

"Fuck!" I roared, which caused the half-dozen or so people on the street, all of whom had been staring at me the whole time waiting to see how this was going to end, to draw their heads back like a strong gust of wind had just buffeted them. "It means the splendor of holiness," I said to them—which is what a journalist for a Yiddish daily apparently wrote upon experiencing the Vilna Troupe's premiere production of *The Dybbuk* in Warsaw—and instead of continuing on to my safe place, I turned in the other direction and made my way back into the JCC, to what I think was a smattering of applause.

DEAR READER...

I have to pause here because Faygen got a hold of the manuscript—thank you, mother—and when he got to this point, he called me up and said we needed to chat.

"About what?"

"The Yiddish."

"What about it?"

"Well, I think that maybe your readers will find it distracting."

"Go fuck yourself," I told him, and hung up.

"*Yingele*," he said when he called back and I answered again. "Would you at least hear what I want to tell you?"

"Go ahead."

"I think maybe you should create a glossary."

"Who the fuck doesn't know what *makher, mentsh, shikshe,* and *narishkeit* mean?!" I told him when I called back shortly after I hung up on him again. "I mean, come on! They've entered the vernacular like *shmuck, putz,* and every other Yiddish word we wish never had."

"You're right, but that's not what I'm talking about."

"Well, would you get to the point already, please?"

"You're holding yourself back."

"From what."

"From being yourself."

"I'm gonna hang up on you again."

"I can see where you used English when you wanted to use the Yiddish, but were afraid nobody would understand."

"How do you know?"

"*Yingele...*" he said again, and although he wasn't standing next to me, if he was, he'd be staring right through me.

"Well, they won't," I said petulantly.

"So, use a glossary."

"Nobody's gonna read the fucking book if they have to keep flipping to the back every two seconds!"

"You're exaggerating," he said calmly. "Just write what you want them to read and when appropriate, insert a footnote at the bottom of the page and explain. No one will begrudge you."

"Yes, they will."

"They'll be grateful."

"No, they won't."

"And you'll be happier."

"Jury's out."

"I think you should do it," he said before adding, of course..."and so does your mother."

"Oh, come on!"

"We agree you shouldn't edit yourself."

"Fine, *genug shoyn[1].*"

"See, that wasn't so bad, now, was it?"

"I'm hanging up on you now."

"*Zay gezunt.*"

"Am I gonna have to translate that for them, too, now?"

"I think they'll get it."

"Fine, *ciao.*"

Fucking Faygen.

---

1. Enough already.

7

"No, no, no!" I could hear Luba's voice screaming from outside the theatre just as I was about to walk back in. Entering through the rear doors, I could see that she was already pacing back and forth on stage where she had begun rehearsing the play and figuring discretion was in order, I quietly chose a seat in the back so as not to disturb. Although I had followed Sue-Ann back into the building, I didn't see her in the room. What I did see was a small group of the *nokhshleppers* from the meet-and-greet who were sprinkled throughout the theatre, sitting and sipping their coffees and finishing off what was left of the buffet. If you know anything about the world of theatre, it's not normal for this kind of an "audience" to be present at rehearsal, except in Luba's Yiddish theatre, where she encouraged it. Even though I didn't make a peep in taking a seat in the back row, it took no more than a split second for the eyes on the backs of their heads to see that I had returned. They soon turned in my direction, the looks on their faces grim and serious as they began whispering to each other things that I probably was relieved not to hear. "Turn away, people, nothing to see here," I wanted to yell at all of them, "it's just the fucking withdrawal." Besides, the drama in the room at that moment wasn't with me and my surprise return, but rather on the stage where the opening scene of the play was being rehearsed, and already it wasn't going well.

Luba, with her back to the actors, was leaning into the table at the foot of the stage with her arms pressed firmly into it like it was some kind of giant stress ball, her head all the while hanging downward like she was taking a moment before something explosive was about to happen...again. Not that it would be the actors' fault on stage, mind you. Nor, for that matter, Joseph—the soft-spoken, punctilious stage manager I'd been introduced to earlier in the day—who was sitting at the table facing Luba and, true to form, saying very little. And it certainly was not due to anything that the lady sitting next to him might have done either. Wendy was her name, a sixty-something-year-old volunteer whose sole job was to sticky-note Luba's ramblings over the course of rehearsals, that were more than likely going to be spoken in a language Joseph would be unable to decipher. As Faygen tells it, she always carried a bag of assorted candy with her, which was the primary *raison d'etre* for this longtime member of Luba's group being by the director's side during rehearsals. At this particular moment, she was sitting at the table with Joseph directly opposite Luba, who was making quick work of a stack of Twizzlers Wendy had given her and was about to explode.

I could see it coming from when I walked into her office earlier in the week. She was a fuse ready to be lit.It wasn't enough that she was about to take on the biggest theatrical challenge of her career, with only eight weeks to do it, to boot. Even with me agreeing to be in the play, she still wasn't fully cast and knew full well that she wouldn't be hitting the ground running on the first day of rehearsal. This was the case, by the way, as the actors on stage—Faygen among them—hadn't bothered learning their lines in time and kept tripping over the words on the page as they referred to their scripts, while Luba attempted in frustration to stage the scene. Even then, some of the opening lines of the play came courtesy of Joseph, who had to read aloud for actors who hadn't shown up, including the guy who was to play the part of Reb Sender. Sitting with her in her office a few days earlier, she said she had to offer it to someone who couldn't act for his life but happened to do her taxes pro bono and insisted this was what he wanted in return. Thankfully, although it's a lead role, it's not particularly meaty, and the fact that he was missing on the first day of rehearsal wasn't the biggest deal.

The absence of the actor playing the part of the *meshulakh* however, was, and I assumed that's what set her off. When she told me that she'd given the part to Norman—a.k.a. Nokhem—I figured that was a solid pick. Although there were no stars in her ensemble, I distinctly recall that back in the day, he was the shit, her go-to leading man for nearly everything she produced. I couldn't conceive of such things back then, but looking back on it now, it was obvious they were fucking. What else could've explained the irrational, passive-aggressive, petty arguments they would have in the open, in front of the whole company during rehearsals, including us kids, which amounted to little more than, "I swallowed last night and you didn't call me, you asshole." According to Luba, however, time hadn't been a friend to Nokhem, and he was no longer the actor he once was. A man in his late seventies now, it had been quite a few years since he'd appeared in any of her productions, and his memory, never that sharp to begin with, was diminishing due to early-stage Alzheimer's. However, that didn't stop him from calling her up when he heard she was producing the play to insist that he had to play the part of the *Miropoler Rebbe*. There was not a chance in hell she was giving him that part, particularly when there was someone she had in mind who she was still holding out for.

Moreover, she told him that because he was really out of shape—to put it kindly—she couldn't see herself giving him a part that would tax his brain and that the alternative, simply having him on stage as part of the company, would embarrass the two of them and she wasn't going there. She'd save him a VIP ticket for opening night, she told him. Of course, he was having none of it and it took no time at all for him to lobby enough people in the company, including Faygen, I later learned, all of whom impressed upon Luba that for the good of the company, its legacy and the sake of the play, she needed to give him a part. "If you won't let me play the *Rebbe*," Nokhem said when they eventually met in her office to discuss the matter in person, "I'll play the *meshulakh*." You'll notice it wasn't a request. As if the *chutzpah* of that statement alone wasn't enough, he followed up with this too: "And I also want the monologue," he told her, and pointed to one of the most memorable monologues in the play, words of pure poetry which An-sky put into the mouth of the *Miropoler Rebbe*, when he introduces him into the play for the first time. You can imagine Luba's reaction. She told me she nearly fell off her chair. However, when Nokhem put on her desk a version of the script he revised himself, which had the play beginning with him on stage alone delivering, you guessed it, the *Rebbe*'s salient monologue. Apparently with an addition he felt was required to give a little of the backstory. For a septuagenarian on the verge of losing his mind, apparently, he turned impressively spry when he ran out of her office as she began raining upon him pretty well everything on her desk, in its drawers, and whatever else she could easily grab and toss in his direction when he proceeded to read *his* lines aloud, by heart apparently, to demonstrate that he had he still had the chops.

Which all goes to explain why Luba totally lost her shit the moment rehearsal began with Joseph reading the following at the top of the play in place of Nokhem, who apparently was taking a nap that day to conserve his energy:

Once a year
At the appointed hour, at the appointed moment
There would assemble all that is most exalted in this world

And all that is most holy from the other world
And that took place on Yom Kippur, the Sabbath of Sabbaths
When the High Priest would step foot into
The Holy of Holies in the Temple in Jerusalem
And there, would utter the unutterable name—the true name of The
Master of the Universe

And while this hour and this moment
Was the most hallowed of all,
It was also the most perilous for the High Priest—and for all of Israel
For, if, at that instant, heaven forbid
Had the High Priest had but one sinful thought,
The whole world could have been destroyed

And so it is with human souls
That the innocent
The pure souls are drawn
To the source of all sources
To the spring of all springs
To the seat of holiness, high above,
To the throne of the Lord
And become one with the holy flame

Yet it transpires, that a soul commits a transgression
And even though that soul has attained the uppermost plane
And has ascended up to the gates of heaven
Should that same soul break one rule
It will stumble and fall
It will plummet from the highest heights
To the deepest depths of perdition,
It will descend from the dazzling light
To the darkness of the abyss
And it will be barred from both worlds

And so it was
With Nisn ben Rivke and Sender ben Henye
Who shook hands on an agreement, gave their word, made a vow, a
promise

While their wives were yet with child
That should one of them bear a son
And the other a daughter
That the pair would be betrothed
And in time
The wife of Nisn bore a son—Khonen
And at the same time
The wife of Sender bore a daughter—Leah
And a deep voice rose from the heavens
And blessed the sanctified vow
And let it be known that Khonen and Leah
Were a predestined pair
For shaking hands on an agreement is sacred and awesome
And by breaking that agreement
Even a pure soul
Can lose this world and the right to enter the world to come.

Sinful thoughts and deeds
Can slay a person
As it could have been with the High Priest in the Holy of Holies,
And thus destroy
Not only the makers of the vow and their children
But an entire world.

Beautiful, right? Regardless, Luba clearly wasn't at peace with the Faustian bargain she'd made to both keep her company together and to get the most important production of her career produced, by having those words open the play; delivered, no less, by someone who she couldn't be sure would be able to remember the lines from one performance to the next. That was a matter for another day, however. In the meantime, she had a bunch of men standing idly by on stage, the *batlonim*[2], waiting for her to turn around and tell them what to do.

"Ok, *khevre*[3]," she eventually said in exasperation, referring to them in the collective. Then, while still with her back to them as she

---

2. Poor, benighted men who hang around the synagogue or study hall in the hopes that they'll get some money tossed their way for being available to make up a religious quorum.
3. Gang.

stood at the stage manager's table at the foot of the stage, her head hanging between her arms that were pressed firmly into it, she added, "just let me hear you read your lines."

The first of the *batlonim* to mangle his one sentence describing Reb Dovidl of Talna and his chair made of gold, was Paul, a fellow in his sixties who by day was a foreman in the sole unionized ladies' garment factory in town and who also happened to be one of Faygen's closest friends.

"And it is said," Faygen now followed in perfectly-spoken Yiddish, "that Reb Shmuel Kaminker walked around in golden slippers, golden slippers!"

"*Zeyer gut*, Avrom" Luba commented approvingly of Faygen's fine delivery while chewing on another Twizzler, still with her back turned.

"The holy Reb Zusye of Anop..." Joseph now began reading the next line aloud in place of the absent Nokhem before Luba cut him off: "Skip it," she said coldly, waving her red candy stick at him in response to his beginning to read the *meshulakh's* part. "Next line!" she yelled out.

Now it was this guy George's turn to talk about how, when the *Rebbe* of Apt first met the Tzaddik of Ruzhin, he threw himself to the ground and kissed the wheels of his chariot. But the bald, diminutive, erstwhile plumber, with a hand tremor and a stammer something awful, could barely hold the script in his hands while making a tepid attempt to get the words out of his mouth that seemed to be stuffed with a handful of marbles. Luba, her head still hanging between her arms as she stared down at the table, just shook it side to side, and I wondered if she was already giving up before she'd even begun. "Avrom," she called out while throwing one arm up in the air, indicating she knew what the next line was and who was to deliver it.

"In my hometown, there is a rabbi who works miracles...!" Faygen delivered his next line excitedly, which to me suggested, because I know him like I do, that he was trying to get Luba back in the game. He may have succeeded, as her head began moving forward and back as if to suggest she was somewhat pleased. "He knows such sacred names," he continued and, while turning to face his fellow stiff-as-a-board, rank amateur thespians, began to gesticulate awkwardly as he called out each of the following great wonders of the miracle worker: "He can create a Golem! Raise the dead! Become invisible! Call forth evil spirits...even the Devil himself!" The latter wonder work he followed up with a spit towards the ground that I don't recall being in An-sky's stage direction, but which nevertheless garnered a few chuckles from the *nokhshleppers*[4] in the audience. "I heard all of this with my own ears!" he added.

"Where is he?" I yelled out from my perch in the back row of the theatre before Joseph could read the next line in the script—mine —which caused every head in the theatre to turn and look up in my direction, including Luba's. I now made my way down the aisle towards the stage, all the while looking over at Luba, whose face lit up as I grew closer and by the time I hit the stage to join the company of men in the opening scene, had completely lifted herself from the state of resignation she'd been in at the stage manager's table and now turned toward the stage to begin directing the play.

"Who?" Faygen responded to me as I walked up next to him for the little conversation Khonen has with the man whose mention of this miracle worker sparks his interest. Like Luba, he, too, couldn't contain his excitement at my return to the theatre, and gave me a little hug.

"The rabbi who works miracles," I said.

"Where should he be? In my hometown, of course! If he's still alive."

"Is it far from here?"

"Far, very far. In lower Polesia."

"How far?"

"A good month's journey, if not more. Why are you asking? You want to visit him, maybe?"

"Perhaps."

"The name of the town is Krasna. The man's name is Rabbi Elkhonen."

"Elkhonen?" I asked him, expressing great curiosity at how close the name resembled my own.

"The god of Khonen?"

"Okay, *khevre*!" Luba exclaimed after I'd finished my line, exhibiting a renewed sense of vigor likely attributable to a massive sugar rush, judging by the nearly empty bag of Twizzlers on the table behind her. "Let's run it from the top, now that *Itzik!*'s here...," she said with that trademark giggle, and came over to give me a kiss before heading back to the stage manager's table where she barked at Joseph, "but without the

---

4. Plural of a groupie with a heart of gold, but who needs to get a life.

meshigoner meshulakh monologue!" and took a bite out of the last remaining Twizzler.

"You okay?" Faygen said as he approached me while Luba huddled with her stage management team for a few moments before we began running the scene from the top.

"For now," I replied with a shrug. "Ask me in five minutes."

"Should I bother asking what brought you back?"

I threw him a look to suggest he knew very well what the answer was.

"I'm glad she convinced you," he said with a wink regarding the street scene Sue-Ann had instigated a little earlier.

"You just had to explain to her what *hadras koydesh* meant, didn't you?" I said to him accusingly.

"She couldn't bear the thought of doing the play without you," he said with a wink. "None of us can."

"Where is she?"

"Coaching."

"What the fuck are you talking about?"

"Her lines. She wants the words to come out of her mouth like *mame loshn.*[5] So, Luba got her a Yiddish coach."

"Right," I replied sarcastically.

Just then, the pallid, *gevezener*[6] Hasid with the notepad and the Coke-bottle glasses, who had been standing on stage the whole time, approached me and Faygen and tapped me lightly on the shoulder.

"Excuse me," he said gently, almost in a whisper. "I wish to tell you how moving the words were that you spoke," he said earnestly but awkwardly, a clear indication that he was not long out of the fold and newly arrived to the English language as well.

"He made me do it," I said and pointed at Faygen, who rolled his eyes at my stupidity as the young man stared at me with a look of confusion. "I'm fucking with you," I said, and extended a hand. "I'm Isaiah."

"I'm called Shmuly," he said, then told me he was playing the part of Henekh, Khonen's best friend in the play, while shaking my hand effeminately.

---

5. Literally, "mother's tongue." Practically, it means the Yiddish language.
6. Lapsed, this is what Faygen meant when he said I should just use the Yiddish word that's in my head and let my agent tell me it makes the book unsellable.

"Yeah, I'm not calling you that," I said and squeezed his hand firmly to get him to adjust to how it's actually done, "how about we go with Sam?" I asked and he looked at me dumbfounded, saying nothing but then turning to Faygen, who didn't have time to smack me upside the head and explain my idiocy to him because Joseph had now called for the scene to start.

Sam and I now stood together quietly, watching as Faygen and his pals once again repeated their lines about the various miracle-working *rebbes*, which had Sam hanging on every word.

"What's going on?" I asked him, noticing how intently he was listening to the men once again tripping over themselves to deliver their lines about the Apter, Ruzjiner, the Talner, et. al.

"It's remarkable," he answered.

"What is?"

"What they're saying."

"Hardly," I scoffed, and said that An-sky was just writing about superstitions he'd recorded people telling him about during his travels to document Jewish folklore and that, moreover, none of this nonsense about holy Hasidic rabbis and their purported miracle-working was real.

"Oh, it's very real," Sam said earnestly, then turned and looked at me directly as his eyes widened as if he was speaking like a true believer. "I know of one myself."

Sam would turn out to be an interesting fellow. The next time I found myself in his company was a week later, when we were scheduled to rehearse the scene that takes place in the synagogue early on in the play. The one in which Khonen and Henekh—sitting in *khevrusah*[7] at a table by candlelight—do a deep dive into the age-old debate between the merits of strict adherence to the tried-and-true practice of studying Torah and *gemara*, versus allowing for expanding one's mind and consciousness by delving into the mysteries and secrets of the world that can be found in the books of Jewish mysticism, known as the Kabbalah. Specifically, whether even dipping one's toe into this unpredictable and perilous sea was rife with the potential to cause one who explores it to lose their mind to madness. In the play, An-sky has Henekh—Sam in this case—arguing

---

7. The traditional way of studying the Talmud—a.k.a *gemara*—typically in pairs.

for the safety and predictability of Moses' five books and the oral law that followed it while Khonen—me—goes to bat for the sexier, although possibly mind-altering world of the Kabbalah. Yup, typecasting.

As it happened, we were delayed in getting our debate on because while we sat waiting to rehearse our scene together on one side of the stage, Luba was locked in a raging battle royale with one of her longstanding female actors on the other side, and it was getting uglier by the second.

Apparently, things began to boil over even before I entered the theatre that day a little in advance of my scheduled call time where, in the days since our first rehearsal, the stage was now set with makeshift elements that gave the sense that a play was actually in production. For the scene in the synagogue, it included a few tables with some aged books strewn about made to look like *sforim*[8]; some benches; a *shtender*[9]; and even an *oren koydesh*[10] with a red *paroykhes*[11] draped in front and a *ner tamid*[12] hanging just above it. The actors on stage that day included the men playing the *batlonim* and Nokhem, the *meshulalkh*, who were running the scene from the top, where they discuss Reb Sender being on the lookout for a match for his daughter.

Everything seemed to be going smoothly up until the point when the *meshulakh* delivers his retort to the men that perhaps Reb Sender could find a suitable match in the local yeshiva. It seems that's when Luba went after Nokhem with both barrels blazing, unleashing a diatribe of fire and fury so virulent that it clearly had nothing to do with his innocuous line in the script and everything to do with her seemingly still seething from the negotiation she'd lost to him in her office only days earlier. She escalated her verbal assault with a barrage of books she began hurling at his head from each of the tables on the stage. As Joseph told it to me later, when she ran out of ammunition, she threw *herself* at him and it was only thanks to Faygen and his pals getting in between the director and her aging, erstwhile star that either one of them was still breathing and we had a play to continue rehearsing.

---

8. Holy books.
9. Standing lectern to read said Holy Books.
10. Ark.
11. Curtain covering said Ark.
12. The light hanging from the Ark meant to represent the presence of the Almighty.

You'd think the time-out Joseph called for would have allowed for cooler heads to prevail by the time rehearsal continued. It didn't. While he was out having a smoke, Ronda entered the theatre and quietly took a seat in the first row, waiting for her part to be called. She looked nothing like I remembered her: A knockout blonde with proportions that made you want to run to the bathroom and whip it out every time she walked into a room. Mind you, the looks were just a plus because when it came to the chops to handle pretty much anything Luba threw at her, no one in her company held a candle to Ronda. Truthfully, she came by it naturally with not a stitch of training. It was while waitressing her way through college that a friend who was in Luba's company at the time told her the director was desperately looking for the female lead for one of the Bashevis productions she was about to begin rehearsing. I forget which one, maybe *Teibele*. Whatever, *nisht vikhtik*[13]. Suffice it to say that it called for the lead actress to reach deep to deliver the kind of psychological gymnastics the bald, Nobel-prize winning author was renowned for creating in his characters. You'll read many books on the subject of acting technique, each one riffing on the same, tired subject of "method-this" and "sense-memory that," as a way of explaining how an actor can just be a fucking human being in front of a paying audience. I'll let you in on a little secret. It comes down to this: The best actors know how to walk the fine line that separates what's raw and true from flat-out bat shit crazy. That was Ronda...then.

The woman I saw in the theatre that day struck me as an impostor. The long, flowing blonde hair was now a mess of matted grey. The svelte pow was now a sixty-something round, and the blank, distant stare I noticed on her face suggested that maybe she'd ended up on the wrong side of that fine line mentioned above. As I observed her from my place on stage at the table I was sharing with Sam, I thought to myself that she didn't look like she wanted to be there. Although the reason she was in the room that day made perfect sense, I would learn soon enough that my hunch was right.

When we began rehearsing again, Luba invited Ronda to join us on stage, where she was greeted warmly by Faygen, Nokhem, and some of the other men with whom she'd shared the stage over many years, all the while whispering things to each other that I was too far out of earshot to

---

13. Not important.

make out. When Joseph called the scene, we took it from where things had left off, which was just at the point when a widowed woman, who has seemingly gone mad, runs into the synagogue crying and throws herself at the Holy Ark, threatening to rip out each of the Torah scrolls as she wails at the Almighty to intercede on behalf of her one and only daughter, who is on her death bed. Although it's only a few lines in the script, they're remarkably haunting and unsettling. At first, Ronda read her lines from the script in her hands without any hint of emotion, almost as if monotone. The second time through, by heart now, her delivery didn't change. I looked over at Faygen and then at Nokhem, and judging by the looks on their faces, I knew something was wrong.

"Okay! Let's really do it now!" Luba barked at Ronda, and clapped her hands impatiently as she stood at the foot of the stage, clearly not having cooled off from the break.

Ronda did as directed: Entered the synagogue and delivered her lines, but this time around, her energy was only slightly better.

"I need to hear you, Ronda. Let's go!" Luba shouted at her again. "You're running, you're crying, you're screaming. I want screaming!"

Ronda did none of it.

"Come on *mamele,* you can do it," Luba said, lowering her volume a tad and addressing the woman affectionately, likely in an attempt to draw out the actress she instinctively knew was trapped somewhere in that body. But the next thing she said totally nullified it. "Think of Debbie," she said for everyone to hear, which I later learned referred to the barely thirty-year-old daughter Ronda had lost only a year earlier. "Give me your emotions, the loss, the pain, all of it!" Luba shouted.

Directors sometimes will go there, it's true. They'll say and do things to elicit performances from their actors that the average person would rightfully consider abusive. Luba should have known better and whether it was her nerves; a lack of sleep; being overwhelmed by what she was trying to do; or any number of reasons that got the better of her in the moment, they were all irrelevant. She'd said it, it was out there, and that's when all hell broke loose...again. I'll spare you the details because I'm sure you can picture the scene perfectly well, but between the crying, the yelling, a chair flying across the stage on the wings of a "how could you even!" to several books that also saw liftoff accompanied by a "you call yourself a director, you monster!" It was an all-out *mêlée* that, as you might imagine, took not a small amount of time to resolve itself. Meanwhile, on our side of the stage, Sam was concerned that we weren't doing anything to help resolve the situation. His worry became particularly acute when Ronda stormed out of the theatre with a vow never to return and when Luba responded that she was not an actor, never was one, and that it was the biggest mistake of her life to ask her to play the part, *s'hot by im di hent getzitert*[14].

"Relax," I told him. "You'll see, in a few minutes, it'll all blow over and they'll be hugging and kissing and making it like it never happened."

"From where do you know this?" he asked earnestly.

"Call it a hunch," I said. "Just sit tight for now."

He looked at me dumbfounded.

"Seriously?" I asked, and looked at him similarly, then told him in plain English: "Sit here, next to me at this table and don't move. We'll be rehearsing our bit soon, *farshtanen*[15]?"

He smiled, and I guess with the Yiddish grounding him in familiar territory, he calmed down a tad.

"Tell me, Isaiah," he now asked me, "what do you do in life?"

"What do you mean?"

"Are you a scholar?"

"Sorry, I'm not following."

"What you spoke with a few days ago, about An-sky. I understood that maybe you are an intellectual with a specific knowledge of him."

"Hardly," I said with a chuckle.

"But what you know of him, it's impressive."

"Yeah, I saw you taking notes."

"I'm very fascinated."

"By what?"

"Yiddish."

"Fuck me, not another one," I said aloud by mistake, but not really.

"I don't understand."

"Never mind, sometimes I think things that I end up blabbing, when I shouldn't. It's a condition I'm working on." Thankfully he was too fresh off the reserve to even begin comprehending the stupidity.

"Since my time with Luba, she has given me books," he said, his eyes beginning to widen.

---

14. He nearly shat his pants.
15. Understood.

"Yeah, like what?"

"I'm reading now Peretz, *Bontshe the Silent.*"

"Of course, you are," I said dismissively, and rolled my eyes in response to his mention of one of the de facto introductory short stories for all newbies to Yiddish lit.

"Such a remarkable character, so pious, a true Hasid!" he said about the protagonist, Bontshe, a "strong silent type" possessing absolutely none of the former qualities but all of the latter ones, such that he goes about his whole life being stepped upon and dismissed that even in death, nobody gives a shit.

"Yeah, no, that's exactly *not* what Peretz was doing with that story," I replied, and struggled mightily from slapping the dilettante upside the head.

"I don't understand," he said again, and stared at me with a look that suggested he was waiting to be taught something.

"All right," I said, and then leaned in: "Bontshe goes through life basically in silence, right? Hence the title."

"Yes," Sam said, placing his elbows on the table and resting his chin in the palm of his right hand as he looked at me, like a child eager to hear a story.

"Then what happens?" I asked him Socratically.

"He dies."

"Right, he dies. But he doesn't just die. He goes to heaven and the angels make a big *tzimmes*[16] about him having arrived, correct?"

"Yes, he sits on a golden throne and they place a golden crown upon his head!" Sam answered, excited like he was sitting in *cheder*[17] again and getting the *melamed*[18]'s answers right. "A just reward for a life lived in piety," he continued.

"Fuck man, no!" I snapped at him, demonstrating that I was never meant to be a *melamed*. "What happens next?" I then said in exasperation, hoping to tease out of him what he should have gotten out of the story the first time around.

"He is offered anything he wants," he answered.

"*Nu*, so what does he ask for?"

16. Literally, a traditional East European Jewish stew made with dried fruits. Practically, to make a big deal.
17. Traditional Jewish elementary school
18. Teacher in a *cheder.*

"*Broyt mit puter,*" he said to me in Yiddish, indicating that my hunch about him feeling like he was back in *cheder* was right on the money.

"That's right, a hot roll with fresh butter every morning for the rest of his life," I repeated back to him, and he smiled at me like this, too, might be good enough for him in the afterlife. "Yeah, *tam* fucking *gan eden,*"[19] I said, and now tried to get to the end of the lesson. "Then what happens?"

"The angels are silent."

"That's right, 'a silence more terrible than Bontshe's had ever been,'" I said, quoting from the story.

"And they laugh."

"They certainly do."

"But why?" Sam asked, the tone of his voice lower now, almost as if a sudden sadness had befallen him thinking about Bontshe being the laughingstock of the heavenly hosts. "He was such a pure and pious Jew," he said innocently and childlike.

"Sam, do you know what a parable is?"

"Of course," he answered, returning to life a little. "There are many in the *gemara.*"

"Correct, like the one in our scene we're going to rehearse together about the Four Who Entered Paradise."

"Yes, yes!" he exclaimed excitedly, and listed off the great sages discussed in the parable, "Ben Azzay, Ben Zoma, Rabbi Elisho Ben Avuoyo, and Rabbi Akiva!"

"Yeah, okay. Great, whatever, we're on the same page," I said, waving a hand like I didn't want us getting sidetracked. I then gave it to him *kurtz un sharf*[20], because I could feel I was starting to lose my patience and slipping: "Guess what, Sam...it's a fucking parable! That's Peretz's brilliance! With this stupid little story, he's giving his readers a character they know well because that's who the Jews were for centuries. They were silent, meek, feckless, and powerless to control their own destiny. But he's telling them very clearly that the world is changing and it will not survive the upheavals if people don't speak up in the face of injustice, if they don't stand up for themselves when they're being

---

19. Uh...when something tastes good, you say it's like it came from the Garden of Eden.

20. Short and sweet.

mistreated, and that the Jews, in particular, had to stop being silent fucking Bontshes, and instead to take their place in the world and make sure at the same time that it's one filled with social justice!"

In contrast to the cacophony emanating from the other side of the stage, at our table, it was suddenly quiet as Sam said nothing in response to my little treatise. However, looking at him opposite me, through the thick layers of glass that covered his small, recessed, brown eyes, I could see a world of wonder and amazement reflecting back at me. It must have been the same countenance that Luba told me she saw as well when he first walked into her office less than a year earlier without being able to speak a word of English.

"He sat in the same chair you're sitting in," Luba said to me when I visited her, and Sam's name came up as we talked about some of the members of the cast I would be interacting with if I agreed to be in the play. "Although a grown man like you, he had the demeanor of a child on their first day of school. He was so frightened. But then..."

"Let me guess," I jumped in.

"Yeah..." she then said as if we were building the sentence together.

"He couldn't believe that *der goy ret Yiddish,*" I said and we both laughed knowingly at the predictability of an ultra-Orthodox Jew, in this case, a once-was, bewildered that a Jew unlike one of their own can speak Yiddish.

"When I started speaking to him in Yiddish, in an instant, he changed," she said, "he couldn't believe what I was telling him about the Yiddish theatre, our literature and culture, a world he never knew existed, and he became so fascinated."

She would go on to describe in detail how Sam—well, actually, Shmuel ben Yankev ha Levi, a.k.a., Shmuly Melamed—the sixth and youngest child of Topshe and Reb Yankev, the *rosh yeshiveh*[21] of their insular, ultra-orthodox community, had come to be sitting in her office looking nothing like a Hasid. His father, it seems, had passed away suddenly from a heart attack just over a year prior. Even though the doctor who studied *daf yomi*[22] with the esteemed rabbi had warned him for years that his wife's *gevaldik*[23] Ashkenazi recipes were going to be the death of him, which turned out to be true, the family chose to ignore the

---

21. Head of a Jewish seminary.
22. The process of studying a page of the Talmud daily.
23. Otherworldly...

facts. Although the doctor might have been on to something when it came to the *schmaltz*[24] clogging his arteries, they placed the blame for his death squarely on the stress Sam was causing the family when his wife Freydl wasn't pumping out the kids as quickly as is expected of newlyweds in "frumland."[25] Apparently, when they were summoned by the parents to explain the shame that they were bringing down upon the families, Freydl said it wasn't at all for a lack of trying. In fact, they didn't wait for *shabes*[26] to do it twice or more, but the fault lay squarely with her husband, who she claimed couldn't keep his cock hard longer than for two seconds, and that even when he could, he must be firing blanks. I know what you're thinking. But believe it or not, *bobe mayses*[27] like that actually fill the dockets of *beit din*[28] the world over. But that wasn't the reason and Topshe and Reb Yankev knew it. They knew from his earliest days in *cheder*, when they were called into the office because Shmuly wasn't getting a hard-on for Rashi like he was supposed to but rather, ironically enough, for the meat between the legs of his bench mate, Benny the butcher's son. "He's fucking gay!" Freydl yelled at the top of her lungs, to everyone's shock and surprise at the family conclave, though it's unclear whether their reaction was over Sam's outing or the fact that she had a surprisingly good command of English.

Regardless, it wasn't long after that debacle that Yankev died and Shmuly had no option left but to leave the community. Because that's how they roll in frumland, where it's marriage and kids and if you're a *faygele* or some other kind of sexual aberrant, you're shown the door and end up "off the derekh;" that fucked-up term of derision conceived in frumland to describe those who've literally lost their way from the one true path of torah, *mitzves*,[29] and men using their peckers for nothing other than impregnating their wives. Apparently, those who've been shamed with the title of OTD have reclaimed it, turned it on its head, and use it as a term of loving self-expression. *Az okh un vey*[30] that it's even gotten to that point but good for them, I guess.

24... typically due to copious amounts of *schmaltz*...chicken fat.
25. Frum = ultra orthodox. Frumland, where they live. I made it up.
26. The Sabbath.
27. Literally, grandma's stories. Practically, fairytales.
28. Jewish rabbinical court.
29. Commandments.
30. Downright shame.

"He's so gentle, sensitive, a *gutskayt*,"[31] Luba said as I continued listening to her describe Sam and the relationship they'd developed in the months that ensued following his initial visit to her office. "He's curious about everything, always asking questions," she said about the fact that she'd introduced him to the world of secular Yiddish culture, which instilled in him a sense of security and belonging.

"So he's basically become *your* Hasid," I joked, and began to hum the melody to "*undzer rebenyu*,"[32] which caused Luba to smile and unleash one of her charming giggles before she joined along.

"When he read the play," she soon said, her voice trailing off to suggest that there really weren't any further words to describe the impact it had on him.

"Of course," I said, assuming she told him something about An-sky and the time period, and that Sam could relate to Jews who left the *shtetl* looking for a new way, only to get lost somewhere between the old world and the new world that never came to be. Lost souls. Searching yet never finding, but very passionate about their journey.

"Like you," she answered with a glance in my direction that penetrated a part of me that few people could access.

As I continued looking at Sam while we sat together at the table on stage, I couldn't tell if his silence was because he found my thesis on Peretz problematic and was therefore taking his time in building a counter response or, given that English was still a relatively new thing for him, that he was simply having trouble finding the words. It was probably both. Regardless, something eventually did begin to make its way to his lips because he started to nod his head like he'd conceived of the thought already and agreed in advance with its conclusion.

"And you say you're not a scholar," he said to me earnestly as he leaned across the table slightly and stared me in the face like maybe he was seeing something just as clearly in my eyes as I'd seen in his. He then raised his right hand, and rather than point a finger at me, he did that thing Jews typically do when engaged in serious Talmudic debate: He thrust his thumb in my direction, which was a signal that he was about to become even more impassioned because he now dipped it downward

---

31. A sweetheart.
32. Literally, our rabbi. Originally sung by the acolytes of I.L. Peretz—not a rabbi.

then circled it back up in a motion, which, if you've studied Talmud, means serious business.

"Not only are you a scholar," he said with the thumb turn for emphasis, and then added in Yiddish, "*bist an ilui.*"

I looked at him briefly before breaking into laughter. "Are you fucking high?" I chided him in response to his suggestion that I was some kind of genius.

"You are, Isaiah, you are!" he said, unwilling to let go of the absurd thought. "What you said about An-sky and the feelings you showed for him, and now Peretz, who you know so intimately. You have a knowledge and a passion for Yiddish that is something remarkable!"

"Sam!" I snapped at him while simultaneously slapping his hand away because frankly, I just thought he was being an idiot. "It's not remarkable," I said, and tried to end the discussion. "I'm not a genius. It's just our history, plain and simple, and it's fucking dead, okay?"

Clearly taken aback, he recoiled slightly but remained firm and leaned in again. "How can it be dead," he said while staring at me almost without blinking that caused me to start shifting uneasily in my chair, "when here we are discussing it on a stage where we're doing An-sky's play, and I can see how much it matters to you?"

I couldn't come up with anything clever. "Can you let this go, please," I said to him instead, then my tone turned harsher, "it's starting to piss me off."

You know, I was right in telling Faygen, when I walked onto the stage, that it probably wouldn't take long for things to change again. They did, and as usual, I didn't see it coming. And, as always, I was mad at myself for it. Maybe I wasn't being totally truthful with you in how I dispassionately described what was happening on the other side of the stage, simultaneous to my discussion with Sam, like it was nothing. He was probably right to be frightened by the insanity, and I guess the truth is that it took me a little longer to recognize that I didn't have the bandwidth for it either. However, things had settled down a bit over there, where it seemed that the *batlonim* had begun to play gin rummy at the table in the middle of the stage to pass the time while Faygen and Nokhem were huddled with Luba. After her actress stormed out and had not yet returned, I assumed it was to counsel her about how to proceed. I dunno. Maybe that wasn't it. It's weird, right, that "Jeckling and Hyding" that happens when you're off the meds, when you know you're fucked up but you think you'll get past it, so you get this sense that like "nope, I'm good..." when you're so not?

"Izzy," I heard Sam call out my name.

I didn't answer at first; my attention was still focused on the other side of the stage.

"Izzy, *bist* okay?" he said again earnestly, and I now turned to face him.

"Wait a second, what did you just call me?" I asked him, nonplussed.

"Izzy. You just said a few moments ago that it was only right I should call you Izzy, when you decided that you would call me Sam?"

Nope, *so* not good.

"Should we continue with the scene?" he now asked me, and suddenly, I could feel that cold touch start to make its way through my body along with my chest starting to tighten, which I instantly recognized as fear coming to the surface in response to the fact that I had no fucking recollection of anything he was talking about.

"What scene?" I asked him.

"We were reading our scene together before you turned away. You were telling me about the Kabbalah and about the mysteries behind the number thirty-six. How Leah's name comes out to that number, three times that number spells your name, Khonen, but it also means not God."

"Right, yeah," I answered, and quickly quoted my lines from the play, "not through God, but through whom? The thought makes you shudder." In that moment, although I was starting to shudder with my own thoughts that had me questioning if what I knew was up might actually be down, I shared none of it. I turned instead and gazed out into the empty theatre, not wanting to look directly at Sam for fear that he might see something that would make him delve into places I didn't want him going to. Not that it mattered, since he went there anyway.

"You're somewhere else," he said.

"Nope, still here," I answered as calmly as I could, and continued looking out at the theatre. "I was just thinking."

"About what?"

"Sue-Ann."

"Leah, you mean," he answered forthrightly.

"That's what I said," I responded and turned back to him again. "I said Leah, the name in the script is Leah."

"Yes, I know that. But you said Sue-Ann," he replied, and stared at me for a second like maybe I was the acting expert and, as the neophyte at the table, he should just follow along with whatever theatre game I was playing though I, of course, wasn't. "*Nu*, so let it be Sue-Ann," he said in a tone that sounded like he was humoring me. "About what is it that you're thinking of her?"

"I dunno," I began and then somehow babbled my way sheepishly into "it's just that...well...I...maybe if I wasn't fucked in the head, she might be..." I didn't finish the thought. I didn't want to. I don't even know why it even started to come out of my mouth, given that I was sitting across the table from someone I didn't even know. Regardless, Sam didn't offer a reply. It was quiet for an awkward little while as I sat, hunched over now, my forearms resting on my thighs, my head hanging down, and my eyes fixed on the floor as I contemplated thoughts of shame and embarrassment and a whole lot of self-flagellating *narishkeit*.

"Izzy," Sam soon whispered to me from across the table. He spoke in a tone of voice that you hear in the *beys medresh*[33] when someone's reciting a passage from the *gemara*, as if they're telling a story.

"What?" I answered, still looking at my feet.

"You remember the parable of The Four Who Entered Paradise...Ben Azzay, Ben Zoma Rabbi Elisha Ben Avuyo, and Rabbi Akiva?"

I nodded.

He then went on to recite the story in the Talmud of how each of the aforementioned *gedoylim*[34] reached the gates of paradise but none managed to cross the threshold. "Rabbi Akiva was the only one who successfully entered and left unharmed," he said. "You know why, Izzy? Because he was true to himself."

I looked up and saw him smiling.

"I see what you just did there, Sam," I said, "and that's really nice of you." I now sat upright, turned to face him and gave my counter argument: "But frankly, we don't know what really happened to the great sages and how far they got. Maybe they never even reached paradise.

---

33. Study hall.
34. Intellectual giants.

Besides, let's not make such a big deal out of Rabbi Akiva, okay? After all, we know that both the Baal Shem Tov and the holy Ari came and went from paradise unharmed. And you know why, Sam? Because maybe they stayed on their fucking meds!"

Judging by his reaction, Sam seemed on the near side to gobsmacked at how I managed to contort the parable in a way that probably no one on the planet would have ever imagined possible. "You're comparing yourself to them?" he asked incredulously.

"I'm not comparing myself to anybody. I'm on my own path."

"What path is that?"

"You don't understand me."

"I will understand you!" he exclaimed, slapping his hand on the table.

"No, you won't!" I shot back at him. "Only one person understands me, and he's fucking dead, okay?

His face quickly took on an ashen countenance, and his mouth dropped as I now unleashed a diatribe that I didn't see coming but was powerless to keep bottled up: "I'm nothing, absolutely nothing. Just a toy for the fucking whitecoats to play around with and slap labels on other than 'human being' and for women to dismiss as weak, worthless, and something they 'don't need,' because without the meds, I'm a fucking wacko to them and being on them makes me less than alpha. And God forbid a man should be anything but alpha, like it's some kind of sin, right?

"I couldn't get it published, Sam. The story's dead. The legacy dies with me. Do you know what that means? What it's like to live with that kind of guilt? What am I saying, of course you do. Trust me, if the withdrawal doesn't kill me, the fucking coronary will. You know the saying 'God won't give you more than you can handle?' What am I saying, of course you don't. It's fucking Corinthians and your Bible experience ends with Moses kicking the bucket atop Nebo at the ripe old age of a hundred and twenty. And that's bullshit, by the way, right? I mean, nobody lives that long. Give me a break. You know, I sometimes wonder if I just confessed all this to one of those boy-buggerers in a frock, he'd simply wave his hand this way and that, perform some ablution, thank me for my atonement—probably more for not calling the cops—and then presto, wacko, I'd be purified of the sins and guilt. Mind you, now that I think about it, if He isn't giving us more than we can handle, then I suppose there's something godly in this fucking morass of guilt and sin, right?"

Although it appeared like his jaw couldn't have dropped any further towards the floor after I'd finished delivering my barrage of non-sequiturs, I have to say that I was really impressed by the fact that he stuck through it all and managed to find something in the drivel that struck a chord.

"Godliness and sin together?" he asked me sincerely.

"Well, sure. We're all God's creatures, so even if He's dealt us the shittiest of hands, I mean, still, He's the one who did it, so there has to be some kind of redeeming holiness in it, right?" He looked at me dumbfounded and truth be told, I was probably piecing together the logic of what I was spewing for myself as well. "Forget the card-playing analogy," I said, "the point I'm making is that maybe guilt and sin aren't such a bad thing."

"But Khonen, sin has nothing to do with *hashem*[35], it was created by the Devil!" he answered me and for some reason, again called me by my character's name.

"And who do you think created the Devil, Sam? God!"

"Holiness and the Devil?" he answered incredulously, "I don't have the capacity to understand such contradictions!"

There was a slight pause in our little debate as he looked at me like a deer caught in the headlights, which allowed me the opportunity to reflect on whether I was, in fact, arguing for anything at all or just, well...Regardless, that's when the light bulb went off in my head.

"Tell me, Sam," I began to ask and leaned closer to him, "what's the greatest sin?"

"I don't know," he said, and although he addressed me as Khonen again, something powerful was building up in me that I didn't bother trying to get him back on track.

"Come on, I know, you know," I said, and leaned in closer still, "but you won't say it, right?"

He hung his head, and I could see that I'd nailed it.

"That's right, Sam. It's men taking it in the shitter from other men."

---

35. Literally, The Name. God-fearing types use it because God forbid you call him by his name, God.

"Yes, Khonen. You're right," he said in a soft whisper that shouted shame.

"Fuck, Sam. Stop calling me that! I'm trying to get *tzum posek*[36] here. Look at me!"

He lifted his gaze in my direction, and what I saw was a frightened child who'd been exposed. I took his hand in mine and at the same time, looked at him dead in the eyes and summarized what I guess I'd been trying to get to the whole time, but it only came to me now: "What if we own our deepest flaws, our greatest sins, the things that God himself created in us," I said to him, "like you *shtupping* men and me just being crazy, and we embrace them openly, honestly, and purely to the point that they become the highest form of godliness? You know what happens then, Sam?" I asked him, and I could tell by his eyes starting to widen and his head nodding that he was with me. "That's right, they become *Shir Hashirim,* the Song of Songs!" And I began to sing:

> The Song of Songs, which is Solomon's
> Let him kiss me with the kisses of his mouth
> For thy love is better than wine
> Behold thou art fair
> Thou hast doves' eyes
> As sweet as wild grapes

"*Itzikl,* you sing so sweetly," Luba now interjected, and Sam nodded in agreement. Turning to look over my shoulder, I could see that she was slouched in a seat in the first row of the theatre. Everyone had left, and she looked spent. "What do you need a director for when you can deliver a scene like that with no rehearsal," she said, and smiled in our direction.

"Actually, we were just having a chat," I responded. "We were waiting for you to finish with the other part of the scene."

"That's exactly as I would have rehearsed it with the two of you, it should sound like a conversation," she said, focusing on the first part of my statement and letting the other part go without an explanation as to how things turned out with the drama that went on earlier. "You did such

---

36. To the point.

a great job of figuring it out without me. You have good chemistry, the both of you. I'mglad."

"Luba, we didn't rehearse the scene," I said insistently, turning to Sam to back me up. "We were just chatting, tell her," I told him, but judging by how he looked at me, it seemed he was with Luba.

"It's okay, *Itzikl*," she said softly, perhaps meaning to mollify. "It's been a long day and maybe all of us are tired. Let's end it here. I now have an idea about how to handle the next part of the scene." She then closed her eyes and fell asleep almost instantaneously.

"Why didn't you back me up and tell her we were just chatting?" I said to Sam incredulously as he stood from the table.

"Maybe you need to get some sleep as well," he said to me, placing his hand on my shoulder. "I wish you a good night, Izzy," he added, and left the theatre through the back stage.

After he was gone, I once again hunched over, looking down at my feet, trying to make sense of what had just transpired. But it was hopeless. There was too much to unpack, and although I disagreed with the two of them, both Luba and Sam probably had at least one thing right. I was exhausted. But there's a world of difference between being tired and.... As I shook my head side to side while staring at the floor, all I could hear myself repeating over and over was, "Nope, *so* not good." Eventually, I got up from my chair, walked over to where Luba was sleeping and covered her with her coat draped over the chair at the stage manager's table nearby. As I did so, something caught my eye and looking up, I could see that we weren't alone. Someone was sitting quietly in the seat in the last row of the theatre I had occupied earlier on, and she was staring directly at me. It was Sue-Ann. I hesitated momentarily, not knowing whether I should make my exit by walking up the stairs in her direction or following Sam through the backstage door. It didn't matter because when I turned my head to see if maybe he was still there, by the time I looked up again she was gone. I think.

————————

"You have a beautiful voice," Sue-Ann said to me when we found ourselves together on stage a few days later, about to rehearse the play from where Sam and I had left it off.

Pressed for time, Luba was anxious to start getting to the "set pieces," the points in the play that had the most moving parts and the first one she was eager to knock off was, well, me — that is to say, the death of my character, Khonen. It called for all the men in the play to be present in the synagogue following my character and Sam's discussion. And they were, Faygen, Nokhem, and the *batlonim*, all of whom were on stage waiting to receive an important bit of news that kicks the play into the next gear. In the interim, however, there was the matter of Leah's unannounced visit to the synagogue, which was why I was now standing center stage while all the men and everyone else in the theatre sat quietly and watched as Sue-Ann made her entrance.

"So you *were* there?" I responded to her with a tone of relief in my voice.

"I was," she answered, and I could tell by how she looked at me that she didn't get it. Which was fine, and I didn't bother explaining. But you can imagine my slight thrill: "Great," I noticed the thought running through my head, "only kinda nuts."

"Okay, *meydele*..." Luba began to speak, addressing Sue-Ann from the stage manager's table where she was making her way through a bag of Starburst candy Wendy had given her, all the while looking at the two of us intently. "Do it now." Sue-Ann, who was standing about a foot or two opposite me, looked me straight in the eyes and I don't know if it was when she began to smile and those dimples appeared, or when she followed that up by starting to speak her lines in Yiddish that my *bubbe* would have approved of but I...

"How lovely and peaceful it is here," she said in a pure and heartfelt tone while looking around to indicate the synagogue. "I've never been here at night, except on *simkhes toyreh*.[37] But then, it's so bright and cheerful here. Not like now, gloomy and sad, the synagogue is so sad, as if it were crying." When she finished her line, she momentarily returned her focus to me before taking a step to her right. As she did so, she cocked her eyes left to hold my gaze, and I soon felt my head turning in her direction as she walked past me slowly before disappearing behind me.

"It is said...that every morning at daybreak," I now began my reply, speaking the words from the play while at the same time thoughts unrelated started to press for equal time in my head, "when the Almighty weeps over the destruction of the Temple in Jerusalem, His holy tears

---

37. A Jewish holiday celebrating the Torah.

fall on the synagogues. That's why the walls of old synagogues are tear-stained."

"It is so old," she replied earnestly as she reappeared in front of me and cocked her eyes in my direction to hold my gaze again before beginning another turn. This time, she moved in a little closer towards me, and when she disappeared again behind me, I felt my senses heightening as the scent of her hair lingered, which caused me to get a little light-headed.

"Yes, old," I replied, my heart beating faster now too. "They even say it was found fully built beneath the earth. So many times the city has been burnt to ashes, withstood pogroms and devastation, but this synagogue was left untouched."

"How sad it all is," she said while completing another circle. As she began again, she moved in even closer to me so that when she spoke, I could feel her warm breath on my face. "Sad, but so friendly and cozy that I feel like staying here," she continued and turned behind me again, this time brushing her hand on my shoulder that the sense I now began to feel was raw, sexual, and growing in my pants. "I want to embrace the tear-stained walls," I could hear her saying behind me but feeling her moving in even closer still, "embrace them with all my heart and ask them 'why are you so pale and sad?' My heart is melting with pity." She had come full-circle again, and there was now barely a sliver of daylight between us. Although she had finished her lines and I had none more to say to her, she nevertheless leaned in even closer so that I could feel she was warm and moist as I was hard. Then, brushing her cheek against mine, she pressed her lips to my ear and whispered to me breathlessly: "Sing it to me again. I want to hear you sing the words to *Shir Hashirim*."

My eyes must have been closed as she spoke because when I opened them, in what honestly felt like barely a second after I felt her soft lips brushing past my ear, she was gone. Although Luba had called for us to run the sequence through to its conclusion and the next beat was mine to initiate, I stood facing upstage in silence feeling kind of disoriented, a little unsteady on my feet and frankly, grateful that the pause, which isn't in the script, had yet to call attention to itself. Actually, aside from feeling woozy and beginning to notice myself trying to unpack what had just transpired, what really had my mind going was the not-so-slight matter, which isn't in the script, of my raging boner that felt like it was about to break through my pants. Compounding matters was that I didn't have time to run the requisite multiplication tables to speed things along, and I couldn't stand there indefinitely with my back to Luba and everybody else, waiting for flaccidity. Thankfully, with the help of the mock *sefer raziel*[38] I happened to be holding in my hands, I placed it where no holy book should be and closing my eyes, I began *shockling*[39] like mad while starting to sing *Shir Hashirim* again, all the while doing my best to think about anything other than my *shmeckl*, Sue-Ann and well, *ir veyst dokh shoyn vus.*[40]

"Izzy, are you okay?" Sam said with great concern as he rushed up next to me on stage for what I assumed was us continuing with the scene, "you look like you're about to fall from your feet!"

"You have no idea," I wanted to answer him and pressed the ersatz kabbalistic tome more firmly against my crotch. "I think so. Why?" is what I responded instead and continued to sing and rock back and forth, hoping that what I was doing was calling attention to itself only because that's what the play has Khonen doing right about now; though without the hard-on, but maybe An-sky had that written into one of his early drafts. Who knows?

"She circled you seven times," Sam whispered to me and then leaned in more closely, "do you know what that means?"

"What are you talking about?" I answered without looking at him, "it was like one or two times."

"No, Izzy, it was seven. I counted," he said. "It couldn't have been an accident. It must be a sign."

"Of what?" I said and turned to look at him now. Judging by the intense look on his face, it seemed that he was closer to being in a trance than I was.

"That it's *bashert*[41]," he said and I could see those eyes of his, the ones that emanated a sense of wonder at the world, starting to widen.

"What are you talking about?" I asked him.

"Luba didn't tell her to circle you seven times," he said, "she just suggested she try it to see if it works."

"So?"

---

38. A kabbalistic tome, supposedly mind blowing for revealing the secrets of God's world.
39. Rocking back and forth – usually in prayer.
40. It might be Yiddish but I won't translate because it's NSFR.
41. Divinely ordained.

"Only a bride circles her bridegroom seven times," he said and leaned in close to me again. "Izzy, maybe it's a sign."

"You said that already," I said and nudged him off."A sign of what?"

"Of *hashem* intervening," he said, insinuating that some kind of divine intervention was going on.

"What the fuck are you talking about?!"

"You said when we last spoke that you were thinking of her, *nisht emes?*" [42]

"And you told Luba we were rehearsing the scene, you asshole!"

"We were, but you used her name. Maybe he heard you?"

"Who?"

He pointed towards the ceiling and simultaneously raised his eyes in that direction.

"Oh, fuck off!" I shot back at him, and my legs suddenly turned to jelly.

"Izzy!" Sam shouted as I stumbled into his arms.

"I think I need to sit down," I said to him, and as he helped me to a nearby chair, I looked up and saw Luba standing by the stage manager's table, popping another Starburst into her mouth. The only thought that came to me was why she didn't seem the least bit concerned. Actually, it was the opposite. "Good! Good!" she exclaimed with approval and then, with a clap of her hands, signaled for the scene to continue to keep the momentum going.

"Reb Sender! Welcome! Will you join us for a drink?" one of the *batlonim* yelled out, greeting the man playing the part of Leah's father, who had now entered the synagogue. Faygen had told me his name, but for the life of me I couldn't remember it at the moment because for whatever reason, as I sat slumped in the chair, I started to feel myself growing weaker and more disoriented.

"Fool!" the man said. "The refreshments are on me. You can congratulate me. My daughter is engaged!"

To which I heard everyone on stage respond: "*Mazel tov!*"

"Wait, what? Engaged?" I heard myself say as the room started to spin, which caused me to grip the chair tightly. "How is that possible?"

---

42. Literally, not true. Practically..."duh!"

"Good *Itzikl*, good! I love what you're giving!" Luba shouted approvingly in my direction.

"Has anyone heard anything from our *rebbe*," Reb Sender said. "A parable maybe?"

"A parable?" I could now hear the *meshulakh* say, "I'll tell you a parable: Once, a Hasid paid a visit to his *rebbe*. This Hasid was very wealthy but a miser. So the *Rebbe* took him by the hand, led him to a window and said, 'Take a look. What do you see?' The rich man answered, 'I see people.' The *Rebbe* then led the man to a mirror and said, 'Take a look. What do you see now?' The rich man answered, 'Now I see myself.' The *Rebbe* now said to him, 'Pay attention...the window is made of glass, and the mirror is made of glass. But the glass in the mirror is covered with a little bit of silver, and as soon as the glass is silvered, one stops seeing other people and only sees oneself."

"Holy words!" the *batlonim* all responded. "Sweeter than honey!"

"Hey, what's the big deal!" Reb Sender now chided the *meshulakh*. "You trying to needle me?"

"God forbid," The *meshulakh* replied to him. "But at some point, every individual will be judged and made to account."

"Hey!" Fagyen now said, "why don't we sing a song, a dance in celebration, ah!"

A moment later, I could feel the chair I was sitting in begin to shake as all the men on stage came together in a circle and began dancing and singing the Lubavitcher *niggun*:

> Yesterday is gone
> Tomorrow has not yet arrived
> There is still a little bit of today
> Let's not distract it with worry

"Ay ay ay!" they sang and as their voices grew louder, their stomping becoming more fierce with each rousing, repeating chorus, the ground beneath me shook with such intensity that it threw me from my chair and onto the floor where I landed faced down near the foot of the stage. What was happening, and why was it happening? I couldn't tell you. What I can say is that it wasn't like any of the other *mishegas* I've told you about up to this point. I don't even have the words to describe it, but it felt like something was sucking the air out of me. I could barely breathe, but with what little spark of strength I had left, I managed to bring myself up onto bended knee to speak Khonen's parting words before he leaves this world for the better one: "My Leah is getting married? How is that possible? What can I do to stop it?" Everything around me was a complete blur now. I couldn't make out the men dancing on the other side of the stage from me, and I had gone deaf to the words they were singing. I could barely see Luba, who I knew was standing not a few feet away, watching me intently. Ascribe what you will to it, but one thing did appear clear as day: The person sitting in the last row of the theatre whose eyes I could feel were locked with mine. It was Sue-Ann, and she was crying. "At last," I said while looking up at her, and although I could feel myself beginning to smile, my eyes suddenly started to well up. "The secret of all secrets is revealed to me," I said, addressing myself to her as the tears now rolled down my cheeks. "All worlds have opened to me...the Almighty is seated on the Holy Throne...I see him. I've won!" I exclaimed before collapsing on the floor.

"Where is Khonen?" Reb Sender said as the men soon finished their dance.

"He died!" the *batlonim* all exclaimed, and everyone on stage rushed to my side.

All but one, that is: The *meshulakh,* who stood alone on the other side of the stage, observing the scene before delivering in a foreboding tone of voice, the final line of the act that portended ominous things to come: "Khonen has been mortally wounded."

8

Upon my next visit to the offices of Manley, Manley and Faygenbaum, I was mildly disappointed to see that the people who occupy themselves with such things didn't get the memo that ancient stacks of magazines in the waiting room aren't a good look. The true buzzkill however, was sitting around in anticipation of being greeted by Ms. Napolitano, Faygen's phenomenal *tsastke*[43] secretary, who never arrived to let me in and escort me to his office. What I got instead was a dyspeptic Irish spinster who happened to be stepping out for a smoke just as I began raising my voice, asking anyone who could hear me that I was stuck in purgatory and starting to get a little impatient. Judging by the look of death she gave me as we passed each other on my way in, which she accompanied with a reference to her Lord and his parents along with some pointed Catholic greetings of which I'm not familiar, I must have made my presence known a little too colorfully. It's possible. Anyway, I returned the gesture with a Jewish one of my own that I won't bore you with, other than to say that it amounted to wishing her the good fortune of visiting her aforementioned saints *bimhera biyamenu*,[44] but that the journey to get there would be a long and tortuous one.

Once in, I paid no mind to the fact that I got her and not the *tstastke*,[45] and also didn't make much of the fact that no one noticed as I made my way down the hallway towards Faygen's office, not even turning to look as I helped myself to a bottle of water and a bag of pretzels from the kitchenette *en route*. That all changed, however, when I arrived at Faygen's office where, aside from discovering he wasn't around, I came face to face with a floor-to-ceiling mess that was on an exponentially unholier scale than I'd recalled from my first visit. My concern grew with each precarious step I took as I entered and tried my best not to disturb anything in my path for fear that Faygen may have purposefully curated the detritus I was stepping on. It was only when I clocked the garbage bin by his desk overflowing with empty plastic containers of dental floss, however, that I knew something was up. Big time. It felt like an eternity that I was alone in his garbage hole but eventually, Faygen showed up,

---

43. I shouldn't say. It's not nice...
44. Swiftly, in our days.
45...I promised Faygen I'll work on it.

looking stressed out of his mind. I don't think it helped that when he did, he found me tossing pretzels in my mouth while I sat in his chair with my feet kicked up on his desk.

"Where have you been?" I shouted at him accusingly as he entered and closed the door behind him. "I've been sitting here for half an hour."

"Meetings," he said matter-of-factly, and motioned for me to keep my voice down.

"With the silver-haired asshole?" I remarked about the guy I recalled seeing last time I was there.

"Yes, the senior partner, Mr. Manley," he answered and threw me a look of displeasure, though I could sense a smile because he then added, wryly, "I see you've been recovering well."

Right, I forgot to tell you. I wasn't bullshitting when I told you about what happened when I collapsed on stage. I totally passed out and apparently, it was bedlam when I did because it wasn't just good acting on my part, and no one knew what the fuck to do when the scene was over and I didn't get up. When I eventually came to, it was in an ambulance accompanied by Faygen *en route* to the nearest hospital. It was there that we were greeted by the head of the ER, a mild-mannered man in a turban named Sanjit, who promptly apologized for being short-staffed because the rest of the scrubs had their hands full with a crazed woman in Triage room number two suffering from all manner of afflictions, the most acute of which at the moment was the fact that she was my mother. It took what felt like two seconds for Sanjit to check my vitals. Then when he heard what had happened, he cracked a smile and determined that there was absolutely nothing wrong with me other than maybe a severe case of over-acting. The smile disappeared swiftly however, when Faygen decided to open his big mouth and express concern to the doctor about my meds situation and that maybe I ought to, you know, use them. While contemplating whether to throw something Faygen's way, it occurred to me that things had gotten quiet in the room next door, where I assumed that the ladies in blue had probably managed to IV a shit ton of the smooth stuff into my mother's veins.

Turning to the Sikh doctor, I told him in no uncertain terms that he'd have to whip out his kirpan and kill me first before I let him do the same. Without hesitating, he instantly corrected my intake chart from his original diagnosis of stage-induced-comatosis to a clear-cut case of stupidity-induced panic disorder, then threw the chart in the trash. Despite my protestations that what occurred was something that I had no vocabulary for, other than to say that it felt "other-worldly," a few days' rest accompanied by a concomitant return to my medication regimen and a promise never to return again was Sanjit's parting message as he escorted us out of his workspace.

"You disappoint me, doctor," I began to say to him as he left us and headed down the hallway, likely in the direction of a real medical emergency. "Given where you're from, I'm surprised you're all over psychotropics," I said, which caused him to stop, turn back to us, and say to Faygen that he should look out for me and above all else, make sure I take my meds. "In case you're wondering," I yelled out as he disappeared behind a corner, "my shit is perfect, thanks for asking!" Faygen now threw me a look like maybe the doctor finished up with me a little too quickly and needed to be called back, stat.

"What're you looking at me like that for?" I accusingly told him, "it's an Ayurveda thing, look it up." He didn't bother with a reply but shook his head instead as he led the way into Triage room number two to look in on my mother, who was sleeping soundly when we entered.

"Feels like I've been asleep for days," I now answered Faygen in response to his question about my recovery.

"Good, so you're back on your meds?" he followed up, and motioned for me to get out of his chair so he could take a seat, which he did, and promptly began flossing.

"No," I answered.

"Goddamnit, Iz. What the hell's the matter with you!" he yelled at me in a way that he never had before, which only served to reinforce that something major was going on that had nothing to do with me.

"For fuck's sake," I shot back, "why won't anybody listen to me? It wasn't a panic attack. It was something else!"

"Oh yeah, what?"

"I told you already; I can't describe it."

"Well, you better come up with something soon because we're all worried, and your non-compliance isn't helping."

"Thank you, Dr. Faygenbaum. And who's this 'we all'?"

"Well, how about we start with your mother and me. I'm assuming you've spoken with her?"

"You have to ask that question?"

"Given what happened to you? Yeah."

"We've spoken. She's on her meds," I quipped.

"This isn't funny, Iz."

"Take it as a sign that I'm well."

"We'll see about that," he said, looking at me disapprovingly.

"You didn't answer who 'we all' is," I continued prodding him.

"Me, your mother, Luba, and almost everyone at the theatre."

"I hope you didn't tell them anything about..."

"Of course not," he cut me off before I could continue, though we both knew I was referring to not wanting to be outed to everyone there. "But you know, Iz," Faygen continued, "what you're going through isn't unusual. There's really no shame in it. Maybe if you opened up..."

"Yeah, let's just not, okay?" I said, taking my turn to cut *him* off.

"Okay," he said, throwing his hands and the lengthy floss string that was getting a good workout up in surrender.

I could sense the frustration. I'm not saying it's easy, especially for those who love and know you best. But sometimes, no one gets it and you just don't want to explain, particularly if you're having a decent day, which I was.

"What did you tell Luba?" I asked him after a brief moment of silence that hovered between us.

"Nothing, other than that you were okay, resting, and that you would be back to rehearsals soon." For those of you who've actually been keeping track, you're right...Khonen's dead, but Luba has ideas for this production which explain Faygen's statement. "She loves having you there, by the way," he said, "it keeps her calm."

"...ish," I quipped.

"Yes, you're right," he answered. "But I'm concerned."

"Clearly," I said, and made with my hands to display the disaster that was his office.

"About Luba, I mean."

"Why?"

"I don't think she can take the stress."

She isn't the only one, I thought to myself while observing him engaging in his oral hygiene *mishegas*.

"I'm sure she'll be fine," I told him. "She's been doing this for years."

"Not this."

"Meaning?"

"On top of being worried sick about you, she's now dealing with Ronda quitting."

"I'm sure that's *a sod far gantz brod*," I said sarcastically, using a Yiddish aphorism to suggest that the aftermath of the battle royale between Luba and her once-upon-a-time leading lady, which resulted in the latter vowing to never step foot again in the theatre, was probably the worst-kept secret in town.

"Yes, I suppose you're right," he replied. "And on top of that, she still hasn't heard from the actor who's supposed to be playing the *Rebbe*, and it's making her crazy."

"Who is it, by the way?" I asked, curious to know who the mystery actor was.

"No idea. That, *davke*[46], is a well-kept secret," he answered. "Anyway, I'm worried about her...and you!"

"Relax, she'll be fine," I said, "and I'm fine. Today at least," I continued before changing the topic. "So, you wanna tell me what the hell is going on here? Where's your *shikse* secretary?"

"Stop that!" he yelled at me. "You know it's not funny."

"Well, where is she?" I shot back at him. "And why is this place a fucking disaster?"

"I have a big case."

"*Nu*," I replied insistently, and waved my hands to make the point that her absence was all the more relevant. "So, where is she?"

"She quit."

"Why?"

"I couldn't afford to pay her anymore."

"So that's what the meeting with the asshole was about?"

"Enough!" he yelled at me again before vacillating on his answer to my question: "Yes and no," he said.

"Okay, I'll shut up now. But could you just tell me straight-up what the hell's going on?"

"I need your help," he said honestly, then proceeded to tell me about a massive class-action case he'd been working on for months that, due to its nature and the way he was choosing to handle it, explained the

---

46. As a matter of fact.

reason why he was out a secretary, up to his eyeballs in a mess of paperwork, and seemingly hanging on to his job at the firm by the thread of a piece of dental floss, pardon the shitty metaphor.

Actually, what he described made for the stuff of good TV. It all started with a random note that his erstwhile secretary slipped him months earlier, in which an anonymous "Deep Throat" asked to meet him in the middle of the night in a back alley in a part of town near the *shmatte* business factories. There, he learned about the abuse of a government-created program, sanctioning the import of cheap foreign labour, to help the flagging industry compete in the global marketplace. Actually, it was worse than that. What the anonymous source described to Faygen was a massive scheme that saw the unwitting immigrants having to sign reams of byzantine documentation that amounted to them kicking back half their wages, in cash, to the company that "hired" them and that any disclosure of the matter would result both in their immediate dismissal as well as reporting to the authorities for trumped up nefarious activities that would speed the way to their deportation. As it happens, there was only one shop in question, but it wasn't just any old shop on the block. It was Manky's, the largest manufacturer of ladies' bras and underwear in the world.I'll spare you the rest of the details, but guess who's manning the barricades, defending the rights of the oppressed workers of the world against the corrupt, rapacious bosses in the case...pro bono?

"Faygen," I told him sincerely, "you should be charging your clients *something*. You have the right to earn a living."

"I will, when I win."

"How long is it gonna take?"

"The trial is in a few weeks."

"And your world falls apart until then?"

"It's not falling apart. I just need to figure some things out."

"*Unzere mentschn?*" I assumed, though I'm not sure why, about the company he was suing and making an educated guess that they were in the tribe.

"Unfortunately," he replied.

"Whatever, we're no better or worse. Scum is scum," I said. "I don't even know who you're talking about, and already my blood's boiling."

Maybe that's why.

"That's how I've felt from the moment I heard the story," he said. "Now you understand what's going on."

"Actually, scratch that," I said concerning the offending Heebs. "They should fucking know better," I said, my voice now rising with emotion. "Hopefully, you get them the chair. Do we still do that? How are we killing no-goodniks these days?"

"Easy there, Moyshe Getzl," Faygen replied with a smile while referencing my *zaide*, who would of course be apoplectic after hearing the sordid tale of immigrant and worker abuse, *especially* at the hands of our own, though he wouldn't have slipped in the bit about capital punishment. That's my *narishkeit*. "I'm only seeking justice for my clients," he added.

"I assume you already told the fuckers that they should be behaving carefully with the poor?" I said to Faygen.

"Yes, An-sky," he answered sarcastically about my quoting a line from the play that has Talmudic roots but in more legal phraseology. "Mind you, Mankiewicz would have appreciated the sentiment," he said about the man I assumed was the name behind the name. "He studied *gemara*. He would never have done this. He must be spinning in his grave."

"Who's there now, the kids?"

"No, his former partner, Mel Seal. A *chaser, a zoyns un a zelkhes*," he said; a real piece of work, to put it politely.

"Lovely, I'll look him up," I answered sarcastically. "So, is this why you asked me to come in today? You need help with the trial?"

"I'm overwhelmed," he answered, and I could sense a tone of desperation in his voice.

"I can't be your Girl Friday, Faygen," I said to lift his spirits, "you need someone with a pair of tits for that."

"I'm ignoring what you just said!"

"Relax, I'm fucking with you," I chided him. "I mean, I'll help out any way I can," I added in all sincerity, "but honestly, you can't do this alone. This is a big fucking deal."

He replied with a perfunctory "Thank you" when his phone began buzzing on his desktop, and suddenly he was engrossed. "Tell me," he began to say to me without looking up from his device, where he was single-finger typing a message intently, "why haven't you responded to any of Sue-Ann's texts over the last few days?"

"What're you talking about?" I replied and for some reason, it started to feel like the office was getting warmer.

"*Nisht sheyn,*[47] Iz," he said, calling my bluff and still not looking up from his phone. "She's been worried, too, you know."

"I told you, I've been sleeping," I offered pathetically, to which he didn't reply but lifted his eyes up instead and gave me a stare that required no commentary. "Is that her?" I asked him nervously.

"Yes."

"You've been texting each other?" I asked incredulously.

"Considering you've been unresponsive to her, yes," he said while continuing to compose his message.

"What're you telling her?"

"That you've made a full recovery," he began to answer out loud while seemingly tapping the same with his finger, "and that you're looking forward to meeting her for a coffee so you can apologize for not being a *mentsch.*"

"Woah, hold up, you can't write that!" I shouted and sprung from my chair onto his desk to grab the phone out of his hands.

"Too late," he answered, with the familiar "whoosh" sound emanating from his phone only serving to confirm the same; though he rubbed it in by shoving the phone in my face so I could see that the message was immediately received. "It's a date," he said with a smile while I slouched back into my chair and assumed a posture my five-year-old self would have approved of.

"Why did you do that?" I pouted.

"Because apparently, there's something stuck between there and there that's preventing you from doing it yourself," he said, pointing at my head and chest for emphasis. "And don't even try to come back at me with something clever because you know I'm right."

I said nothing.

"I knew it the moment she looked at you," he said.

"When?"

"Don't play dumb, you know when. You had your eyes down the whole time, but when you started talking, *boychick*, I'm telling you..." he said, clasping his hands together and then began smiling ear to ear, as if in his mind, he already imagined my depressive progeny. "And *you*," he

---

47. Not nice.

continued while pointing his finger at me again, "I haven't seen you like this with a woman since...."

"Okay, stop!" I interrupted him, "I don't wanna talk about Her."

"You didn't let me finish," he said, waving his hand. "I was *about* to say I've never seen you like this with a woman since, well...ever."

Again, I said nothing.

"Your mother thinks it's a great idea, by the way."

"Oh, come on!" I shouted and threw my hands up. "She's in on this too?"

"You're not being fair, Iz," he came back at me. "You got rushed to the hospital. She was right to be scared."

"And what does that have to do with what we're talking about?"

"She wanted to know what happened at rehearsal when you collapsed. I told her I didn't know. But what I did know, I told her, is that something nice was happening between you and Sue-Ann."

"Nothing is happening."

"There's coffee," he joked.

"You know, I could throw this back at you and ask why you're not doing the same with my mother."

"Nice try, *yingele*," he said, and although he shut me down with a wink, it occurred to me that his use of the Yiddish term of endearment for a young boy might have suggested that I was onto something. The truth is, I don't know why I'd never brought it up over the years; I mean that it made no sense to me that Faygen and my mother were alone, when maybe they should explore being together. But bringing it up now was fruitless. "This isn't about your mother or me," Faygen politely admonished me, "it's about you and, from where I'm sitting, maybe something very nice." It was quiet between us for a few moments as I started unpacking the euphemistic possibilities of "something very nice," while my mind also started racing with the even greater black hole that is...coffee.

"I don't think I can do it anymore," I eventually said aloud with my head turned away from Faygen and in a voice that was low, soft, and fragile.

"What, coffee?"

"Yeah, but no," I whispered.

"It's coffee, Iz. Not *shtupping*. I think you can handle it," he said in a clear demonstration that he knew me all too well. And although it was clearly offered to build me up, I kind of took it the wrong way, and I don't think he, nor I for that matter, could have predicted what came flying out of my mouth next.

"I don't think so. I mean, isn't coffee just the *forshpayz*[48] before the meal?" I asked rhetorically, using a lousy analogy, I admit. "So we'll go for coffee, and then what?" I asked him again rhetorically. "I'll tell you what," I began answering my own question, my voice rising as I turned to face him directly: "*Shtupping*! Because that's what coffee is a euphemism for! And I don't think I can do it anymore, so thank you very much for putting me under the gun to figure out how the fuck I'm gonna get it done! Okay, I mean, look, *got tzu danken*[49] I got it working again and by the way, Dr. Faygenbaum, *zolst visn*[50] that's because I threw the fucking meds in the garbage. And you didn't even think to ask before you tapped with your finger that *maybe* there could be a problem and *maybe* you should ask me first? Fuck, I don't know if it'll even work if someone else is there aside from my own hand! Text her back and cancel the coffee. I'm not going."

Yup, it was *definitely* hot in the room, and there were crickets now, too. Thankfully, his phone buzzed again before he could offer up a reply to my petulance.

"Would you look at that," he said as he stared at his device, "Sue-Ann must have heard your *narishkeit*."

"What did she say?"

"Coffee's cancelled."

"Great!" I exclaimed, then allowed myself to relax in my chair and let out a huge sigh of relief. Prematurely, it seemed.

"Looks like you're going dancing instead," he said, looking up at me from his phone with a massive grin starting to build from ear to ear.

———————

Later that week, I again found myself in the same part of town as that hipster bar I'd visited with Luba, the Vulgar Vulva. This time however, standing in front of a take-out Portuguese rotisserie chicken outlet, wondering if I'd messed up. Although the address above the entrance was correct, there was nothing to suggest that dancing of any kind was

---

48. Appetizer.
49. Thank God.
50. Please be advised.

taking place in the cramped space inside, where a dozen or so birds were quietly rotating on spits. Before I could take my phone out to double-check, the Joao doing the slicing behind the counter motioned to me with his knife through the shop window that I should enter, and pointed in the direction of the back of the restaurant. I did as instructed and in an instant, was carried past him on what felt like a magic carpet of sweet-smelling, burnt chicken fat wafting through the air, past a tiny kitchen in the back where his Ana was hand-peeling potatoes. She, too, pointed with a knife, this time towards a curtain at the other end that opened onto a narrow staircase that seemingly led to a place where I could begin to make out what sounded an awful lot like *klezmer* music. As the sound grew with each step I took up the three creaky flights of stairs, so did the beating of my heart, and at that moment frankly, I felt kind of bereft of the "protection" the meds offered in situations like this. I should tell you that in the intervening days since Faygen's office, I had broken his phone numerous times with all manner of verbal detritus that amounted to not much more than the simple fact that I hadn't gone out with anyone in forever and didn't know what the fuck to do anymore.

"Just be yourself," he said on one of our calls, to which I responded that I didn't think the date would last long if I took his advice. "You see what you just did there," he said, "that self-deprecating defense mechanism you use to mask your insecurity? Let it go. You're human and being nervous on a date is perfectly normal." There's nervousness, sure. But then there's that feeling when you're off the meds, you know what I'm talking about, when you're totally out of your comfort zone that invariably leads to the kind of insane dry mouth, shortness of breath and a thin line between lightheadedness and depersonalization that makes you stop at almost every step on a flight of stairs towards somewhere that you're fighting your hardest not to turn back from. It didn't help matters that the music kept growing louder as I climbed, to the point where as I neared the entrance to the room it was emanating from, the sound was unmistakable: It was *klezmer* music...and I can't fucking stand it.

Nothing outside the chicken restaurant suggested there was room amongst the birds for live music, let alone a hall three-floors-up replete with a full bar, stage, and a dance floor big enough to accommodate a hundred people which, on the night I walked in, seemingly held that amount and more. Once inside, the pleasant aroma of roasting birds that had accompanied me on my journey upward was instantaneously overtaken by a fetid stench emanating from a sea of sweating millennials on the dance floor. Although to be fair, there appeared to be a sizeable cohort of pensioning hippies among them contributing to the massive cloud of foul effluvium that covered the room. As it happens, they were all dancing trance-like to an incessantly repetitive *doina* being offered up by the mediocre *kapelye*[51] on stage that was seemingly led by a crazed Rasputin with a fiddle, busily rousing the crowd with nonsensical bursts shouted into a microphone in a language I couldn't identify but wouldn't have been wrong had I guessed the former Soviet Union. "Great," I began muttering to myself as I inched my way through the throng toward the bar where Sue-Ann and I agreed to meet, "a fucking *tantshoyz*."[52]

I could feel my palms sweat when I got to the bar and she wasn't there. And it was pointless scouring the room for any sign of her because aside from the *nebekhdik*[53] stage lighting focused on the musicians, the place was too dark to make anyone out. Well, there was the faint light behind the bar, where things had begun inauspiciously with my ordering a pitcher of water from the ladies tending; they could have been men, I wasn't sure, as my head was kind of preoccupied. *Nisht vikhtik.*[54]

"You have the tools in your box," Faygen said to me when I'd brought up what would happen if I started having a panic attack, which I knew would come and explained the need for the pitcher of water. But that wasn't what soured the bartenders on me. Seriously, who tips on water? Anyway, as I drank and breathed in one-two-three, then out the same, wondering how long I would wait before skedaddling, something caught my eye. There, carved into the wood paneling above the stage, were the letters "A and R," but arranged in a way that was unmistakable to anyone familiar with the logo of the Workmen's Circle, known in Yiddish as the *Arbeter Ring*. Was this the place the original home of the fraternal society my grandparents devoted their lives to? By the time I began walking this earth, it had long since moved to the venue I had recalled as a kid, but this space was legendary. I could see them before me now: My grandparents, newly arrived after the war, in this hall filled to the rafters with their fellow survivors, all of them day laborers whose sweat, tears, and every hard-earned penny were put toward establishing

---

51. Band of musicians.
52. Klezmer dance party.
53. Feeble.
54. Whatever, not important. Seriously, it means...not important, or whatever.

and nurturing this humble but noble place and others like it, to be sure. A venue with a stage—the same one where the crazed Slav was presently giving me a headache—the kind that would witness the greatest writers, poets, artists, and intellectuals of their generation, delivering lectures that lifted their spirits, expanded their minds, and grew them as individuals as they struggled to rebuild their lives after Hitler. *Bildung*,[55] hidden three creaky floors above roasting chickens. Go know.

"Izzy!" I suddenly heard Sue-Ann's voice yelling over the music and felt her shoving my shoulder gently. "You okay?"

"Yeah, why?" I turned to her, and shouted back.

"Are you sure?" she said, coming in closer and looking straight at me with genuine concern. "I just screamed your name three times, and you didn't respond," she added while touching my cheek with the inside of her hand, which felt warm and moist. My mind must have truly been lost in a time warp to have completely ignored her arrival at the bar, where she had already poured a glass from my pitcher and was now standing close to me so that I could feel her breast against my arm as she drank.

I haven't talked much about her, it's true. You're in good company. I haven't shared with anyone, including my mom and definitely not Dr. G. Only Faygen, which as you know was a result of circumstance. Besides, I'd prefer not to bore you with language describing what it feels like in her presence, which I'm afraid you'd dismiss as pathetically jejune. And like you don't already know, right? That said, everyone's got their distinguishing character traits, and hers, in the little time I've gotten to know her at rehearsals, I'd describe as "casual confidence." It's expressed not only in how she walks into a room or how she knows to brush herself against you just enough that you notice how it was precisely that. It's also in the simplicity of how she chooses to present herself, like on this night, dressed down in faded jeans ripped at the knees, suede cowboy boots, and a white tank top that exposed two black lace bra straps clinging perilously to her shoulders, which at the moment were gleaming with beads of sweat from dancing that were hard to ignore.

Ugh. I just reread all that. See what I mean? Jejune, fucking drivel.

---

55. Self-cultivation.

"Sorry, it's just really loud," was my pathetic attempt to reply to her concern. "Besides, I was focused on the stage," I added, which was totally valid.

"Aren't they awesome?" she asked jubilantly about the crazed fiddler and his merry band of *klezmorim*.

"You read my mind," I replied, feigning sincerity, which seemed to have gone over.

"My friend and I brought them in from New York," she said proudly.

"They're phenomenal," I lied.

"And so authentic, right?" she added enthusiastically. Rather than get into it with her, like asking how on earth she would know *vos heyst*[56] authentic *klezmer*, I said nothing and offereda smile instead.

"You're beautiful when you smile," she said, again caressing my cheek. "You should do it more often," she added with a wink.

As my mind raced with thoughts of what I was supposed to do or say next and my heart started to beat faster, the band intervened by launching into an up-tempo *bulgar* that caused Sue-Ann to down her glass of water, grab me by the arm, and attempt to lead me onto the dance floor.

"Come dance with me!" she shouted over the music and seconds later, when some of her tattooed friends I vaguely recognized from the Bushy Pussy came calling as well, the panic rushed in.

"I want to dance with the bride!" I could swear I heard one of them shout as she tugged at Sue-Ann's arm and began pulling her away from me.

"Me too!" another said, swooping in and grabbing Sue-Ann. "I put my arms around the bride and danced!" she shrieked with a piercing, grotesque laugh that plain hurt, then began twirling Sue-Ann in a circle.

"Izzy, come! You're such a good dancer!" Sue-Ann shouted to me as the music grew even louder and the room started to spin, causing me to suddenly grab hold of the bar for fear of collapsing to the floor.

"Why does the bride only dance with the women?" I heard the voice of a young man say. "I want to put my arms around her and dance with her too!"

---

56. What means.

"Izzy!" Sue-Ann called for me one last time, her voice trailing off, and I could barely see her reaching out to me as her friends pulled her quickly towards the dancefloor.

"*Kaleh!*" I then heard myself yell out the Yiddish word for bride in Sue-Ann's direction, where she got swept up in the sea of humanity and disappeared.

———————

On the day I returned to rehearsals, it didn't take long to corroborate that Faygen was right about the toll that mounting the production was taking on Luba.

No sooner had I walked into the theatre where the greetings I received from cast and crew were genuine and heartfelt than Luba, allowing for a quick hug and a *vos makhstu,*[57] nervously rushed me onto the stage to cover for Nokhem, who was MIA for a change. Walking past the stage manager's table and onto the stage, it occurred to me that his absence alone couldn't account for the rate at which Luba was plowing through Wendy's bag of candy. Judging by the volume of empty wrappers and similar detritus at the foot of the stage where Luba was pacing anxiously, it had to be something more. In fact, as Faygen would later confirm for me, Nokhem was the least of it.

Apparently, Luba had allowed the budget for the production to spiral out of control, the news of which had reached the board of the JCC, where changes were in the offing. Although Faygen was fuzzy on the specifics, suffice to say that they wouldn't accrue to the benefit of Luba and her theatre. Apparently, the rationale for the red figures was the short timeline given to mount the play, which although doable in Luba's mind, didn't match up with the reality of what was required to deliver the production elements, which had fallen severely behind schedule. Ironically, although Luba had given the green light to go red, so to speak, on the day that I returned, everything seemed to be as it was when I was there last, passed out on the floor in the synagogue. Well, that's partially true. The one element Luba did manage to get was some basic lighting from the dyspeptic French-Canadian designer, which to the untrained eye, gave the sense that some kind of theatre magic was about to happen. It did nothing to keep Luba from muttering some choice

———————

57. *Comment ça va*

words for him under her breath in Yiddish, which had me thinking that it was probably best that only a few of us in the room could understand. Without getting into the scatological specifics of her sugar-high diatribe in *mame loshn*, let's just say that she took issue with the fact that his *farshtunkene* spotlights shone brightly in all the wrong places. In this case, it happened to be on the *oren koydesh*, which only served to remind her how behind the eight ball she was, having to direct the intimate cemetery scene smack dab in the middle of a brightly-lit synagogue, which was where Sue-Ann and the actress playing her aunt Frade were seated next to each other on one of the study benches finishing up their chat about the souls of the departed, when I walked onto the stage and stood a few feet away from them.

"Izzy, go, *kaleh!*" Luba barked at me while pacing at the foot of the stage, where she was in the process of breaking open a bag of candy, then waved at me to get going before popping a handful in her mouth.

"*Kaleh,*" I said and looked to Sue-Ann, "the bride," to whom Nokhem was supposed to be addressing his lines as the *meshulakh*. I'm sure you're wondering why it was me up there and not somebody else — let's say, Joseph, reading Nokhem's lines aloud from the stage manager's table, where it appeared he was preoccupied trying to get Wendy to translate for him what Luba was *plapling*[58] about in Yiddish. The truth is, like my speech on the first day of rehearsals, there was no plan. Luba took for granted that I knew the script *fun oysn veynik,*[59] which was pretty well the case. I should add, however, that in spite of the fact that she was bereft of her production elements, there was acting happening on stage, a poignant intimacy between Leah and Frade "in the cemetery," and Luba was right to want to keep it going to the extent that she could.

"What do you want?" Sue Ann replied to me as Leah, earnestly and slightly frightened. Although she wasn't about to break character to welcome me back, I clocked her dimples trying to take shape ahead of a smile, which was enough for me to know that she was pleased. It was the first time I'd seen her since my collapse and not long after my *rendez-vous* with Faygen, so I very much wanted to respond to the question openly by apologizing for having ghosted her, which I knew was wrong.

---

58. Babbling on.
59. By heart.

Faygen was right to wrap me over the knuckles for it. But I stuck to the script.

"Souls of the departed do return to earth," I replied, "but not as evil spirits without a body. Some souls pass through several bodies before they are redeemed. Souls that have sinned transmigrate into animals or birds or fish, or even plants, and those souls can't be redeemed by their own efforts and wait for a holy sage to cleanse them of their sins and free them. Some souls enter the body of a newborn and redeem themselves through their good deeds."

"Speak. Go on," she said, then stood from the bench and approached me.

"Good *meydele*, I like that," Luba commented from the foot of the stage, observing the scene intently and motioned with a subtle gesture of her hand for Frade to quietly exit the stage in the opposite direction so that Leah could be alone with me.

"But then," I continued as Sue-Ann and I were now standing face to face, "there are the homeless souls that can find no peace, so they force their way into the body of a living person as a *dybbuk*. In that way, they achieve their redemption." Although I was standing in for the actor who was supposed to be there, the moment seemed to work as it should. It was intimate, with Leah expressing genuine interest in the words the *meshulakh* was saying to her and what they portended. But the fourth wall came crashing down, so to speak, when she spoke the first words of her follow-up line, which are technically delivered once the *meshulakh* has left her alone on stage and she unabashedly shares the thoughts on her mind. But there I was, and it was unavoidable.

"Why did you leave me, Khonen?" she asked, and in an instant, everyone in the room burst out laughing in response to how the question was so apropos. Even Luba allowed herself to partake in the timeliness of the line and let the moment play out, even though it temporarily killed whatever happy vibe she had created on stage. "Now I must go to the wedding against my will," Sue-Ann continued, playing up the lines more for the audience in the room than anything else. "Everyone will rejoice, except me!" she added with a melodramatic flourish to uproarious applause.

"Okay, *khevre*," Luba said, and started waving her arms at everyone as if to suggest that some decorum was in order to let Sue-Ann deliver the last of Leah's poignant lines. Admittedly, as a stand-in for a no-show at rehearsal, it felt beyond awkward to still be on stage at that moment, and I began to wonder why Luba hadn't called for me to step down. In fact, it was the opposite. She said nothing as Sue-Ann brought herself closer to me and directed her lines to me like we were the only two people in the room.

"Without you, my life is no life," she said quietly in a dulcet voice while simultaneously looking at me with beseeching eyes that caused my mind to start racing with the thought that there was a shit ton that needed unpacking in what she'd just said. Before I could look over to Luba for a sign that what was happening was kosher by her, Sue-Ann took my hand in hers and continued speaking. "Come, Khonen," she said, and now caressed my cheek with her other hand as she finished with Leah's lines, "protect me, save me." But she wasn't done, and it seemed like Luba knew it because the director didn't move from her spot by the foot of the stage, where she was keenly observing what was transpiring. Without averting her gaze from Sue-Ann's bit of *improvizatsye*, she simply raised her arm to signal that no one was to move, speak, or breathe until whatever was happening on stage was finished. Sue-Ann then took my face in both hands and lifted it so that we were staring deeply into each other's eyes and after she whispered softly to me, "I'm so glad you're okay," the room erupted with a collective gasp when she then flashed her dimples at me before suddenly closing her eyes, bringing her lips to mine and kissing me deeply.

―――――

I don't recall how long it was after the *klezmer* band had finished its *geferlekh geroysh*[60] and the hall above the chickens had emptied that my eyes fluttered open to see Sue-Ann and her merry band of millennials standing over me, looking gravely concerned. For that matter, I also don't have the faintest as to when it was that I managed to find my way from the bar to the one quiet place in the room, which turned out to be the stairwell behind the stage, where I could lie down and ride out the storm. It's not early onset, I don't think. *Meyleh,*[61] the family tree only goes as far back as Auschwitz, so who knows.

―――――

60. Abominable caterwauling.
61. However.

127

"Oh, thank god!" Sue-Ann said when my eyes finally opened completely, and I could see her breathe a deep sigh of relief. "We've been looking all over for you!" she exclaimed. "What on earth are you doing lying here? Are you okay?"

"Yeah, fine, just needed to lie down," I answered as she and her gang lifted me gently by the shoulders and propped me up against the wall nearby like a rag doll. "It's over?" I asked about the din in the dance hall, and breathed my own sigh of relief when the group nodded collectively in the affirmative. Sensing that all seemed okay, her friends retreated back into the hall, leaving Sue-Ann and me alone in the stairwell.

"Did Luba tell you to do it?" I asked her as she plopped herself down to sit beside me.

"What are you talking about?" she replied, wrapping her arm around mine.

"Yesterday, in rehearsal, you kissed me. Was that something Luba told you to do?"

"No," she answered somewhat incredulously.

"The two of you planned it, then?"

"Again, no," she replied similarly.

"So, was it something you just went with because it felt like the right thing to do in the moment?"

"Uh-uh, still no," she replied with a slight giggle as she rested her head on my shoulder.

"So why did you do it, then? I can't figure it out."

"Because I didn't want to wait for you to get out of your head and kiss me first," she replied, and nudged me playfully. "Besides, I wanted to kiss you before I even met you."

"I don't get it," I said clumsily.

"No, you don't," she replied before lifting her head and turning to face me. "Here's where you say how good it felt and that you'd like to do it again," she said, staring at me longingly.

I said nothing because she was right: I didn't get it. It had been forever and a day since I had, if in fact I ever did. Had I opened my mouth to offer words of any kind, I would have wanted them to be along the same lines of what she just had confided, except that it seemed to come to her more easily than it did for me. More to the point, I didn't know how to tell her that from the moment she whizzed across the bar into Luba's lap at the Cunning Clitoris, I, too, felt something I wanted to explore. Unfortunately, like I need to tell you, it immediately got lost in the maelstrom of my *mishegas* that it was left to her to act on what was obviously mutual. I ought to have thanked her for that.

All told, in spite of the fact that my thoughts began to coalesce into something I felt comfortable sharing, I should have realized that she wasn't expecting me to say anything at all. Rather, without hesitation, she pressed her lips against mine, and although I began to shake nervously, I instinctively let mine part just wide enough so that I could truly feel her for the first time. I'm not ashamed to admit the fragility, by the way. I think we should cop to it more often than we do. I haven't gotten into it with my doc as to the specific connection between the shit that goes on in my head and the concomitant physical manifestations that result in the ridiculously awkward convulsions I'm overcome by in moments like this. I didn't tell her, but I was grateful to Sue-Ann that rather than call attention to it, she somehow knew that so long as we were flesh to flesh, eventually, my heart would begin to move in sync with hers, and the discomfort would subside, which it did.

"You should have said something," she whispered to me when we eventually stopped to take a breath, but continued holding my hand, which she had brought to her chest near her heart.

"About what?"

"That you're agoraphobic. We could have just gone for coffee if it would have made you more comfortable," she added, and nudged me playfully again for emphasis.

"Funny," I deadpanned, and thought better than to point out that among the grab bag of labels I've been tagged with by the whitecoats, I've actually never been diagnosed with social anxiety disorder. I think. It also occurred to me that it seemed a little soon, in what was really our first heavy, for the labeling to start and what the unintended and inadvertent emotional consequences of that might be. Regardless, her coffee suggestion was unlikely to render a different emotional and physical reaction on my part than had the *klezmer* dance party she'd invited me to.

"I'm serious," she said, wrapping her arm around mine again. "I thought it would be fun. I'm sorry," she added sincerely, and snuggled even closer.

"You don't have to apologize," I said while looking down at my lap, where she was now tracing the lines of my palm with her fingers, which felt calming. "*Klezmer's* not my thing."

"Clearly," she giggled.

I knew better than to open my mouth any further on the topic, but I feel like I need to pause here to explain to you my *klezmer* aversion. It's not so much that I can't stand the music, which I can't because, to my ears, it sounds like fingernails scratching a chalkboard. But that's an aesthetic argument we can quibble about some other time. What drives me up the fucking wall about *klezmer* is the "scene" that's been built up around the music that amounts to this bizarre Jewish revivalism, whose adherents have appropriated the music and the Yiddishland roots from which it sprung, to match whatever convenient Jewish identity they've crafted from themselves today...but who knows what will suit their fancy tomorrow. Or, as I like to call it, the "shoe-storization" of modern Jewish identity. To wit: "Ooh, I really like that one over there, but do you have it in my size?" A *kholeria*.[62]

"Do you do these parties a lot?" I asked her.

"Actually, it's the first time,"

"All downhill from here," I quipped, resulting in a playful punch from her part to my shoulder.

"You're weird."

"That's one way of putting it."

"That's not what I meant," she said, her tone serious. "Faygen said you'd really be into it."

"Ah, our matchmaker," I joked. "So, what did the *shadkn* tell you?"

"The what?" she asked.

"It's Yiddish for gossipers who need to mind their business," I answered.

"Stop it!" she replied with another slightly firmer punch to the shoulder.

Dear reader, *zayt moykhl*, but I'm dead fucking right: It's exactly what it means. Look it up.[63]

---

62. Like being hit with the plague. Scout's honour, that's what it means.
63. Literally, it means matchmaker. But if a matchmaker isn't a gossip who doesn't mind their business....

"*Nu*, what did he say?" I asked, genuinely interested to find out the answer because Faygen knows damn well how I feel about the whole *klezmer* thing.

"A lot, actually."

"My shoulder's starting to get sore," I responded lightheartedly, "but can I suggest that I'm highly skeptical that he told you that I'd be into this?"

"You're right. He didn't," she said, and mercifully held her punch. "I just assumed."

"Why?"

"Because of what he told me."

"About?" I asked, genuinely curious.

"You. Your family..."

I didn't respond immediately, as it was hard to discern whether her statement was innocuous or dreadfully loaded. Nevertheless, my mind went straight to the latter, wondering how much more Faygen might have blabbed about my mental instability and how intimately interwoven it was with my flesh and blood, which you can imagine I was really looking forward to having labeled again, imminently. My heart really skipped a beat, however, when she opened her mouth and finished her thought.

"...mostly your *zaide*," she said and then turned to look at me. "He said what you had with him was really special."

Shit, forgive me for these interstitials, but I need to share this with you, and I'm fine about it because we've come this far together. But I'm telling you right now that the next time I meet with my doc, I'm putting Faygen on the agenda...the only topic. I never told you, but following that first rehearsal, when I ran into him having dinner at my mother's, I gave it to him but good for doing what he did. He knew my state of mind very well when he shoved me into the abyss to speak on his behalf because he was too nervous to put two words together. And now, when I haven't been with someone since I tossed the meds and I can't control what works anymore above or below, he goes there?

"Izzy?" Sue-Ann asked me when it seemed I took too long with my reply.

"Mmm?" I muttered, because a lump was building in my throat, and I knew what came next once it got stuck there.

Fucking Faygen.

"He basically told me that if I really wanted to get to know you, I should ask you to talk to me about him," she said.

I didn't respond, taking a moment instead to release my hand from hers to wipe the moisture that had begun to fall from my eyes.

"Izzy?" she asked me, concerned.

"I'm fine," I said. "He's right, but not tonight, if that's okay?"

"Of course," she replied, retaking my hand in hers and pressing the two together in a gesture of sensitivity and compassion. "I wish I had what you have," she continued, likely sensing that I probably wouldn't be saying much for a while. "Well, I sort of did," she went on. "I mean, nothing like what Faygen told me. But whatever, it's gone," she said cryptically, without explaining further. Suddenly, her eyes brightened, and she soon began to speak about her experience the previous summer at the intensive Yiddish program. "I had this professor who just blew my mind," she said. "She didn't just teach us the language, you know? Every day, she would talk about the world before the war and how vibrant it was: The Yiddish street, the politics, the culture, the newspapers, and the literature. In the afternoons, she'd take us to lectures or *klezmer* concerts, anything that would help us understand the bigger context. Even at night, in her free time, we'd go to bars with her and just talk about what Yiddish was, what it is today and what it could be in the future. She always told us that if we really wanted to understand what Yiddish means, we had to go deep and not just appropriate it for what we think it means today."

Whoever that person was, I would've wanted to tell her that she deserved a medal.

"Sorry, I'm rambling," Sue-Ann said.

"Not at all," I quietly replied. "It was meaningful, I get it," I added, and was relieved that I'd dodged the bullet thanks to not having shared my reflections on the revivalist *narishkeit*.

"It really felt like I belonged," she said, lifting her head to look at me. "I feel like that with the play."

"And that's why you're producing *klezmer* concerts too?" I asked her.

"I'm not producing, just searching."

"For what?"

"Belonging again," she said. "Aren't you?"

I didn't say anything because it occurred to me that the best I was gonna come up with was an "I guess," which I feared would come out of my mouth sounding like an insult. Besides, even if I'd thought about it a bit longer, I'd probably just get myself caught up in an analysis of whether our journeys were at all symbiotic. If they weren't, I was scared that I'd let out something to that effect, which would be no less hurtful to her. I felt she deserved the protection of the moment she had just created. Although I was mired in the incapacity to come up with a simple confirmation of the honesty and truth she spoke, I was relieved that at the very least I managed a nod, which elicited a smile on her part.

"Not that this has anything to do with what we're talking about," I soon said, "but are you related to the family that makes bras and underwear?"

"Not that I know of," she giggled. "What made you think about that all of a sudden?"

"Just curious," I replied. "The name Mankiewicz came up in a recent conversation, and I was told that it's the family behind Manky's. It's not a common name, so I figured you're related."

"You were conversing with someone about women's bras and underwear?"

"I know, it's kind of retarded."

"We don't use that word anymore," she said lightheartedly, but matter-of-factly enough that it came with another punch to my now bruised and sore shoulder.

"Right, sorry," I said. "Anyway, it might have been with my mother," I lied about the ladies' undergarments. "But it was kind of cool to learn that the company is based here."

"Don't know anything about them," she answered forthrightly, and went no further because just then, her gaggle of friends walked back into the stairwell to announce that they were leaving; but not before one of them, who I got introduced to as Amber, proceeded to announce to Sue-Ann the minor financial success of the evening, then kneeled down to give her a big hug, all the while thanking her profusely for her help, guidance, and motivation.

"You feeling better?" Amber then asked me when she was done rocking back and forth with Sue-Ann.

"Yeah, thanks for looking out for me," I replied, and looked up at the rest of them so that the message was conveyed to the bunch.

"All her," she said regarding Sue-Ann with a wink and a smile. "She's the absolute best!" she added, and hugged her friend one more time, and gave her a big kiss on the lips before they all said their goodbyes, leaving Sue-Ann and me alone again in the stairwell.

"Okay, Marlo Thomas," I soon said with a chuckle, "what was *that* all about?"

"What?'

"The way she thanked you. It was kind of over the top. What did you do?"

"That's just the way she is," Sue Ann began answering. "Amber's my best friend. The party was her idea, and she tried organizing everything, but it was kind of over her head. So, I stepped in to help. Who's Marlo Thomas, by the way?"

"Seriously?" I asked incredulously.

"Yeah, *seriously,*" she said, returning it to me with a concomitant punch to the shoulder.

"Whatever, it's not important," I said, which it wasn't. "It's just something you say to someone who always gets up on the right side of the bed."

"Nobody does."

"Based on what I've seen so far, it seems like you're someone who does."

"You don't really know me," she said in a way that wasn't at all aggressive, but at the same time, I could detect just enough bite in her voice that it was clear to me I'd touched a nerve.

"You're right, I don't. I guess I was just trying to pay you a compliment for having personality traits that I'm envious of."

"Thank you," she said then turned to face me and smiled before planting a wet one on my lips. She then quickly jumped to her feet and stood before me with both arms stretched out for mine. "Come," she said, and helped me to my feet. "I want to show you something," she said as I took her hand and she led me out of the stairwell.

The neighbourhood streets surrounding the rotating chickens were still. They felt like they belonged to us alone when a little while later, Sue-Ann and I were walking hand in hand towards a nearby destination that she wouldn't divulge. In the quiet of the darkness that surrounded us, broken only occasionally by the sounds of crickets late to bed and, on one occasion, the piercing screech of fornicating ferality emanating from behind a dumpster we passed *en route*, I felt comfortable beginning to flesh out for Sue-Ann the parts of my biography she'd heretofore been unaware of.

As you might imagine, she had a hard time picturing me as a wedding planner, though she got a kick out of hearing all about it and the particularly pointed and colorful way I described my Uncle Hank and cousin Manny for her. Although she was rather taken, though not surprised, that I had a knack for putting words together on a page, I didn't get into the book I couldn't get published because I wasn't there yet. For her part, she began to speak passionately about the poorly-paid but profoundly meaningful work she was doing for an NGO tasked with delivering desalinated water to sub-Saharan tribe folk. I say *began* because as we turned a corner, my mind immediately shut down, and I was stopped dead in my tracks because there, in a pool of light emanating from the streetlamp directly above, its immense shadow appeared.

CHIRP.

Shit.

"What's the matter?" Sue-Ann asked me playfully when she tried moving us toward what I assumed was our destination, while I stood frozen. "You've never been to a cemetery in the middle of the night before?"

"That's not it," I responded. And yes, we had in fact arrived at a cemetery, a place which even in the brightest of a warm, sunny day I wouldn't begin to know how to explain to her, let alone in the middle of the night with that thing hovering overhead.

"Are you afraid that dark spirits lie hidden and buried in every corner?" she said jokingly, referencing a line from the play. "Come on, scaredy-cat," she added with a wink, then let go of my hand and soon disappeared into the darkness among the graves.

CHIRP!

On the day that I returned to rehearsal, despite Luba's intention to run the end of the first act of the play through to the final beats before the curtain without interruption, it was painfully obvious that in the wake of Sue-Ann's inspired improvisation and the bedlam that erupted in the room immediately thereafter, her plan was out the window. Truthfully, when Joseph rightfully called for everyone to take five, I was hoping that Sue-Ann would explain her motivation to kiss me as I stood in for Nokhem. But amidst the hooting and hollering from the *yentes* sitting in the audience, who it seemed had begun casting lots as to how soon we'd be getting biblical and likewise, Luba's fulminating that they should keep their mouths shut and let her work or she'd replace them all, I didn't get the chance. In fact, I was immediately ushered off stage by Joseph's new intern, Francine—a stern, four-foot-something stage hand with a crew cut, struggling mightily to keep an adult-sized electrician's belt around her waist—who dutifully led me out of the theatre and to the rehearsal room, where I was apparently needed urgently for a choreography session.

"Oh, excellent, the zombie's here!" was the sarcastic, if not exasperated, introduction I received when I walked into the rehearsal hall a short while later and was greeted by Zeke, the flamboyant and utterly dyspeptic choreographer. Despite the abrupt greeting, I nevertheless found his reference to the dead Khonen, the missing piece it seemed he needed to complete the Beggar's Dance, kind of witty. Not that he was one to joke around because no sooner had he gestured to his assistant to cue the music shortly after I'd walked in than the invectives began to fly fast and furious, and with a vulgarity, I should add, that made the opprobrium that occasionally spewed from Luba's mouth sound tame by comparison. Now granted, although I didn't know the man from Adam, I could imagine the pressure that he, of all the creative professionals on Luba's team, was under; especially on this day, when Luba insisted on seeing his Beggar's Dance on stage in rehearsal for the end of the first act sequence.

I don't want to get sidetracked here but suffice to say that in the annals of its storied history, nothing contributed as much to *The Dybbuk*'s lore as did the iconic Beggar's Dance, whose reputation reached its apotheosis almost from the moment the play was first introduced to the public. Although it was An-sky who had written the dance into his work, basing it on the traditional Jewish custom of granting the poor a right to dance with the bride on her wedding day, it was *where* he placed it in the context of the story that made all the difference — coming, as it does, at a pivotal moment where the two worlds made explicit in the title of the play meet, quite literally. It was all the inspiration needed for Stansislavsky's star student, Yevgeny Vakhtangov, to put his stamp on the play that would resonate for ages. Indeed, it was the famed director who helmed the second-ever presentation of the play, the Habima production that used Bialik's Hebrew translation, which An-sky himself had desperately lobbied the famed Hebrew poet to agree to produce not long before the playwright's death.

Vakhtangov's own choreography of the Beggar's Dance in that landmark production, in which he incorporated his signature expressionistic style bordering on the grotesque, set the benchmark by which every subsequent production of the play would be judged. Luba knew this in her bones and there's not a doubt in my mind that, in her inimitable way, she conveyed as much to her choreographer, who was surely expected to rise to the occasion for *her* production. None of which, of course, would have provided any solace to the handful of *nokhshleppers* in the rehearsal room who Luba, for some reason, had assigned to the Beggar's Dance because the music, which I can only describe as a bizarre mash-up of electronica married in compound time to violins and a clarinet that I assumed were meant to evoke an old-world authenticity, was utterly bereft of anything resembling a beat that could be followed by rank amateurs, let alone pros in leotards who I would bet money couldn't find the downbeat. Mercifully, Zeke had allocated only half a minute's worth of his brand of grotesquery for my walking dead entrance and exit into the dance, which didn't take me long to figure out. As for the *nokhshleppers,* who had been at it for weeks on end and were still struggling to deliver on Zeke's vision as he harangued and mercilessly whipped them into shape in time for that afternoon's showcase for Luba, it was a macabre scene that I was glad to have not been a part of for very long.

The atmosphere in the theatre when I returned following my dance break was more akin to what I suspected Luba had in mind all along for this important afternoon. It was dark, quiet, and the mood solemn as Sue-Ann and the actress playing Frade sat together again on a bench in the middle of the stage, carrying on their introspective discussion in the cemetery. In contrast, Nokhem, on stage this time around, observed stoically from just off to the side. "Dark spirits lie hidden and buried in every corner," Frade admonished Leah in response to the latter's assertion that in the cemetery, aside from asking her mother and other close relatives to come to her wedding in the customary fashion, she would go in search of Khonen's grave to ask of him the same.

In that moment, as I watched Sue-Ann deliver Leah's passionate rejoinder, I saw for the first time what Luba said she picked off almost instantaneously when they first met. I should add that I don't know to what extent it resulted from what had transpired between us only a short while earlier. Still, the sheer rawness of emotion Sue-Ann exuded as she spoke, was more than an accurate interpretation of the lines on the page. There was more to it, and I was both stunned and captivated watching as she pleaded her case to Frade for why the souls of the departed mustn't be forgotten, especially those who've left this world too soon. She was referring of course to Khonen, and although the words An-sky gives Leah to speak about him are beyond moving, it wasn't enough to explain how, from my perch sitting in my seat at the top of the theatre, it felt like Sue-Ann was grabbing me by the throat with every word she uttered. It wasn't just me who felt it. Luba and everyone else in the room did too because after the actress playing Frade delivered her line to Leah that the Almighty knows very well what he's doing and that we are nothing but blind sheep who know nothing, it felt like a collective punch to the gut when Sue-Ann bellowed Leah's next line: "No, Frade!" she shouted, and as she stood from her bench to continue speaking, it felt like the walls of the theatre began to shake. "No one's life is ever completely lost," she continued. "If someone dies before his time, his soul comes back to earth to live out his lost years, to experience the unlived joys and sorrows. But where does the homeless soul go, Frade?" There was nothing for Frade to say figuratively and literally, because her lines were done. Although the next thing for her to do was to exit the stage quietly so that the *meshulakh* can be alone with Leah to give his point of view on the matter, Sue-Ann, apparently overcome with emotion, wouldn't let Frade leave but instead kept repeating to her over and over: "Where does the soul go, Frade? Where does the soul go? Answer me, Frade! Frade!"

"Izzy, hello!" Sue-Ann said while shaking me slightly as we stood by a gravesite in a far corner of the cemetery; a spot which, honestly, I haven't the slightest recollection of having arrived at. "Did I lose you again?" she asked.

I didn't answer at first, as I was preoccupied trying to get my bearings and stuck in particular, on what otherworldly force could have propelled me forward into the cemetery.

Moreover, my ears were now sharply attuned to what I expected would be its imminent re-appearance, and I wouldn't be overstating the matter to say that I was scared out of my wits at how close it would be this time around.

"You didn't answer my question," Sue-Ann noted in response to my silence.

"What question?" I replied honestly.

"Where do the homeless souls go?" she said. "I literally just asked you that, like two seconds ago."

Again, I didn't answer. I couldn't. The God's honest truth is that I wasn't at all sure that she had, in fact, spoken those words or if I had gone somewhere I didn't want to be, to a place way beyond anything I could control. You know what I mean. "Who's this?" I said, my voice fragile while attempting to change the topic, and pointed at the small, unmarked grave we were standing next to.

"My sister," she whispered.

If I'd learned anything throughout my life as it pertained to our people's ways in death and mourning, in moments like this, discretion is the better part of valour, and being there to comfort while saying little to nothing is where the mitzvah lies. So I listened silently as she spoke of the sibling she never knew but felt intimately connected to. She was born a few years before her arrival to this world, yet died tragically less than a month later of massive complications associated with a congenital heart defect.

"I always wanted a sister," she said by way of introducing the topic of how she was an only child. Although she'd never addressed it matter-of-factly with her parents, she just assumed that her whole life to this point was coloured by the tragedy that befell them. "I wanted you to see her," she said to me.

"I don't really have the words," I answered awkwardly but truthfully, as I didn't know why she had brought me to this place and, given the circumstances, I felt it was neither appropriate nor wise to delve.

"When Faygen described to me the loss you felt when your *zaide* passed...," she began to say, but cut herself off abruptly.

"It's okay, speak," I said to her. The thought of Faygen sharing the most intimate parts of my life didn't even cross my mind because it was elsewhere now.

CHIRP!

It was too dark. I couldn't see it...

"I know it's not the same," she said softly, if a little sheepishly, "I guess I just wanted to show you that I could relate."

...but I could definitely hear it, and it was really close.

Shit.

CHIRP! CHIRP!

"Fuck!" I blurted out, and grabbed my ears with both hands as I froze.

"Oh my god, I'm so sorry!" Sue-Ann said, and recoiled in horror.

"Ahhh!" I shouted.

"Izzy," Sue-Ann said, with some relief this time, because she quickly turned to look at an apartment building overlooking the cemetery, where music began to emanate from one of the units with an open window. "It's just people singing."

"It's not!" I yelled out, panic-stricken.

CHIRP!

"You're trembling!" she answered, her voice disconcerted again and without the slightest hesitation, proceeded to wrap herself around me in a protective embrace.

"Hey! She hasn't danced with me yet!" I thought I heard someone yell at me from the open apartment window. "I've waited a whole hour to dance with the bride!"

CHIRP!

"Stop it! Just stop!" I shouted back before falling to my knees. As the voices I thought I heard coming from the open apartment window combined with the piercing squawks into a deafening cacophony that I couldn't bear, my shoulders began to heave, and I started crying uncontrollably.

"It's okay, shh. You're okay," Sue-Ann whispered to me repeatedly as she lay down on the grass and gently pulled me down next to her so that we were pressed tightly to one another. "Take my hand," she said, and wrapped her fingers in mine while bringing my hand to her breast so that I could feel how rapidly her heart was beating. "You don't need to be afraid," she said. "I'm nervous, too," she added, then began to kiss me, and as she did, I could feel her nipple harden under my hand as her heart started beating faster still.

CHIRP!

"Alms! Alms for the poor!" the actor playing Reb Sender shouted out enthusiastically when he walked on stage immediately after Sue-Ann and Nokhem had finished their beautiful dialogue in the cemetery on the afternoon I returned to rehearsal. "Ten *groshen* for each one!" he continued overzealously and in a tone that sounded like he'd just pinned the nail on the donkey, which caused Luba to shout at him to get off the stage while frantically waving her arms like she was yanking him off with the proverbial cane. She didn't say it explicitly, but from where I was sitting high atop the theatre, what had just transpired on stage was, to put it simply, a moment. Sue-Ann had begun to deliver on the promise Luba had for her. And Nokhem, I have to give it to the old man, showed for the first time since the rehearsal process began that he was an actor's actor, when he then spoke the *meshulakh's* lines to Leah about what happens to the souls of those who've left this world too soon. It was poetic and wholly incongruent with the blurting out of Sender's line from the mouth of Luba's accountant. If you want my opinion on the matter, I don't think it was his fault. As lousy an actor as it appeared he was, although enthusiastic, I think she was just impatient to get to the Beggar's Dance and hadn't yet worked out the transition to the wedding that happens prior to it. In any case, after Joseph and his assistant Francine took a few moments to clear the stage, the theatre soon reverberated with the music I'd heard earlier in the rehearsal hall, and Sue-Ann and the *nokhshleppers* took to the stage where Luba witnessed, for the first time, what would be *her* Beggar's Dance.

"Hey, she hasn't danced with me yet!" one of the female beggars chided another, who had taken Sue-Ann and began twirling her around in the sequence's preamble. "I've waited a whole hour to dance with the bride!" she continued, and yanked Sue-Ann away and into her own arms, where she engaged with her in an intricate maneuver Zeke had choreographed. "I don't want alms!" another one of the dancers shouted, and pulled Sue-Ann towards her. "Just dance with me! It's been forty years since I last danced," she added, swirling Sue-Ann around in a circle to dizzying effect. "More!" she cackled as she sped up. "More! More! More!" she shrieked even more loudly and then let go of Sue-Ann, who exited the stage briefly so that the beggars could now segue way into the dance. Taking that as my cue, I stood up from my seat atop the theatre and went down the aisle toward the stage. When I neared, I looked at the stage manager's table where Luba stood with Zeke, observing his choreography being played out by the dancers.

Although their movements were imprecise and their gestures grotesque for all the wrong reasons, she kept her mouth shut and let what was happening run its course. It only occurred to me afterwards that what she had her eye on was less the distraction of the first part of the sequence but rather the short part that followed it that would be unique to this production's version of the Beggar's Dance. Hearing the change in the music that hastened Khonen's arrival in a beggar's disguise, I quietly maneuvered myself to the back of the stage. I watched as Sue-Ann returned to the dance, where the beggars performed a ballet of pulling and pushing her in concert to the music, which began to swell with the sound of a wailing clarinet. Only a few musical bars later, when the clarinet stopped to allow the violin to start playing a lugubrious, dirge-like melody, the beggars drew Sue-Ann upstage, where they released her into my waiting arms.

CHIRP!

As we lay in the grass together by her sister's grave, Sue-Ann kissed the tears dripping down my cheeks and soon whispered to me breathlessly, "you can touch me more...if you want." She gasped momentarily when she brought my willing hand to the warm, uppermost region between her thighs.

CHIRP!

I don't recall hearing any music or having the sense that I was in a rational moment when I took Sue-Ann into my arms and danced with her to Zeke's sensual choreography, which metaphorically unites this world and the better one to come. Although Leah's intersection with the undead at this point in the play is fraught and perilous, Zeke nevertheless has her relinquish herself to Khonen, who proceeds to twirl her gracefully. At the same time, she arches her back and revels in a brief moment of ecstasy with her one true love. Holding her so soon after we had first kissed, my senses were heightened to the point that with every motion we made in unison, each gesture that had me holding her torso where it curves subtly but perfectly, just above her hip, or as I gently caressed the nape of her neck, I was jolted into feeling things for a woman I don't recall ever having had. A few beats later, when the violin slowly fades, heralding the moment in the dance when she parts with her *basherter*[64] and Khonen supposedly returns to his heavenly home, Sue-Ann brought herself upright in my arms and before letting me go, whispered in my ear.

CHIRP!

"I want to feel you," I could make out Sue-Ann's lips whispering to me just as I felt like it was hovering directly above us, but I was too afraid to look up to see if that was the case. Instead, I held her gaze as she stared at me longingly, as if waiting for an answer on my part, and I didn't stop her when she gently began moving her hand down my chest toward my belt, which she started to unbuckle.

CHIRP!

After finishing my part in the dance, I quietly exited the stage and entered the audience to see how Luba intended for the rest of the act to play out to its dramatic conclusion. The music grew increasingly discordant as it rose to a crescendo, signaling that the Beggar's Dance was nearing completion. On stage, the beggar's movements were likewise becoming ever more exaggerated in their grotesque expressionism as they took turns grasping at Leah, who was frantically searching among them for the one beggar she longed to continue dancing with.

"Beautiful *meydele!*" Luba shouted out to Sue-Ann and began gesturing excitedly for everyone in the room to amass on stage for the act's finale, even though she hadn't yet rehearsed it.

"Good *mamele,*" she again called out to her lead actress, "let yourself go!"

CHIRP! CHIRP!

Holding them in my hands, I could feel the goosebumps running up and down every inch of Sue-Ann's naked thighs as she straddled me in the graveyard. With her shirt lying on the ground beside us, she brought her chest close to mine and pressed her breasts against me so I could feel her erect nipples through the thin layer of lace in her black bra. While we continued to kiss each other deeply, her breath started to grow heavier, and she likewise started rocking her hips forward and back in perfect rhythm so that soon, the warm moisture from beneath her underwear started soaking through mine.

CHIRP! CHIRP!

---

64. Predestined.

"Layale, what's wrong with you?!" the actress playing Frade exclaimed when all the actors were on stage where Sue-Ann, following Luba's direction, was spinning around ecstatically in search of Khonen. "You're falling off your feet! Oh, my goodness!" Frade shouted in a panic when, eventually, Sue-Ann twirled herself to a point where she collapsed into the arms of the actor playing her father, Reb Sender, and exclaimed in a plangent and foreboding tone of voice: "I'm not going to the wedding," she yelled, to which everyone on stage responded by recoiling in shock. "I'm not going!"

CHIRP! CHIRP!

In the midst of our passion on the grass in the cemetery, while it continued to screech incessantly in the darkness nearby, Sue-Ann suddenly stopped. After a brief moment, during which time I looked at her as she cradled my head in her hands and likewise gazed deeply into my eyes, she kissed me deeply before lifting her chest to sit atop me upright, where she placed one hand between her thighs and looked at me again one more time. When I nodded that it was okay, she soon gasped as she gently put me inside her. Not a moment later, after she'd closed her eyes, tilted her head back, and let out a deep, ecstatic moan...it suddenly stopped and the cemetery and everything around us became eerily quiet. Everything except for the next sound I heard, which was that of Nokhem' voice delivering the *meshulakh*'s ominous message that concludes the first act of the play: "The bride has become possessed by a *dybbuk*!"

9

It was while stroking it in the shower the following *shabes*, when it occurred to me that the boner in my hands had less to do with thoughts of Sue-Ann's nubility than it did the fact that I was up early, on a weekend no less and, *got tzu danken*, happily rededicating a vital part of a man's daily washing ritual that had been abruptly ripped away from me by the meds years earlier. I know I don't need to explain because when it comes to what we go through, mornings are always touch and go; let alone on days of the week when there's no apparent reason to get out of bed and mingle with the masses. As for the ability to successfully do it again under the soothing cascade of the showerhead, do I even need to? *Gevaldik.*[65]

In the days since the cemetery, not a moment had passed that Sue-Ann wasn't on my mind, a fact abetted by the incessant electronic communication I was now receiving from her. To be fair, although her texts were utterly innocuous and for the most part, built around the theme of how I was doing, the sheer volume and rapid-fire pace at which they came was new territory, and it was making me anxious. Further to that point, although Faygen had also been breaking my phone, undoubtedly seeking a status report on "how I did," and likewise my mother, who I just assumed Faygen had given a head's up to because I certainly had said nothing to her, I managed to keep them at bay. With Sue-Ann however, I could do no such thing because even though it had been a long while, and I'd forgotten most of the protocol, I took for granted that if you lose your shit on someone shortly before cumming inside them in the middle of the night in a dark cemetery, the least you can do is reply to their early morning texts asking how you're faring. Not that any of this explains what I was doing in the shower early that Saturday morning. As it happens, I'd decided to take Sam up on an offer he'd made to me earlier in the week to join him for services at his "*shul.*"[66]

I know, another thing I forgot to tell you. Sorry. On the day I returned to rehearsal, it was Sam's turn to welcome me back. He hugged

---

65. Orgasmic.
66. Synagogue.

me so tightly that it took the Jaws of Life to extricate myself from his embrace before I could help Luba out of the bind she was in on stage. Apparently, during my absence, he was overwrought, inconsolable, and racked with debilitating guilt that he could have played even a little part in my on-stage collapse. When I walked through the door that day and he set his eyes on me, you'll believe me when I tell you that he gave out such a *geshrey*[67] and made with his hands in that way believers do while looking heavenward like he was witnessing some kind of *t'khiyes hameysim,*[68] he nearly fainted.

I'm not kidding. His euphoria grew to be such a distraction to Luba that at one point she kicked him out of the rehearsal, with a warning not to come back until he'd finished his holy rolling *narishkeit,* and sent me after him into the lobby with a bottle of water to monitor his time out.

"I knew *hashem* would bring you back!" Sam said to me ecstatically while we sat together on a leather bench in the lobby of the JCC. "He told me he would!"

"Who did?" I asked.

"*Hashem,*" he said, referring to God with the word that believers use that literally means "the name" to steer clear of the biblical Tetragrammaton.

"You spoke with God about me?"

"Oh yes, a lot."

"What did you talk about?"

"I told him it's too soon that he should take you, that you're a *mentsch* and that he should give you a *refuah shleymah*[69] so that you could come back and be with us in the play. And he did it!"

Though a man in his adult years, his words were innocent and pure as if spoken by a child who believes in all that isn't real.

"Sam, do you know what a panic attack is?"

"No," he responded, looking at me bright-eyed like I was about to explain.

"Never mind," I said, and rubbed his shoulder gently. "Thank you for the good wishes."

We sat silently for a little while as he drank from his water bottle before I spoke up again. "So, you still speak to God, huh?" I asked him,

---

67. Shout.
68. Resurrection of the dead.
69. Swift and complete recovery.

honestly curious to hear why he still had a relationship with religion when it had done him wrongly.

"Sure!" he said incredulously like it was a bullshit question. "I talk to *hashem* frequently."

"Wait, hold up. When you say you talk to God, you mean you pray, right? You don't actually speak out loud to him?"

"Certainly, I pray to him, *and* I talk to him."

"When?"

"Every day," he answered, then turned to ask me in kind: "You as well?"

"Usually at night, when I'm alone in my bed," I quipped, assuming he'd be clueless.

"You mean the bedtime *shema*?"[70] he answered, proving me right.

"Sometimes it's the *shema*," I continued, "other times I use different *psukim*[71] for inspiration."

"Yes, I do as well," he said.

"Let me guess, the Book of Samuel," I asked, having too much fun at his expense at this point.

"Yes! How did you know?"

"Lucky guess," I said with a chuckle.

"It's one of my favorite books in the Torah."

"Of course, it is," I replied, biting my lip so as not to laugh.

"It's yours as well?" he then asked me earnestly.

"Fuck man, no!" I snapped at him, and as quickly as he recoiled in shock at my unprovoked outburst, I felt overcome by a rush of guilt for having toyed with him needlessly. Fortunately, I managed to keep my mouth shut, rather than take it any further and have to get into it with him about why I couldn't give a rat's ass whether David and Jonathan stuck it to each other or were strictly platonic buddies, even though he clearly fell within the camp that held by the exegesis of the former. He, too, had nothing further to add on the topic, and it was quiet for a while between us as I now sipped from his bottle of water and stared at my feet, doing my best to simply observe and breathe through the myriad thoughts of self-loathing that were busily wafting through my brain.

---

70. The first word of the prayer: "Hear oh Israel...."
71. Religious passages.

"I knew you were religious," Sam eventually whispered to me, and took the water bottle that we were now sharing from my hands.

I didn't answer him immediately, because despite having interacted with him plenty up to that point, it was only at that moment that it occurred to me that Sam's *tabula rasa* wasn't something to be trifled with. His genuine intellectual curiosity in anything and everything we discussed, although absurd, was a rarity that left him vulnerable and exposed to all manner of influence. To that end, I pledged that for however long I could make it last, I would begin to tread a bit more carefully when it came to opining on matters he wanted to delve into and to do my best to handle him with kid gloves.

"I don't know that our terms are defined the same," I eventually said in reply to his latest question. "My religion," I went on to tell him, "consists of a humble admiration of the illimitable superior spirit, who reveals himself in the slight details we are able to perceive with our frail and feeble minds."

"Ooh vah, beautiful!" he said excitedly, looking at me like more was coming.

"Yeah, not me," I said, waving him off, hoping to take him down a notch. "Einstein," I added.

He stared at me blankly, and I don't know if my crestfallen response had more to do with the fact that my self-pledge had lasted all of a nanosecond or the fact that he had been so wronged by that fucking inbred community of his that they had rendered him utterly clueless.

"Sam, where's that *farkakte* little notepad of yours?" I asked him, and watched as he dutifully took out from his pocket the scratchpad I recalled him having at the first rehearsal, along with a tiny pencil that he took up in his right hand. "Good, write down the name, Albert E. Einstein." He didn't at first because his hand started to shake, and it fucking killed me to watch him struggle with the fact that he hadn't the skills to do what I told him to do, at least not from left to right on the page. Even from the opposite side, he was hesitant. "Albert, *mit an aleph*," I encouraged him in Yiddish, so that he would understand where to start writing the name in the Hebrew alphabet. "*Lamed, beys*," I continued until we spelled out the name together in Hebrew letters.

After he'd spelled it out in full, he looked the name over before asking, "a rabbi?"

"A *godl hador,* you could say," I quipped, referencing a rabbinic ranking system he could relate to, which placed Einstein right up at the top.

"And his writings, you read?" Sam asked with great interest.

"Hardly. It's heavy stuff. You need to really know your shit to get into him."

"Like the *kabbalah!*" he jumped in immediately, and to his credit, offered up a pretty good analogy.

"Right, kinda like that," I said with a smile, suggesting he'd scored one.

"It's a beautiful way of describing *hashem.*"

"Actually, I don't know if that's what he was saying, exactly. His views on the whole God thing were kind of complex."

"A rabbi, but he didn't believe in *hashem?*"

"Uh..." I hesitated a moment as again, I was stuck trying to find the right response to the latest mash-up to come out of his remarkably fecund brain, which I recognized I'd played a large part in concocting. "How about we forget about Rabbi E. for now, okay?" I began to respond, and then tried to tack in another direction to what were hopefully calmer waters: "Let's just say that one can struggle to be a Jew without the capacity to believe in the holy one, but it is impossible to be a Jew if one does not believe in holiness."

Again, he stared at me like I'd just delivered *toyre fun sinai.*[72]

"Yeah, not me," I said, slightly exasperated, and pointed for him to begin writing again. "Shmuel Niger. Shmuel, *mit a shin,*" I said, and again helped him spell it out in *oyses*[73] from right to left. "Not a rabbi, don't worry."

When he was finished writing, he again looked over the notes he'd taken and when he was done, he lifted his gaze and rested it upon my face. "Such beautiful words," he said before his voice began quivering with fear and confusion as he asked me the following pointed question: "But *you* Izzy, you don't believe in *hashem?*"

In that moment I was grateful that it was only the two of us on that bench in the lobby of the JCC because had anyone been there other than the neophyte by my side, they would certainly have long since called me

---

72. Literally, "Torah from Mt. Sinai." Practically, an idea that blows someone's mind.

73. Hebrew letters.

on the self-conscious deflecting *narishkeit* I'd managed to get away with up to this point. Frankly, my response to his latest weighty question would be no different: "What can I say, Sam," I began without delving into the meat of his query other than to add, solemnly, that when it came to my disbelief, "*der got fun mayn umgloybn iz prekhtik.*" I didn't bother waiting for his reply. "*Shrayb arayn,*" I instructed him in Yiddish to begin writing the name of one of the towering Yiddish poets of the twentieth century, Jacob "Yankev" Glatstein. His phrase describing "how beautiful the God is of his disbelief," while seemingly contradictory on its face, was actually redolent of a theme as old as the Jewish faith itself, whereby wrestling with the Divine, *krign zikh mit got,* was axiomatic of what it meant to be a Jew.

"I recognize that name," Sam said excitedly after he'd written it out.

"I'm sure," I replied. "Luba has no doubt talked to you about the great poets."

"No, I think I saw his name in the *siddur*[74] at my *shul.*"

"Your *shul* has Glatstein in its *siddur?*" I asked him incredulously. "Are you sure it's a *shul?*"

"Of course, why do you sound surprised?" he responded.

"Cause...uh...well." Actually, I didn't have a quick answer but last I checked, I don't recall having come across *siddurim* in any self-respecting synagogue that had included in them radical Jewish poetry anywhere in the pages between the *moyde ani*[75] and the bedtime *shema.*[76]

"Our *shul* does," he answered confidently, ignoring that my internal monologue must have clearly gotten away from me again, which disturbed me. "I feel very welcome there," he added. He then went on to say that this "*shul*" made him feel like he belonged in a similar way to how he felt being with Luba and her theatre.

"The rabbi is very nice. He believes strongly in *kiruv,*" he said, referencing the Hebrew word for what essentially means bringing people together. However, I think he was kind of confused, as it typically refers to Orthodox Jews proselytizing to bring lapsed ones back into the fold through Torah. But given Sam's recent personal exodus, he could be forgiven the nuance. "If you'd like," he then offered, "I wish to invite you to join me for services this *shabes.*"

---

74. Prayer book.
75. The prayer one says upon waking.
76. The prayer one says before sleeping.

The curiosity was too much to ignore, so I accepted.

Shoyn eyn mol[7] a "*shul*." The Holy Temple of Righteous Seekers, they're called. The name had me fearing for my impressionable friend that he may have landed somewhere he shouldn't have, so much so that I actually took the time that evening to look them up. Indeed, that's the name, but I suppose for tax purposes it's much longer: "An egalitarian congregation perpetually on the fence as to locking down a definition of Judaism and what a Jew is that feels safe and welcoming, and we're not exactly certain about the whole God as a Him thing either, but do join us weekly as it's a work in progress that's fun for the whole family." Or something to that effect. *A kholeria*. At all events, neither the short nor the full description of his "*shul*" instilled me with any confidence whatsoever that he hadn't fallen into the hands of a bunch of charlatans who were going to lead him down an ugly road to perdition.

My first impression of the blasphemy I was invited to participate in began even before I walked through the front door that Saturday morning. It wasn't long after I'd finished up my shower that I found myself in an industrial part of town, standing in the lobby of a warehouse seemingly retrofitted to accommodate a multitude of communities of worship, judging by the list of names on the roster of tenants, where each one had its own take on "holy this" or "divinity that." The Righteous Seekers could be found on the fifth floor by buzzing in a very *shabbesdik*[78] four-digit code to gain entry.

A few flights of stairs later, when I opened the door to the loft with their name next to its number, I thought to myself that my instincts were spot on — it wasn't the little closet on a folding table in the far corner with a red curtain hanging down in front of it, which I assumed held a holy scroll, that had me wondering. Rather, it was the two dozen or so individuals of various shapes, sizes, genders, and colors, a seemingly motley assemblage whose collective asses were thrust to the ceiling in a communal downward dog and who were chanting something foreign to my ears, that the first thing that came to mind—with apologies to the prophet Nehemiah—was that they were speaking the language of Ashdod or other peoples and did not know how to speak the language of Judah.

---

77. Hardly.
78. In keeping with the Sabbath.

That said, at the very least, by my count, it appeared that they had a *minyan.*[79]

"Actually..." I now heard the voice of a young man begin speaking behind me, quietly so as not to disturb the vibe in the room, "....prayer requires preparation to be able to focus and direct the mind on its intention."

"Shit, you weren't supposed to hear that," I apologized to the thirty-something dude who was now standing beside me. He was tall, looked like he took good care of himself, and was dressed in clothing that suggested he might be the yogi leading the class. "I say things sometimes that I shouldn't," I added without getting into it further.

"All good," he said in a calm and accepting tone. "Our sages teach us," he continued, "that one should sit a while both before and following prayer to meditate and let it all sink in. We adhere to that."

"The Rambam, *touché*," I replied, and observed as the hamster in my mind hopped onto its wheel. I began calculating the minimal likelihood of a yogi being familiar with Moses Maimonides and his Laws of Prayer, which he just cited.

"Indeed, we incorporate yogic elements and other mindfulness modalities from various traditions to heighten the *kavana*[80] of our prayers," he said before extending a hand, and with the other removing a multi-colored knitted *kippa*[81] from his pocket and placing it on his head. "I'm Rabbi Rob. You must be Sam's friend."

"Izzy," I responded, and made a mental note to look up what maharajas bestow *smikheh*[82] as I also took the opportunity to grab from my pocket the *kippa* I had brought, just in case I was totally wrong in my assumptions.

"It's a pleasure to have you," he said. "Come, we're about to begin the Torah service," he added, and led me in as the congregation wrapped up their asanas and the room suddenly reverberated with a collective "Om."

A few minutes later, after I'd wished Sam *gut shabes* and he introduced me to some of his fellow "worshippers," the room was transformed for the Torah service. The yoga mats were rolled up and

---

79. Quorum.
80. Intention, sincerity.
81. Yarmulke.
82. Rabbinic ordination.

placed against the walls and, in their place, rows of folding chairs facing forward to the far end of the room opposite the entrance, where the table with the little closet with the red curtain hanging in front of it was brought to the middle to serve as an ersatz *bima.*[83] Sam invited me to sit with him in the first row, where he handed me the *"siddur"* he had spoken of during our conversation earlier that week, which as it turns out, was a few dozen photocopied pages stapled together. I began to flip through it as Rabbi Rob introduced that week's Torah portion, *Ki Tissa,* which if you recall your Exodus, discusses the building of the Golden Calf. No joke, I swear. I enjoyed a slight chuckle at the irony as I looked through the stack of pages in my lap for the Glatstein poem Sam said was contained therein, while the rabbi began to summarize, in English, the story for the room full of what I assumed was the Hebrew-impaired.

The joke was on me however, because after the rabbi finished his summary, he approached the little closet, moved the red curtain aside and took out a pee-wee sized Torah scroll, and everyone stood as if on cue as he cradled it in his arms and began the *Gadlu.*[84] When he did so, I could feel a lump building in my throat, and it wasn't long before my eyes started welling up as he began marching the Torah through the room, which now resounded with the voices of all the assembled singing the *Romemu,*[85] in the language of Judah.

While wiping away the moisture, I could see Sam looking at me with concern and for some reason, the countenance that reflected back at me from his Coke-bottle glasses wasn't me at all. At least not the *me* of today, but rather the man I apparently became according to the Law of Moses and Israel on the day of my bar mitzvah, when I stood before the open *oren koydesh* together with the rabbi, who removed the lightest Torah scroll from the ark and placed it in my arms. When I turned to the congregation to sing the *Gadlu,* the only face I recall seeing at that moment was that of my *zaide,* who stood quietly against the wall in the back, wiping tears from his eyes.

I don't know that we ever discussed that moment specifically, he and I. In thinking about it now however, as I contemplated a rationale to explain my tears in the sanctuary of The Holy Temple of Righteous Seekers, it became clear to me. There was pride in his tears for the

---

83. Platform where the Torah is read.
84. Opening lines of the Torah ceremony.
85. Psalm 99:5-9

accomplishment I had achieved or was about to achieve. When my mother insisted that I was to be bar mitzvah'd, my *zaide* dutifully obliged her request that, absent a father, he be the one to escort me to *shul* every *shabes* in the weeks and months leading up to my special day. As you know, studying for your bar mitzvah is no small thing, so there's no doubt he was *shepping nakhes*[86] that I'd gotten the job done. But I know it was more than that. Although he had abandoned the religious life of his childhood home for a secular ideology that held out the promise of bringing about a better, more equitable world, both approaches to Jewish life were rooted in the same place. It was one of the things I had to explain to Sam earlier that week in our discussion when I gave him another name to look up, the secular Yiddish writer and philosopher Chaim Zhitlovsky, An-sky's childhood friend. Zhitlovsky argued that Judaism is vital because of what it idealizes - its universal, humanistic values - and not as a tool simply to perpetuate Jewish existence. Indeed, that if you strip away the dogma, all that is "holy" in the Torah remains no less important to a secular Jew. For that reason alone, I could only imagine what it must have felt like for my *zaide*, after all he'd been through, to see his *eynikl*[87] cradling the Torah in his arms. Although he didn't sing along with me as I paraded the Torah from the *oren koydesh* towards the *bimah* because the dogma no longer applied to him, his tears were proof enough that the profound words that follow the *Romemu* were no less foundational for him as a secular Jew than for those who believed: *Eytz khayim hi la makhazikim bah—* "It is the tree of life for those who lay hold of it."

"Izzy!" I suddenly heard Sam calling my name excitedly as he simultaneously tugged at my arm. "Come, you're getting the first *aliyah!*"[88]

Fuck.

It took me a moment to get my bearings but when I did, it appeared that Rabbi Rob had finished parading the Torah around the room, and it was now lying flat on the table at the front where the show was about to get started. Joining him at the "*bima*" was a heavy-set, curly-haired blonde woman wearing a *kippa* and a *tallis*[89] draped around her neck, as well as Sam, a *tallis* covering his head in the traditional

---

86. Deriving pride and joy.
87. Grandchild.
88. Literally, "to ascend." Practically, given the honour to read from the Torah.
89. Prayer shawl.

Orthodox fashion. Sam was apparently *gabbai*[90] for the occasion, as he was bouncing excitedly from one foot to another like a kid in a candy store while he called for the congregation to "give honor to the Torah" before calling up the first *aliyah*.

"Arise..." Sam began to say aloud boldly and dignifiedly so that everyone could hear. He then turned to look at me for guidance so that he could complete the sentence because I hadn't told him my formal Hebrew name in advance. Not only wasn't I expecting the honor of being called to the Torah, but I also didn't even know if these people did Torah.

Ugh.

"*Yitzhok elioho ben chane bas mordekhe-hirsh...hakohen*," I said to him as I reluctantly approached the table where Rabbi Rob handed me a *tallis*, which I draped around my neck so as not to offend. Meanwhile, it seemed I'd stopped Sam cold when I told him my name, *sans* my father, choosing to reference my matrilineal lineage instead. "It's okay," I whispered to him, "I had it *paskn'd*[91] once. It's kosher."

"A *Kohen*, but how?" he whispered back at me, not only confused at the unconventional construct of my Hebrew name, but apparently gobsmacked that I also happened to be a descendant of the priestly class on my father's side, which I threw in as I knew it would make an impression upon someone like him.

"We'll get into it some other time," I whispered to him, and urged that he not hold up the proceedings and get on with it, which he did by adding the blessing for the almighty who gave the Torah to his people. Rabbi Rob then handed me a laminated step-by-step for *amoratzim*[92] that explains what to do when called to the Torah, complete with pictures. I waved him off. "I know the drill," I said to him, then nodded at the corpulent lady, who I presumed was the *bas koyre*,[93] to open the scrolls, which she did, and pointed at the first words of the *parshah*[94] with the silver *yad*[95] in her hand. I then touched the margin of the parchment with the fringes of my *tallis*—not the words themselves, heaven forbid—brought the fringes to my lips while touching one of the handles of the scroll and

---

90. Someone who helps run Jewish religious services.
91. A rabbinic ruling on a matter of Jewish law.
92. Ignoramuses.
93. Official title of the person reading from the Torah.
94. Weekly Torah portion.
95. Pointer.

then with a wink at Sam, began to recite the blessings over the Torah like I meant business.

When I was done, I stepped to the side and listened as the woman chanted the first verse of the *parshah,* in what was admittedly a beautiful operatic voice inflected with a modern Hebrew accent. Likewise, I got a kick out of watching Sam dutifully fulfilling his role as *gabbai* by following along in a *chumesh,*[96] all the while conducting the *trop,* a.k.a. the musical cantillations that the woman sang, ensuring that she got every note right. When she finished the verse, and after I wrapped up my *aliyah* with the post-reading blessing, Sam turned to me and asked if I'd like to *bentsch goyml,* which is to give thanks to the Almighty for having made it through an ordeal.

"Yeah, no, I'm good for today, but you can ask me again tomorrow," I told him with not a little bit of sarcasm, as I was kind of done and antsy to get back to my seat. Regardless, he then launched into a *mishebeyrakh* on my behalf, beseeching the Holy One to "protect and deliver me from all trouble and distress, affliction and illness....to send blessing and success in all my endeavours," and called upon the congregation to respond to him with an Amen, which they did. He then broke protocol, and rather than shake my hand with the accompanying "*sh'koyekh,*" which is typically said as a compliment when you don't fuck things up at the *bima,* he wrapped himself around me instead and held me in an embrace that felt embarrassingly long. He let go eventually but held onto my shoulder so that I was stuck beside him as the next *aliyot* were called. Mercifully, the Righteous Seekers didn't hold by the traditional seven on *shabes,* and only two more batters came up to the plate after me. The second *aliyah* went to a lesbian couple who had just given birth, followed by the *maftir aliyah,*[97] a Black former gang-banger named Harold, who was so taken with Rabbi Rob when he pastored him in prison that he was now in the process of converting. When I was introduced to him a little earlier, he asked that I refer to him as Haggai, or what he proudly called his new Jew name. Not a word of a lie.

While standing at the "*bima*" throughout, it was hard to brush aside the thoughts running through my mind at the incongruity of it all, but more particularly, the self-consciousness that I was probably the only one

---

96. Literally, "the five books of Moses." Practically, the Torah in printed form.
97. The last *aliyah.*

in the room even thinking about it. I can't tell you if I smiled back at Sam when he occasionally looked at me, his face beaming with what I could only interpret as a profound sense of feeling at home and belonging, because I don't know if I shared it. It could very well be that from the moment the rabbi removed the Torah from its little ark, I was taken to a place in my mind that I chose to stay in throughout the entire service. Even though I was able to get through the honor bestowed upon me, I couldn't help feeling that everyone in the room saw right through me, and although they were too nice to say it, I was an impostor in their midst.

With the thoughts building upon themselves, I could see myself struggling to fight them off, and I started to get scared that my next move would be to run. As much as that concerned me, I was equally afraid of the embarrassment it would cause Sam. I was frozen. That is until I heard Rabbi Rob beginning to sing Psalm 29, which heralds the closing of the Torah service. As he did so, he lifted the Torah from the table, placed it in my arms, and motioned for me to lead the processional of parading the Torah through the room so that the congregants could kiss it before its return to the ark. With each step I took, the voices of the assemblage grew louder as they sang through the verses of the psalm, which extols the seven voices of the Almighty. As I passed through the room and the congregants showered me with all manner of kind-hearted good wishes and heartfelt *gut shabes,* while beaming at me in that way Sam did, for some reason I randomly thought of Spinoza and wondered if he might feel that by the grace of communities like this "the kingdom could yet rise again and God might likewise elect them."

When we returned to the front of the room and the singing of the psalm was complete, there was a pause as I stood before the ark with the rabbi to my left and Sam on the right, and I started to feel a sense of relief that it was over. Yet, it wasn't. The rabbi didn't take the scroll from my arms to put it back in its resting place as I expected he would. I certainly didn't anticipate the next moment, when the woman with the curly hair opened her mouth and began to sing the passages from the Book of Psalms, "Return O Lord, to Zion your resting place and in the place of your choice, that every mouth and every tongue may glorify the splendor of your holiness." This caused the lump to reappear in my throat because I knew what came after it. On the day of my bar mitzvah, after I had paraded the Torah back through the congregation, past my *zaide*, who with tears in his eyes, kissed me on the head, this was the passage that I sang before handing the Torah back to the rabbi so that he could return it to the *oren koydesh*. When I turned around to look at my *zaide*, I found that my eyes began to well up just like his were, because although I was only a child, I understood the weight of the words I was singing, that they were more than Biblical poetry. Rather, in the context of my life, they reflected a hope that after all that my *zaide* and his generation had been through, what they had done to hold fast to their beliefs, and surviving through that long dark night of Hitler so that the golden chain of the Jewish people would not be broken, a great responsibility had now been placed upon my shoulders: I was now the bridge that united that past with the present and the future. Standing between Rabbi Rob and Sam, a tiny Torah once again cradled in my arms, the tears poured down my cheeks as the room full of the Righteous Seekers raised their voices and now sang together the passage from Lamentation that held the fate of the Jewish people in its final words: "Renew our days as of old."

"Izzy!" Sam called out to me with great concern as the collective voice in the room rose to its crescendo. "Are you okay?!"

I said nothing, nodding instead that I was all right despite the fact that I was making a mess of the mantle covering the Torah with my tears.

"Then what's wrong?" he asked.

"Nothing," I began to say. Through the jumble of emotions that I honestly was not expecting to experience that morning in his *shul*, I believe I managed a little smile: "It's just really fucking Jewish," I added before handing the Torah back to Rabbi Rob, who then returned it to the closet and pulled the red curtain in front of it to bring the Torah service to a close.

The room was silent as everyone listened attentively to Rabbi Rob as he now read in English the *haftorah*[98] from the book of Kings, which told the story of how Elijah disproved the existence of the false gods Baal and Asherah by challenging his rival prophets who believed in them to a good, old-fashioned cook-off. As the story goes, each would sacrifice an animal to their god, and whichever one could deliver fire to the spit to get the barbecue started would be the true God. As we all know, it works out well for Elijah, as the Almighty is the only one who sparks the fire

---

98. Reading from Prophets following a Torah service.

and the assembled fall to the ground and cry out the words familiar to all from the end of the Neilah service, "The lord is God! The lord is God!" which the Rabbi began to chant multiple times in unison with his congregation which to be honest, was kind of creepy. When he was done, he said a *mishebeyrakh*[99] for his holy congregation, for some reason, dispensed with the "yukum pukum,"[100] which I'm guessing he didn't know was designed for his sake. Then, rather than recite the half-kaddish, the Rabbi began a Buddhist *niggun*[101] that everyone in the room seemed to know was the signal to rearrange the chairs yet again; this time into a circle of friends, "AA"-inspired formation for a show, tell and share portion of the *shabes* program that I quickly deduced was definitely not *musaf*.[102]

Once the chanting was done and everyone was seated, the session began with Rabbi Ron doing his clergical shtick by tying in the themes of the *parshah* and the *haftorah* with whatever might be on his mind that week. Then each member was given a minute or two to share their thoughts, feelings, and whatever else Rabbi Rob encouraged them to be unburdened of in the moment. It started with the lesbians, whose cups were unsurprisingly running over with their new bundle of joy; followed by Haggai, who went on and on, testifying about how his life was changing for the better because of his righteous soul brother, Rabbi Rob. And then I wasn't paying attention, as I was back to flipping through the *siddur* where I'd found the Glatstein poem that Sam told me was there. I'm no *mumkhe*[103] on Yiddish poetry, so the fact that it was unfamiliar to me was beside the point. But there it was, called "*Shabes*," together with a wide variety of other poems, texts, and meditations, many attributed to names I recognized as Jewish, and others like Confucius, Gandhi, and Mother Theresa, who definitely were not — all of them under the rubric of "Making *Musaf* Meaningful," which I assumed was Rabbi Rob's copyrighted millennial *mishegas*.

---

99. Prayer for people in need.
100. "Not funny, Iz" Faygen said when he read it. It's "*yekum purkan*"– may deliverance arise — a prayer for students and teachers of the Torah. Read it fast... yukum pukum.
101. Melody.
102. Additional service, performed on the Sabbath and the Holy Days after the Torah reading.
103. Expert.

"Izzy," I heard the Rabbi's voice call my name now, and I looked up from the *siddur* to see him and every other face in the room staring at me, because I guess it was my turn to blah blah. Before I could tell the Rabbi that I'd kind of had enough for one *shabes,* and I was only sticking around for Sam's sake, he preempted me: "I understand from Sam that we have a native Yiddish speaker with us today, is that true?" he asked in a voice that rang to me like that of a kindergarten teacher asking if the fat kid wouldn't mind sharing some of the candy with the rest of the class.

"It is," I answered, and watched as Sam bounced around the outside of the circle excitedly while passing out sheets of paper, one of which landed on my lap.

"Well then, what a treat," the Rabbi said happily. "Would you be willing to share your knowledge with us by reading the poem you have in your hands in its original Yiddish? I've decided to add it to our *siddur.*"

With all eyes on me rapt with anticipation, I could only give one answer. "Sure," I said reluctantly, and then was momentarily taken aback when I looked down at the sheet of paper Sam had handed me to find Avrom Sutskever's poem *Ver vet blaybn,* "Who Will Remain."

As my heart skipped a beat at seeing the name of not only one of the greatest Yiddish poets, but a partisan who had fought the Nazis alongside my *zaide* and *bubbe*'s friends in the forests outside Vilna during the war, my phone started ringing. "Shit, sorry," I said awkwardly while I fumbled for my phone in my pocket with a trembling hand. It was Faygen, who I ignored, and switched the phone to vibrate before putting it back into my pocket. I then took a moment to gather myself and clear my throat, not simply to deliver the poem properly, but mostly as a stalling tactic to keep the emotions at bay that started percolating the minute I scanned the page and saw the words I knew by heart. I closed my eyes and hoped for the best as I began to recite the first stanza:

Who will remain, what will remain?
The blindness of the blind man, who disappears,
will remain.
A hint of the sea will remain: a thread of foam–
A wisp of cloud, entangled in a tree,
will remain.

As my phone started buzzing again in my pocket, and as I imagined everyone in the room would be distracted and tell me to answer it if I opened my eyes, I tried my best to ignore it and kept going.

> Who will remain, what will remain?
> A word will remain....
> Genesis-like, growing the grasses.
> The rose will remain, because it must
> And seven of those grasses will understand.

But it wouldn't stop buzzing, so I stopped. "I'm really, really sorry," I said to everyone and no one in particular as I fumbled again for my phone in my pocket. However, when I took it out and saw the message on my screen, I lost my apologetic composure. "Fuck, no!" I screamed, and leaped from my chair. I may have apologized to the Rabbi, Sam, and the congregation for desecrating the Sabbath with my outburst, and I may also have thanked the Righteous Seekers for their hospitality. But I honestly can't remember, because as soon as I jumped from my chair, I was out the door even faster. Within seconds I was outside, running as fast as my legs would take me. The sound of my *zaide* reading Sutskever's final stanza reverberated piercingly in my ears as the sky fell all around me.

> Of all the heavenly stars, the one that falls
> In the tear will remain.
> A drop of wine will always remain in its jug.
> Who will remain, God will remain.
> Does that not suffice?

Over the course of my life, the few experiences I've had with intensive care units have been less than propitious. In fact, they've been downright traumatizing because in each case, the ICU led straight to the morgue. I didn't hold out much hope that this time would be any different when on this day, after I ran into the ICU at the hospital where I'd been only days earlier, I found Faygen pacing, flossing, and looking like death warmed over. His response when I asked him where things stood confirmed my worry: "*S'halt zikh shmol*," he said in Yiddish. The window was closing fast.

"Shit," I said as we sat near the nursing station, buzzing with activity nearby.

"What happened?"

"Stroke."

"When?"

"Middle of the night."

I then asked a series of rapid-fire questions to ascertain the extent of the damage, for which he had no reply, as it was too soon to know. Just then, a nurse turned a corner and approached us.

"She's awake and stable," she said to Faygen. "You can go in to see her if you wish."

"Thank you," Faygen replied as she returned to the nursing station, then he turned to me: "She asked for you."

"Can she speak?" I asked, my heart skipping a beat.

"Haltingly."

"Faygen..." I began to say before my voice trailed off. I hunched over and held my face in my hands.

"I know," he said, and patted me on the back. We'd been here together before during those times when it didn't end well. "But she said it's important."

"Can we go in together?" I asked in a fragile, childlike tone.

"You'll be fine," he answered, which provided no solace coming from the man who pulled out another package of floss from his pocket. "I'm not going anywhere," he added, and gave me a slight nudge like there wasn't much point in talking it through any further. He then told me the room number and pointed in its direction. After taking a deep breath, I stood and made my way over.

Upon entering the room, when I heard the slow, steady beeping of the heart rate monitor, it wasn't lost on me that, by comparison, mine was beating at a rate a zillion times faster. There wasn't much I was going to do to change that fact, particularly when the frail, pallid-looking woman lying in the bed hooked up to a myriad of tubes and machines turned to gaze at me with a smile that caused the beating to grow even faster, opened her mouth and said to me in a barely audible Yiddish, "Itzikl, *bist gekumen*."

"Yes, Luba," I answered softly in her mother tongue. "Of course, I came."

She then held out her fragile hand as if to suggest that I should approach from where I was standing, which admittedly was with my back hard against the door, my hand squeezing the handle for dear life. For some reason, although it was an ICU, she not only had a room, but it was all to herself. To be sure, it was sparse, windowless, and eerily quiet, but for the sound of her lifeline beating out a steady rhythm. Although there was no chair to speak of, there was a rolling stool, which I brought to the bedside, where I took her hand in mine. Judging by her appearance, it seemed she was too frail to engage in a conversation, so I kept my mouth shut, although I wanted very much to ask about the circumstances that led to her hospitalization. Moreover, as curious as I was, according to Faygen, she had specifically asked to see me of all people, so I kept that in my vault too. It was quiet for what felt like an awfully long, awkward while, as I sat with her, saying nothing, watching her with her eyes closed, holding her hand and assuming that's how it would be until Faygen would eventually check in and relieve me. To my surprise however, she eventually spoke again, and the strange conversation that ensued was conducted in Yiddish.

"You don't need to be angry anymore," she said as her eyes remained closed.

"Angry?" I responded, unsure of what she was referring to. "I'm not angry."

"You are," she responded, and nodded just enough like she was confident about what she was saying. "The book," she said.

She was right, of course, but for the life of me, I don't recall ever bringing it up with her. As with every other intimate part of my life that ended up in the public space, I assumed Faygen must have shared.

"Not Avrom," she said about Faygen, and I could feel my heart pounding against my chest because I could have sworn my internal monologue didn't leave my lips.

"Then who?" I asked her nervously.

She then turned towards me, opened her eyes, and stared at me like what she was about to say should have seemed obvious from the moment I walked into her office. As her eyes widened and she opened her mouth to speak, she was suddenly possessed with the strength of Samson that I let go of her hand and recoiled in terror at what I heard next: "The bird," she said in a voice so thunderingly loud that it shook the room, all the while holding my gaze in hers, which had now taken on the appearance of something I could only describe to you as not of this world. But in a flash, before I could process what was happening, it was over, and it became quiet again as she lay motionless in the bed with her eyes closed once more; that I wasn't sure the moment had occurred at all. The silence grew deafening before she eventually spoke again, but now in a whisper so soft that it was barely audible.

"I've known the whole time," she said, and as she looked at me, I could see my reflection in her eyes that started to grow distant. "You can still tell the story," she added.

"But how?" I asked apropos of both, and brought myself as close to her as possible, hoping for the whole world that she would explain what she knew.

"The theatre," she whispered before closing her eyes again.

"What about the theatre?" I asked her, but there was no reply. The only sound that could now be heard in the room was the steady beep of the machine monitoring her heart, which was still beating. Although I sat there a few moments longer, continuing to hold her hand in mine, hoping that she would speak again, it was wishful thinking on my part because it appeared that she had fallen back asleep. I eventually relinquished my hand, gently placed hers on the bed by her side, and got up to leave. When I reached the door, however, she spoke.

"*Itzikl*," she whispered, and lifted her hand just barely as if to signal that she and I weren't entirely done.

"Yes, Luba?" I responded to her while standing by the door.

"Soreh," she said, referring to the Hebrew name she had given Sue-Ann, and I now re-approached the bedside.

"What about her?" I asked, sitting down on the stool and rolling it close to hear what she had to say.

"She's not what you think," she added, looking at me briefly before closing her eyes for the final time and turning her face away.

"Luba," I said and nudged her gently. "What do you mean?" I continued to nudge her. Despite the room being silent again, the machine's beeping increased in frequency.

"Luba?" I said and as the beeping became more rapid, so did my repeated calling out of her name.

164

"*Zaide*! *Zaide*, wake up!" I began to shout, and as the beeping increased more quickly and its volume grew, it was now joined by my *zaide*'s voice reverberating throughout the room as he spoke his last words to me before he left this world: *Zay a mentsch, Itzikl. zay a guter yid:* "Be an exemplary human being, be a good Jew."

"*Zaide*, don't leave. Wake up!" I shouted. "Tell him to wake up!" I bellowed even more loudly as the door to the room flew open now, and the nurse rushed in with Faygen behind her.

"Get him out of here!" the nurse yelled at Faygen, who grabbed me by the waist and attempted to pull me away from the bed that I was holding onto for dear life while a handful of other white and blue coats came rushing through the door to attend to Luba.

"*Zaide*, wake up! Wake up, *zaide*!" I shouted over and over as Faygen eventually pried me away from Luba's bedside and dragged me from the room while whispering into my ear that it was okay, that I would be okay.

Over the next few days, I cloistered myself in my room where I lay in my bed in darkness, purposely shutting myself off from anyone and everyone. I thought of nothing other than what had transpired, and more specifically, the news that followed shortly after my visit that Luba had slipped into a coma. Although I refused all communication from the outside world, including from the young woman who deserved better from me, I did make one phone call to my mother shortly after Faygen sent me a text a few days after the ICU that simply said that it was *nokh alemen.*[104]

When my mother answered, she put me on speaker because Faygen was with her. After apologizing profusely for what I felt was my fault, there was silence on the other end of the line and on mine. Nothing but deep, mournful, interminable tears at the indescribable loss.

---

104. When all is said and done.

10

I'm sure it won't come as much of a surprise when I tell you that I have a neurosis something fierce concerning electronic forms of communication, specifically as it pertains to the issue of not knowing in whose hands my missives might end up after sending them into the ether. I mention this merely to provide some context as to why, when on the morning following the news of Luba's passing, it felt like I took an eternity and a day to not only type but to eventually send a few, but honestly very polite, words of regret to Sue-Ann apropos of a dinner party she was hosting that evening; one whose timing, I think I can be forgiven, couldn't have been worse.

With a show of hands, how many of you think it took a heartbeat for that message to make its way back to my handlers? Congratulations to all who voted in favor of "duh," because that's how quickly Faygen and my mother began breaking my phone with their pointed replies. I'll spare you their contents because it wasn't much longer after that when they appeared together live at my apartment door to conduct an intervention in support of my not only retracting but most definitely attending Sue-Ann's shindig.

Forgive me. I don't mean to make light of interventions, as they truly are a serious and solemn matter. However, given what you know to this point, you can imagine that over my lifetime, I've been the subject of not a few of them. And each was conducted by the dynamic duo of Faygen and my mother. I could be off by a couple, as there might have been whitecoats on particularly challenging occasions. *Nisht vikhtik.* I should point out parenthetically, that as irony would have it, the occasions typically devolved into a therapy session focused not on me, but rather on the latter "interventionista," someone who could always be counted upon to use the opportunity to blame herself as the root cause of all my *mishegas,* which as you might imagine, rendered the interventions counterproductive and ultimately pointless. Come to think of it, I shouldn't be that flippant because absent a decent bottle of Chianti or a pack of cigarettes, turns out that obsessive cleaning is the next crutch on my mother's list of things to lean on in moments of emotional crisis, like on this occasion when it wasn't long after she and Faygen walked through the door that she put herself to work.

"What?" I asked despondently when they turned their gaze toward me as I opened the door, finding me naked except for my briefs and my *zaide*'s slippers. "You were expecting a fucking greeting party?"

"Again with the fucking," my mother responded with tears in her eyes when she walked in. Then, exasperated, she threw her hands in the air and turned to Faygen to handle the situation, as she was already heading for my kitchen, where Soffy had told her to look for the cleaning supplies she had used the last time she was here—well, I don't want to tell you when. Upon Faygen's first question about my well-being, to which I replied that it would likely be touch-and-go while he and my mother were around, I dutifully complied with his request to put something on so we could have a chat.

Knowing her as I do, it was while heading down the hall to my room that I counted seconds, maybe fractions, before the expected scream came bellowing from the kitchen. "Yes, mother, I know..." I shouted back at her over my shoulder, and there was a slight delay before I completed my thought as I reached into my room and grabbed whatever was strewn on the floor amongst the empty Kleenex boxes, which happened to be a towel. "I haven't gotten around to taking them down," I shouted back at her again as I wrapped it around my waist and made my way back to my living room, where Faygen was now sitting on my sofa shaking his head at my absurdity, while my mother was apoplectic about the dozen garbage bags filled to the brim and lining my kitchen.

"For fuck's sake," I yelled at the two of them, "can we just stop for a moment and acknowledge that the garbage is at least *in* the bags?" It was crickets for a little while after that as my mother started to cry while simultaneously taking to finding things to scrub in the kitchen, and I took to pacing back and forth, not wanting to engage with Faygen...until I did.

"I know what it looks like," I eventually said regarding the physical manifestation of my condition piled up neatly in the kitchen, then sat beside him. "I just haven't had the *koyekh*," I added in Yiddish, which he clearly understood had nothing to do with the strength required, literally, to bring the garbage bags downstairs.

"You don't need to explain, *yingele*," he replied like he meant it, and I was grateful that he was with me on that, at least concerning the nuances that lie hidden between the lines that required no further explanations.

"Why did you tell her?" I asked him about my mother, who was seemingly in a world unto herself in the kitchen.

"She had a right to know."

"And you didn't think twice about what it might be like for her to relive it?" I asked, and looked over my shoulder to watch as she was now scrubbing my sink, which happened to be in no need of any cleaning whatsoever.

"I did. But she's your mother," he replied wistfully.

"I don't know what came over me," I said to him, thinking not only of what had transpired a few days earlier, but also of the time all those years ago when it occurred similarly and which I imagined, as I glanced over at my mother, was haunting her again as well.

"You wanna talk about it?" Faygen asked me.

Actually, I did, but not with him.

Unfortunately, the person I wanted to chat with was *en route* to *oylem habeh*,[105] leaving me with a bucket load of questions I hadn't the faintest about how to answer.

"What's there to say?" I replied to him instead, which led us into a brief discussion we'd had many times before when we lost someone from the generation that shaped our characters and our understanding of what it meant to be both a Jew and a citizen of the world.

But they didn't come to eulogize Luba.

"We called Dr. G," Faygen said softly, which I interpreted as a preemptive measure against the inevitable pushback on my part. Actually, I didn't reply immediately, as not only didn't I know where he was going with his line of thinking, but I was reminded that as much I loved the man, it always pissed me off when he took certain liberties I didn't feel he had a right to. "She believes it's urgent that you meet," he went on, and the next bit out of him got my back up: "She'll come here for the session."

"Nope," I replied matter-of-factly with an accompanying cold stare and watched as he looked over to the kitchen where my mother had stopped scrubbing, and suddenly it was "high noon" in my apartment. "For fuck's sake, I don't need to see her!" I began to lash out at the two of them as I jumped from the sofa, leaving the towel behind as I did. "What's the matter with you guys?" I continued while pointing at them

---

105. The world to come.

accusingly. "We know what she's gonna say," I now began, and watched as Faygen nodded along in agreement as I illustrated how well I knew the doctor's script, pardon the pun: "That I have to go back on the meds not because I relived a childhood trauma, but that it played out so irrationally in public, providing a clear signal that I'm not in control of my faculties. Moreover, my exhibiting of classic signs of guilt and shame in direct response to my uncontrolled outburst, which resulted in my shutting myself off from the world, is an additional sign that I'm out of control, at risk and that taken all together, could lead to something much worse if left untreated."

Faygen stared me up and down, as if to submit for Exhibit A that I wasn't making a good case for myself by arguing on my own behalf, while half-naked in the middle of my garbage-laden apartment. "Well, couldn't it?" he said.

"Yes. If you trigger me again!"

"Me?" he answered, and recoiled in disbelief.

"Yes, *you*. You're the one who made me go in to see her. You should have known it could be a problem!"

"Faygen's only trying to help," my mother finally chimed in as she exited the kitchen with a bucket full of soapy water, rubber gloves, and a sponge. "You know that's what we're here for, *mamele*," she added before beginning to make her way down the hall toward what I knew was a disaster in the making, but I didn't even bother getting in the way.

"Good," I replied, and began pacing again, already contemplating a response to the eruption I knew was imminent from where she was headed. "Then, fuck the doctors," I continued, "because they don't understand that this is about a pain no medication can fix."

"Then what's it about?" Faygen asked.

"What are you asking *klotz kashes*[106] for," I replied sneeringly. "Loss! Life, for chrissake!"

"And what are you gonna do about your...life?" he asked and waved at me as I continued to stand in front of him in my briefs and my *zaide*'s slippers, like there was a lot I needed to figure out on that front.

"While the two of you are here, nothing."

And then....ka-boom!

---

106. Idiotic questions that don't merit an answer.

"Oh my god, Faygen!" my mother shrieked from the bathroom, and although I could see he was tempted, I held him back.

"What is it?" he asked me nervously.

"I told you already. I just haven't had the *koyekh.*"

"There's no toilet paper!" my mother yelled and he looked at me again, dumbfounded like he wasn't sure what fire was burning, where, and what he was supposed to do about it.

"Just wait," I said, knowing full well what was incoming and not a minute later, my mother appeared before us carrying a stack of shredded newspapers, discount flyers, and various other detritus that made up the carpet of my bathroom.

"Tell me you're not using these," she said, thrusting them toward me, her voice choking with emotion as she looked at me beseechingly in the hope that while I may have been losing my marbles, at the very least I was managing to hold onto my dignity as I descended.

"Can I just say that it bugs the living shit out of me that I have no fucking privacy with the two of you," I said petulantly, and began to feel even more exposed than I already was, literally.

"Faygen," she said, desperately turning to him while clutching the offending shards of paper in the hopes that he would do or say something because she was paralyzed with fear. She then turned to make her way back down the hall.

"Ma, I'm okay. It's not your fault!" I called out to her in futility because she didn't stop or look back over her shoulder in response. All I could do was stare in her direction and watch as she walked back into my bathroom, fell to her knees, and began scrubbing my toilet while she wept, the site of which felt like a punch to the gut. I then turned back to Faygen, and tears began streaming from my eyes as well.

"It's not her fault," I whispered to him.

"I know," he said softly, "but she's your *zaide*'s daughter, and you're her son," he added as if to suggest the genes were what they were and it was pointless trying to make sense of it otherwise.

"I'm just trying to come to terms with what's happened," I said.

"I know, but you don't need to shut yourself in or off to do that," he replied, "it's not doing you or anybody else any good."

I said nothing.

"She wasn't expecting this," he then started again about my mother and I suppose referencing the train wreck that I appeared to be, and my place of residence no less. "Believe it or not, she's really happy and excited for you."

"What are you talking about?"

"Sue-Ann."

"I'm not even gonna bother asking what you've told her."

"Nothing you haven't told me, I swear."

I threw him a look like he was the worst bullshitter on the planet.

"What? It's true."

"I haven't told you anything," I said to him.

"People express themselves beyond words, *yingele*."

"Yes, coffee, we've gone through this already," I said to him, exasperated.

"And dancing," he replied, smiling like a Cheshire cat.

"Fuck, what did Sue-Ann share with you?"

"Only that you're a good dancer," he said again, his grin wider now. I actually didn't know what to make of it because if Sue-Ann divulged details of what transpired in the cemetery, it's not the kind of thing Faygen and I have traditionally shot the shit about, and now wasn't the time to start.

"What will it take to get you to reconsider attending her dinner?" he asked me point-blankly.

"Faygen," I hesitated before he chimed in again.

"I'm choosing to believe you," he said.

"What are you talking about?"

"As your friend," he began to say, "I'm telling you that I've sat here, I've watched you, and despite appearances, I've listened to you advocate strongly on your own behalf that you don't need to see your doctor, but all that you needed was some time to wallow in your self-loathing for a few days."

Actually, I thought he did a good job with that.

"However, neither your mother nor I believe for a second that you should be off your meds," he continued. "But that's for another day."

"Thank you."

"Then, what excuse do you have not to go to Sue-Ann's? She's incredibly disappointed."

I said nothing, as it occurred to me that I never did ask Faygen why he felt comfortable opening up my life's story to Sue-Ann after I'd hit the floor at rehearsal. But, like he said, it was for another day.

"She'll be disappointed, too," he added, nodding toward where my mother was still prostrate before my toilet, doing work I wished she wouldn't have undertaken.

"Guilting me into it isn't the best approach, you know," I fecklessly told him.

"All we wanted to do was come here and share our thoughts for your consideration," he replied, and I guess he was finished because he then stood up like he was preparing to leave. "Promise me you'll at least do that," he said, and I looked at him and nodded that I would.

"But I can't do anything until you pick my mother off my bathroom floor and take her home," I chided him.

"Go ahead," he said and motioned in her direction to emphasize it was something that, between the two of us, I was the one who should do it. He then stood in my living room and waited patiently as I headed down the hallway and into my bathroom, where I got down on my knees and kissed my mother on the forehead before taking her in my arms and holding her close for a long while.

———

As I reflect on that afternoon, I'm grateful that the time between Faygen and my mother's departure and when I rang Sue-Ann's buzzer was so short. I was practically left with no time to rethink my decision to override the one I had taken that morning when I sent an otherwise benign text message that actually sparked the entire drama that followed. In fact, the aforementioned "long while" turned into a few hours alone with my mother for what was an overdue heart-to-heart, one that took us from sitting by my toilet to eventually lying together on my bed, where we shared a pack of cigarettes and a bottle of Chianti that Faygen had smartly gone out to procure.

Although it began with me sharing what had transpired by Luba's bedside, it naturally evolved into a discussion of the trauma that it awoke within me, which of course, led to a long conversation about my *zaide* and how much we each missed him. Please forgive me for not sharing what we said to each other about the night he died and the scene I caused at the hospital, when as a frightened boy barely into adolescence, he called me to his bedside, because although he knew his time was up, he still had something important to tell me. I don't recall exactly how our back-and-forth went, and I don't think it matters.

I'm sharing, mostly, I think, to tell you how grateful I am for my mother; that despite myself and despite the burdens she likewise carries, we can have these moments together where we acknowledge that the pain which runs deep, like a perpetual mourning, is our common bond. Of course, we discussed my doc and the meds. Yet, I was relieved that despite her worry and although it was a topic she wanted to keep at the top of the agenda, she didn't come down hard on me. She accepted my heartfelt plea that the valley into which I had fallen in response to Luba's death was legit and that I felt I had the strength to climb out of it on my own.

When our discussion invariably turned to Sue-Ann, I felt comfortable sharing—at the very least filling in the gaps Faygen hadn't already—minus the cemetery stuff, of course. The tears she cried in response didn't concern me because I could tell they were shed in joy. Not as a result of what came out of my mouth, mind you. But rather, how it sounded when it did and maybe most importantly, because I think I was smiling. The latter statement I kind of knew instinctively because me smiling while sharing was the kind of moment that, given our life's journey together, seldom occurred.

When the chat invariably turned to that evening's dinner *chez* Sue-Ann, she asked a critical question I suppose any loving mother would do in that situation: "What would I be wearing?" I likely shrugged in response, as if to suggest I had no clue and wasn't sure why it mattered, then got a kick out of watching how quickly she hopped from my bed and began rummaging through my closet for an outfit that befit the occasion, something her own mother would have described as *pasndik.*[107] I will share something with you however, that I ask that you please keep to yourself. As I lit a cigarette and observed her going to work in my apartment on something I actually didn't mind her doing, I knew full well that there were items that I hadn't shared with her during the course of our discussion, topics that I didn't know if and when I ever would. As a result, after she had picked out an outfit that would show me off well, then left with Faygen shortly thereafter, a cloud descended upon me as I invariably began ruminating again over the cryptic bread crumbs Luba left for me on her death bed, which had been haunting me ever since,

---

107. Appropriate.

including those regarding Sue-Ann, who I was about to see for the first time since the cemetery.

Although I was nervous about the idea of attending dinner at Sue-Ann's from the moment I got the invite, it was only once the buzzer rang to let me into her building that I wanted to shit my pants. You know the discomfort I'm talking about. I mean the heart-pounding, palm-sweating kind of stuff; to say nothing of the fact that I wasn't two steps in when I wanted to rush back home to replace the shirt that my mother had just pressed special, which my pits had already drenched and I could start to smell myself something awful. "Nice going, dickhead," I castigated myself in frustration as I stepped into the elevator and punched number fifteen, which happened to be the top floor of a warehouse full of lofts where Sue-Ann seemingly occupied the penthouse. Yeah, sure, I was uneasy about not having attended a sit-down dinner in I couldn't remember how long and I was out of practice as to the pro forma stuff used in service of avoiding the awkward. But that's not what was causing my body to start shaking as I watched the numbers tick away on my ride up. Of course, Luba's parting words to me about Sue-Ann felt like they were burning a hole through my forehead. But that wasn't it, either. So I was stuck for the brief journey like a prisoner in my now convulsing, pathetic self while fecklessly attempting to figure out what was making me so uneasy.

All of it pointless, by the way, because when the doors opened to the fifteenth floor, with an accompanying "ding" so loud I thought I'd have a heart attack, I stepped out, and after an initial glance to my left, my knees buckled when I turned to my right. In an instant, it was clear: Here, at the end of the hallway about ten feet away, standing with her arms folded comfortably one atop the other as she leaned against the doorway to her apartment, her head tilted just slightly to the side and at an angle that struck me as both vulnerable yet frighteningly confident all at once, was Sue-Ann waiting to greet me. Ten feet felt like a hundred as I began to approach, watching as her lips began curling upwards just before she cocked her eyes in that way, which by now I was under no illusions as to the mysterious, disarming effect she knew it possessed. Unlike my initial encounter with her ocular phenomenon, which of course, caused me to look at my feet in a way that was embarrassingly childish, on this occasion I didn't avert my gaze, and I was glad I didn't.

Dressed in black pants that clung perfectly to hips that I could still feel rocking gently in my hands, matched with a delicate white blouse buttoned only where it needed to be, she wore her hair pulled back in a way that exposed features in her face that I could swear I was being introduced to for the first time. With all that had transpired in the short time since we were last together, coupled with the *narishkeit* rushing through my head about not wanting to mess things up at her dinner, I don't know why the thought only hit me as I neared her doorstep that, on top of everything, I was falling for someone in a way I never felt before. And that, in and of itself, is a hurricane most of us are ill-equipped to handle.

"Hey, you," she whispered to me breathlessly when I eventually arrived at where she was standing and presented her with a bouquet of flowers, which I had been holding in my now trembling hands. After taking a moment to enjoy their aroma, she stared at me briefly, looking at me as if the time between our last encounter and now was far too long an interlude, but she wanted to be certain she wasn't the only one feeling that way. She must have seen something in my reaction, because rather than thank me for the *farkakte* flowers, Sue-Ann said nothing. Instead, she began caressing my cheek with the palm of her hand, which was soon wet with my tears that cascaded over her lithe fingers. She then touched them with her lips to gather the moisture before bringing them to mine. "It's okay," she whispered to me, and I was suddenly overcome with emotions that I hadn't allowed to rise to the surface in the days since Luba's passing and would no longer be held back. "I'm here," she added softly while pulling me in close to her as I sobbed uncontrollably and bringing my hand to her chest so that I could feel the calming rhythm of her heart. After we stood together at the threshold of her apartment for what felt like an eternity, my heaving eventually subsided, and she gently released me from her embrace. When she then looked at me in the way people often do to see if I was done, so to speak, we instinctively took to that strange but naturally human emotion that immediately follows an awkward, tear-filled moment such as this one. Both of us began laughing. "Can I introduce you to my friends now?" she said charmingly, and when I nodded my "yup," she kissed me, took me by the hand, and led me into her apartment.

I know nothing from architecture and interior design, so to try and describe for you how a once industrial space had been retrofitted into a place to sleep, eat, and do your business, would be an exercise in futility. And it's beside the point. Suffice it to say that the first thing that came to mind as I took in my surroundings when we entered Sue-Ann's loft was that I needed to get in on whatever desalination racket she was engaged in with the tribes *ergetz dortn*[108] in sub-saharan Africa. It's true, a maven I'm not. Still, I know enough to calculate that the king-sized bed with a gigantic frame that I spotted up a small flight of stairs and the non-ersatz, granite kitchen countertops in what was, *keynhore*,[109] a kitchen, didn't match up with the salary of an NGO worker. Now, if maybe you *funded* the NGO, a totally different story. Yes, I wondered about this as we made our way towards the back of her high-ceilinged, open-concept living space where a half dozen of her guests were already seated around a table that could fit ten comfortably, and behind which was a floor-to-ceiling window that offered up such a view of the city, you could *khalesh*.[110] After introducing me briefly to her friends, some of whom looked familiar from the millennial hipster bar whose sexual name I'm forgetting at the moment, Sue-Ann motioned me to the chair directly opposite hers, then took her glass of wine in hand and officially kicked off the evening's festivities with a toast to the young lady sitting beside her, in whose honor we had gathered. It was her best friend Amber, who was recently engaged and apparently flying solo on this occasion as the fiancé, a musician, was the first to send regrets, because he was in the studio with his band cutting their first record. Believe it or not, the proposal came via text on a cigarette break in between takes, the proof of which Amber delighted in passing around the table for everyone's viewing pleasure. Strangely, no one but me was the least bit phased by the casual absurdity of a one-line message full of emojis asking if she was "into it," which left me wondering if maybe he wasn't the band's lyricist.

I didn't bother asking. Soon enough, after Sue-Ann finished her toast and took her seat, she invited everyone at the table to offer their own good wishes to Amber and her absent ramblin' man. For some reason, she skipped over the woman sitting to the right of Amber, who everyone seemed to be in on the fact that she wasn't in any shape to say anything. She then quickly moved over to the other side of the table where, sitting to my far left, was an exuberant, fantastically inarticulate twenty-something-year-old fellow who, despite not having said much of anything in his brief remarks, seemed to have made a big impact; mostly

108. Someplace, somewhere.
109. Literally, "no evil eye." Practically, knock on wood.
110. Faint.

on me, truth be told, as I marveled at his capacity to use the word 'lovely' as a noun, verb, and adjective all in one sentence. After him, the two smartly dressed men to my immediate left said nothing in the way of good wishes but had everyone at the table in a tizzy over the ideas they already had for the big day. Then, apparently, it was my turn.

"Izzy," Sue-Ann said as all eyes turned to me. "Would you like to say something?"

In fact, I did, but I knew that if I shared it, I'd be shown the door.

Moreover, judging by how she both phrased the question and looked at me earnestly, it didn't sound like saying nothing was an option either.

"Uh...sure," I replied, stalling for some time to devise something that wouldn't offend. As I did, it felt to my ears at least like the table got quieter in anticipation of what would come out of my mouth. While my thoughts began to coalesce, I wondered whether the silence I was probably making more of than I should have been was the result of whatever Sue-Ann might have shared with the assembled about us before my arrival. I started to worry that they were standing by for what I was about to share to judge whether I was worthy of her. Although she was smiling in my direction, I didn't take the way Sue-Ann looked at me as anything resembling assurance that there was no pressure. There was, if only because I was putting it on myself to rise to the occasion and to just say something fucking normal, a string of innocuousness that wouldn't cause anyone to recoil in horror and then look to Sue-Ann, aghast at the choice she made to be with that wacko sitting across the table from her.

"It's okay, you don't have to if you don't want to," Amber chimed in and offered up a way out, when I suppose it was silent for too long.

"No, no. I'm good," I answered apologetically. "I've got something," I added, and noticed that I suddenly shifted forward to the edge of my seat, and my hands likewise unwittingly began rubbing my thighs. "I think," I whispered to myself before gesturing the following in Hebrew:

> May the Lord bless and protect you.
> May the Lord's face shine upon
> you and be gracious unto you.
> May the Lord lift his face unto you and grant you peace.

Don't ask how or why it occurred to me in that moment to recite the oldest Biblical passage to have ever been discovered: The priestly blessing from the Book of Numbers. I thought it appropriate, and considering I'm a *kohen* I figured that if it's in my arsenal, it was worth a shot. Yes, I'm aware: No *minyan*, so not kosher *k'halakhah*,[111] but for all you believers out there...fuck off.Anyway, judging by the blank stares around the table after I'd finished, I should have realized that sourcing something Biblical would have most likely gone over their heads, which it did. In addition, considering my hands were still busily attempting to rub holes through the fabric in the pants my mother had just pressed, I realized I wasn't done. So I followed up with an interpretation of the blessing that has come down to us through the ages by men much wiser than me on such matters. "May you be blessed with lots of good stuff," I explained to Amber plainly, "but be protected from it swelling your head." I then continued that she should feel the presence of something bigger than herself resonating within, so that it may serve to inspire good in others. I concluded by telling her that no matter what road she travels, no matter who she may come into contact with, she should be blessed with the good fortune of knowing inner peace, that who she is and what she brings to the world, is a gift.

Remember back in the day, when the disgruntled, alcoholic clown at the birthday party of one of the kids in kindergarten class pulled off a two-bit trick that our impressionable four-year-old brains couldn't yet fathom and everyone's collective face took on the expression of something akin to "what the huh?!" I was taken back to that place when I was done with my Rashi and nobody said anything, but stared at me instead, mouths agape like the fucking clown on this occasion was *me*. Well, actually that's not true. Amber was making with her hands like it suddenly got really hot in the room, while simultaneously revealing herself to be one of those *farkakte* "umm-like-you-knowers," as she tried desperately to string together a thought resembling what I assumed was a thank you.

"I know, right?!" Sue-Ann suddenly exclaimed jubilantly, like she was clearly aware of what everyone was thinking and was over the moon that I'd delivered on expectations. She then jumped from her chair and came over to my side of the table, where she plopped herself down in

---

111. According to Jewish law.

178

my lap and planted a deep, long, wet one on my lips before adding, for everyone's edification, "and he has the most amazing tongue, too!" She then hopped right back up and invited everyone to dig into the appetizers that were already placed around the table and before turning to head into the kitchen, she brought her lips to my ear, which she touched gently with her soft, moist tongue and whispered breathlessly to me, "you're a rock star." She pecked me playfully one more time before making her way to the kitchen.

The mood quickly lightened once the formalities had been dispensed with, and I had seemingly passed the first of what I anticipated would be several more trials before the night was through. Throughout the next little while, as a variety of tapas-sized appetizers made their way around the table, accompanied by the uncorking of bottles of both red and white—yes, organic; no, I stayed dry—I started to get a better picture of Sue-Ann's colorful circle of friends. When it finally hit me that the woman sitting to Amber's right was the bartender on the night I first met Sue-Ann at the Laughing Labia, she responded to my reintroducing myself with nothing but a blank stare to somewhere way beyond me, which I couldn't decipher as anything other than just plain weird.

"Oh, don't mind Jess, she's still tripping," the exuberant fellow to my far left blurted out indiscreetly and seemingly on everyone's behalf, as they all nodded in agreement and didn't seem the least bit concerned that she appeared on the verge of falling face first into the bowl of gazpacho on the table in front of her. In light of her incapacity, I took for granted that she'd given power of attorney to her friends to share with the complete stranger in their midst because they were perfectly comfortable describing for me that Jess, despite the fact that there wasn't a substance with which she was unfamiliar if not struggling with an addiction to, every so often made a valiant attempt to try whatever mechanism was available in the service of giving the world of sobriety a try.

To that end, I soon learned, she'd just returned from a Mexican peyote and Ayahuasca retreat, whose stated purpose was purification. Yet she'd neglected to read the shaman's fine print in the online advert, which said, in effect, that if you show up high, uncleansed, and full of toxins, you're gonna leave in a state of all kinds of messed up. Which she apparently was. I didn't know whether to feel sorry for her or burst out laughing as Amber caressed Jess's hair gently, while dutifully wiping away the drool that periodically dribbled from her mouth when she attempted to speak, but the sounds that emanated were nothing but gibberish; or maybe they were some kind of voodoo chant those familiar with such things would understand. Honestly, I couldn't say.

Turns out the exuberant fellow at the far end of the table had an interesting story of his own, which I'm only sharing because I couldn't believe it when I heard it. Max was his name, a lifelong friend of both Sue-Ann and Amber who shined, I was told, not only because of his near-constant state of good cheer, but also his preternatural capacity to be open to anything and all; or what the more seasoned among us who've travelled the road of life would euphemistically characterize as highly impressionable. More to the point, as my chain-smoking, non-nonsense doc from Bedford-Sty might put it: A fucking idiot. I offer up as illustration the latest stop in his life's journey to find his purpose, a place he delighted in describing as an organic farming collective near the town of New Putz, which is apparently *nisht vayt*[112] from Poughkeepsie. I swear that's what I heard, but I could be wrong. You can look it up.

Regardless, the place isn't the story. In fact, what they grow there is also *nisht vikhtik.* Although, to tell it fairly, it's supposedly a real farm, with happy chickens and various other sundry *freylekh beheymes*[113] churning out overpriced, chemical-free sustenance for those who are mindful of and willing to pay for such *narishkeit.* Not a big place, you should know, the farm that is, with maybe two dozen denizens working the land. Among these, apparently, Max was the only one with a penis. My curiosity piqued; I asked him if he found that kinda strange.

"Oh no, we're all searching," he said with no hint of irony in his voice.

"For what?" I prodded a little further, though I knew where this was headed. Admittedly, his response lacked coherence, so I'll spare you except to say he circled around the theme of "identity," which was, as you might have guessed...very lovely.

"It's so non-judgmental," he added apropos of nothing that I had asked specifically.

"Tell me, Max," I began to ask him leadingly, "what do you guys do in your free time?"

---

112. A hop, skip and a jump.
113. Contented animals.

He didn't reply, and nobody at the table answered on his behalf because either they had no idea what I was getting at or they were too embarrassed for him to get into it, particularly with the stranger at the table. Suffice to say that this *farsholtene*[114] farm was nothing of the sort, but rather an LBGTQ sex commune and the joke was on him because despite his fellow farmers' adamant profession of non-adherence to any predefined gender or sexual orientation, none were the least bit androphilic, but rather perfectly content to reside in their gynephilia, munching each other's rugs while he wasn't getting any at all. Well, except maybe from the sheep, but who knows? I didn't delve further.

Now, in contrast to Max, the gay couple to my immediate left seemed on slightly more solid footing: He, on the one hand, the money in the marriage, apparently from daddy's wildly successful business building communal work spaces he let them play with, and then, sitting right next to me, the other he, who I learned took care of the nuts and bolts of it all. And really, it just goes to show you how you never know how these things come together because if I told you that the gent to my immediate left—tall, blonde, a Sven when he could also have been a Dieter—was the neurotic, disheveled one and the other—about half a foot shorter, Saville row bespoke suit freshly-pressed, with a head of hair Bruno Marslike—was the suave, GQ'd of the two, you'd never believe me. We made fast friends me and them, as the blonde and I bonded over the fact that we were both C-sectioned at birth, which I said explained our common neurosis, as it's now well established that because we didn't flow out of our mothers' vaginal canals, we were bereft of the commensal bacteria that helps in brain development. Shit, sorry. I was totally off, his name was a very pedestrian Sean, and he was blown away by what he perceived to be my *teef kentenish*[115] from all things birth-related. As for the Bruno Mars doppelgänger, real name Josiah, he was likewise blown away when I shared with him and the assembled, all apparently ignorant of such celebrity *narishkeit*, that in fact, the diminutive, famous funkster was half-Jewish.

"It's true," I replied when they all said they didn't believe me, and I went on to recount for them: "There was a little-known Hasidic court in the Polish town not far from Modzhitz that gave the *Modzhitzer Rebbe*

---

114. Accursed.
115. Profound understanding.

fits. As the story is told, he nearly died of exhaustion from having to keep coming up with newer *niggunim* to keep his flock happy because he was losing members to the *rebbe* from this other town, from which his Hasidim would return occasionally on a *moytze shabbes*,[116] snapping their fingers and tapping their feet to the funkier *niggunim* of that other town's *rebbe*. That's why *ad hayom*[117] the *Modzitzer* have such awesome melodies. But in the annals of Hasidic apocrypha, it's known that they were really second-rate to the funk that emanated from the little town of Marstchych."

"He's kidding," Sue-Ann yelled playfully from the kitchen when I was done with my story and somehow knew, without even turning to look back, that there was a collective confusion at the table in response to my Hasidic BS. "He's a great writer," she added for good measure, which she knew would serve as an *araynfir*[118] for her guests to begin prodding me with questions of their own when she returned to the table with some mains that honestly smelled delicious.

Between you and me, as much as I had obsessed about the evening, especially in the context of Luba's passing and what she had shared cryptically about Sue-Ann in the seconds before she died, the god's honest truth is that I didn't give a moment's consideration to the fact that if I did attend, I would quite likely be put in a position of having to present myself. And when it was my turn to do just that, I immediately regretted my decision to attend. Yes, I'm aware of the hyperbole; thank you very much. However, as I observed the people at the table—all displaying a remarkable lack of even the most basic forms of verbal expression, and none exhibiting a hint of self-consciousness about it—what I saw and felt was an empirical engagement with life and the world that, if nothing else, starkly reflected my own incapacity to do so. Fulfilled by inanities, while seemingly bereft of a sense of self and centeredness, they were of a kind with which I wasn't familiar. Mostly though, they were happy, and as I contemplated having to describe myself and the fact that I wasn't, it fucking pissed me off.

"Oh my god, that's so Jewishy!" was the next thing I heard as Amber exclaimed excitedly in response to what I assumed was Sue-Ann's synopsis of me when I must have been stuck inside for too long. "We

---

116. End of the Sabbath.
117. To this day.
118. Intro.

have such good stories, right?" she then added and admittedly, in addition to trying to keep my *mishegas* at bay, I now found myself instantly flummoxed with trying to not only take in the idiocy of the former statement Amber uttered, but most definitely stuck on deciphering what on earth she was getting at with the latter.

"I'm sorry, you lost me on *we*," I eventually replied. "Are you Jewish?" I then asked genuinely, as I never would have suspected. Yet no reply was forthcoming, at least not at first because Sue-Ann chimed in.

"Amber's studying anthropology," she said on behalf of her friend like she wasn't in the room and apropos of I'm not quite sure what, but the ventriloquy struck me as more than awkward. Then again, maybe Sue-Ann had gotten to know me well enough to this point and likely recognized that I had already pegged her friend as a complete dolt, and her preemption on the lightweight's behalf was right in the nick of time.

"It's okay, I don't mind sharing," Amber said, which immediately caused me to worry, as her statement in her defense dovetailed perfectly with what I had been thinking, which I assumed hadn't been shared aloud. However, rather than confirm that my filter had collapsed yet again, which of course had been its wont of late, I bit my tongue instead. "I'm doing my Master's in Jewish food," she added.

I don't recall responding immediately because, like I just said, I was busy chewing. That said, my first response probably was to bite a little harder while simultaneously thinking something akin to, "yeah, great, sure...so that's what passes for higher learning these days, huh?" At any rate, I was still stuck on a previous question I had posed that had gone unanswered.

"Good for you," I said genuinely, I think, "but can we go back to the 'Jewishy' thing for a sec," I then added, which I can confirm had more than a slight hint of sarcasm attached. "I was kind of hoping you might expand on that a little," I continued before looking to her for a response. I'll spare you her drivel. Suffice it to say that my heart skipped a few beats when she began to expound upon the topic of her Jewish identity in that inimitable way common to the "umm-like-you know" set, which seems to prejudice their case *prima facie* due to what I'd describe as a congenital affliction of inarticulation that by its nature belittles whatever argument they're making, thereby compounding how silly it comes across. To wit: When she proceeded to tell me, without a hint of self-consciousness, that despite having never converted, she nevertheless considered herself Jewish because she "kinda liked how it felt," and wasn't into the whole religion thing besides because it was like "so, umm, like you know...serious," she had me on the edge of my seat with my teeth clenched. You'll believe me when I tell you that when she concluded by proudly offering up her thesis statement that it really wasn't important because in the end, "we'll always have our food," *s'iz mir nisht git gevorn.*[119]

Now, before you jump down my throat: I'm fully aware that there's a valid and significant historical basis for the claim that folkways, culture and art could serve the same anthropological purpose as religion when it came to keeping the Jewish people *geknipt un gebindn.*[120] It's what An-sky, Dubnow, Peretz, and others of their ilk argued post-Kishinev and 1905, when the revolution didn't go quite as planned. It was time to look elsewhere to plant the flag heralding the salvation of the Jewish people because religion alone wasn't gonna cut it anymore in a world moving fast into a modern era that didn't take kindly to it.

I believe somewhere till here I've given my *shpiel* on An-sky and *The Dybbuk,* so you know I get it. Yes, according to these gods of Jewish secularism, you'll pardon the wordplay, creativity in all its forms was as "Jewishy" as those who held fast to Torah and *mitzves* and even those folksy Hasidim with their *shtreimlekh*[121] and *zokn.*[122] Forgive me, maybe I'm simply blinded by the fact that they spent a lifetime agonizing over the Jewish future, dedicating their careers in search of a solution and their articulation of the same point Amber was making was thus more artful, if not slightly more intelligent than the fucking banality of "we'll always have our food." But I could be wrong.

In any event, although I don't recall having offered up a reply to Amber of any kind whatsoever, her sexually deprived farmer friend Max decided he couldn't help himself and now added her to the list of those around the table he felt obliged to defend. "Why is her truth any less valid than yours?" he asked me in a tone that sounded as aggressive as you might have imagined. All eyes, including the ones that mattered most, turned to me for a rebuttal, which wasn't initially forthcoming as there was a shit ton of unpacking to do with that absurd post-modern

---

119. Nearly lost my shit.
120. Knotted and bound.
121. Furry hats and...
122. Socks.

shibboleth that is unfortunately alive, well, and thriving by the millennials. I'm not sure why, but at that moment, which seemed fraught with peril at what would be my eventual response, I thought of my *zaide*. It's true. That's where my mind went. I wondered how he'd want me to act on my instinct to call BS on their "I'm all right, you're all right," relativist, meta *narishkeit*, which from my vantage point seemed to be leading them nowhere but down the road to perdition.

Although my *zaide* was tough on the idea that you broke the rules only when you had a good understanding of why they were there in the first place, his heart overflowed with compassion matched only by an even greater abundance of patience. Admittedly, despite his painstaking efforts over the years to instill in me, at the very least, a passing familiarity with both admirable qualities, the fact is I failed him. "*Hob geduld*, Itzikl." I could hear his loving if firm admonishment ringing in my ear to marshal at least a modicum of patience and compassion.

At the same time, I sat there struggling with a response to the absurdity of "truth" as a relative concept that no one at the table seemed to have a problem with. Neither was forthcoming. I felt pity as I observed the company around the table. These people rightfully had nowhere to place themselves in a world where they could find no center because they were fighting so hard for everybody to have their own "truth." They're "searching for identity," Max said earlier, or Sue-Ann similarly on a previous occasion, calling it "belonging." Semantic *narishkeit*. It's no wonder they're all wracked with anxiety because in their search for such nebulae, so long as they refuse to believe in, let alone acknowledge, that some things are shared or common, all they're doing is chasing their tails. Yes, that came from me; I'm fully aware of the pot and the kettle. I dunno, when even knowledge and truth fall under some "Foucaultist" suspicion as having been dictated by authority and are therefore suspect, if you ask me, they're just royally fucked.

"I suppose you're right," I eventually began responding to Max before I tossed the ball back into his and the rest of the gang's court: "But you'll forgive me for thinking that this 'truth' business you're apparently so passionate about strikes me as very much the definition of the Precession of Simulacra, which seems to me kinda problematic, wouldn't you agree?"

So...uh...that clown reference earlier? Yeah, it happened again.

"Really, Baudrillard?" As I asked in disbelief, I looked at Amber, the so-called academic, whose countenance was filled with confusion that seemed on par with my question, which made me wonder how she got into an institution of higher learning, let alone a program that would officially award her letters after her name when she completed what I guessed was going to be... a cookbook?

"Izzy, tell me something..." Sue-Ann began to speak, and when I turned to look at her, I knew it was all problems. "Are you religious?" she asked, finishing her thought before leaning back ever so slightly in her chair, crossing her legs and folding her arms across her chest while looking at me menacingly. Having spent enough time around Faygen, I recognized a leading question when I heard one. She knew full well what my answer would be and at the moment, I couldn't think of anything to counter other than to answer truthfully because, judging by what I was staring at across the table from me, it seemed I was on thin ice.

"No," I said quietly, and began girding myself for what I knew was coming next.

"So, then you're just a hypocrite," she said aggressively, like it wasn't on her behalf alone that she was knocking me down a rung or two but that of her guests as well. Combined with a stare that was just pure venom, I knew better than to try and respond in kind, and it didn't help that the words I believe she then mouthed for my benefit alone were, "don't be such an asshole." Although Luba's dying words about Sue-Ann not being who I thought she was began to rush to the fore, I swear to you I did my best to keep them at bay and that what I did next was a genuine attempt to steer the conversation back to calmer waters. But I couldn't have anticipated what transpired next.

"So, what Jewish foods are you studying specifically?" I asked Amber in a soft and gentle tone of voice that conveyed a genuine interest in learning more about her chosen field of study.

"Really from everywhere, but my focus is going to be on the culinary expressions of Jews from Arab lands," she began to respond. Truth be told, I was kind of interested...until she said: "Palestine specifically."

"I'm sorry, you lost me," I responded. "You mean Israel?"

"No, no, not the Zionist entity," she said matter-of-factly and in such a way that it honestly felt like she hadn't a clue what she had just uttered. "Palestine!" she recapitulated enthusiastically. She then began to expound excitedly upon her course of study, propagated by an erstwhile wealthy Upper East Side Jew, who apparently came under the spell of the lefties when her father's boiler room got busted by the SEC, leaving her to a life of penury, bitter, angry and in search of a new identity. Apparently, she found it across Central Park while jerking off with Said's acolytes. She was now drilling into Amber's head the "laws of intersectionality," which, in this case, specifically placed the white, privileged, colonialist Jews squarely at the root of all humanity's problems. As she went on waxing orgasmic about the professor, with the cutest little lap dog named Derrida—I swear, not a word of a lie and I don't even fucking know why I'm even bothering with describing this to you—she was oblivious to the fact that not only had she already lost me, but her best friend and I were staring at one another and without uttering a word in either direction we both knew the die had been cast, we were on opposing sides and the question was how it was going to shake itself out once the yapping subsided.

So, that bit earlier about An-sky and the others, where I kinda wavered on the whole folklore thing and that maybe I was wrong? Yeah, fuck that. Not for a second do I think they considered that their ideas would be used as a Trojan Horse to destroy the Jewish people from within, which is all I heard ringing in my ears as Amber spoke. I don't think I said as much, but my expression must have signaled it because Sue-Ann then let me have it again.

"Are you a Zionist?" she asked me pointedly when Amber finished, and it seemed no one at the table understood why she would have asked me that question. But she knew what she was doing, and for the life of me, I didn't know why she felt the need to back me into a corner where it was unlikely that I was going to come up with the correct answer to her question. I could have gotten into it with her and insisted that before I enter into any kind of debate on such a volatile subject, we'd need to establish context, terms of reference, definition of terms, historical timelines, etc. But what good would it have done me? She had the room, and of all the people at the table, *she* wasn't the one I wanted to fight with. In fact, I didn't want to be fighting at all.

"No," I answered, and looked to her pleadingly not to choose sides by saying what she was going to at my expense.

"So again, you're just a hypocrite," she said, and my heart sank instantly when I didn't detect an ounce of reluctance in her tone.

Just as quickly, my mind returned to Luba's bedside, where I could hear myself screaming for her to tell me what she meant about Sue-Ann. It was all I could do not to shout out to her then and there and plead for her to tell me the truth about what she knew but couldn't explain before she passed away. I kept my own counsel, but I also knew that what I had promised my mother earlier, telling her that I could get through this, was being put to the test. I knew it because just like the signs have always been there whenever I took steps beyond where I should have, one appeared again. In this case, as I looked across the table, I didn't see Sue-Ann anymore. What I saw was Her, pointing at me, saying the things about my flaws and weaknesses that she never in fact ever said but that I put in her mouth for her to say because that's what we do, we who suffer with the illness. And her piercing cackle was deafening.

"You know, I might very well be," I eventually managed to respond to Sue-Ann, "but at least I don't go around pronouncing on things I know nothing about." I didn't hold back as I now turned to everyone at the table and let them have it too: "You people can't have it both ways and argue out of both sides of your mouth. Either you believe in your relativist, virtue signaling, post-modernist bullshit, where there is no truth other than what you feel, or there is in fact truth and you're just choosing to ignore it because your coddled fucking minds can't handle it." I then looked to Sue-Ann and gave it right back to her: "So who's the hypocrite now, huh?"

As you might imagine, we stared at each other for a long while and the words that weren't said between us spoke volumes.

"Your micro-aggression is making me very uncomfortable," Amber said.

"Actually, it's very macro," I responded coldly.

"Why are you attacking her!" Max chimed in from the far corner of the table to defend his friend again. "You don't even know her!"

"Based on everything I'm hearing," I replied, "that's probably for the best."

And that's when Sue-Ann finally spoke again, for the last time.

"I'd like you to leave," she said quietly but firmly as can be and with a stare so cold that as I got up from the table, I knew full well that something beautiful, if however short-lived, had just shattered into pieces.

When I stood on the dais at Mendelman's funeral home a few days later, looking out at a sea of people paying their last respects to Luba, the only face I could see was the one in the first row with that cold stare, which had haunted me ever since Sue-Ann dismissed me unceremoniously at dinner. In the intervening period, despite my countless attempts to reach out and make peace, my efforts were for naught as she simply wouldn't engage. Rest wouldn't come and sleep never set in as I watched the sun rise and set over multiple days while cloistered in my apartment, a prisoner to my mind's incessant ruminating over the circumstances that had led to the debacle and to the interminable self-flagellation over what I should, could, would have said or done differently. Of course, as these things typically go, I eventually crashed from the sheer mental and emotional toll that the entire mess of my own making had taken, so that by the time Faygen had arrived with my mother to take me to Mendelman's on the morning of Luba's funeral, they literally had to peel me off the floor of my apartment.

Despite their attendant poking and prodding all along the car ride, I had enough strength to withstand and shared nothing about what had transpired. Instead, I chose to expend what little energy I did have ripping into Faygen, who upon seeing how large the turnout was for the funeral based on the traffic jam in the parking lot, decided at the last minute to once again plead with me to take his place at the lectern to speak about Luba. This, even though she had apparently left specific written instructions that *he* must give the eulogy.

It was indeed a large crowd that morning at Mendelman's, where the sign in the lobby's entrance indicated that Luba's funeral was taking place in the main room, the Judah. The entire cast of the play was there, to be sure. As we gathered in what was already a crowded lobby, however, it felt like hundreds more were arriving, people whose lives were touched in one way or another by the one-of-a-kind force of nature who everyone knew simply as Luba. Although I spotted Sue-Ann a dozen or so heads in front of me as we waited to enter, when she turned back and our eyes caught one another, she was stoic and looked right past me like I wasn't even there. You can believe that between the fatigue and the frustration I now had percolating in me apropos of Faygen, what I internalized as her dismissal of my presence didn't help much in settling my nerves as we began to make our way into the grand sanctuary. Of course, it helped not a bit that as people started taking their seats among the red velvet cushioned pews, I found myself sitting squarely in the middle of the front row with only Sam and Faygen between us to my left and my mother to my right. Meanwhile, it felt like a massive hole of ignominy was about to be drilled into the back of my head as a combination of her friends and Luba's admirers from the Vulgar Vulva happened to seat themselves conveniently in the row directly behind us.

Given the morbid circumstances, no one paid any attention to the fact that we didn't say a word to each other in that awkward time before things get serious, when people typically greet one another with variations on the wholly appropriate, "better occasions," along with absurdities like "you're looking fabulous," together in the same breath. If however, you say nothing, like me on this occasion, nobody's a critic.

Soon enough, after the doors to the side of the dais opened and someone official-looking appeared asking for silence, everyone stood when Luba's small, simple wooden casket was wheeled into the hall and placed at the foot of the dais, not three feet away from where we sat. Walking a few steps behind the casket were two bearded men in black suits and matching leather *kippas*—one tall and slim, the other short and slovenly—both of whom climbed the dais and seated themselves on either side of the lectern. Although neither looked familiar, as soon as the one with his shirt tucked in approached the lectern and dove maudlin into *tehillim*,[123] I pegged him as the rabbi. I assumed that the disheveled one playing with the toothpick in his mouth was the *chazen*,[124] waiting his turn. For the life of me, I couldn't understand why either of them was there, as I couldn't imagine it's what Luba, staunchly secular, would have wanted. Regardless, when the rabbi's high-pitched, nasal voice began reverberating over the sound system throughout the grand hall—and it was, replete with Chagall images on stained glass windows on every side and a chandelier the size of Texas hanging from the massively high ceiling—my mother made nothing of the fact that I started to shift nervously in my seat and my legs started shaking. It wasn't an unusual reaction on my part whenever clergy spoke, and to that end, she simply took my hand in hers and probably assumed that I'd be fine once he shut his trap. That she had no clue what else was on my mind, which was more at the heart of the matter, was beside the point.

---

123. Psalms.
124. Cantor.

She likewise probably assumed that there's something about caskets being wheeled into the room that triggers things primordial in us that are nothing to worry about, as it's perfectly fine to be mildly freaked out in the presence of the dead; to say nothing of the fact that it was barely days since the last time I was this close to Luba and I kinda didn't handle it all that serenely, to say the least. I don't think she expected, however, that I would squeeze as tightly as I did when the rabbi segued from the valley of death into *pirkey oves*[125] and began reciting *eyshes khayil*,[126] which I absolutely know for a fact Luba would have responded to by throwing a mug at his head and telling him, rightfully, to get off the stage for deigning to recite that piece of misogyny in her "honour." If you don't believe me, take as proof that Faygen couldn't control himself and pulled a roll of floss from his pocket because he also knew *s'hot nisht gepast.*[127] At some point around the third verse of the many, which I guess on paper you can say the poetry is pretty, I let go of my mother's grasp and hunched forward, allowing my head to rest in the palms of my hands as I waited impatiently for the misfortune to end.

It did, although it was then followed by some ill-timed, hollow drivel about Luba and her life that probably checked off all the boxes that I imagine are on the clergy's to-do list at funerals but were totally off the mark. I suppose the rabbi felt obliged, given that it was a paid gig and all. Yet it seemed to me that the absence of any next of kin to keep him in check didn't, by its nature, give him license to get a little too comfortable improvising a life's story about someone he didn't know. I dunno. Maybe it was just me, but among the series of perfunctory hosannas he threw Luba's way, I could have sworn that he never got the crux of the matter that she fucking saved Yiddish theatre from the dustbin of history. I kind of told him as much when, after he was done and Faygen looked to me and nodded that it was my turn, I stood, took a moment by Luba's side in order to gather myself and then, after walking on to the dais and approaching the lectern, I turned to the clergyman and said: "You know, you would have been better off just sticking with *tehillim* and keeping your mouth shut."

As a collective gasp went up among the sea of people, I leaned against the lectern. I said nothing for a while to gather myself and let the

125. Ethics of Our Fathers.
126. Proverbs 31:10-31
127. It was inappropriate.

myriad murmuring critiques of me subside so that I could hear myself think clearly enough to begin saying something coherent about Luba. Unfortunately, whether it was fatigue; my anger boiling in response to the paid hypocrites seated behind me on the dais; or the fact that as I looked out at the assembled, I could only see one face looking up at me, which was the one I truly wished wasn't shooting venom at me; the words didn't come.

At least not the words Faygen likely imagined I'd speak to eulogize Luba. Frankly, I knew full well that I was at my wit's end, and it was hopeless to think that I had my shit together to stick to protocol. So rather than address the mass of humanity in front of me, I looked up at the ceiling instead and let Him have it:

"Good morning to You, Lord, Master of the universe," I began, which elicited another collective gasp that went up around the room and even though I'd barely uttered a few words, I could already hear the worried tone in my mother's voice when she whispered Faygen's name, followed immediately by Sue-Ann's similarly-toned question to him as to what I was up to.

"He's doing Levi Yitzhok," I could hear him say to them reassuringly, referencing the Hasidic *rebbe* of Berdichev, renowned in his day as the great interceder on behalf of the Jewish people before God and who for some reason in that moment *iz by mir in kop arayngefaln.*[128]

"He's fine..." he added but didn't lower his voice much when he finished his thought, "I think."

"Good morning to you, Lord, Master of the universe," I repeated, and suddenly the room fell silent as I continued, quietly at first:

I, *yitzhok elioho ben chane bas mordekhe-hirsh hakohen,*
come to you with a din Torah from one, simple soul among your people
Israel.
What do you want of this tortured soul?
What are you demanding of this tortured soul?
For every step along the road you have set for me I hear you say,
"speak to the children of Israel."
And in every deep valley into which you take me, you say,
"go, tell them the story of my people, Israel."

---

128. Came to mind.

And over and over, "they must know, they must know."

"But father, sweet father in heaven," I continued, and with each word I uttered into the microphone, it felt like the walls were starting to shake as my voice reverberated throughout the hall:

How can they know?
When you have destroyed the world whose story you've asked me to tell
and have now taken into your heavenly kingdom
yet another witness to the splendor of its holiness.
The *amoratzim*,[129] what do they say?
That it matters not, for whatever they feel it to have been will be
sufficient.
The heretics, what do they say?
That the thousand-year-old Yiddish treasure you burned to ashes in
Auschwitz, Treblinka, and Majdanek should stay buried there.
And the Amalekites, what do they say?
That what remains of the story should be destroyed forever.
Still, I *yitzhok elioho ben chane bas mordekhe-hirsh hakohen* say
yisgadal v'yiskadash shmey raboh
Magnified and sanctified is Thy Name!

"And I, *yitzhok elioho ben chane bas mordekhe-hirsh hakohen*, say," I went on, the thoughts now coming to me extemporaneously amidst tidal waves of emotion, that I was completely unaware of my fists raining down on the lectern with such ferocity that it started teetering to the point of breaking into pieces as I gave it to Him one final time:

From my journey, I will not waver...
From my place, I will not move...
For so long as a single spark of strength remains within me...
I will continue the struggle until there be an end to this madness!
The story will be told!
Over and over again, it will be told.
So that the golden chain will be strengthened,
from this generation to the next one and then to the next.
yisgadal v'yiskadash shmey raboh

---

129. Ignoramuses.

Magnified and sanctified is Thy Name!

I recognize that it wasn't a eulogy, and it was likely nothing that Faygen expected me to say, but it was all I had at the moment. I instantly regretted what I had done in such a public and somber forum. I would have apologized for it, but I was collapsing from fatigue and was leaning on the lectern to keep from falling to the ground.

When I felt the corpulent *chazen* rise from his chair behind me, however, I suddenly experienced another surge of adrenaline that caused me to turn and shout at him in full voice, "Sit down! I already spoke to Him!" before ripping the pocket of my shirt above my heart with my bare hands. Turning back to face the sea of humanity in front of me, it honestly felt like there wasn't another soul in the room but Luba. To that end, I walked mournfully from the dais to where she lay and placed my hand on her casket. "*Zol di erd dir zayn gring, Lubenyu*," I whispered to her in Yiddish as my eyes began to well up, wishing for her a speedy and peaceful transition to the better world to come. I then took my place at the front of the casket, and while looking straight down the center aisle that we were now going to lead her, my voice began to crack as I started to sing the *niggun* from *The Dybbuk*. Almost instantly, Sam, whose cheeks were streaked with tears, rose from where he was sitting in the front row, took his place on the other side of the casket from me, and joined in the singing. Faygen was next, rising and taking his place behind me, followed by Nokhem, who stood behind Sam. Then, one by one, members of the cast joined us until we were enough pallbearers to carry Luba toward the exit at the back, where the hearse awaited the journey to the cemetery.

As we began to walk Luba down the aisle, even though most in the room weren't familiar with it, the *niggun* swelled like it rightfully should have as everyone in the room fell in behind us and raised their voices in tribute to Luba.

When we reached the back of the room, Sam stopped abruptly and recoiled in horror while simultaneously letting go of the casket. "What is it?" I asked him after we instinctively grasped the casket's handles to avoid dropping it to the ground.

"That man," he whispered to me, and nodded in the direction of the back corner of the room, where a man in a sharp suit and a black fedora covering a head of silver hair was standing by himself.

"What about him?" I asked, and motioned for him to retake hold of the casket so that we could continue moving.

"He's a bad man."

"You know him?"

"No."

"So, why would you say that?" I asked, and we had now reached the opposite corner at the back of the room, where the professionals wearing dark glasses motioned for us to step aside so they could put the casket into the hearse idling by the doorway.

"He killed Luba," Sam said, shaking with fear.

"What on earth are you talking about?" I replied incredulously and looked back at the man whose face I didn't recognize from the hospital, assuming Sam was referring to the docs who attended at the end.

"He's the boss."

"Of what?!"

"The JCC," he replied.

"So?" I asked again, this time wondering in what other context I might be able to place the man as I didn't recall having bumped into him in the building during rehearsals, but I couldn't.

"He's destroying the Yiddish theatre," he said, still shuttering with fear.

When I turned back to where the man had been standing to get a really good look at the *soyne yisroel*,[130] he was gone. As I stood there pondering Sam's cryptic yet ominous statement, the bright blue sky above us darkened almost instantly. In the distance, I began to hear the sound that reverberated in my ears seconds later:

CHIRP!

---

130. Literally, "anti-Semite." Practically...douchebag.

11

No *shiva*[131] is not unheard of these days. People will do what they do. However if, according to the balls and strikes in the ways of Jewish death and mourning, there are relations who are tasked with sitting but don't, or even in the case where there are none to sit, I'd argue that not having a place to gather after you've buried someone near and dear is simply weird. For that reason, Faygen was right when, shortly after Luba had passed, he asked Joseph to reach out to the cast of the play and likewise all those in Luba's larger theatre family to inform them there would be an opportunity to gather at the theatre following the internment. If not to sit *shiva,* then to reminisce about the giant little woman everyone had just said goodbye to.

And I arrived late for reasons I don't know why...

It hadn't been a week since I was last in the theatre. Nevertheless, given what had transpired in the interim, it felt like the play had receded from my mind. It was a falsehood I quickly disabused myself of, because when I entered the JCC that afternoon, specifically when I reached the doors to the back of the theatre, I froze before entering. Although I had no idea what was transpiring in the theatre on the other side, my hesitation in turning the handle on the door had nothing to do with what Faygen had planned. Instead, I was suddenly overcome by a surging cascade of thoughts and emotions from the last time I saw Luba. Not the woman I witnessed expiring in front of me just days earlier; instead, it was of the vigorous, artistic force of nature, who was in full flight only hours prior, standing at the foot of the stage orchestrating a stunningly dramatic finale to the first act of *The Dybbuk,* the play that would serve as the rightful capstone to a remarkable career built against all odds.

As if the day we said goodbye to her couldn't have gotten any gloomier, standing there with my hand on the door to the theatre, hesitating to enter, the notion that her life's masterwork was destined to die along with her started to cut deep, and it just plain hurt.

...Maybe that's why.

The emotions surged when I eventually walked in, where, upon seeing the stage and the set of the play we had been rehearsing, it

---

131. Week-long mourning period.

honestly felt like Luba was about to enter from the wings and yell something unintelligible, amounting to a charge for everyone to get to work or she'd throw something. Alas. So I stood there inconspicuously for a while, at the top of the theatre, letting the thought pass and the emotions subside somewhat before joining the gathering in her honor taking place on the stage below.

Speaking of which, if the volume emanating from the throng of people gathered there was anything to go by, including occasional spikes of laughter, it seemed that in contrast to what I was feeling, the mood in the room was anything but somber. That's not to say that when I finally began making my way down the aisle towards the stage, it wasn't accompanied by what felt like a sudden deafening silence, which fell over the proceedings as everyone turned to look at me cockeyed as I approached. It may have well been a projection on my part. Still, given that it was the first glimpse they were getting of me since I unloaded on Him at the funeral that morning, which I just assumed they all thought was wacko, combined with the fact that I was a no-show by the graveside, which only Faygen could understand, I wouldn't have blamed them if my presence somehow rubbed them all the wrong way. In any case, I didn't help things much by arriving at what seemed to be the end of the gathering.

No one said anything, however, or paid me much mind when I stepped onto the stage and joined the immense crowd that packed every inch of it, which only served to remind me of the amount of bandwidth our self-conscious selves consume and utterly waste in the course of such things. Indeed, their collective focus was in the middle of the stage where Faygen, Sam, Sue-Ann, and dozens of others were seated among the tables and chairs, or sitting on the floor in "the synagogue," where at the moment, everyone was listening attentively to Nokhem as he reminisced about some of his more personal experiences with Luba. I don't recall what he said exactly, but people laughed more than they cried. Likewise, as he was followed by some of the other members who were around during the theatre's fledgling years, people whose faces I could recall from the meet-and-greet but whose names I just couldn't, the smiles outweighed the frowns and the tears. For as much as they spoke about their dramatic experiences with her on stage, which if you've read 'till here, you know was likely the truth, it was the impact she had on their lives off the stage that formed the common thread that wove its way through each of their recollections.

"It's amazing how she knew us," Sue-Ann was inspired to say in a tone that was gentle and full of appreciation, following one of the older guard's moments of memory. "Who we *really* are, I mean," she added, which elicited a collective nod in agreement that was remarkable to me, not only because I was already thinking about her comment in ways no one else in the room could have been, but also for the fact that the newest member of Luba's theatre family, one who barely knew her, could speak words about her that resonated truly and profoundly across the generations who were there on the stage; a fact that spoke volumes about the kind of impact the woman we all loved had on each and every one of us.

Although she didn't once turn her gaze in my direction, Sue-Ann was all I could focus on as I stood not ten feet away from where she was sitting on the floor next to Nokhem, wanting for all the world to be alone with her so that I could plead for her forgiveness, because whether I was right or not, I blamed myself for the fiasco. As it turned out, I was so focused on her that it took the person next to me, the woman with the walker from the meet-and-greet, who quickly brought my attention back to the proceedings when she shoved the metal apparatus smack into my hip, shortly after Nokhem raised the topic of the play and what was to be done now that Luba was gone. Although he posed the question to everyone and no one in particular, if the steel *zetz* she gave me when again she drilled her walker into my side was any indication, clearly she felt I was the one who should answer. I didn't, and kept myself from pushing back, although I strongly considered it because the fucking thing hurt.

"*Khevre*," I heard Nokhem repeat his question, now that she had me paying attention: "*Vos vet zayn?*"[132]

Despite the cacophony of whispering, murmuring, and general *yentifying* that now went up in the room, no one answered his question because there was no response to give. There was no rainy-day plan for what would happen if Luba died, not for the play or her theatre, because she was *sui generis*. As I stood there holding the woman next to me back while she was busily weaponizing her walker in my direction, I actually

---

132. *Que sera.*

did want to yell out to everyone in response to, "*vos vet zayn.*" That it was fucking over and the sooner we got on with it, the better. Well, leave it to the autistic fellow pacing back and forth at the back of the stage to blurt out the answer that I, for one, never would have thought of in a million years:

"Izzy direct! Izzy direct!" he shouted repeatedly in full voice, and kept at it until some saint with the requisite bedside manner approached him and whispered him down. But the damage was done because in an instant the mass on stage had turned towards me in unison and seemed to be anxiously awaiting a response from my part, including the handicapped woman to my left who finally relented and gazed at me longingly in anticipation of *ziyse verter*[133] that were hopefully forthcoming from my lips.

"Guys, he was kidding," I said self-consciously about the afflicted fellow who blurted out my name. "I mean, come on," I started to add, "he's...," and didn't.

"But your eulogy?" the supposedly fragile woman beside me said, with a mighty shove of metal into my hip for good measure.

"It wasn't a..." eulogy, I wanted to say. Still, I felt—rightly, I think—that now wasn't the appropriate moment to delve into a contextual analysis of whether what I blabbed that morning rose to the level, met the definition, or whether I was just selfishly bitching to Him about the failure of my book and perhaps my life.

Regardless, aside from keeping focused on the fact that Sue-Ann just wouldn't look my way, I also had my eye on Sam and Faygen, who were now busily whispering to each other as they sat side by side only a few feet from me and seemingly up to no good. "What are you doing?" I chided them, though it was mainly directed at Faygen because well, he's typically the crafty mastermind behind moments like this that make me nervous.

"Nothing," he began to answer, and then started smirking as he continued, "just reminiscing about the things you said about the play and about An-sky at the meet-and-greet."

"What about it?" I asked in what I immediately recognized was an embarrassingly petulant tone.

---

133. Sweet words.

"You seemed to really know your stuff," he replied in that fucking expert lawyerly way that he knew would have everyone in the room nodding their "uh-huh's," which caused his smile to grow wider. As sick as it was, I immediately thought as I looked at him that this moment we were having was pre-ordained, and that somehow he had a role in making it happen. But I dismissed it as quickly as it came because all the things that would have had to happen to arrive at this moment, including Luba's passing away, was too obscene to contemplate. That didn't stop me however, from taking my mind back into the hospital to Luba's bedside, where among the breadcrumbs she left me as she lay dying was some disjointed talk about my book, that I could still tell the story, and...the theatre.

Fuck. Me.

"It's okay, Khaveh, he's fine," Faygen called out to the woman with the walker, when my legs suddenly gave out from under me, and I instinctively leaned on her metal contraption for support.

"You said the play was produced on the *shloyshim*,"[134] I heard a voice call out from the crowd, but the room started spinning, and I couldn't tell whose it was.

How long did Faygen know? Why didn't he say anything to me? Was this, in fact, Luba's plan all along? I was to be the heir apparent and would take over after she was gone? I couldn't keep track or make sense of it all, as the thoughts were coming too quickly and the massive Greek chorus chattering around me wasn't helping.

"That only gives us a month to produce the play. It's impossible!" another voice called out with great trepidation as I continued leaning against the walker, ironically the only thing keeping me from another ignominious visit to the floor of the stage.

"He can do it!" another voice called out on my behalf, eliciting the rabble's rousing response. Clinging to Khaveh's metal contraption for dear life as my breathing grew short, the only thing I could hear clearly was my own apologetic whispers to Luba: "I'm sorry, I'm sorry," I repeated over and over to her that I just wasn't up for the task she had apparently set for me, one which I was only now piecing together in my mind, and it was scaring the living shit out of me.

---

134. The thirtieth day from burial, when the mourning period concludes...except for parents.

"Izzy," I could now hear Sam's voice calling to me. "Do you remember what you said that day?"

Of course I know what I said, but I couldn't respond out of fear. "It's the most beautiful thing I've ever heard anyone say," Sue-Ann told me when we stood outside the JCC that first day and that I thought I heard her say again as I now teetered on the brink of another collapse. "You said that if I could say that about the play and walk away,"I whispered to her now almost inaudibly, "then I wouldn't only be hurting myself."

"*Hadras koydesh,*" I could swear I heard her voice speaking to me for the first time since the disaster days earlier. As I finally lost hold of the walker and spilled onto the floor of the stage yet again, the sound of her voice began ringing in my ears along with the myriad of others who had gathered to honor Luba that afternoon in the theatre: "The splendor of holiness!" they joined together in rousing unison. "The splendor of holiness!"

A while later, after everyone had left the theatre and Faygen and I were alone on the bench in the synagogue, Joseph entered the room and jumped onto the stage, handing me a water bottle and an ice bag.

"He's okay," Faygen said to him reassuringly, when I guess my hunched-over pose with my head resting in my hands must have given the opposite impression. "He really is," Faygen added, waving him away politely so we could be alone again.

"When it rains, it really fucking pours, huh?" I asked Faygen rhetorically apropos the conversation we had become engrossed in, after it was quickly established that my fall to the stage was nothing serious, the bump on my head would hurt but heal and no, Khaveh couldn't be sued for any perceived defect in her *farkakte* walker that I fecklessly argued should have done a better job supporting me from my embarrassing tumble. I know you're wondering, and yes, he threw it in my face in a tone that sounded to me a little bit too sing-songy and too patronizing that "maybe... if I was on my medication..."

"Stop! Enough with that fucking cop-out!" Medications or no medications, he should know better that nothing can protect you from the kind of shock I experienced after the autistic fellow had a conveniently timed episode that centered around me. In fact, when I threw it back into Faygen's lap and asked how someone "normal" like him might have reacted in my place in front of hundreds of people, he rightly went mute, and I rested my case. Shit, I keep calling him the autistic fellow, and it just occurred to me that his name's Emmanuel. Sorry.

Know this: After I woke up from a little *driml* [135] on the stage floor that they must have allowed me to fall into when somebody in the room determined that an ambulance wasn't needed, but just some air, a cushion, and blanket, they said that one person wouldn't leave the building following the Luba assembly and that he was pacing back and forth inconsolably in the lobby. When I awoke, and they brought him into the theatre to demonstrate that, in fact, I was alive, well and that it wasn't his fault, he hugged me most awkwardly. But I mean awkward in a good way. Shit, that read awful. Again, sorry. What I'm trying to say is that he's a good egg, Emmanuel. Truly.

As to my little tiff with Faygen, we were past that now and onto bigger *tsures*. [136] The "man who killed Luba," as Sam put it at her funeral. As it turns out, although he didn't know the specifics, he wasn't totally off the mark. Not long before Luba passed away, Faygen told me about something going on at the JCC that compounded the stress she was already dealing with trying to mount the production of her life. I don't recall, but I think I mentioned it already. Well, now he laid it out plainly: They were shutting it down. Her theatre, I mean. That's right, they were throwing her a bone by letting her do *The Dybbuk*, but once the curtain came down, it was going to be *oys* [137] Yiddish Theatre at the JCC. Apparently, Luba had confided in Faygen and asked that he serve as her *shaliakh* [138] to the fuckers upstairs because what did she know from "shrinking envelopes," "value propositions," "repurposing of visions and mission statements to maximize engagement," as well as other such nebulous consultancy bullshit that's infected Federation boardrooms across the land. Although he started getting into the particulars, I soon tuned out, because the more I heard about how they were tossing aside Luba's Yiddish theatre willy-nilly and the decades-old legacy she'd built

---

135. Nap.
136. Problems.
137. No more.
138. *Consigliere.*

to boot, which I should add had become synonymous with the whole fucking place's reputation, the angrier I got.

"So, who's the *soyne yisroel* from the funeral who Sam said killed Luba?" I asked Faygen, still hunched over and pressing the bag of ice to my head, which was now pounding.

"The new chair of the board," he answered. "Mel Seal."

"Hold up," I replied and in an instant was back upright on the bench staring right at him. "Isn't that the fucking douchebag factory owner you're suing?"

"One and the same," he replied and momentarily forgave me...me.

"And this is all *his* doing?" I asked concerning the travesty he was describing that was about to befall the Yiddish theatre as my voice grew more animated.

"He is the chair," he replied, which I took to mean that whether there was consensus around the table, it didn't matter because there was a new sheriff in town.

"Well, I'll be fucking damned!" I blurted out, then hunched over again and pressed the bag of ice rather firmly against my head with the fist that now formed in my hand.

"That's one way to put it."

"Faygen..." I soon began to say to him with respect to something else before he interrupted me, assuming he knew what I was thinking.

"It's okay, *yingele,* I've already hired someone to help me in the office," he said with a smile. "You're off the hook."

"Shit, I'm sorry. I totally forgot about that," I answered, and he was wrong because that actually wasn't on my mind, at least until that moment. "Someone good?" I asked.

"Actually," he began to answer, and I could hear a sense of confidence in his voice as he did. "I worked something out with the partners, and Ms. Napolitano has already returned to her desk for this important case."

"You mean the one with..." I began to ask as I turned my head and looked up at him, but he cut me off again, assuming he knew what I was thinking.

"Yes, and that's enough of that," he said forthrightly, and this time he was right.

There was a brief pause in our conversation, and although I managed a chuckle while he rubbed my back, it wasn't long before my mind turned to dour thoughts again. Despite his comforting me, I could feel a sense of hopelessness start to build, which caused me to start shaking my head from side to side.

"I don't think I can do it," I said to him softly as I began tossing the bag of ice in my hands. "I've got a lot on my mind."

"Don't worry, you'll see..." he began to answer. Although I didn't bother looking up at him to ask what he was referring to, I knew in my heart he was talking about Sue-Ann, and when he added apropos in Yiddish that "*s'vet zikh oyspresn,*" that it'll all work out, I started to cry because I just didn't know it to be true.

"You can do it, Iz," he soon said, getting to the heart of the matter that Emmanuel blurted out a little while earlier and in a tone meant to instill confidence.

"How could I possibly?" I blubbered through the tears, "I don't know the first fucking thing about directing a play."

"And Luba did?" he responded immediately, and suddenly we were laughing. "She had a vision and a purpose," he continued, and then added, patting me on the back like a good coach would, "just like you, kiddo."

The theatre was eerily quiet for a while after that as we sat there together on the bench in the middle of the stage, me hunched over, nursing my head with the bag of ice that was quickly turning to water, and wondering if this was something I really wanted to take on.

"Anyway," Faygen eventually started again, breaking the silence with a more lighthearted tone. "You really should think about it because your *Miropoler Rebbe* just walked into the room," he added and patted me on the back like I should straighten up, which I was in the process of doing anyway, as I thought the comment kind of strange.

But it wasn't, because standing right in front of us, alongside Joseph at the foot of the stage where Luba always took up her spot, was a rotund hulk in his late seventies, with his signature bald head and curly white hair that draped dramatically over his shoulders like a cape. My mouth dropped at the sight of him because whatever the timing, the missing piece of the puzzle that Luba had alluded to when we first met, the actor who she was holding out for to play the iconic role of the *Miropoler Rebbe,* without whom she honestly couldn't have produced the play, had arrived: And it was none other than Karl King, aka Khatzkl

Katznelnbogen, the last and arguably greatest living actor of the Yiddish stage.

12

As if the day of Luba's death couldn't have ended any worse, what broke my fall from the couch in my living room in the wee hours later that night was my head, which was taking a beating on all fronts. After getting up and heading to the kitchen to fill another bag of ice, I soon returned to the living room where, before my spill that awoke me from a nap of five seconds, I was back and forth and upside down the apartment, my mind all a jumble over what had transpired in the theatre that afternoon. Specifically, what Faygen shared with me when we were alone together after my ignominious collapse and the pressure I was now feeling. Not in my head, but yes, in my head. Oh! And that's to say nothing about the fact that I was nowhere with Sue Ann, which was just flat-out maddening. I should also mention that it helped not a bit that while lying on my sofa, where I was reading the sacred copy of the script to *The Dybbuk* Luba had entrusted me with, my heart started skipping too many beats when I hit the meat of the play. Specifically, the part after Leah's possession, which I don't need to remind you, Luba never got to, and that Khatzl started pestering me about when Faygen and I took him out for deli a short while after he'd made his grand entrance into the theatre.

"So, is it true?" Khatzl asked me in his heavily-accented English, which rang to me as an interesting hybrid of pre-war acquired Yiddish, with not a small dose of Hebrew spoken *sabra*[139]- like, shortly after handing his menu back to our waitress who, I should point out, looked at him cockeyed and not a little bit nauseous after taking down his order. Indeed, although she asked him rather innocently if he wanted his smoked-meat sandwich "lean," it nevertheless caused him to let out a dismissive laugh so thunderously loud that it shook the walls of the joint, which in turn resulted in every head in the packed restaurant turning in our direction to hear, I guess, what he was in fact gonna order. On that front, he quickly made the young lady feel two inches tall by pointing out to her, in his caustic, irascible *basso profondo* tone of voice, that it was something akin to waitress malpractice in a deli to ask anyone the question she had posed. He then proceeded to tell her that not only should the cured meat in between the two pieces of rye that she was to

---

139. A Jew born in Israel.

bring him be dripping with fat, but that they should come *shmeered* with chopped liver, topped with fried onion and...speck.

I should pause here to tell you that even though the tone in which he asked me his question had a real sense of urgency to it, like you'd imagine from someone after they'd gotten wind that *moshiakh ben dovid*[140] had finally returned, and they had more than a passing interest in knowing his whereabouts, I held off, as I needed to get the hamster in my brain off his fucking wheel. Firstly, the last time I could recall someone ordering deli like he just did was my *zaide*'s friend Milner and my mind was taken back. I recall one winter, when my *zaide* and I were visiting Miami Beach for a Bundist gathering he was organizing at one of those hotels on South Beach that used to be fancy, before they became fancy again, he took us out for dinner with his tailor friend. Their prices were never above deli or similar, and he ordered exactly the same Ashkenazi, artery-clogging concoction. But if memory serves, he was more polite about it. Secondly, before our waitress looked like she was gonna throw up, Khatzkl told her to hold the fries, and then with a wink at her like he was maybe suggesting that he was still "capable," to bring the Coke diet because he was, you know, watching himself. Come to think of it, maybe that's what caused her face to turn that shade of jaundice before she walked off. The geriatric lothario *narishkeit* aside, the last piece of ordering was a remarkable assertion on his part, because not only was I still marveling at the fact that he'd defied the laws of physics by somehow managing to wedge himself into the booth opposite me and Faygen, but I don't think I'd be lying if I told you that once he did and his belly was allowed to find a place for itself, the table between us somehow started moving in our direction and began pressing into mine. On that note, I had no appetite and ordered nothing except a bag of ice for my head. Faygen, I think, chicken soup.

"Yes," I eventually answered Khatzkl, even though I was starting to feel short of breath. Although Faygen had no idea what was happening, I knew exactly what Khatzkl was getting at. It wasn't hard to figure out that it was matters of importance because when he smacked the table with his fist in response to my reply, with an accompanying "I can't believe it!" that reverberated throughout the restaurant, he gave it such an emphatic *zetz* that it caused Faygen to jump and look at the two of us in utter

---

140. The Messiah.

bewilderment. He was referring to An-sky's copy of the play, and don't ask me how I knew. It's a shitty analogy, but I suppose if someone was guarding the Holy Grail in a shoebox in their closet, they'd also filter every question posed to them through that reality. And for Khatzkl, to learn that Luba had not only kept safe the treasure Mikhoels entrusted her with, but that her production of *The Dybbuk* was being produced from An-sky's very own script, he could be forgiven his outburst because, for a man like him, such things were the essence of life itself.

Don't bother looking him up because you won't find anything on Khatzkl other than B-list credits for an impoverished actor using the stage name "Karl King" to make a living and hawk product, despite being a generational talent who deserved so much more. I only knew of him through Luba, who I could recall speaking of Khatzkl in terms she never would anyone else. Such was the respect and admiration she had for him. Indeed, that they had for each other, because from the earliest, they each knew that Yiddish theatre would be their calling. And just like Luba and her connection to Mikhoels, Khatzkl too could claim *yikhes*.[141]

He was born before the War in Lodz, the industrial beating heart of interwar Poland, to a mother who worked in a mill and a father who came from a family of Ger Hasidim, but who left the fold. If you know your history of that branch of Hasidism, then you're aware that there were a shit ton of them in Lodz at the time. Not all of them, however, could claim the kind of eminence that Khatzkl's family could. Indeed, the Katznelbogen name meant something. Yet although his father could claim direct lineage to Rabbi Meir, the Maharam of Padua, among others—go ahead, look it up, it's kinda cool—like many of his generation who got caught up in the ferment of the times, the draw of secular life and the radical, socialist politics that were promising to change the world for the better, was too much to withstand. That's how he ended up as a stagehand in Broderzon's Ararat theatre company, which was known for its strong socialist beliefs and whose famous alumni included none other than Dzigan and Schumacher: Two actors who would go on to become the greatest Yiddish comedic duo of the twentieth century. His father cast his lot with them, and as their star rose quickly, leading them to move to Warsaw to start their own company, Khatzkl's father moved his family of three to be with them. It was in the Polish capital where, by day, Khatzkl

---

141. Prestigious lineage.

obtained his formal education in the Bundist school system. By night, however, and at every other opportunity, he developed his calling for a life in the Yiddish theatre by soaking up everything he could in the lap of the two icons who paid his father's salary.

When the war broke out, the Katznelbogens fled east along with Dzigan and Schumacher, and the rest of their troupe to Bialystock, where, under Soviet occupation, they managed to keep their theatre afloat until the Nazi invasion in June of 1941. At that point, the story gets kind of murky, and what happened to Khatzkl and his family is unknown. Did they flee further east into the Siberian hinterland? Did they join Anders' Army together with Dzigan and Schumacher? What we do know is what Luba told us, which is that she met Khatzkl in a DP camp in Germany, where he and his parents survived to at war's end. As Luba told it, Khatzkl had long admired Mikhoels, who he learned about directly from Schumacher himself, who always considered himself a "serious" actor, and unlike Dzigan, aspired to do real theatre, the kind of stuff Mikhoels was renowned for. When Khatzkl learned of Luba's direct and personal connection to Mikhoels, they became fast friends. Why he never joined her or came to perform in any of her productions during the years that followed, was a mystery lost in time, except to say that he was simply an enigma, his own person who marched to a singular beat. In fact, you won't find his name listed among the august alumni of the Royal Shakespeare Company, because apparently, he quit early.

Likewise, every other academic institution or theatre academy he attended because he had a raw penchant for bucking authority and simply didn't take direction: A pattern that began in Israel, where the family ended up settling, because that's where Dzigan and Schumacher did, which lasted throughout his life. You also won't find his name mentioned anywhere in the biographies of acting icons like Lee Strassberg or Stella Adler. However, according to Luba, they were his friends, particularly Stella, with whom he bonded over their shared connection to the Yiddish theatre. When it comes to Khatzkl, what you need to know is that, aside from ensuring the existence of her theater over the decades following the war, Luba always maintained an eye on Khatzkl's whereabouts, which was tricky, because he traveled to the corners of the earth in search of roles that would allow him to perform in Yiddish on stage. And he played them all...except one, by design.

Strange as that may sound, there's a reason for it. When they were together in the DP camp, and Luba revealed to Khatzkl the treasure Mikhoels entrusted to her and that she managed to safeguard during the War, the two new friends, young and uncertain of what the future held for them, made a *t'kiyes kaf*, a pact: That before their time was up on this earth, they would come together to produce *The Dybbuk*, using An-sky's script, a production which Luba would direct and that would feature Khatzkl in the iconic role of the *Miropoler Rebbe*.

"Where is it, now that she's gone?" Khatzkl asked me about the script, his voice dripping with concern that the treasure was, *kholileh*,[142] at risk and in danger of falling into the wrong hands.

"*I* have it," I answered him confidently, which caused him to look at me askance.

"*You?*" he replied incredulously, and I wasn't sure if the next thing to come out of his mouth was going to be a series of invectives directed at me or maybe something more refined on the topic of "I/Thou," which would have come natural to a distant cousin of Buber — like I said, Katznelnbogens, look them up. It didn't matter because the waitress had now returned, and suddenly his eyes brightened and his breathing grew heavy, which I guess was some sort of Pavlovian head start for the mess of meat, accompanied by a bowl of pickles and sauerkraut she placed in front of him, which took about a nanosecond for him to begin hoovering.

"Can I ask what you two are going on about?" Faygen asked as he tucked a white napkin into his collar and started blowing on the ladle of soup he'd brought to his lips.

"The script," I answered, took the bag of ice the waitress had brought to the table, and placed it against my head.

"But why you?" Khatzkl chimed in, chewing a mouthful of meat that sounded like it was a lot of work to manage.

I didn't answer him because, as you know, from the moment Luba slipped it to me that day in her office, I honestly didn't know if the reason why she'd given me An-sky's script was anything more than just a good PR job on her part to get me to do the play. No, wait, hold on. That's not fair to her. Sure, now that I'm thinking about it, it's about as good a pitch as you can think of, and it worked. But honestly, up until

---

142. Heaven forbid.

that day of Luba's passing, the events that immediately ensued and even up to that moment in the restaurant, I guess I hadn't given it more thought.

"Because that's who Luba wanted to have it," Faygen replied assertively on my behalf. I was immediately taken aback and, well, kinda touched.

"This *pisher*?" Khatzkl scoffed in reply, emphasizing the insult by looking at Faygen but pointing at me with a pickle.

"This *young man*," Faygen continued in my defense, "happens to be the individual Luba wanted to take her place." He then looked at me like I was supposed to say something, or maybe, I dunno, applaud. Whatever the case, he was clearly riffing on a case he was building, and I just sort of waved my hand at him as if to suggest that better I say nothing and he should just keep going. Mistake.

"And *he* will be directing the play in her absence."

Fucking Faygen.

"And who is *he*?" Khatzkl again asked Faygen accusingly while not bothering to look in my direction.

"Okay, can we just stop with the fucking pronouns, please?" I snapped at the two of them as my head began pounding again, and I turned to look for the waitress and waved for another bag of ice. "You're right," I said to Khatzkl, "I'm a *pisher*, a nobody, and I'm not directing the play."

He didn't say anything in reply but grunted smugly instead before taking another bite of his sandwich. Actually, that's not true. Before he shoved the meat in his mouth, he gazed over at Faygen with a look that suggested he wanted to ask him if I was playing with a full deck.

"Stop that," Faygen jumped in and scolded me as he wiped his face with his napkin, which he then folded neatly and placed under his bowl, before attempting to redirect after my comment and continued to advocate on my behalf: "Khatzkl...," he began to say, addressing the large man opposite him in a deferential tone, "...may I call you that?" The legendary dyspeptic actor across from us, who seemed to be growing larger with each bite, grunted his approval that it was kosher, so to speak, so Faygen continued: "Khatzkl, there is *nobody* on the face of this earth other than you and Luba, *zol zi hobn a likhtikn gan eydn*,[143] who feels this play in his bones like Izzy does. He knows it by heart."

Again, Khatkzl didn't say anything. This time however, as he washed the first half of his sandwich down with a sip from his soda, he gave me a once-over as if to get the measure of me.

"Besides," Faygen then continued confidently, which he had no right to feel because he added, like an idiot: "Luba already completed the first act, so Izzy only has to concern himself with the second."

Khatzkl said nothing. I said nothing. In fact, we both simply looked at Faygen and shook our heads in exactly the same way and probably for precisely the same reason, though under different circumstances, I likely would have slapped my head with my hand in frustration as well.

Fucking Faygen.

"Tell me, *yingele*," Khatzkl began to address me, and I was immediately struck by his choice to use the Yiddish term of endearment for "young boy," which sounded genuine, though he was probably setting me up. "Have you ever directed a play?"

"I haven't," I answered him, and I sensed that I was right about his motive.

"What's your vision for how to handle the ex-communication?" he asked, in reference to one of the key plot points in the second act of the play that prominently features the *Miropoler Rebbe*.

"I don't have one," I answered meekly, because it was the truth.

He didn't respond immediately, choosing to grunt smugly while shoving a spoonful of slaw into his mouth. A few chews in, however, he opened his mouth again and asked another pointed question: "The trial, as you know, has confounded directors since the Vilna Troupe's production. You have a plan for it?"

"I don't," I answered forthrightly, because what was the point in lying about the fact that there was none.

"So, Luba shared nothing with you about how she wanted the rest of the play to be dealt with?" he followed up.

"Like what, for example?" Fagyen chimed in because he could rightly sense that I was growing impatient with the line of questioning. Or maybe he was feeling likewise, what with how I took no time to consider my replies.

---

143. May she rest in peace.

"Like what?" Khatzkl repeated his question aloud, scoffing so that Faygen could hear the stupidity of it. "Plans, notes, a bible, sketches, some kind of roadmap for how to finish the play!" he bellowed dramatically with an accompanying wave of his hand before finishing with a flourish by letting out a *zaftig* burp.

Faygen and I looked at each other after he'd finished and knew better than to open our mouths for fear of revealing a truth about Luba that would put her in a lesser light than Khatzkl would have otherwise expected. I'm referring, of course, to the fact that the woman operated on instinct and wouldn't know a plan or a roadmap if it hit her between the eyes.

"There's no pla...," I began to say before Faygen cut me off.

"Luba shared everything with Izzy before she died," Faygen chimed in with an air of confidence, and for the life of me, I couldn't figure out why he was making this shit up. "All her plans for the play, to the last detail," he added.

I looked at him blankly, and it was all I could do to keep myself from saying to him, "What the fuck are you doing?" But it wouldn't have helped, so I refrained.

"But the young man just finished saying the opposite," Khatzkl said incredulously as he sipped the last bit of his soda and burped again. "Which of you is telling the truth?" he asked and began to maneuver himself out of the booth.

Of course, Faygen and I both responded simultaneously that each of us had the story right, which only confounded Khatzkl even more and generally turned the situation into a shit show.

"Well, whatever the case, it's immaterial," Khatzkl said as he finally wrested himself out of the booth and let out another gust of wind, this one loud enough for the restaurant to once again turn in our direction and unfortunately pay attention to what he had to say: "I came here to fulfill a promise I made to Luba," he said as he stood looking down at us as we continued sitting in the booth. "Now that she's no longer with us," he continued, and now pointed at me, "although you say that this young man here knows something about the play, but has no plans for how to direct it, or to direct it at all for that matter, I have no reason to stay."

Faygen and I looked at each other, speechless. Actually, it was more Faygen giving me the look of death.

"Excuse me," the heavy-set man said as he turned his gaze toward the back of the restaurant. "I have an urgent need for a toilet," he said as he began to walk away. "When I return," he added, "I'll ask that you take me to the bus terminal so I can return to New York."

———————

It's amazing how many components go into a phone you never pay any attention to until you've thrown it against the wall and smashed it to pieces. It's like a million of them; that's what I felt as I was on my knees in my living room trying to collect the zillion shards into a dustpan, after I destroyed the confounded device and made a mental note to be angry at myself another time over the hole I made in the drywall. Ostensibly, actually between us not so ostensible, but let's go with that, it was because I just couldn't take that she wasn't returning my calls, texts, or any other electronic channels I could find to reach out to Sue-Ann. After the last failed attempt I made when I'd returned to the living room after falling off the couch, feeling particularly embarrassed for myself and generally pathetic, I'd just had it. Granted, it was the middle of the night, so maybe it would have been wiser to have waited a couple of hours to be rid of the offending apparatus, but *azoy geyt es*[144] sometimes. Regardless, like I was telling you above, she was just the last straw, as it was really a confluence of issues that led to me being on the floor in my underwear, looking for every last piece of metal, plastic, and whatever else they put into those handheld machines, if only because I didn't want anything to tear into my *zaide*'s slippers, which I happened to also be wearing.

Apart from Sue-Ann, there was also the issue of Faygen's "grand bargain" with Khatzkl, made following the latter's return from the deli's toilet. Despite me voting against the deal, which called for the irascible artist to stay in town an extra *mesles*[145] in return for me getting back to him by sundown the following night with my vision for the play; despite the pressure, I had not even committed to directing the play. From the moment I stepped foot in my apartment, shortly after dinner with them, I was in a panic, thanks to Faygen, who had now put me on the clock. Unfortunately, the bump on my head felt like it was growing bigger, fast and in direct proportion to the amount of garbage piling up in my brain

———————

144. So it goes.
145. 24-hours.

no less swiftly; after countless hours reading An-sky's script back to front, in reverse, then over again, likewise screaming at the top of my lungs for Luba and even An-sky himself to come and help. By the time the phone hit the wall in the middle of the night, I was just plain out of my mind bonkers because the god's honest truth was that I had *bubkes.*

Fucking Faygen.

There was another item stuck in my head that night, however, which was compounding matters and really kept me up until I saw the sunrise the following morning: The douchebag who was shutting down the theatre, Mel Seal. After I'd finished collecting as many shards as I could find lodged in my living room carpet, and likewise concluded that I wasn't going to get any further with the play, I decided that since it was also unlikely that I was getting any sleep that night, maybe it was finally time to look into the man. You'll recall that I promised Faygen I would do so when he first told me the story of how the bazillionaire was sticking it to his employees in the scheme that Faygen was now betting his career on, by leading a class action suit against him.

Although I'd caught a glimpse of the man that morning at Luba's funeral, when Sam nearly dropped her casket at the sight of him, I'll tell you honestly that it wasn't until I opened up my computer and started Googling him that I began painting an honest portrait of the man. Weird how these things go. I mean when you think of something, and then you're presented with the real McCoy and it's like nothing you imagined. In this case, I'm referring to the physical figure, his presence, if you will. Based on what Faygen told me about him that day in his office, which admittedly wasn't much, when he said that the guy was *the guy* in the ladies' underwear business I had this image of, I dunno, maybe a tall, strapping *goy* with matinee idol flowing hair, who could make ladies swoon upon entering a room. Yeah, that wasn't the troll-like figure I was looking at on the screen who made Louis B. Mayer look like Cary Grant by comparison; a diminutive *yidel* with a visage that, suffice to say, Der Stürmer would jizz over.

"My name is my word, get it? Seal?" That seemed to be the headline in every *farkakte* puff piece about him, which he apparently used as his calling card. For *brekhing.*[146] I don't want to get too much into

---

146. You could vomit.

it here because it's just gonna get me upset, but the guy's story isn't so special. He's basically a Duddy Kravitz.

You know what I mean: A street kid, or someone without much formal education whose parents, typically simple folk, didn't pay much attention, or maybe paid too much attention, and the kid's got a complex something phenomenal that the only thing that matters is to make it big, to become a somebody. Back in the day, they didn't know from such things, but every Duddy Kravitz by definition has ADHD, maybe even a *bisele* bi-polar, ridiculously insecure because of their lack of education and refinement, which they compensate for brilliantly with social skills that could make your head spin. My doc wouldn't be happy with me saying all this, but it's coming from someone who can appreciate these finer points on the spectrum, so I just hope she's not reading and doesn't start charging me more for being an asshole. If you want my take on it, a Duddy Kravitz type's one goal in life is to die and have the largest tombstone in the cemetery that, if it had nothing else written on it, would say: "A somebody." Maybe Gebirtig pegged these douchebags perfectly in *Avreml der marvikher.* Look it up.

I know what you're thinking. You're on *shpilkes* wanting to know how he made it big. Dunno, none of the articles pointed to anything other than him feigning sincerity by telling the reporters that he got lucky. "Things fell into place," or "Right place, right time," and other such trite nonsense. What I can tell you is that maybe, just maybe, he worked for it.

Apparently, he's got a bad case of dyslexia. His father got him a job sweeping the floor in the factory he worked at making ladies' bras and underwear. Yeah, that's right...Manky's. Word eventually got to old man Mankiewicz about the Duddy Kravitz on the factory floor who had a Rain Main-like capacity to not only grasp the intricacies of how the machines did what they did, but in fact how things could be improved. The boss then takes him under his wing and the rest is headlines. What can I tell you, all very nice for this supposed "self-made man." Truthfully, I didn't give a shit reading about any of it as none were getting to what was in my head, why the *soyne yisroel* was shutting down Luba's theatre.

"My wife got me into it," is the line I kept coming across in the articles, in reference to how he got started in philanthropy, otherwise known as the rich douchebag's guide for how to get your name on a building while destroying lives and institutions in the process. She was his secretary before becoming the missus, and judging by the amount of photos with them together showing her with a cocktail in hand, I'm guessing an alcoholic; which wouldn't be stretching the bounds of credulity, given how I described him and the fact that she, *lehavdl*,[147] looked like a Swedish goddess. No wait, sorry, that's not accurate, a more careful reading indicated that she owed her trophy appearance to not much more than clean genes from a Brahmin family in Boston, or maybe a good surgeon in Beacon Hill. The articles didn't say. Whatever. For some reason, I hear it's not atypical in circumstances of Jewish philanthropy, where the husband being the *yid* and the wife the convert, it's she who gets him involved in the giving of *gelt*.[148] And that's the case here, supposedly. Although the douchebag grew up Jewish, apparently it was in name only. By him, Passover was always the Jewish Easter and Chanukah, the Jewish Christmas; and maybe, in the case of both, the day he wondered why his employees weren't busily working. In any event, he was ignorant of all of it, as it just got in the way of getting ahead. Who knows, maybe the nose with a slope like the Himalayas put a massive chip on his shoulder that even if he foreswore all of it he is, was, and always would be a little Jew. I'm guessing. But I don't know how off the mark I'd be if I said that the reason he probably followed his wife's advice to get involved in community and to start plastering his name everywhere had nothing to do with *ahavas yisroel*[149] and probably everything to do with the fact that he'd likely be hobnobbing with the kind of people who'd give him advice on how to avoid paying taxes. But I could be wrong.

Whatever the case, by the time the rooster crowed the next morning, I felt I'd read enough about the man for a lifetime, and I don't know that I was the better for it, because after hours of reading it all, there wasn't even a hint of an answer to the question that was vexing me and keeping me up: "Why was he closing the Yiddish theatre?" The one thing I was grateful for however, was the fact that whatever anger I felt toward the troll was quickly being overcome by a long overdue somnolence that soon had me passed out on the floor of my living room. But before the sheep started jumping over the moon, I promised myself

147. By comparison.
148. Money.
149. Love for one's fellow Heebs.

that the first thing I would do when I woke up was try to get an answer to my question.

It was around dinnertime the following day when I found myself walking up the stairs of a massive walkway to a house larger than I'd ever seen in my life; itself the biggest of the big at the top of the mountain in a part of town I'd never visited, because I'd heard that, to this day, no Jews and dogs. By the way, I say dinnertime, but it was more like late afternoon, as that's when the secretary at Manky's told me that Mr. Seal took dinner at home.

I know what you're thinking, but it's not her fault. When I told her I was calling from the JCC on important matters and that my own secretary misplaced his address, she was more than happy to oblige. Two things occurred to me when I finally got to the door and rang the bell which, I kid you not, reverberated like the bells at Notre Dame. First was that I missed Philip Roth z"l.Second, I completely forgot to email Faygen after I woke up mid-day to let him know that I was both *sans* phone and bereft of any vision whatsoever for how to direct the play. The sun was close to setting, my time was nearly up according to the deal he'd made with Khatzkl, and I could only hope that he was doing something to keep the guy around.

It took a few minutes but eventually, a housemaid in an outfit came to the door. Although I was deaf to the series of questions she asked before letting me in, due in no small part to the gaudy bells that for some reason didn't stop ringing when the door opened, I made sure not to ask her the one that popped into my head as she spoke, because although she looked like my Soffy, they probably weren't related, I had likely never seen her before, and better to just keep my stupidity to myself. They did talk alike, though. At all events, I told her I was there on important JCC business, and although she threw me a look that suggested she found my claim more than dubious, given that I wasn't wearing anything other than sweats and a t-shirt, she let me in regardless. I don't think it hurt that she giggled and crossed herself when I told her how much I envied that she got to work in a church every day. I know what you're thinking, but I'm not that far off the mark because it wasn't just the bells that, once you were inside, reverberated even more loudly against the sky-high ceiling. The building she ushered me into was so massive that the foyer alone felt like it needed a welcome desk with a docent to point you to the appropriate wing. As it turns out, she led me down a hallway towards the one in the east where five priceless impressionist paintings are located. I think I counted twenty steps between each. She opened a door, motioned for me to enter, and asked that I wait while she let Mr. Seal know that I'd arrived, but that it might be a while because he was already entertaining guests.

You know me well enough by now that when I tell you I haven't spent much time around *fineshmeckers*[150] and their smoking rooms, you'll believe me. I'm only guessing that's what this room was that the woman made me wait in, because despite no humidor or ashtrays, the fucking place reeked from cigars. That being said, the few times I have had the misfortune, I've noticed certain commonalities that fall into two broad categories. First, the décor. Again, knowing me as you do, we're aware that I know from nothing when describing these things in any way that would give you a good feel for setting. So, forgive me...but s *'makht nisht*.[151] As if you need to know that the leather on the weird-looking *chaise* in the corner of the room was so soft that the moment you sat on it, your *tukhes* slid right off? Of course not. Or that all the half-dozen paintings on the walls were done in neoclassical style, each with a variation on the theme of hailing the conqueror? Likewise, not important; mind you, on that point, I should add that although none featured Mr. Seal, from what I could tell, the subject in each painting did seem to feature a relatively diminutive, Napoleon-like figure. Suffice it to say that everything in the windowless room, from the dim lighting to the similarly dull color palette used on the walls, and the upholstery on the chairs, lent a sense of foreboding that I'm just guessing was meant to make its guest feel intimidated.

Now, to the second category: The books on the shelves. I don't know if you agree, but there seems to be consistency among the fucking *g'virim*[152] whereby among their collection, you're guaranteed to find a copy of the following, which is in no particular order and by no means exhaustive: Ayn Rand's *The Fountainhead*, Martin Gilbert's multi-volume biography of Winston Churchill, something by Milton Friedman or the Chicago School, likewise anything penned by Kissinger, *Leviathan*,—of course,—the Steinsaltz Talmud...and maybe *Mein Kampf*. In this case, I couldn't be sure about the latter, because as I was checking

---

150. Literally, fine tasters/gourmets. Practically, rich douchebags.
151. Not important.
152. See *fineshmeckers*.

to see if the Steinzaltz was in unopened plastic wrapping—yes, all twenty-two volumes—I was distracted by a dense plume of cigar smoke that suddenly wafted into the room when the woman opened the door. Moments later, I got walloped by a wall of Latin American tobacco when a balding gnome with a prominent paunch, proudly pronounced by his suspenders, entered the room chewing on a cigar.

Interestingly, he looked way shorter in person than the photos I'd seen had suggested. When the housemaid threw me a cautionary look, then gazed skyward and crossed herself before closing the door, leaving me alone with Mr. Seal, I knew it portended something ominous.

"Mel Seal," he said, introducing himself as he approached and extended a hand.

Admittedly, I hesitated momentarily in returning the gesture as I was instantly blinded by the reflection coming off of the needlessly oversized, gold-plated cufflinks he was wearing, which featured his initials engraved that aroused something familiar in me, not too pleasant. At the same time, I was suddenly overcome with more than a mild case of dyspepsia when I saw the sea of eczema covering the whole of his stubby little hand that I was being asked to take hold of.

"Your name is your word," I eventually replied emphatically and sarcastically while swallowing the vomit that had quickly made its way up my esophagus as soon as I shook his hand.

"You got it!" he said excitedly, and I'm guessing impressed that I was familiar with his dime-store catchphrase, but deaf to my tone nonetheless. I then watched as he took a seat in his high-backed smoking chair, which I'm guessing he had custom-designed special to make it look throne-like. But judging by the way he sank into it, with his feet dangling slightly above the floor, it made him look anything but regal.

"I get it, all right, you imbecile," is what I wanted to say, but kept my mouth shut as he gestured for me to sit opposite him on the slip-and-slide that I wanted no part of, but on which I nevertheless managed to find a place at its edge that seemed marginally safe.

"Do I know you?" he asked me without waiting for an answer, as he followed up with questions delivered in such rapid succession that I wondered if maybe, along with the auto-immune disorder manifested on his skin, he also suffered from some kind of nervous tic syndrome. "You look familiar," he said. "But I don't think I know you," he repeated. "Do I know you? My secretary said there was an urgent call from the JCC about a meeting I missed, but I don't know you," he continued while taking a puff from his cigar. "Do I know you?"

"You don't," I answered succinctly.

"You're from the JCC?"

"I'm not."

"But you look familiar," he said, and looked at me, twisting his face and trying to put the pieces together in his mind. "No, wait," he said, "it's your voice."

I said nothing, as an instant later, he figured it out. "Got it," he blurted for an audience of no one but me: "The funeral."

"That's me."

"I'll tell ya, that was some eulogy."

"It was hardly a eulogy."

"Now that you mention it, you're right," he said forthrightly. "I'm not sure what it was."

"That makes two of us," I replied.

"Anyway, you caught me in the middle of entertaining," he said, moving on swiftly. "But you're here, so what can I do for you, *kid*?"

Between us, I hadn't planned for my uncle Hank to get in my head during this ad hoc meeting I'd called, but I couldn't have foreseen the gaudy cufflinks Seal wore, which were too much a reminder of him. So, already I wasn't in a good place, as you've experienced what being in my uncle's presence does to me. When you add to the fact that this not-too-dissimilar boor just referred to me in that infantilizing way my uncle always does, I had my back up even before we got into anything of substance.

On that front, I'll be transparent and tell you that between the time I awoke earlier that afternoon and that particular moment in Seal's smoking room, I hadn't given much thought to what I would say to him or how I wanted the meeting to unfold. Look, it's just us here and we already know from what we've shared together that if Faygen, my mother, my doc, or anyone for whom it mattered, knew that I had taken it upon myself to ring the guy's bell on a horrible night's sleep, without an ounce of preparation, or having even the slightest inkling as to what I was gonna say if I was actually let in the front door, they'd be right to be concerned and maybe even mad as hell. Well, fuck 'em. Meds, no meds; I felt something in my gut, I trusted it was right, if perhaps not rational, and I chose to act upon it.

"I don't want you to close the theatre," I blurted out in reply to Seal's putting me on the clock, and maybe with a slight tone of pissed off at being called 'kid'.

"The Jewish theatre, you mean?" he answered. I was immediately struck by the fact that he didn't call it Yiddish, but also by the way he pronounced the word theatre, emphasizing the "a" in a really atypical fashion. In the first case, I instinctively understood his substitution of Jewish for Yiddish as being either common, especially among those benighted and therefore maybe harmless or, purposefully mocking and derisive, something akin to the centuries-old reference to the Yiddish language as a "jargon" by those who looked down upon it as anything but legitimate. I couldn't tell you for sure, but my gut went with the latter. Concerning the fucked-up way he pronounced "theatre," I guess the polite thing would be to say that perhaps it was a word with which he wasn't familiar. It's either that or, as the news articles suggested, the douchebag did indeed suffer from a severe case of dyslexia that he would call it a "the-atre." In all events, by my calculations, we weren't off to a good start.

"Yes, the *Yiddish* theatre at the JCC," I replied, emphasizing its unique character.

"You're involved?"

"Sort of."

"I thought there was only the old lady?"

"Her name was Luba."

"Right," he said without apologizing. "I didn't know there was anybody else."

"There isn't," I replied, and instantly regretted prejudicing the case I was trying to make by offering that statement.

"Okay, then, who are you?"

"Nobody," I answered, and let's not get distracted over the self-defeating psycho-underpinnings of that statement either.

"Not if you managed to convince my secretary that you had something important to discuss with me," he said, and I couldn't tell whether he was impressed with what I'd done, pissed off, or maybe both.

"I'm an actor in the play," I answered Seal truthfully, and for some reason, he didn't immediately come back at me with something clever or insulting. In fact, as he put the cigar in his mouth, I noticed he was biting into it more heartily than he had been, and also that he was looking at me in a way he hadn't previously. In the silence, while he was taking a deeper look, I decided to follow up: "Can I ask you why you're closing the theatre?"

His reply was akin to what Faygen had discussed with me a day earlier in the theatre after my fall, when he shared the various rationale for why the JCC Board was shuttering the theatre. Still, Mr. Seal was a tad more insensitive and downright vulgar about it. Aside from regurgitating the Federation corporate-speak that rang hollow to me, which I wasn't so convinced he believed in all that much either, he was pretty forceful about the "numbers" he was seeing and how it all came down to dollars and cents. He didn't see the point in spending valuable community money, his, I guess, on something that was living on borrowed time and that wasn't meeting the "needs of the community." He didn't elaborate on that latter point and frankly, I didn't ask, as I could feel myself growing angrier by the second as he mocked the irrelevance of the "Jewish the-*a*tre," a fact he claimed was born out by the rapidly aging and continuously dwindling audiences, which he may not have ever seen himself personally, but that appeared in the "data." So, it was only a matter of time that, like Luba, her theatre would die off, too.

All that aside, the guy's focus was on Israel. "I noticed," I replied when he segued to a topic that mattered to him.

Sorry, I forgot to tell you when I was describing the room to you that, like a lot of Diaspora Jewish douchebags with *gelt*, he had all manner of plaques, photos, and various other signed memorabilia from the organizations and institutions he'd given to in the Holy Land.

Interestingly, when I looked them over more carefully, it occurred to me that most of them had to do with religious matters, particularly houses of study.

"I give," he said in a tone in which I could sense just a hint of modesty. A hint, it was like infinitesimal.

"*Oylem habeh* insurance, I get it," I answered him. When he looked at me dumbfounded, I didn't bother getting into it with him, not wanting to have to explain the concept that, since time immemorial, wayward Jews have always given to those who've supposedly stayed on the righteous path, if only to give them a sense of comfort that it'll help when the time comes for the man upstairs to decide whether to let 'em in for eternal rest. Think I'm kidding? Take it from the horse's mouth:

"They're the real Jews, kid," he said to me, and pointed at the various photos he had on the bookshelf of him surrounded by black-clad men with long beards either holding up a giant cheque or pointing to his name on a *bes medresh*[153] or a *yeshiva*[154] he'd just endowed. "When you and me are gone," he continued, "they're the ones who'll still be around."

"Like cockroaches," I said, I think in jest.

"Jewish ones, nonetheless," he replied, in all seriousness. "You ever been?" he then challenged me, I assumed in reference to visiting Israel.

"Many times," I said, and confessed that I cried when I first stepped foot on the ground at Lod Airport because of how much it meant to me. "And I weep for it to this day," I added.

"What for? It's the greatest place on earth," he scolded me, then rattled off all the great things about the Start Up Nation that you can read about in the papers.

"Not yet," I replied whimsically, "but I'm rooting for it."

"I don't understand how you can say that," he said, taking umbrage. "I'm sending kids there every year by the thousands, they have the time of their lives!"

"I'm sure they do," I said to him calmly, "but the Jews having a state is not the final piece of Jewish history."

"Which is?" he said gruffly like I was talking down to him, and I guess I was.

"I'm just saying that the Jewish people were chosen for a much bigger role than ensuring your 'kids' have a good time, getting drunk and *shtupping* each other on the promenade in Tel Aviv?"

He looked at me like a deer caught in the headlights.

"The *tayelet*?" I asked by way of offering a synonym in Hebrew for the pedestrians-only stretch along the beach in Tel Aviv that maybe he would understand. *S'hot nisht geholfn*,[155] he was clueless. "Look," I said, exasperated. "I'm just saying that the Jewish people have a lot of work to do."

"Which is?" he asked me again, emphatically, like I should have maybe gotten the picture that he wasn't too pleased.

---

153. House of study.
154. Seminary.
155. It didn't help.

"To redeem the *fucking* world through absolute justice!" I yelled back at him, and instantly I could feel my heart racing a thousand miles a minute, unsure of what was going to come back at me in return. Strangely, he didn't seem the least bit moved either way by my outburst.

"That's deep stuff, kid," he said dismissively, and began lighting the tip of his cigar again.

"Yeah, not me," I whispered. "Ahad Ha'am."

"What's that?"

"Not what, who," I said, referring to the pen name of Asher Ginzburg, one of the greatest early Zionist thinkers. "You can visit him in Trumpeldor next time you're in Tel Aviv," I said somewhat in jest, referring to the "old cemetery" where he and other greats are buried and forgotten.

As we sat together for another moment or two in silence, I wondered why he continued looking at me like he was still trying to size me up. I didn't understand why, given that I'd done such a great job of it, I hadn't been shown the door, though I suspected that was coming soon. Regardless, I knew I was on the clock, so I returned to the topic at hand.

"I don't understand something," I began to say. If you don't care for the arts and think it's a waste of money, why is your name on the art museum downtown?"

"That's a damn good question," he replied, smiling at me. "My wife thinks it's important for our names to be on things like that, it keeps her in good with the girls. Personally, I couldn't give a shit."

I swear that's exactly how he said it.

"So *that's* why you're closing the theatre, because you just don't care?" I asked him forthrightly.

"Let me ask you something, kid." He then began to speak, and again he did it in such a way that it just got to me, and his crass follow-up only stirred the pot: "How are you gonna do a play with a dead director?"

As a result, my blood began boiling and I felt that trusting my gut had been a huge mistake, since I didn't know what would happen if I lost it, as it seemed like I was about to. As much as I wanted to jump at him and choke him to death, the "rational" side of me was still around and unfortunately not only did it keep me at bay, it did a fine job reminding me of what a total idiot I was for coming up with the idea of ringing the guy's doorbell in the first place. Oh yeah, and of highlighting the fact that I had no answer to his question. So, I stayed silent.

"Well, given that that's the case, I'm not wasting another nickel on the thing," Mr. Seal said when I didn't come back with anything.

"What does that mean?" I finally spoke up, and I could feel the fear of where this was headed starting to build up in me.

"The play, I'm cancelling it.'

"You can't do that!" I yelled back, just as there was a knock at the door and the housemaid walked in.

"I can and I will," he said, and started to get up from his chair. "Time's up kid, I gotta get back to my guests."

"No, Hank, wait!" I shouted, and tried to grab him as he was turning towards the door. "You can't just say that and walk away!"

"There something wrong with you, kid!" he said, and looked at me like I was out of my mind.

"No, why?"

"You just called me somebody else's name."

"No I didn't," I said and I honestly don't know if he was right, as my mind was focused on the reason I'd come to see him, and not on my mind: "It doesn't have to be like it was, it can't be," I said, for some reason apologetically about the topic I'd come to speak with him about. "I know that, I get it. But you can't just say you're shutting down the Yiddish theatre and walk away. If you do that, it won't just be me you're hurting, you know that right?"

He didn't respond and for a moment my mind was taken elsewhere and I didn't quite know how those words, those exact words spoken to me by someone else, entered my mouth such as they did. But in that instant, a sea of people rushed into my head and I could feel that I was no longer speaking in my own voice. "It's not about me," I said to him. "There are people for whom the Yiddish theatre really matters. It's their identity, and they'll be lost without it. For others, it's a way they're coming to discover their sense of what it means to be Jewish, for the first time. Believe it or not, in its own little way, it's flowering. That has to mean something, doesn't it, Mr. Seal?"

"It's a dying language, kid. Let it die with her," he said coldly, and that was that. He then started to walk out of the room and, judging by the gesture the woman made for me to follow, I quickly fell in with him as she closed the door behind us. Once in the hallway, Mr. Seal extended his hand to me, and despite all my misgivings, I shook it. "My housemaid will show you out," he said. "Gotta hand it to you kid, it took real balls coming here," he added. "But I think you need to get some help," he finished, and turned to leave.

"Wait!" I shouted a few seconds later when I noticed something in my surroundings that hadn't caught my eye until now. I waved for him to come back so that we could both look out the window to his massive backyard, complete with a perfectly manicured French garden and a patio where, as he mentioned, were a shit ton of people he was entertaining. "Tell me, Mr. Seal, what do you see out there?" I asked him.

"People," he answered me nonchalantly.

"Right," I said, and then I turned him toward this massive mirror on the opposite wall and crouched behind him as he looked into it. "And what do you see now?" I asked.

"I see myself," he answered.

"Right again," I said, and stood up straight.

"What's this about, kid?"

"Well," I began to answer, and I could feel a little hint of a smile building as I did because I suddenly felt that I wasn't alone. Luba was with me, An-sky, my *zaide* too: "The window is made of glass, and the mirror is made of glass, but the glass in the mirror is covered with a little bit of silver, and as soon as the glass is silvered, one stops seeing other people and sees only oneself."

"Geez, there's something truly wrong with you, kid," he scoffed at me after I'd finished sharing the parable with him that comes straight from the play.

"Actually, nothing's wrong," I said with a slight chuckle. "Just felt like it needed pointing out."

"Why's that?"

"I dunno, I guess to show that everyone will be held to account one way or another," I replied confidently, and for the first time since ringing his doorbell, I felt like trusting my gut was the right thing to have done.

After throwing me a look of derision, he barked at his housemaid to show me the door and quickly began heading in the opposite direction. "By the way, you never did me the courtesy of asking me my name!" I yelled out to him as he quickened his pace. "It's Izzy!" He didn't turn back, and I was left there with the woman, who just shook her head and led the way toward the front door. "It's true, he didn't," I said to her and no one in particular as I followed behind. "Fucking douchebag," I muttered to myself, but clearly loudly enough that, even though English likely wasn't her first language, the housemaid knew enough to let out a little giggle.

It was only a minute or two later, but by the time we'd turned the corner from the east wing and made our way back through the mansion's rotunda, I was spent. The truth is, the whole time I was with Mr. Seal I must have been riding such a wave of adrenaline that I didn't realize I was still nursing a massive headache, which suddenly returned with a vengeance, just as the chimes of Notre Dame rang when we reached the vestibule. "Jesus. Fucking. Christ! Make that stop!" I yelled out while covering my ears and probably blurting out a series of non-sequitur "la-la-la's" to boot, that I couldn't hear what the woman was shouting back at me as she crossed herself and looked at me sternly before opening the door.

"Oh my god!" Sue-Ann shrieked when the housemaid opened the door, and she both saw me and...uh...heard me.

"He no feel no good!" the woman shouted to her over the god-forsaken din of the broken doorbell, and made with her hand to her head like I was crazy while pushing me gently out the door; probably to her own relief, but from the looks of it, not Sue-Ann's.

"Close the damn door!" I shouted at neither of them in particular with my hands still pressed against my ears so that the racket would stop. The housemaid obliged. "Thank you!" I yelled out in exasperation, though by this point, the chimes had stopped, and I sensed that I sounded ridiculous.

"Your papa left the envelope in his office," the woman said to Sue-Ann as I moved slowly to the cement ledge nearby and sat.

"Thanks, Linda," Sue-Ann replied, "I'll be in soon."

No, I never would have guessed in a million years, Linda. I felt only a little bad not knowing, but not that much, considering her own fucking boss couldn't muster the courtesy to refer to her by name. You are probably thinking, had I called her Maria, which wouldn't have been a bad guess, would it have been any better? Regardless, now that Linda was made known, I wanted to ask her if she wouldn't mind maybe bringing a bag of ice. Judging by the looks on their faces however, I kept it to myself, and watched as Linda turned and walked back into the house, leaving Sue-Ann and me alone together for the first time since the disaster in her apartment.

"Your what?" I asked her accusingly as she leaned against the doorway; I guess *davkeh*[156] so as not to sit next to me on the ledge, although it had plenty of room for the both of us.

"Don't play dumb," she came back at me coldly, and did that thing like at the dinner, straightening her back and crossing her arms against her chest like she was donning some kind of battle armour. "You heard correctly."

"Envelope for what?" I followed up, and took a moment to observe that although she was dressed down like I was, in sweats, with her hair up and tied, she looked spectacular.

"It's none of your business," she shut me down.

"Your father?" I asked more directly this time, but she wasn't having any of it.

"I told you once already. You don't know me."

"But your name is Mankiewicz, not Seal. I don't get it." I continued, generally confused and kind of anxious, because Luba had now started chatting in my head.

"There's nothing to get," Sue-Ann continued brusquely, which was also not helping matters. "Like I said, it's none of your business."

"It is my business!" I shouted at her and felt my head start to pound again as I did. "You're not what I think!" I added, and immediately recognized that regardless of her quizzical look, even I didn't quite understand what I had just said or why.

"What are you talking about?" she rightly asked, and threw me a look that I guess was equal to how strange I must have appeared, with my palm firmly pressed into my head to relieve the pressure.

"Luba!" I kept shouting as the pain grew. "She warned me about you! She said you're not what I think. Now I know!"

"You know nothing," she responded like I was a fool, and asked me to stop shouting, but didn't inquire as to why I might be slightly off. "What else did she tell you about me?" she drilled me again.

"Nothing," I said matter-of-factly, "she died right after warning me."

---

156. On purpose.

She didn't say anything, and didn't have to, because the next look she gave me, this time in response to my crass reference to Luba's death, said enough. "You're so angry," she said pointedly and with contempt.

"*I'm* angry?" I replied incredulously. "Really, *me*?"

"I have a right to be mad at you!" she shot back while looking at me with disdain, and it appeared she was finally going to engage with me like I'd wanted her to do, and I frankly didn't care if she was about to let me have it. And she did: "I invited you into my home to meet the people I care about, and what did you do?" she began by asking me rhetorically, though I knew better than to do anything but shut up and take it. "You didn't just insult my friends. You were rude, obnoxious, demeaning, pompous, and self-righteous, when you had no right to be. No one attacked you, Izzy. It was all you. You tore each of them down for nothing other than the fact that you can't control the mess that's going on inside your head. But that's your baggage, not theirs. What you did was self-serving and juvenile. And at the end of it all, you didn't think for a moment that you may have been hurting *me*. So, yeah, I'm mad at you. I'm more than mad. I don't want to see you or talk to you." She paused for a moment before continuing, and her voice modulated slightly lower, and the words she spoke cut even more deeply: "I'm not an angry person, Izzy," she began to say while pointing her finger and staring at me venomously. "But you," she continued with derision in her voice, "you're not just an angry person. You're angry at the world and everyone in it for no reason. It's pitiful."

It was what I was expecting. In fact, I'd actually played this moment out in my mind a zillion times in anticipation of whenever it might come, but it still hit me like a ton of bricks when she finally delivered her harangue. When she took a moment to catch her breath however, I kept silent because not only was I searching for the words I might eventually speak, I also didn't know if she was done or if there was more invective incoming that I needed to gird myself for. The truth, however, is that regardless of whatever words she might have continued to use to keep chopping me down, what really gutted me was the realization that she was just taking a moment to compose herself and wanted me to play no part in it, a fact made plain by the way she calmly wiped a tear from her eye with her little finger as she turned away from me so that I wouldn't see, rather than coming to sit by my side and letting the tears flow into my shoulder and share in her pain. Fucking hell and its fury.

"Why are you here?" she soon whispered accusingly, like the incongruity only set in and my being there was more than a minor irritant.

"I came to save the theatre," I replied truthfully, and while I fully expected the conversation to head in that direction, it didn't.

"I opened myself to you like I never have to anyone," she said, returning to the previous topic of conversation. "Nobody knows about my sister," she continued, pointing at me again and then, out of nowhere, she added, "but *you* won't say a word about your *zaide* to me."

That I wasn't expecting.

"Wait, what?" I answered her dumbassedly, really as a stopgap because I was confounded by the combination she'd just put together. Not only did it require some diligent unpacking, which this moment was not going to tolerate, but it immediately had me thinking that I in fact couldn't remember the last time I was in one of these "wacko-a-womano's;" but if memory served at all, they never followed any logical path and this one seemed to be playing out to form. Additionally, with the throbbing of my head serving as a lovely foundation upon which Luba's arrival seemed to pile on perfectly, compounded now by my *zaide*'s unexpected entrance on top of that, whatever bandwidth I had was pretty well used up, and we're all now familiar with where that leads.

"You just contradicted yourself," I eventually came back at her. "You said I don't know you, but you show me your sister's grave... so I know you?"

"Why are you so hung up on him?" she asked, I assumed about my *zaide*, and for the life of me, I couldn't figure out how he got into this conversation.

"I'm not!" I shot back at her. "What on earth does he have to do with what we're talking about?"

"Everything!" she yelled back at me and again went on a tear: "I had to hear it from Faygen, not you, that he was a leader, forthright, respectful, honest, and always did what was right..."

"Okay, stop," I said to her, because as soon as she began speaking about him it wasn't just my head and everything swimming in it that was hurting anymore. She'd pulled a knife from an invisible scabbard tucked somewhere in her sweats, found the perfect spot, and thrust it in.

"And you're nothing like him," she continued, and I could feel it twisting inside me.

"Please stop," I pleaded with her because things were now stirring within me that she couldn't see but that I knew I couldn't control.

"What's the point of carrying a torch for him if you're nothing like him?" she continued, ignoring me and the fact that I started sobbing, which I guess she thought was due to a headache, but of course was the result of my having gone somewhere else, a place she couldn't see, which would explain how she could follow up cruelly with, "don't profess to be something you're not, Izzy."

"I asked you to stop!" I cried out to her as I began heaving. "I can't fight with you," I said while gasping for air. "I don't want to fight....*ikh...ikh...*" and in the delirium that suddenly overtook me, Ansky now reappeared and joined the chorus inside my head, whose collective voices now burst forth from my mouth and shouted Khonen's words from the play when he's finally forced out of Leah, whose body he'd possessed: "*ikh ken zikh mer nisht ranglen!*[157]" I shouted before collapsing onto the cement walkway.

Sue-Ann looked at me aghast as if I'd just spoken in tongues, and rather than bring herself over to console me, she did the opposite and took a step backward.

"You're not well, Izzy," she said. She may have been right on technical grounds. Nevertheless, the truth of the matter is that something had just transpired that I would be loath to try and explain to any whitecoat because although there was no physical evidence of me purging anything, thank God, everyone and everything had gone now, and my head was fine. But she wouldn't have known it. "You're gonna be miserable and lost until you find yourself, Izzy," Sue-Ann said while looking down at me, twisting the knife one last time, and at that moment, it was clear to me how much she was her father's daughter. Although the words I wanted to speak had somehow managed to coalesce quickly, they came too late because Sue-Ann had by now turned her back to me, opened the door to the mansion, and slammed it shut a second later, leaving me a pathetic mess at the doorstep.

"I think I have," I would've responded to her had she stayed outside just a fraction longer. Still, instead I started to chuckle, which soon turned into an uproarious laugh that came from somewhere I

---

157. "I can fight no more."

couldn't explain as I simultaneously shouted at the top of my lungs: "I'm gonna do it...I'm gonna direct the play!"

13

"Oh, Izzy!" my mother cried out, and looked at me gobsmacked after I turned on my computer during our online chat and she caught sight of the bandage I'd triaged onto my head, following my spill at the doorstep of Castle von Seal.

"Ma, I'm fine!" I yelled at the screen as she started bawling, and I immediately regretted giving in to her ultimatum — either she would get to see me or call the cops. Okay, maybe that wasn't the exact threat, but by this point in the conversation, she was fit to be tied and on the verge of calling in the big guns.

"You did what?" she responded soon after the conversation began with me telling her what happened to my phone and why I hadn't been returning her calls. She stepped away to grab a bottle and a glass, choosing to ignore me when I added that, despite the gadget having attained a *borukh dayen haemes*,[158] I felt liberated without it and encouraged her to give the "heave and hole" a try with her own phone. "You did what?" she said again upon returning, when I told her about my unscheduled visit with the diminutive douchebag and how well *that* went. She didn't bother searching her vocabulary for three words of like meaning when I described how I'd been possessed by the three-headed *dybbuk* of Luba, An-sky, and my *zaide*, whose arrival into my head presaged my hitting the cement on Seal's walkway. And you can rest assured that a feral animal in some alley blocks away from my apartment likely shrieked in sheer agony in response to my mother's voice hitting G above high C when she yelled out a final "YOU DID WHAT?!" after I told her that moments before us being together online, I'd sent a letter to Seal's office threatening his life if he dared follow through on his decision to shut down the theatre before we'd presented the play. It didn't matter that I'd made that last part up, as she was already half a bottle deep and beside herself over my first three offerings of how well I was doing. What? You know that with my mother, I'm nothing if not truthful.

Anyway, regarding the made-up story on Seal, I will say that I hadn't gotten any sleep since I'd left him and his daughter. Nor was I

---

158. Literally, "Blessed is the true judge." Said when someone or a vital electronic device dies.

expecting to get any moving forward, now that I'd done a bang-up job of causing a sword of Damocles to hang perilously over me and the Yiddish theatre.

Our fruitful conversation took a brief pause when the sound of my mother's doorbell caused her to be physically off-camera momentarily. I mention that with a qualification, only because I could hear her voice clear as a bell as she full-throated a conflated recapitulation of where we had arrived at this point in the discussion. Assuming she wasn't shouting *glat in di velt arayn*[159] and likewise taking for granted that she probably wasn't confiding in Soffy, I immediately got this feeling of "ick" because somehow, I just knew that when she returned, it was gonna be with Faygen.

"You did what?" were the first three words that magically rolled off his tongue when he shoved his face right up against the camera.

"Oh, for fuck's sake!" I yelled at the two heads squished together on the screen in front of me, which made me wonder if crazy was actually on the other end of our digital "can-and-string" sideshow.

"What's on your head?" Faygen then followed up quizzically.

"I don't wanna talk about it."

"He fell," my mother answered, and lit up a cigarette while pouring herself another glass, and one for Faygen too.

"Again?" Faygen asked legitimately, and suddenly my head started to hurt because my mother now threw him a look of displeasure, like she wanted to know what she wasn't in on.

"Ma, I'm fine!" I yelled again, pressing my nose against the screen to cut them off at the pass: "Can we just not? Please?"

"So that explains why I didn't hear from you last night," Faygen said, to which I didn't respond, and I guess it didn't matter because he then offered up his Cheshire grin. "So, you're gonna do it, eh?" he asked me rhetorically; I just assumed he meant the play, and then he explained the situation to my mother, who finally smiled for the first time in the conversation. "That's good," he added, "because I convinced Khatzkl to stay." I didn't ask by what means he managed that impressive coup, as I just assumed it came down to a monetary transaction that had Faygen out of pocket to the fat man, which immediately made me feel guilty and anxious because now it was real.

---

159. To no one in particular.

Shit.

"Izzy?" my mother asked with concern when it seemed the absence of my yelling at the two of them created a vacuum of awkward silence.

"It's nothing," I said to her, and at this point wanted to shut my computer down because she was seeing right through me, and not because she, too, shoved her face up close to the screen for closer inspection.

"There's something wrong," she whispered to Faygen after pulling back, like the few inches made a fucking difference in the sensitivity of the computer's microphone.

"There is," I chimed in. "It was a mistake," I added, and although it was understood that I'd established a nice laundry list of items to which that statement could have applied, I was talking about my decision to direct the play.

"Izzy, you don't have to...," my mother started to respond before Faygen cut her off politely by placing his hand gently over hers, which could have been because he saw that I needed to talk things through, or maybe it was that he didn't want her upending any of the progress he'd made in inching me along. I couldn't tell you either way.

"I can't do it," I told them, and as soon as the words left my mouth I wanted to throw my computer at the hole I'd made in my living room wall, as I had grown tired of hearing myself repeat the same fucking self-defeating maxim ad nauseam of late and was plain pissed off that I couldn't get my head out of that cycle.

"So why did you say yes?" Faygen then asked softly.

"I didn't. I just blurted it out."

Silence.

"I dunno," I shrugged, "the douchebag said he was cancelling the play, so it felt like the right fuck-you-asshole thing to do."

My mother looked at me, cockeyed, then at Faygen, perplexed.

"He means Seal," Faygen clarified for her, and she then threw me a look of displeasure.

"Okay, whatever," I said to them exasperated. "That's not the point."

"What is?" Faygen asked.

"What is?" I repeated his *klotz kashe* back to him. "He says he's shutting down the theatre, and the next thing you know, I get possessed by Luba, An-sky, and my fucking grandfather!"

"So, it's *bashert!*[160]" Faygen chuckled, but my mother remained stoic.

"It's not funny," I said, and started to cry because as interesting as it might have been for him to hear how it all transpired, and maybe even for you, dear reader, it scared the living crap out of me. "Ma," I then said to her softly, "I'm scared."

"Of what?" she whispered.

"My head."

"You'll heal," Faygen tried to reassure me and my mother. But he didn't get it.

"That's not what he meant," my mother said to him, because she did, and I could see the pain registering on her face.

"I blurted out lines from the play like a fucking psycho!" I shouted.

"Izzy, it's okay," she whispered and began crying again.

"I can't control it, Ma," I continued, while wiping the tears from my eyes with the back of my hand.

"*Yingele,*" she said to me in Yiddish, trying in vain to reach out and comfort her little boy.

"Ma, I'm not okay," I said to her, got up from where I was sitting on the couch, and started pacing in my living room.

"Faygen," I then heard her say to him pleadingly.

"Izzy, are you there?!" I heard him call out to me.

"Yeah, I'm here, but I'm not here," I responded to him through the tears as I continued pacing while scratching the bandage on my head with one hand so feverishly that I tore a hole in it. As bad a sign as that was, it didn't bother me so much as it was simply a matter of discomfort. What I began doing with the other hand, pulling the hair from my eyebrows, was of real concern. Indeed, if the Trych was back, it was a clear sign that I'd once again reached a place in my head -off the meds - that, if my medical chart was any indication, was perilous and likely beyond my control.

"Izzy, can you come back so we can see you, please?" my mother shouted into her microphone.

"You don't have to yell," I replied. "I can hear you."

"Iz," Faygen then began to speak. "Do you realize how you're exactly where you need to be at this moment?" he said, his voice

---

160. Fated.

brimming with pride and confidence, which if you were there to witness the incongruity of what he said and what I was up to, you would have had to laugh, or maybe cry, too.

"What do you mean?" I called to him, still from a distance.

"I'll tell you if I can see you," he said smartly, and I gave in.

"It's been a long time since you've been on stage, *yingele,*" he said once I sat back down in front of the computer, where I found both of them smiling, even though I was wiping tears from my face, looking like a total hot fucking mess. "But do you realize that everything you're going through now is in fact what you should be feeling?" Faygen finished.

I could have said something but I chose otherwise, as I didn't feel like sharing the fact that the return of another of my mental disorders probably didn't meet the criteria he was confidently outlining.

"You're more than okay," he said, and I let him. "You're living the experience in the rawest and truthful way possible."

He had that right, and this from the guy with the floss in his pocket.

"You'll be better for it. You'll see."

The jury was still out on that one.

"I have no vision," I blubbered to him sheepishly.

"Oh yes, you do," he said with a smile, suggesting he'd gotten me where he needed me to be. "More than even you know," he added, and I could see my mother nodding in agreement.

I didn't say anything further at this point as I was out of words and emotionally spent. I simply asked if it was all right if we ended the conversation so I could reapply to my head and go lie down. They agreed, but not before Faygen told me that he'd already informed Joseph that I would be at the next production meeting, which was taking place the following morning at the theatre.

"I'll go with you if you'd like," he offered earnestly.

I replied that while the gesture was well-intentioned, he'd be more of a headache to me than anything else. I didn't intend for it to be a pun or funny, but Faygen and my mother took it as such, and started to laugh. And maybe that was precisely how the conversation needed to end because, although the sword of Damocles was still hanging over me and my fear hadn't subsided, by the time I closed the cover on my computer and tossed it to the floor I had instinctively joined them, and for that little moment alone, I was grateful.

No one remarked upon it, but it was hard to miss: The equal amounts of blue and red pens, together with perfectly sharpened pencils and fresh erasers, all placed in cups similarly distributed across the stage manager's table in the theatre, which was itself elongated exactly double its size for the following morning's production meeting. Similarly, the way the chairs for us to sit were just-that-much width apart from each other, so the place cards with our names and titles on the table in front of them could have room to breathe. Like a lot of things in my life that I've been accused of seeing but not paying any attention to, it was only now, weeks into spending time around him, that I noticed Joseph's OCD. And it was amazing.

That being said, as much as I appreciated the gesture on his part to add some pomp to what I imagined are usually pedestrian proceedings, it was more than a tad contrived. So, as soon as I took my seat in front of the card that boldly declared me the *capo di tutti i capi,*[161] I quickly folded it face down on the table, as I was nervous enough as it is without the added bull's eye on my forehead. Not literally, of course, although there was much consternation around the table about my well-being, what with the latest piece of latex I'd applied to my noggin that probably looked as ridiculous as I felt being there that day. Not that I was the only one on *shpilkes,*[162] as I could see it on the faces of the designers around the table that they were likewise all on edge. We were only a few weeks from opening, and nobody had a clue what would happen now that Luba wasn't around. Judging by their communal stare in my direction, accompanied by sundry fidgets, ticks, and various bodily expressions of unease, they would have been right to ask outright if I had a fucking clue as to what the hell I was doing or if I knew anything at all about their respective crafts. The fact is, I was sitting around a table with temperamental artists who, on the best of days, struggle to keep their shit together, and my being there, the impostor that I was, probably was just making things worse. That might be my projection, but their being on edge about the precariousness of it all was actual and I didn't begrudge them. It did occur to me, however, to give Joseph a note that next time

161. We all know it's not Yiddish, right?
162. Literally, pins. Practically, ants in my pants.

'round, the liters of coffee they each had in front of them, alongside their digital gadgets and gizmos, should maybe be decaf.

The departmental debrief kicked off with Joseph pointing to the set designer, Mack, who quickly announced that he wasn't pleased with the status of his work. When I asked which part specifically, he declaimed with a grand, sweeping gesture: "All of it!" I found the hyperbole surprising as just prior to sitting down for our roundtable, he gave us all a tour through the nearly completed set that, to my eyes at least, looked spectacular. Again, I'm not sure why I didn't pick up on his progress when I was in the theatre only days earlier for Luba's "shiva." Maybe I got distracted by the sea of humanity on stage that afternoon, or perhaps it was everything else that was happening that day that prevented me from noticing. Dunno...but likely, uh, all of it. On this day, however, when it was just the handful of us, Mack's legendary attention to detail shone through. To wit: When he ceremoniously pulled open the *paroykhes* in front of the *oren koydesh*, I just assumed that the three impressively decorated Torah scrolls inside were stuffed with paper. They weren't. But if they were real, *posul*[163] and whether it was even kosher all together to have anything but stuffed, I didn't think it was for me to *paskn*.[164] That said, even without looking up each one's skirt to take a peek, I kinda had a hunch we were offside with the *eytz chayims*.[165]

Nevertheless, standing there among the circle of *goyim* admiring his work, who I'm just guessing didn't know from these things, I figured it was best to let him have his moment under the circumstances. All were further impressed when he then pointed out that the *sforim*[166] littering the tables of the synagogue weren't just collections of paper covered with *faux* Hebrew lettering but rather the real McCoy. However, when I went over to grab one off the table to see for myself, all hell broke loose.

"Not that one!" Mack shouted, then lunged at me when I quite innocently opened what appeared to be a *siddur*. But rather than seeing the *moyde ani*[167] on page one, a massive flame burst forth from the book, which nearly singed my face off.

---

163. Unfit for use.
164. To give a ruling according to Jewish law.
165. Literally, trees of life. Practically, synonym for Torah scrolls.
166. Holy books.
167. Prayer upon waking.

"*Sefer Raziel?*" I asked him sheepishly, referring to the Kabbalistic tome that gets Khonen into a whole lot of trouble in the play after the book went flying, and he lay on top of me on the stage floor shaking his head back and forth at my idiocy. "Impressive," I added before the assembled helped me up, and Joseph and I agreed that he take a note to make sure that the burning book was marked appropriately and not filled with lighter fluid until showtime.

Back at the roundtable, when I asked Mack what it was specifically that he felt was keeping his design from attaining its desired level of perfection, his answer was simple: A total repainting of the set. "No problemo," I told him with an accompanying thumbs-up that had Joseph looking at me askance while Mack smiled. Although I'm sure he was concerned about how the request would affect the production's timeline, it's more likely that the discussion Joseph and I were gonna have later on was over the lack of money for the request. Frankly, given what I knew that all of them didn't, I didn't give a shit. Moreover, if it was all going to hell in hand basket soon anyways, I was more than happy to saddle the douchebag with a bill he never saw coming.

Consequently, I totally blew Chantal's mind when she presented the photos of the cast in costume displayed on her tablet during her report on how the costumes were coming along. To make them even more fabulous, I said yes to as much fabric as her manic heart desired, making her face shine from ear to ear. "But on one condition," I told her, and pointed to the cigarette in her hands that she'd been tapping nervously on the table. "Just light the damn thing up already because you're driving me nuts," I said, and nodded my approval that she let it rip, along with a hand gesture that she toss one my way as well, for good measure.

This, despite Joseph throwing me a look like the addition of a health code violation to the financial misdemeanors I was already guilty of, wasn't anywhere on the meeting's agenda. "It's all good," I said to him with an exhale that felt delightful, a welcome distraction that kept my hands from reaching for my face and pulling, which I could sense I was going to start doing and I didn't want to have to explain the condition to a group of people who didn't know me and who had likely already declared me *nisht mit alemen.*[168]

---

168. Wacko.

"What's next?" I then asked impatiently, as the discussion 'till now hadn't grown on me like Faygen *et. al.* probably would have wanted, and I was eager to have it end. My luck was that the lighting designer delivered the next department report—that's the dyspeptic fellow I vaguely recalled from the meet-and-greet and whose name I assumed at the time Luba hadn't gotten right. Turns out, she was the maven and me the moron because, as bizarre as it sounds, the French-Canadian's name actually was Fred. Regardless, similar to his presentation on that first day of rehearsal, he kept his remarks brief, and that's being generous. In a sentence or two, and in an English so mangled that I wasn't the only one with the look of "huh" on my face, he waved at the ceiling while using technical jargon with which I wasn't the least bit familiar, then sat back in his chair, folded his arms across his chest, and looked to me earnestly for a response.

"So he basically just said there's gonna be lights on, right?" I whispered to Joseph, who didn't answer but looked down at the computer in front of him, dejected. When I asked him what the problem was, he replied that what Fred *actually* said was that his plan was shot to hell because he didn't have the money he needed to do what he had discussed with Luba.

"What's that?" I asked him.

"Moving lights for you and Sue-Ann," Joseph replied, and I could see Fred nodding like we were all on the same page, though we actually weren't, because although I was thinking it, I didn't bother asking for the technical description of how lights can move. Though I think I recalled something similar during my time with Hank's company, I'd put it in the rearview mirror at this point.

"So give 'em to him," I told Joseph.

"But there's...," he began to say before I cut him off.

"There is," I reminded him, then looked over to Fred, who appeared befuddled at my back-and-forth with the stage manager, who looked like his head was gonna explode as he began scribbling and erasing his way up and down the spreadsheet he had on the table. "You need 'em, you got 'em!" I said to the lighting designer while waving my hands at the ceiling in case he didn't get my French, to which he smiled in return and gave me a "*merci.*" Turning to Joseph, I held his hand and pointed at the mess he was making. "Relax, it's all on me," I told him, pointing at the spreadsheet. "Just make sure there's a line item in there for candy. We're gonna need lots of it," I added and despite my lightheartedness, he, unlike everyone else sitting at the table, wasn't smiling.

"Okay, we done?" I then asked, and slammed my hand against the table to gavel the confab closed, which had everyone around the table kind of weirded out that I was making the meeting quick and dirty. "Guys, you're not gonna teach me how to be a director in a day," I told them. "Either I'm pulling a rabbit out of a hat, or it'll be a fucking disaster," I added, then muttered to myself that in the latter case, I'd be glad to have proven everyone wrong for having been so adamant about choosing me to do it. "So, let's just get on with it," I said finally with another slap of my hand, which they took to mean I was actually serious and we were indeed done.

I'd wanted to add a "besides," but didn't as my mind was preoccupied with thoughts unrelated to anything they were there for. Well, not Chantal, who, when flipping through the cast photos on her tablet during her presentation, happened to conveniently land on the one of Sue-Ann dressed as Leah in her wedding gown and mercilessly left that image up for the duration of the meeting, pointed in my direction. I was nervous enough as it was walking in that morning, but having Sue-Ann looking out at me in that dress gave me palpitations. Shit, I forgot to tell you earlier. As difficult as the chat was with my mom, I didn't share the part where I told her about the debacle with Sue-Ann in front of her dad's *chateau*. Well, it just killed her, and you already know where I was on that front. Anyway, I knew it was all just unfinished business with her, Sue-Ann; I mean, because it would only be a matter of days before she and I would be in each other's presence again. How soon and how intimately, I couldn't have predicted.

Fuck, wait. That's a lie. Although I wasn't used to the whole director thing and being the person who makes the final decision, apparently, I did. After I'd adjourned the meeting and it was only me and Joseph left in the theatre, we then turned to the topic of scheduling rehearsals, which was when he showed me a color-coded schematic that I imagined made Operation Overlord look like something whipped up on the back of a napkin. As he presented my options for how we would get to curtain up in less than three weeks, I was already out of my chair and pacing the stage nervously while thinking about things non-related. I should have paid more attention because rather than easing me into the whole process—like, I dunno, maybe rehearsing the part where the *Miropoler Rebbe's* followers chat leisurely about the *Baal Shem Tov*[169] and his wonders before things start to kick into gear—Joseph took me at my word instead. I mean the point I'd made at the end of the meeting that we should just get on with it, which I think I intended as a rhetorical flourish more than anything else, but that he, unfortunately, took literally. All of which explains how the schedule ended up having me thrust into the heart of the lion's den on day one, directing the meat of the play dealing with the exorcism of the *dybbuk*.

Then again, I should maybe give him credit for the fact that he was perceptive enough to not stick me with Luba's B-team of male actors, the superstars you'll recall from the first day of rehearsals, who couldn't get a single line out of their mouths without messing up. Other than Faygen, of course, who scored aces, but that's beside the point. Regardless, Joseph knew they were a headache for Luba, whose patience was lacking at the best of times and would likewise be for me, whose bandwidth he keenly observed was wanting at best. All told, it seemed I'd made a decision, and I would see Sue-Ann a lot sooner than I had anticipated.

Joseph had no idea what was behind the look I gave him when we returned from break at the end of the day, after getting my feet wet taking Luba's place. But he was right to point out to his overzealous intern Francine that, despite what the official manual says, it was okay for her to just go with it and not shout out, "Thank you everyone, we're back!" to an empty theatre. Well, not exactly empty. There was Joseph; Francine; me; and Wendy, Luba's erstwhile translator whose services were no longer required, except that she was the sugar mamma. Despite our haggling over it, Joseph and I settled on the fact that although he didn't technically need her around anymore and therefore, she didn't require a seat at his table, I did. And since the candy came free, she would have a coveted seat specially reserved for her and the bags of goodies in the front row, not two steps away from the stage manager's table.

But I digress, as that's not what the look was about. What did have my brow furrowed was the fact that we weren't done, we were running on fumes, and rather than a return from a break, it should have been the end of the day. But it wasn't. Instead, while pulling the last of the day's

---

169. Rabbi Israel ben Eliezer, a.k.a. the *Baal Shem Tov*, the founder of Hasidism.

Twizzlers from the bag Wendy placed for me on the table and smarting over the fact that I didn't pay enough attention to the scheduling decisions I'd made, I watched as Sue-Ann walked back into the theatre and onto the stage, where we were now going to rehearse the last scene of the play, which called for the two of us to be alone together, intimately.

"Here goes nothing," I said under my breath to Joseph and Francine, who hadn't a clue, then tapped the table with my fist for courage before turning towards the stage where Sue-Ann was standing, script in hand, waiting for me and my instructions.

"I don't know my lines by heart yet for this part," she said softly and apologetically while staring at the floor, her fatigue palpable. The discomfort she must have felt at the moment's awkwardness, which I shared, was no less obvious.

"That's okay," I said gently while standing at the foot of the stage not more than a few feet from her, and tried to offer a smile, but she didn't see me. "We can just read the lines together if you'd like."

"I don't have the Yiddish yet either," she whispered.

"That's all right, too, you can do them in English," I replied. Although we'd already spent a good number of hours in rehearsal that day working other scenes, I was still keenly aware that despite the position of authority that had been handed to me, it only mattered so long as I had a cast ready and willing to follow along. And where she was concerned, I hadn't a clue where I stood. "Would you be comfortable with that?" I then asked, trying to get her to raise her head.

"Yeah," she said, lifting her gaze and although I wanted to believe it, I honestly couldn't tell whether she was grateful that I'd made the offer.

"Alright then," I said, then looked over my shoulder at Joseph and told him that he could chill, as we weren't gonna be doing any blocking, simply running the lines, to which he gave me a thumbs-up. "Whenever you're ready," I then said to Sue-Ann, and rested one leg on the stage, clasped my hands behind my back, and waited amidst the stillness and silence of the theatre for her to begin.

"Who's sighing like that," she soon said softly, as if it was only the two of us there together, and as she began reading Leah's lines from the script she held in her hands, I could see them starting to tremble.

"It is I," I replied by heart in Yiddish.

"I hear your voice, but I don't see you."

"You are fenced off from me by an invincible wall, an enchanted circle."

"Your voice sounds sweet as a violin moaning on a silent night. Tell me. Who are you?"

"I have forgotten. It is only through your thoughts that I can remember who I am."

"I'm beginning to remember. My heart was drawn toward a radiant star. On silent nights, I shed sweet tears and there was always a blurred figure in my dreams. Was that you?"

"Yes, I."

"I remember you. You had soft hair, as though touched by dew, and gentle, melancholy eyes. You had long, slender fingers. Awake or asleep, I thought only of you."

Sue-Ann then stopped, and it wasn't a secret to me as to why, as I knew the next lines she was going to speak. I didn't say anything to try and coax her along. If she was going to stop there, it would be what it would be.

She didn't.

"But you abandoned me..." she continued, and her voice suddenly modulated to a tone familiar to no one in the room other than me, "...and the light in me was dimmed, and my soul was overcast. Like a forsaken widow was I, so that an unfamiliar man approached me. And then you returned, and in my heart, there blossomed a life formed of death and joy formed of mourning. Why did you forsake me again?"

Although she read the lines while not once looking directly at me, I could tell from the drops of moisture gathering on the stage floor that she was struggling.

"I demolished all barriers and rose above death," I told her, offering Khonen's reply. "I defied the laws of time and ages. I struggled with the powerful, with the mighty, and with the merciless. And when the last spark of my strength was drained, I left your body in order to return to your soul."

"Come back to me, my bridegroom, my husband," she said, and if anyone was listening, they would have thought she was doing a fine job with the part. But I knew otherwise because the tears she was shedding, although suggestive of the dialogue and appropriate, were all too real and needed no cajoling from the words on the page. Indeed, the next lines Leah speaks had profound meaning to Sue-Ann personally, which only I could understand: "I will carry you, in death, in my heart. And in the dreams of the night, we will both rock our unborn children. We will sew them little shirts to wear and sing them lullabies:"

Hush, hush, little ones...
Without cradle, without clothes.
Dead you are and still unborn
Timeless and forever lost.

Although there were more lines for Leah to speak, on this day at least, Sue-Ann wasn't going to deliver them. "I can't do this," she said, then rushed off the stage and stormed out of the theatre, to the shock of everyone in the room but me. Despite feeling sure of what had just transpired and why, I was also aware that my gut could be completely wrong. As a result, I stood for a moment at the foot of the stage, my head bowed, my back to the others, taking a moment to collect myself before turning to face them. When I did, I could see Wendy wiping tears, Francine appeared baffled, and Joseph, who I knew was going to ask the question on everyone's mind: "Did she just..." but I cut him off before he went there.

"Of course not," I said to him, to them, and in an admonishing tone suggesting that she'd just upped and quit was preposterous. "She was moved by the words," I lied. "That's all it was." Even though I wanted to believe her storming out was due solely to the unfortunate confluence of fatigue with the profound lines from the play that struck a little too close to home, both of which were my fault but hopefully rectified by a good night's sleep, I wasn't so sure. I didn't say it to the others, but I shared their concern and was completely aware that we were, quite possibly, royally fucked.

———————————

I don't know that I'd be going out on a limb here by saying that all of us, *ex post facto* a royal fuck-up of our own creation, live with that gnawing feeling that we wish we hadn't. But it's measured in degrees, right? I'm not gonna ask you where you sit on the self-flagellation spectrum.

As for me, well, we're already well-schooled on where I land. Admittedly, the Trych was hard to brush aside as I sat in my bathrobe and my *zaide*'s slippers in the middle of my living room later that night, feverishly pulling the hair from my eyebrows while staring up at the hole I'd made in my wall days earlier. I could have talked to my doc about it, not the Trych, I don't mean, as she knows about that already, and it's been prescribed for. I'm referring to the hole, and if there was anything in the DSM that deals specifically with excessive rumination over a minor disruption in gyprock, along with the outsized significance a disordered individual such as myself would give it, as a reflection of my own incapacities, if not symbolic of fragilities and fallibilities similarly related. Shit, sorry: DSM, the Diagnostic and Statistical Manual of Mental Disorders.

Anyway, I didn't give her a ring; we already know why. Besides, even if she'd made house calls in response to the urgent, middle-of-the-night emails, I also already knew what her response would be to the fact that I'd taken to viewing the physical void I'd manufactured in the heart of my living space as a sort of *memento mori*. "Get back on the meds, or we're not talking," would likely have been quick off her tongue in response to my overdramatizing of the banal. And I know it wouldn't be helping my case much if I followed up shortly thereafter by telling her that, Latin macabre aside, my landlord with a yarmulke wasn't at all sympathetic when I explained to him that, in line with my recent decision to bring God closer to my heart, there was nothing to worry about, as the disruption in the surface of something he owned was my newly created *zeykher l'khurbn*[170] and therefore a holy, uh, hole. On all fronts, she likely would have turned her back on me and walked away, but not before either giving me the finger or telling me, "you're a fucking idiot." Probably both. I explained that she's from Brooklyn, right?

Honestly, I don't know what I would have done differently. I mean the hole, yes... but no... as staring at it invariably got me back to the play and not really the play, but Sue-Ann. I didn't blame her for quitting, if that's what she did when she rushed out of the theatre. I didn't know for sure because although I wanted to reach out, I'd already destroyed the simple mechanism by which to do so. Besides, the phone wouldn't have been of any use to me because she wouldn't have replied anyway. Moreover, as wired and mired in obsessive rumination as I was already deeply into, sending her an email only to pace and pull while awaiting a reply wouldn't have helped matters. You should know, the thought of

---

170. Reminder of the Temple's destruction.

writing had nothing to do with inquiring as to why she jumped ship. There could have been a myriad of reasons why, including the fact that for her, it was all about Luba, who knew her, and to paraphrase some old white man from I don't remember, I sir was no Luba. Correct. But no, the only reason my insides churned was that she simply wanted nothing to do with me. Without a word of a lie, all I wanted to do was compliment her on that day's rehearsal, not the part you already know about, but what transpired earlier, because she was nothing short of exquisite, and I felt she needed to hear it, even from a dilettante like me.

"What are *they* doing here?" I asked Joseph when I walked into the theatre on the day we started rehearsing again, only to find Faygen and the other *batlonim* standing on stage, apparently eagerly waiting to rehearse the top of Act Two. "I thought we agreed that we're skipping them?" I prodded him again as I stood at the stage manager's table where he was sitting next to his assistant, Francine, whose downward-facing gaze, along with Joseph's silence, was a clear sign that someone messed up; a fact confirmed when she started fidgeting and he didn't answer me, until he did.

"We sent out the wrong call sheet," he whispered apologetically, using manual speak for the email that got sent out listing who was coming in, who was not, what scene we were doing, etc.

"Well, that's just perfect," I said with no small amount of dismay and sarcasm in my voice, tinged with an anxiety that was not mine alone. The fact of the matter was that it had been over two weeks since we were last rehearsing with Luba, and the world had turned upside down in the interim. On paper, that doesn't seem like much of a hiatus, but in the world of mounting a play, it might as well have been a lifetime. All told, whatever momentum had been achieved before the tragedy was now effectively gone. Likewise, although they all called for me to take the helm on the day of Luba's funeral and expressed with every bit of confidence that I was going to get the job done in time for opening night, nobody had a crystal ball, and the nervous energy in the room as we began our journey into the unknown that day was palpable.

"So Khatzkl isn't late then," I said to my stage hands rhetorically, now that I knew the schedule was off. "Sue-Ann?" I followed up by asking Joseph directly, who couldn't confirm that he'd heard from her either. The truth was, given the blow-up outside her dad's place, I had no idea whether she'd be showing up that day or ever again. "Best-laid plans," I mouthed under my breath.

Then, don't ask me why because I couldn't explain to you, I naturally assumed Luba's position: Back to the actors, hands pressed firmly into the table like it was a giant stress ball, and head hung low in utter frustration, all before an actor uttered a single word. I guess the one bright spot in the first few minutes of my taking the helm was the family-sized bag of Skittles that soon found its way to the table courtesy of Wendy, who was sitting calmly the whole time in the first row nearby, saying nothing but waiting for the right moment to pull the trigger. And it was now.

"Thank you," I told her as I tore the bag open and dumped a handful into my mouth before turning to face the headache on stage that I knew was imminent. "Nice set, huh?" I mumbled with my mouth full to Faygen and his pals, who looked as dumb as I must have sounded, standing there on stage, lifeless, scripts in hand, waiting for me to tell them what to do. While each of them looked around and grunted some form of acknowledgment at my comment about Mack's craftsmanship, Faygen knew better and kept his gaze focused on me while mouthing an inaudible "are you okay?" in response to what he instinctively knew was a stalling tactic on my part. I shrugged, as it was too soon to know.

"Is it all right where I'm standing?" George, the diminutive fellow with the awful stammer, who just happens to speak the first lines of the second half of the play, then asked me eagerly in anticipation of getting a chance to kick things off. Even though I actually wanted to tell him that he could disappear behind the *oren koydesh* for all I cared, I held my tongue. However, I did make a note to tell Joseph that we were definitely giving the opening line of Act Two to one of the other champs.

"Why don't you guys just sit at the table and let me hear you read the lines," is what I actually said, and they dutifully obliged. I won't bore you with the description of the little table read that ensued as the lines in the play they then started mangling, whereby the followers of the *Miropoler Rebbe* share tales with each other about the *Baal Shem Tov* are about as exciting as you might expect it would be sitting *baym rebn's tish*[171] listening to fanciful tales, hungry as hell and waiting for the

---

171. The festive table of a Hasidic rabbi.

mashke[172] to start flowing. Besides, as soon as George started us off, butchering his one line about a rock sitting atop a high mountain at the end of the world, from which a spring of clear water flows, my mind was already elsewhere. Specifically, thinking about what I was going to do once Khatzkl arrived, as I hadn't a clue and the fear of failure that I knew was incoming had me so consumed, that it took Joseph to get up from his chair and poke me in the shoulder to get me back in the game.

"What is it?" I asked him when he was standing beside me.

"Faygen's been calling out your name, and you didn't respond," he said quietly, looking at me concerned.

"Something wrong?" I asked him, then looked to Faygen for confirmation of the same.

"Nokhem isn't here," Faygen said to me with a look of concern while Joseph skulked back to his chair.

"*Ma nishtana?*"[173] I answered him caustically, but clearly didn't get what he was trying to tell me.

"It's his monologue now," he responded.

"So, skip it," I replied curtly, and judging by the look he gave me, he made no attempt to hide that I wasn't delivering well on the first day at the job.

"Fine, I'll do it," I said churlishly, and without turning back to see that he was already out of his seat again and *en route* to bring me a script, I raised my hand to wave Joseph off, as there was no need. Indeed, regardless of the mess that was going on up there, when it came to the lines in the play, they flowed like clear spring water out of a rock at the top of a mountain at the end of the world. "The holiest and most sacred place in the world is the Land of Israel," I began the monologue in Yiddish while standing with one foot on the stage, facing the actors, my hands clasped behind my back, my eyes closed:

> In the Land of Israel, the holiest city is Jerusalem.
> In Jerusalem, the holiest place was the Temple,
> and the holiest place in the Temple was the Holy of Holies....

"You speak a beautiful Yiddish," I then heard Khatzkl say. "From Luba?"

---

172. Whisky.
173. "How is this night different?" See Passover seder.

"My *zaide*," I answered, then turned around and girded myself for the uncomfortable conversation I expected was about to unfold, only to find him sitting in the first row next to Wendy, smiling, already partaking from her stash of the good stuff. Now, whether it was the sound of what he'd just heard coming out of my mouth or the candy bar he was making quick work of, he seemed impressed, which wasn't a good sign. Why didn't he tell me to go on, with the monologue I mean, as we both knew it was incomplete? More to the point, why wasn't he ripping me a new one for speaking his lines when he was already in the room? Between you and me, I didn't even know where to begin telling him that the script we were working from was a bastardized version of the one he would have been familiar with; a bargain Luba made with the devil—Nokhem, that is—who you'll recall took the better part of the monologue for himself as his pound of flesh for agreeing to be in the play. But I got nothing incoming from my *Miropoler Rebbe*, who didn't seem the least bit fazed by any of it.

"*Zeyer sheyn*"[174] is all he said, a short compliment apropos of I'm not quite sure what, as he'd already turned his attention to what he'd hoover next from Wendy's loot bag, which I took as an ominous sign of things to come that actually didn't take long to manifest and be put on full display for all to see.

"Gimme the line!" Khatzkl called out in frustration a short while later, after I thanked the *batlonim* for their good work and immediately dove in to rehearsing the scene in Act Two when Leah's father, Reb Sender, comes to see the great *Miropoler Rebbe* to plead for his help with regard to his daughter who's been possessed by a *dybbuk*. It wouldn't have been much of a thing that he was calling to be prompted for his line, what with the history of theatre all but synonymous with the role of prompters feeding mindless actors lines they should have memorized. Except that in this case, it was the very first line he speaks, a fact I gently reminded him of while standing at the stage manager's table doing my job.

"I know that!" he snapped at me. "Just give it to me."

"Khatzkl, you know it's okay to have script in hand, right?" I said to him, continuing to do my best...and motioned subtly to Joseph with my

---

174. Lovely.

finger that he not come to the big man's aid by calling out the line. "It's rehearsal after all," I added, but he would hear nothing of it.

"*Yingele!*" he shouted to me from the stage where he was seated at the table among the *batlonim*, who were now playing the roles of his Hasidim, while Luba's accountant, playing Reb Sender, stood nearby. "I know this play like the back of my hand," he continued, waving me off. "The line, please!"

"Sender of Brinnitz, I know," I said to him softly, feeding him his dialogue. I then previewed for him that the next thing he does is turn to his Hasidim and asks that he be left alone with his distraught guest.

"Right, thank you," Khatzkl said, then cleared his throat and in a deep, resonant voice, proceeded to repeat my words exactly, which I think is a classic sign of some stage of dementia, which one I couldn't say, but all bad to be sure. He then gestured to Faygen and the others with his finger. "Leave us alone," he instructed them, and waved for the actors to do just that. Although they all hesitated and looked at me to make sure what he said was what I wanted, I didn't interfere. I nodded in agreement that they should, in fact, get the fuck off the stage so that I could see what was gonna happen next, as I wanted to make sure they weren't collateral damage in whatever disaster might be forthcoming.

It wasn't what I was expecting, I'm sure you can imagine. But then again, the legend of the man was implanted in me a lifetime earlier, and when it caught up with the present-day reality of an obese, geriatric actor seemingly on the cusp of losing his mind and demonstrating as much before my eyes, well..."Lovely, *nokh dus darf ikh hubn,*"[175] I muttered sarcastically under my breath while standing at the stage manager's table. Although I was in no mood to translate, I thankfully didn't need to, because without saying as much, I could see that Joseph and Francine weren't expecting this additional challenge on their plates either. Frankly, it was touch-and-go as we sputtered out of the gate, with every second line requiring a feeding that had even the usually stoic accountant playing Reb Sender growing impatient. "Thank you," I said to him in advance when I asked that he start again so that our esteemed *Miropoler Rebbe* could hopefully get into a groove.

"*Rebbe*, I've come to you for help!" the accountant said his line excitedly, and I was grateful for his energy, despite the stressful situation.

---

175. I need it like a hole in the head.

"Me?" Khatzkl replied to him. "Why would you come to me when there is no me to come to?"

No shit, I caught myself pondering, but I quickly realized I had to jump in again. "I can't anymore!" I shouted to Khatzkl when he was late on his next cue.

"What are you yelling for, *yingele*? Can't you see we're rehearsing?" he shot back, oblivious.

"Not me, Khatzkl," I said. "You! That's your line," though it might as well have been mine. "You say 'I can't anymore' in response to his pleading with you to help save his daughter."

"Yes, you're right. I'm sorry," he said before clearing his throat again. "I can't anymore, Reb Sender, I can't!"

"But *Rebbe*," Reb Sender then said. "You mustn't forget those generations of holy men who can support you," he continued, and suddenly the Khatzkl I was expecting decided to show up.

"Yes," he began to speak. Although I softly mouthed the words along with him, he thankfully didn't need the training wheels anymore, because as soon as he stood to deliver his response to Reb Sender, an actor suddenly appeared, and for the moment at least, he was off to the races. "My grandfather, the great Reb Velvele, the *Baal Shem Tov's* friend," he said while beginning to pace the stage, as if with each step he took, he was starting to mark his territory and taking command of his space. "He would exorcise a *dybbuk* without a spell or an incantation," he continued. "He could cast a *dybbuk* out with one giant shout!" he shouted to Reb Sender in a voice so resounding that the room reverberated. But then, just as quickly, the actor in him knew instinctively to return to where he was sitting and to invite the other actor to join him before delivering the next line quietly, with honesty and sincerity: "In difficult times I turn to him and he sustains me," he said. "He will not forsake me now. How did this happen, Reb Sender?"

"Before they were going to lead her under the canopy," Reb Sender replied.

"That's not my question. What could have caused this calamity? For when a worm penetrates a fruit, it begins to rot from the inside."

"*Rebbe*, my child is a pious soul. She is modest and obedient."

"Indeed," Khatzkl said to him. "But children are sometimes punished for the sins of their parents. Has anyone asked the *dybbuk* who he is and why he has attached himself to your daughter?"

CHIRP!

"Wait, stop!" I interrupted the two of them and rushed to the foot of the stage like a man, uh, possessed. "Say that again!" I then shouted, and I could feel my heart starting to beat faster.

"What again?" Khatzkl asked me, nonplussed.

"Your line," I replied. "Say it again!"

"Which line?"

"About the children!"

"You mean, children are sometimes punished for the sins of their parents?" he asked, and looked at me cockeyed.

"Yeah, that one. Again!"

"Why? I just said it."

"I just need to hear it again."

And he did as I asked.

"Again, please!" I insisted.

"You want me to say it differently, maybe?" he asked me, still perplexed. "I don't understand?"

"No, just say it! Say it!" I shouted breathlessly while waving my hand at him frantically.

"*Yingele*, are you alright? Is there something wrong with the line?"

"Yeah. Fine. No. Nothing wrong with the line," I rambled because suddenly my heart stopped racing, and the moment was gone. "It's fine, just perfect," I said calmly now. "Go on, sorry," I added, and returned to the stage manager's table.

CHIRP!

"Are you sure?" Khatzkl asked me, rightfully, I suppose.

No, I wasn't sure.

"Yeah, please don't stop," I said anyway, then leaned against the table to catch my breath.

"Did you know the young man?" Khatzkl now spoke to Reb Sender, though his attention was still focused on me.

"Yes, he used to come to my house for meals."

"Perhaps you offended him, humiliated him?" Khatzkl replied, returning his focus now to Reb Sender. "Try to remember!"

"I don't know, *Rebbe*, I don't remember!"

CHIRP!

"Very well," Khatzkl then said, but for a reason that I can't explain, so did I. "Bring in the maiden!" the both of us then shouted, and as dramatic as the scene in the theatre now became, what with everyone looking at me to ascertain what on earth was going on, the moment only ratcheted up a notch or twelve when Sue-Ann arrived, as if on cue, just in time for her entrance into the scene as Leah, possessed by Khonen's *dybbuk*.

I thought of Luba at that moment and wondered if I knew her at all. The way she handled things that were planned but not so much, whether she would have thrown caution to the wind, motioned for Sue-Ann to hop onto the stage, and called for the scene to continue, regardless of Luba never having rehearsed everyone together yet. I didn't go there, instead telling Joseph to call for five because although I knew this moment was coming—I scheduled it after all—Sue-Ann walking into the theatre meant something different for me than anyone else in the room that day, and I wasn't ready for it.

You know that feeling when you start to panic, and you wonder if everyone around you can see it all unraveling in real time the way you do? Right. So, you'll believe me when I tell you that I found myself tethered to the stage manager's table, unable to move, as Sue-Ann began making her way into the theatre. I could only tell you that I could hear the sound as she dropped her things on a seat in the front row near Wendy and didn't see it with my own eyes, because for some reason, they were fixed on my shoes again. I couldn't tell you whether she was looking at me in that way of hers, which on the first day of rehearsal, caused me to react similarly. I just assumed and didn't have the courage to keep my head up in case she was, and as a result, I felt pathetic because, despite the nadir in our relations, I was actually glad to see her, so to speak. Turns out I wasn't the only one, what with a room full of men who delighted in the energy she suddenly brought into it. None more so than Khatkzl, who immediately bounded off the stage and introduced himself in a way that I suppose one could describe as cute, maybe funny, perhaps creative, but given how graphically anatomical it was, I'll just leave it at not telling you more.

"You okay?" Faygen whispered to me after he came over while the men huddled around Sue-Ann to check in on me, and took my hand away from my face, where I was starting to pull.

"Dunno," I said, and I don't think I lifted my gaze when I did, as I wasn't sure if he was referring to what had just transpired on stage or the sudden entrance of my kryptonite, though I suspected the latter.

"It's *your* room now, you know," he said to motivate me.

"I know," I said sheepishly.

"Hey, look at me," he said, putting his finger under my chin and lifting it. "You've got this, okay?" he asked rhetorically while nodding simultaneously.

"Okay," I replied without any confidence whatsoever.

"Whatever you're feeling is right; trust it, and just tell us what to do," he said, then kissed me on the head and left me alone.

A few seconds later, Joseph announced to everyone that we were back from break, then took his seat at the stage manager's table and gave me the floor. It was quiet for a few moments as I opened the bag of jujubes Wendy had quietly placed on the table for me during the break, then took a handful and popped one in my mouth before speaking.

"Good work so far, *khevre,*" I began to address them. As much as it pained me to see that of all the faces I was looking out at, the only one whose gaze was focused downward and not at me was Sue-Ann's, I concentrated instead on Faygen's words of encouragement. I told the actors what I wanted to accomplish next with the ex-communication scene. When I was done and the actors began to take their places on stage, Joseph reminded Sue-Ann as she passed by the table that having a script in hand was okay. "All good," she said confidently without acknowledging me at all. "I'm ready," she added before hopping onto the stage and taking a seat next to Khatzkl, who kicked the scene off from where we'd left it when he called for Leah to be brought in to see him.

"*Dybbuk!*" he shouted to Sue-Ann, while the actor playing Reb Sender stood nearby. "Tell us who you are!"

And true to her word, she was ready.

"*Miropoler Rebbe,*" she said to him in a Yiddish that rolled perfectly off her tongue and in a brooding, haunting tone that sent chills. "You know exactly who I am," she added, staring at him confidently and with a defiance that was pitch-perfect.

"Why did you enter the maiden?" he then asked.

"I am her intended," she answered while standing to face him directly...but she wasn't the only one who spoke the line.

CHIRP! CHIRP!

"According to the law of our sacred Torah, a dead person is forbidden to be among the living," Khatzkl said to her admonishingly.

"You must leave the body of this maiden and exit the world of the living."

"I will not leave!" we shot back.

"I command you a second time!" he shouted at her.

"Mr. Seal," I suddenly heard my voice ringing in my head while watching Sue-Ann speak as she began circling Khatzkl, "I know how powerful you are, but you can't control me." I then heard her again: "I have no place to go. All roads are blocked for me, and all gates are shut. There is a heaven, an earth, and endless worlds, but there is no place for me." The voice in my head, my voice, returned again: "And now that my embittered, tormented soul has found its refuge, you want to rid me of my destiny?" And just as quickly as it arrived, it departed, and I could hear Sue-Ann speak: "Have pity! Do not pursue me, do not conspire against me."

CHIRP! CHIRP!

"I do pity you," I now heard Mr. Seal's voice mocking me as I watched Khatzkl's lips move, and I could feel my knees buckling. "You're pathetic, poor, and mentally unstable," he continued attacking me. "You're a totally unfit match for my daughter, who deserves the best."

"I will not leave her!" I shouted and saw Leah doing the same at the *Rebbe* on stage.

"*Dybbuk*!" Khatzkl scolded Sue-Ann as they stood face-to-face like two prize fighters in the ring, and pointed his finger at her. "In the name of almighty God, I command you, for the last time, to leave the maiden!"

"Mr. Seal," I heard myself say threateningly as I watched Sue-Ann bring her face directly up against Khatzkl's, all the while striking a terrifying but perfectly realized pose of someone whose body has been overtaken by otherworldly forces. "In the name of the almighty God," I heard myself continue as Sue-Ann's lips moved in synchronicity to my words, "I am bound to my intended bride and will remain with her for eternity."

CHIRP! CHIRP!

"Izzy," I soon heard Joseph's voice whispering my name as he nudged my arm gently.

"What?" I asked him.

"You okay?"

"Yeah, why?"

258

"You didn't answer about Reb Shimshon," he said, and admittedly, at first, I had no fucking clue what he was talking about and told him so.

"What the fuck are you talking about?" I asked, losing track of where we'd arrived in the scene.

"What should we do about Reb Shimshon?" he then asked me, and as I looked at him, at Francine sitting by his side and then to the actors on stage, all of whom staring back out at the stage manager's table, it became apparent that they'd been waiting on an answer while I must have been M.I.A.

Clearly, they'd gotten past the part where the *Rebbe*, in a standoff with the recalcitrant *dybbuk*, tells Reb Sender to take his possessed daughter away and return with a *minyan*[176] of men, who are to bring with them seven black candles and an equal amount of ram's horns, as well as a duo of judges and a rabbi, the aforementioned Reb Shimshon. The latter, being the Chief Rabbi of the town of Miropol, who the *Rebbe* then asks for permission to carry out the gravest possible means of exorcising the *dybbuk*... excommunication. But for our production, there was no Reb Shimshon.

"She never fucking cast a Reb Shimshon?" I asked Joseph in exasperation about Luba, and when he nodded in the affirmative, I just gasped and looked to the ceiling in frustration. "And I'm only learning about this now... because?" I asked him kinda, sorta, but not really rhetorically, and in any event, he didn't bother trying to come up with an answer because it was pointless. We were stuck.

"I can do it!" Faygen called out excitedly from the stage. "I know the lines!"

"Of course you do," I muttered to myself, because although he was correct, as always, he wasn't the right choice. Regardless, I was up a creek without a paddle.

"Fine, go ahead!" I shouted back at him, and waved my hand for him to just get on with it. I then took the bag of jujubes and started pacing the floor in front of the stage, listening as the two rabbis come to an agreement on how to handle the ex-communication, all the while tossing pieces of candy into the air for me to catch with my mouth, which I guess was my way of avoiding the troublesome fact that it was one thing for Faygen to read Reb Shimshon's lines in rehearsal, it was a fucking

---

176. Quorum.

disaster to think that he could play the part for real on stage. I'd say I went fifty-fifty with the candy. While on stage, they not only discussed exorcising the *dybbuk*, but also the fact that Reb Shimshon couldn't get any sleep the night prior because the ghost of Khonen's dead father, Nissen Ben Rivke, came to him to accuse Leah's father, Reb Sender, of being guilty of his son's death and calling him to a *beit din*[177] so that he can have justice done on his behalf.

"Although I am the spiritual leader of the community," Reb Shimshon says to the *Rebbe*, "I'd ask that you serve as the Chief Judge in the trial."

"Very well, I agree," I heard Khatzkl's voice replying to Faygen, then suddenly stopped dead in my tracks when he offered his follow-up. "I shall postpone the exorcism of the *dybbuk* through ex-communication, and we shall summon the deceased to a trial..."

"No, we're not doing that!" I shouted while thrusting the wrong hand in their direction, causing what remained of the candy to fly onto the stage. "Just keep going," I added, and turned my finger in a circle for emphasis as I didn't want to address the immediate issue of my gaffe nor get into a discussion of the trial, which was a whole kettle of fish I had no idea what to do with. Neither did Luba, by the way. "We've got good momentum going," I lied, and while *en route* back to the stage manager's table, I crossed paths with Francine, who, for some reason, had a dustpan and brush at the ready to clean up my mess lying at the actor's feet.

"Let's just get me out of Sue-Ann and call it a day," I then thought I heard myself say out loud, which maybe I didn't as it seems my instruction to keep going with the ex-communication was heeded without objection and all the actors assembled began getting into position to continue through to the end of the scene. Meanwhile, as Khatzkl called for the maiden to be brought back into the *Rebbe*'s study, Wendy quietly slid a fresh bag of jujubes onto the stage manager's table near where I was leaning on my hand and offered me a thumbs-up. Bless her heart.

"*Dybbuk*!" Khatzkl called out to Sue-Ann as she re-entered the scene, his booming voice reverberating through the theatre more profoundly than I'd heard it up until that moment, and rightfully so as the scene was reaching its momentous crescendo. "In the name of the

---

177. Jewish court of law.

spiritual rulers of this community and the holy assembly of men that surround me," he said, motioning dramatically to the men who were gathered around him, "and in the name of the Great Sanhedrin of Jerusalem," he continued, his voice growing more robust and increasingly thunderous as he now stretched his arms wide like Moses summoning the power of God to part the Red Sea: "In the name of all the forebears and the great spirits of Israel, I, Azriel ben Hadas, order you for the last time to leave the body of the maiden, Leah bas Khana!"

CHIRP! CHIRP!

"I will not leave!" I shouted back as Sue-Ann lunged at him, only to be stopped by the men protecting the *Rebbe*.

"Don the shrouds and light the black candles," Khatzkl now spoke to the men, addressing them sternly and in a tone that echoed the gravity of the moment. "Cover the holy ark with a black curtain and take the ram's horns in hand," he continued while holding his gaze on Sue-Ann, who was lashing out and using every ounce of energy in her beautiful body to try and extricate herself from the grasp of the men holding her back from lunging at the *Miropoler Rebbe*.

CHIRP! CHIRP!

"You're a fool, Izzy!" I now heard Mr. Seal's voice mocking and laughing at me as I watched Khatzkl take a few paces in the opposite direction of the demon in his midst. "Since you refuse to obey my command," he continued while Khatzkl had his back turned like he was hiding something that would only now be revealed, "I deliver you into the hands of the evil spirits who will expel you by force from my daughter." Khatzkl then turned on a dime and with a spectacular thrust of his arm in the direction of the possessed Leah, called for the *shofars* to be sounded. "*Tekia*!" he screamed, and all the men blew into their ram's horns simultaneously, creating a single, unified deafening blast that sounded otherworldly.

CHIRP! CHIRP!

"Leave me alone!" I yelled as Sue-Ann thrashed about ever more emphatically. "Stop pulling me!" she shouted at the men. "I don't want to go!" I yelled. "I can't go!" she called similarly.

"Since the spirits of the upper spheres cannot overpower you," Seal's voice rang out again, "I entrust you into the hands of the dark spirits of the nether worlds so that they shall drive you out!" Khatzkl, again with his arm outstretched masterfully, now called for the *shofars* to be blown a second time. "*Shvorim!*" he yelled, and the men blew three times into their ram's horns.

"Woe is me!" Sue-Ann shouted in response, her body convulsing as if to physically illustrate the exorcism of Khonen's soul from Leah's body taking effect. "All the powers of the world have been arrayed against me and are commanding me to depart," she added, but I could only hear my voice shouting the rest of her line: "But as long as a single spark of strength remains within me, I will struggle and I will not leave!"

CHIRP! CHIRP!

"With the power of almighty God," Seal shrieked again in my ear, "and with the supreme authority of the holy Torah," Khatzkl's voice boomed equally as loud, "we tear asunder every thread that binds you to the living world and to the body of the maiden, Leah bas Khana, and the soul of my daughter, Sue-Ann!"

"Woe is me!" she and I shouted.

"And we excommunicate you from the people of Israel!" Khatzkl shouted, and Seal cackled, before the *Miropoler Rebbe* beseeched the holy assembly of men to expunge Khonen's soul from Leah's body with a final, dramatic sound of the *shofar*: "*Teruah!*" he commanded them. They obliged with nine pulsating blasts of the ram's horns.

"Ahhhh!" I then heard both mine and Sue-Ann's voices yell just before they melded one last time. "I can't struggle any longer," she shouted in English as I joined her in Yiddish: "*Ikh ken zikh mer nisht ranglen!*"

CHIRP! CHIRP! CHIRP!

———————

I know we get labeled a lot for conflating, overdramatizing, and even making shit up. But please believe me when I tell you that the confounded sound was louder than I'd ever heard. And it wouldn't let up. Not even after it woke me up abruptly, causing me to fall off my couch in my living room, where I guess I eventually caught some z's. Although I'd observed from previous instances that, as frightening as this manifestation of my mind was—and I think that's what it was—it eventually flew away, this time was different. The sound never subsided as a minute clocked to five, then to fifteen, to thirty, and even longer. Not when I ran to the other end of the hallway in my apartment and into the bathroom, where I slammed the door shut before cowering in the tub, because there, it was even louder. My bedroom was exponentially worse. The fucking thing was everywhere. That is until I fought back. Kinda. Without any regard to the fact that I was still naked, wearing nothing but my bathrobe and my zaide's slippers, I decided to eventually come out from under my blankets and take to the streets to find it and...well. Actually, my living room is as far as I got, where I was stopped cold and nearly leapt out of my skin because that's where it was: just outside the window, its bulging eye darting back and forth, covering the whole damned thing from side to side and top to bottom. Whether it was taking place in the living room or in my head, I couldn't honestly say, but either way, a cacophony erupted then and there as I confronted it as it fixed its gaze squarely on me, all the while continuing its shrieking. "What are you?" I yelled at it in a primal and subconscious voice that erupted out of me. "What do you want?!" I continued.

I began throwing pillows at the window. It was the strongest course of action I could take in that moment, hoping it would fly the fuck away.

"You're not real! Go away!" I shouted over and over until I was out of ammunition. And eventually it did, if only briefly. For despite the fact that it had grown eerily silent in a heartbeat, the next thing I knew I was taking steps backward and holding my breath for dear life as I watched my window opening, and what soon appeared on my ledge out the blackness of the night sky was the tip of a wing that rested on the ledge and began motioning for me to approach. What unearthly powers motivated me to heed its call, I honestly couldn't say. Yet I soon found myself, bathrobe, slippers, and all, climbing out of my apartment through my living room window and onto the wing of an immense creature that waited patiently as I walked up its wing and onto its back before taking flight into the night sky.

I know what you're probably thinking. Let me disabuse you however, of any of fantasy-infused, cinematic *narishkeit* that probably sees me soaring above and in and out of the clouds, hair waving in the wind, smiling while observing the world from a magical, enviable vantage point, with the whole montage dramatically heightened by a heavenly orchestral score. Yeah, it was like none of that. In fact, I couldn't tell you what anything looked like, or how long the ride took, because as best I can recall, my eyes were shut tight the whole time for fear of shitting my pants, or I dunno, maybe falling off the back of a giant flying creature, only to fall splat onto the ground to an ignominious death. But the thing did eventually touch down, and while I certainly did wonder where the trip would end up taking me, the final destination wasn't anywhere I expected we would land.

In spite of the fact that it was pitch-black outside and I couldn't see two feet in front of me, from the moment I walked down from the bird's wing and felt the gravel beneath my feet, I knew exactly where I was. In fact, my mind immediately became awash with a flood of thoughts, memories, and emotions associated with the place we had arrived to, that I didn't even notice that the bird had flown away. I couldn't tell you what did it because it wasn't my own initiative, yet despite my reluctance to move even one inch from where I stood, an energy soon propelled me forward. Although hesitant at first, my feet soon felt like they were floating as I began to retrace an all-too-familiar path, one that I couldn't bring myself to tread for nearly two decades. And yet, despite the darkness, I knew my surroundings intimately. Kneeling to pick up a few pebbles, I counted the exact steps I knew I had to take before turning into the row to my right. There, three gravestones in, my eyes began to well up as I placed a stone on the grave whose inscription I couldn't read for the darkness but knew by heart. It speaks of a woman, a mother and grandmother, a teacher who lived a life according to the highest ethical and moral values, with a profound commitment to seeing the beauty in all that is life. A devoted daughter of *Vilne*...my *bubbe*. Next to her lay the man with absolute love and devotion to the woman he couldn't have imagined a life without, which was inscribed by my mother on his stone. In addition, a message left for me and anyone who should come across it evermore, that they should know: Here lay a Jewish man, dedicated to family, social justice, to the Yiddish language, and the world from which it sprung. A devoted son, a father, a grandfather, a brother, an uncle. A leader of youth and a lifelong Bundist.

To my eyes, however, the only thing I ever saw written there was, "my *zaide*."

"I'm sorry *zaide*," I whispered to him in Yiddish through quivering lips, the pangs of guilt starting to stab as I stood before him for the first time since the day I watched them lower him into the ground. At the same time, the memory of Faygen having to hold me back that day as I shouted and lunged at everyone for having taken him too soon now rushed to the fore and punched me in the gut as well. "Forgive me," came next. Whether I was consciously apologizing for my inexplicable absence since then, for what I did dishonoring him that day, or for my own perceived lifelong failure in carrying out the legacy he left me, I'm not sure right now. Let's just agree that we'll discuss it some other time, because the dam had broken and a river of pain and emotion, suppressed by a lifetime of diagnoses, medications, and interventions from those who had no clue, started raining down my face and watering the flowers in the dirt that separated us.

I can't tell you how long it lasted. Amidst the pitch-black darkness of that night, when the light of the moon wouldn't penetrate the heavy clouds that hung low, combined with the quiet ethereal surroundings, but for me and my tearful eruption, I couldn't make sense of time and space. It also took me a while to capture the thoughts I wanted to share with him. As I searched, I fought off the fact that I was starting to get upset with myself, because I understood at that moment that if like my mother, I'd visited regularly, I wouldn't be struggling. He'd be up to date. Truthfully, if not for that place, at that moment, I'd have brushed off such *narishkeit*. If only for a moment however, I understood why my mother, despite how emotionally painful it could be, visited as often as she did. I, on the other hand, never could. I began to despair that on top of all of this, I didn't want to embarrass myself in front of my *zaide* for not knowing what to say. Eventually, I just blurted out what was top of mind and hoped he wouldn't judge me for it.

"I met someone, *zaide*," I began to say, and couldn't without crying again. "I like her a lot," I continued, "but I'm afraid I'm going to lose her if I haven't already." Yes, after twenty years, that's what came to mind. I then described to him everything about Sue-Ann that made me feel like, for the first time in my life, I understood what it meant to be alive. "She's special, *zaide*, but I don't deserve her." I went on to tell him that Faygen had told her a lot about my *zaide*, what kind of man he was, the high regard he had for him, and how in his mind, I guess, I was the distillation of all of that he was. "I'm trying, *zaide*, but I'm failing," I said to him with a whimper. "I'm failing you."

Just then, its shadow appeared overhead, a shadow that could only have been visible given the availability of light. And now there was because the clouds suddenly parted just enough for the moon to appear, full and bright, so that I could finally see it for the first time. And there it was, sitting high atop a tree just outside the cemetery, not more than twenty feet away.

"Is that...?" I asked out loud, and suddenly I heard my *zaide*'s voice, as I heard it nearly every night as a child, when he tucked me into bed and sang me Yiddish songs and lullabies. This one, written by Itzik Manger, was his favorite:

> And the Golden Peacock flew Eastward,
> In search of yesteryears,
> In the hills, encountering an old Turk
> On an old white nag, she asks:
> "Any chance that you've seen the yesteryears?"
> Furrowing his brow and giving it thought,
> "Yesteryears haven't seen, nor heard," he declares.
> And yanks the reins and shouts to the nag.
> His laughter resounding in the hills,
> "A golden bird, and such a fool!"

"Sing with me, *Itzik!*" I then heard my *zaide* say to me in Yiddish, and as I continued staring out in wonder at the indescribable creature glowing in the night, looking down upon us with its golden plumage in full expanse, I joined him.

> So the Golden Peacock flew North,
> In search of yesteryears.
> At the seashore, a fisherman, spreading his nets,
> While singing a rhyme, she asks: "Any chance that you've seen the
> yesteryears?"
> Furrowing his brow and giving it thought,
> "Yesteryears...never seen, nor heard," he declares.
> And ends his song, tra,la, la la...
> "A golden bird, and such a fool!"

> And the Golden Peacock flew Southward,
> In search of the yesteryears.
> Seeing a Black man in the field,
> Mending his tattered shelter, she asks:
> "Any chance that you've seen the yesteryears?"
> With a toothy grin, he answers, "Huh?
> A golden bird, and such a fool!"

As the last verse approached, however, I couldn't bring myself to sing along anymore.

> And the Golden Peacock flew Westward
> In search of the yesteryears.
> There...
> Kneeling beside a grave,
> Dressed in black, exhausted, depressed,
> A woman...
> But the Peacock asks nothing,
> For she herself knows,
> That the woman in mourning,
> Keening over the grave, at the side of the road...
> Is the widow of the yesteryears.

"*Zaide*," I said to him, weeping. "It's so sad."

"It's not," he answered.

"I don't understand?"

"Is that how the song has to end?" he asked me in the same Socratic way he did, when as a child we would have these little chats and I could hear a smile in his voice when he did.

"I suppose it doesn't," I replied, although my answer mainly was me thinking out loud.

"*Itzikl*," he said to me in a loving voice. "You're writing the next verse as we speak...and it's beautiful."

"*Zaide?*"

"By living every day, the way you think and what you believe. It's in the play you're directing. You're telling the story and passing it on."

I hesitated momentarily as he mentioned the play, and I wondered..."*Di goldene keyt?*" I eventually said.

"That's right," he answered regarding my reference to the golden chain of Jewish history that he taught me from the earliest to understand and solidify. "*Bist a mentsh Itzikl, bist a guter yid*," he then said, repeating his dying words to me but turning them ever so slightly to confirm that the charge he left me to accomplish throughout my lifetime, to be both an upstanding citizen of the world and a respectful Jew, had been achieved.

"*Zaide*, am I the bird? I asked him. "The golden peacock, is it me?"

There was no answer.

"*Zaide*?" I asked again.

I looked up to the top of the tree to see if the bird was still there. It was gone and suddenly, so too was the moon, and it was once again dark and quiet. In the silence, rather than leave, I chose to lay on the grass next to the flowerbed above my grandparents' graves, planted by my mother every year with the perennials taken from the garden that my *zaide* had built for her. As my eyes began to flutter and the somnolence arrived swiftly, I rested my head next to my *zaide*'s and wrapped my arm around his grave.

"I miss you," I whispered to him before falling asleep.

14

It had been forever and a day since I'd last walked onto a campus, so I'd forgotten that there's something different in the air. Yeah, sure, the weed. But that's not different, just more of it wafting. And I don't go in for all that rarefied *narishkeit*, so that we can skip. The ivy? The oak? Maybe and possibly. Could also be the nubility and the smell of the sweat chasing after it. I can't say for certain. Maybe all of the above. But you know what I'm talking about; it's just different. Kind of uplifting, but I dunno, I could be full of it. The truth? I think I was just thankful to be alive.

Not a word of a lie.

On the morning following my visit to my *zaide*, what woke me up wasn't the cooing of the pigeons on his grave, or the chirping of birds of a different feather in the tree not twenty feet away. Instead, it was the guy on the tractor minding his business while mowing the lawn in the rows between stones, who quite rightfully wasn't expecting the head of someone lying naked except for an open bathrobe and slippers in his path. Mercifully, he managed to avoid slicing my head off by swerving just in time, which resulted in him crashing his John Deere into the Finkelsteins behind my *bubbe* and *zaide*. Although I offered to help the custodian get the blade cutter unstuck from the dirt above the dead, after I'd gotten up and cinched the belt to my bathrobe, he was having none of it.

Actually, besides sharing a few choice words with me that you can guess the order of for yourself, though they revolved around the theme of what kind of deranged individual falls asleep naked by a graveside, he didn't make any phone calls or do anything to hasten my exit from the sacred grounds. For that, I was grateful.

In fact, he simply watched in curiosity as I took a few moments to say goodbye to my *bubbe* and *zaide*, with a promise to them that I would return again, and often, before spending some time walking the rows and visiting the plots where their friends lay as well to say hello and lay a stone. When I eventually exited, returning to the spot where I had been dropped off the night before, I stopped for a few moments to look up at the names engraved on the two granite pillars that mark the entrance into the modestly-sized *Arbeter Ring* section of the Jewish community's cemetery. I was proud to see my *bubbe* and *zaide*'s names up there as heads of the committee that made the section possible. In fact, my heart warmed at seeing all of the names of the Bundists I'd known growing up — simple but proud, hardworking individuals who, as with everything else they made happen after Hitler, gave whatever they could to build the institutional framework in which Jewish life could begin anew and ensure the proper place for when it naturally ended.

I probably knew this already, though it had likely been lost in the recesses of my mind, so I had to chuckle when I saw that their little place in the *beys oylem*[178] was sandwiched between the massive plot financed by the wealthy *Pinsker landslyat*[179] on their right, and the even larger *Lubavitcher shetakh*[180] to their left. There's nothing meaningful in any of that, but the funny part was the thought that in the end...all Jews. I guess that's what caused a familiar tune to pop into my head, and I found myself humming *Ale Brider* as I turned and made my way home.

———————

"Oh my god!" Amber screamed needlessly when she and a group of friends started up the stairs leading into the anthropology department at the far end of campus, and she spotted me standing by the entrance.

"What?" I replied honestly in response to the look of death I got from her, the friends, and a dozen or so other people who were gathered about, minding their business just like I was.

"How did you find me?" she shouted in an accusatory tone that tweaked everyone's radar—because, obviously—so that in a heartbeat, she was shielded from me by a phalanx of thermos-toting social scientists, who suddenly grew militant.

"Uh, I searched the school's site for food classes and just guessed right?" I offered back nonchalantly and was relieved that my statement, although dripping with sarcasm, was determined by the mob to be accurate and didn't result in the end of me.

"Why are you here?" she tossed back up to me over the crowd.

"I need your help!" I yelled, and started to grow impatient at the stupidity of the scene that she, okay, I guess *we*, were causing.

178. Cemetery.
179. People from the town of Pinsk.
180. Plot of land owned by the Lubavitcher Hasidim.

"With what?" she returned the volley, and all the assembled heads bobbed back in my direction for the rebuttal.

"Sue-Ann!" I shouted, and threw my hands up, as the scene had turned a ripe shade of ridiculous. "Can we just..." I then added, and made with my hands impatiently for her to call off her dogs so that we could be alone. Although it took a few minutes of her confabbing with her friends, eventually, there was dispersion. Despite the indignity of stares, snickers, sneers, and sundry other impoliteness that I wholly didn't deserve as they filed into the building, eventually, it was all over with, and I was finally left alone with Amber.

"Thank you," I said in exasperation as we met halfway up the steps and sat down next to each other to chat.

"What's the matter?" she asked me.

"I dunno, that's why I need your help."

"Did you get into another fight?" she followed up regarding Sue-Ann.

"I wish," I responded, and judging by the blank stare, she didn't get it. "I think we're still stuck on the first one," I added for clarity.

"You apologized, though, right?"

"Of course," I replied defensively, though I probably added in an, "I think" because honestly, with everything that had transpired since the dinner, I couldn't confirm for a fact that I had, either to Sue-Ann, or for that matter, to my interlocutor sitting on the step next to me.

"She's hurting," Amber added.

"I know that," I replied in frustration, and despite the fact that my mind immediately started racing with what else I needed to come up with in my own defense, I was totally off the mark.

"About Luba," she clarified, which I wasn't expecting, and felt kind of dumb about it. "She's struggling to process the loss," she added.

"Of course," I said quietly, and my thoughts immediately turned to the fact that from the moment Luba re-entered my life and introduced me to Sue-Ann, I could never place the reason for the connection they had, nor how strong it had become almost instantaneously. For the first time, as I sat there listening to Amber, I wondered if Sue-Ann's repeated accusations about how little I understood her might have more than just a passing connection to Luba.

"Honestly, I've never heard her say that before," Amber replied when I asked her if she might be, uh, wiser to it in ways that I wasn't.

"She's said it to me more than once," I told her, specifically about Sue-Ann's "you don't know me" daggers. "In fact, just a few days ago, outside her father's place," I added.

"You met her dad?" she asked incredulously.

"Yeah, but it's not what you think," I replied, and I didn't get into why I'd met Mr. Seal, the circumstances by which I did, and chose instead to skip right to the point when Sue-Ann and I didn't meet-at-all-cute at the front door when I was leaving.

"Oh!" Amber responded, her eyes widening in a more forgiving tone, once the context became clear. "She was there to pick up some money," she clarified. Once I told her I didn't understand what for, she smiled and began to describe a part of Sue-Ann's life that spoke to the heart of her connection with Luba.

Turns out she lied to me, Sue-Ann that is, about her name. Yes, it was Seal, but it wasn't. No, it wasn't Mankiewicz, but it was. Sordid, but the lie told a tale. You know from the case Faygen's been working on that Mankiewicz and Seal were partners. I didn't realize that Sue-Ann abandoned the douchebag's name and took on Mankiewicz's...*davke.* "They were really close," Amber said. She described a bond to an individual I could identify with: A Jew, with a strong attachment to his *yiddishkeit,* a *mentsch,* and a *guter neshome.*[181] When her nuclear family wouldn't celebrate Jewish holidays, she'd be by him and his family, his children, the siblings she never had. "She took it really hard when he died," Amber went on, describing the void it left in Sue-Ann's life, which she chased to fill almost immediately.

"Luba," I said in a way like I was piecing the puzzle together out loud as the story unfolded.

"Yep," Amber replied on the same wavelength before going on to explain the reason for the cash transfer on the day I bumped into Sue-Ann at her dad's place. "She takes care of his daughter," Amber began to say about Mankiewicz's death-bed ask of Sue-Ann. When she told him that she'd be fine, his daughter that is, and that Sue-Ann didn't understand why he would need to ask that of her, given that the family had means, he disabused her of whatever perceptions she may have had about him and his relationship with her father and put it to her straight: He was broke and worried sick that his daughter, who had down-

---

181. Kind soul.

syndrome, would fall to social services. It was a heartbreaking thought he couldn't bear.

"So, she confronted her father to ask why Mr. Mankiewicz died without a penny to his name," Amber said, "and that's when she learned the awful truth."

"About?" I asked her, honestly riveted at this point.

"I don't know exactly," Amber said, "but they had some kind of deal, and Mr. Seal broke it." I didn't need to pester her with too many questions because although she may not have known the particulars, she certainly knew enough to paint a nasty fucking picture.

"Well, I'll be fucking damned!" I blurted out, and smacked the cement step after Amber finished telling the story that had my head spinning. "A *t'kiyes-kaf!*"

"A what?" Amber responded.

"A deal; an agreement; an understanding; a vow; a handshake," I said to her frenetically. "I'm going through this right now!"

"Really?" she asked, and I could see I needed to elaborate.

"Not me," I said. "It's in the play I'm directing."

"Oh, that's so cool" she said in that clueless way that was oh so...Okay, never mind. Trying to be a better man. I swear I was. I just smiled and invited her to go on.

"That's it," she said, but not before telling me that ever since Sue-Ann learned the ugly truth, she effectively broke off all ties to her family, even going so far as to take on Mankiewicz's name as her own. Whether officially, I didn't ask, and it didn't matter. The gesture alone, to keep his memory alive, to be a caregiver to the only sister she ever had, so that they could be a family, and just to stick it to her father because of what he did...

"My heart aches," I said, and it occurred to me that I was paraphrasing one of Sue-Ann's lines from the play.

"That sounds familiar," Amber replied.

"I doubt it," I said dismissively.

"I'm serious. I think it's one of Sue-Ann's lines from the play, right?"

"You shitting me?" I said, looking at her dumbfoundedly because she was right, and I couldn't even begin. But yeah, impressed.

"I'm right, right?"

"Uh...yeah," I said, and the ache I was now sensing had a lot to do with feeling like a complete dickhead.

"She really likes being in it," Amber said, and it occurred to me at that moment that one of the things I hadn't been able to piece together yet was why the douchebag hadn't already shuttered the theatre, as he threatened he was going to do when I failed miserably at my meeting with him. It didn't seem the least bit plausible to me that the only reason why the theatre hadn't been closed down was that daddy's little girl was the star of its next play. Not after everything Amber had just told me. Did he even know that she was in it? And if so, was he holding off on pulling the trigger because of whatever they have going on between them, so that she visits his house only to pick up envelopes of money to care for Mankiewicz's afflicted offspring?

Although I kept my own counsel because I knew Amber wouldn't have answers, that didn't mean I wasn't on *shpilkes,* and it didn't help that the piece of advice she gave me about Sue-Ann was to chill and to just "give her some space."

"What do you mean, give her some space?" I shouted. "I need her!"

"You need her because you *need* her?" she asked me wisely and calmly. "Or you need her for your play?"

"There's a fucking difference?" I shot back.

"See what you just did there?" she replied with a look of confidence that suggested I wasn't getting away with it. "Yeah, not so much."

"Fine, I *need* her," I relented.

"You want her?" she asked forthrightly.

"Oh, come on, really? I asked petulantly, like a dog being forced to roll over before getting the biscuit.

"Say it," she said.

See.

"Of course I want her," I relented again.

"Then man the fuck up and go get her," she said with a wink and a smile, sticking it to me solid, then slapped me on the knee before jumping up and making her way up the stairs. "Gotta go, late for class."

"Wait!" I yelled out a few seconds later as she pulled the door open to the building. "There was something I wanted to tell you, but you wouldn't stop talking, so I forgot," I said wryly.

"What?"

"I'm sorry," I said simply.

"Gawd, you're so weird," she said with a smile before entering the building.

"Yeah, I get that a lot," I muttered to myself before turning in the other direction and racing down the stairs because I was now running late, too.

"Shit, sorry!" I said when I hurried into the theatre late because rehearsal was already in progress. *"Vu haltn mir?"* I asked Joseph when I got to his table, and true to form in his never-ceasing way to amaze, he understood exactly what I asked him in a language I guess he was growing ever more familiar with, and told me that we were right at the part at the top of the show, when I enter. Khonen, I mean. "Excellent!" I exclaimed with a clap of my hands. "Perfectly timed," I added so only those at the table could hear, which elicited a slight chuckle from Joseph, as he knew full well that the longer I could hold off having to rehearse the *batlonim*, the better off we'd all be. "Okay, give me the line!" I shouted out before hopping onto the stage to join them.

"Excuse me," one of the men began to speak. Murray was his name, I think. I hadn't yet gotten my head around the specifics of putting names to all the faces, so it could have been one of the other champs. "You don't know what we're talking about, yet you mix in!" he exclaimed.

"He pissed at me or something?" I whispered to Faygen, who I was standing next to on stage.

"No, why?" he answered.

"Because he's supposed to deliver that line to the *meshulakh*, not me," I replied, and then realized that Noyekh was absent for a change. "Fuck! Where is he?" I yelled out to Joseph, who just threw his hands up, which I monkeyed, and it took all of two seconds for my plan to skip this fiasco to go to pot. Nevertheless, "that was a good instinct, what you did there," I said to Murray, attempting to summon a tone akin to encouragement. "You addressed the line to somebody rather than to an empty chair." I didn't want to be too hard on him, as it was an instinct. A fucking idiotic one, mind you, but that was for another day.

"Okay, your turn. Go!" I said to Faygen.

"You okay?" he whispered to me, rather than speaking his line.

"Yeah, fine. Why?"

"Dunno, you're kind of frenetic."

"Yeah, no, good. I'm good, go ahead," I replied, and I guess I must have proven him right based on the look he gave me, but he obliged regardless because, after all, I was the director. He then fed me the line that precedes the first words Khonen utters in the play, which you'll recall my sharing with you from that day of the meet-and-greet, when it was due solely to the force of nature, who goes by the name of Sue-Ann of course, that I returned to the theatre to rehearse.

"Where is he?" I asked Faygen again on this day, responding to his wild-eyed description of a miracle-working rabbi in his hometown who can "create a *golem*! Raise the dead! Become invisible! Call forth evil spirits...even the Devil himself!"

"Iz?" I could see Faygen's lips mouthing my name.

"Yeah?" I asked him.

"You sure you're okay?"

"Why?"

"You're not responding to my answer," he said with concern.

"I'm fine, totally," I replied. "I was just thinking about what you were saying about the miracle worker, and it planted a seed of an idea in my head," I added before telling the men to continue with the rest of the lines as I hopped off the stage and started pacing.

"Who is the young man?" Joseph then read from his script in place of the missing Noyekh.

"A *yeshivah* student," one of the *batlonim* answered.

"A genius," said another. "He's from somewhere in Lithuania. Studied here at the *yeshiva*, and was ordained as a rabbi, but suddenly disappeared. But since he's returned, he's not the same young man who left. Always in deep thought, fasts from one Sabbath to the next...they say he's absorbed with the *kabbalah*!"

"Who knows, maybe he's one of the great ones, a *lamed vovnik*!"[182] another exclaimed.

At that point, I chimed in, thanking the men for their "good" work, and told Joseph to call a break. Fuck, sorry, I shouldn't have qualified that statement. To their credit, they were actually off-book, and the

---

182. Literally, one of the thirty-six hidden righteous ones, whose existence sustains the world.

Yiddish was only half garbage. The fact that they didn't know what to do with themselves on stage was totally on me. And I didn't know if I'd ever figure that piece out.

Gosh! Again, sorry. It just occurred to me that I've neglected to mention that the whole time I stood there on stage, and then while pacing in front of it, I had my eye on Sam, as he appeared forlorn and just totally out of it. In fact, when the men left the stage but he didn't, choosing instead to stand by the *oren koydesh* alone, I grew a little more concerned.

"How you doing?' Faygen asked after he came off stage and started collecting his things.

"Why do you keep asking me that?" I said defensively, all the while keeping my eye on Sam.

"Better to ask than the alternative," he answered, and I suppose there was no arguing that point. "Your *keppy*?" he followed up about my head, and he specifically meant the bump, which I said was healing fine, thank you, and then he kissed me on the noggin before starting to leave.

"Oh, shit, I totally forgot," I said as I grabbed his arm and pulled him back. "I think I've got some news about your case that'll blow your fucking mind," I told him excitedly, which elicited some eyeballs from the stage manager's table. "Nevermind, I'll share it with you later," I added in propriety. "Gotta rehearse with Sam now," I added before shoving him away lovingly and returning to the stage.

———————————

"Come, sit," I said to Sam after I hopped back onto the stage and invited him to join me at the table in the middle. As we took our places, it occurred to me that I hadn't spoken with him at all since Luba, and although I had a feeling that his being out of sorts was due to the fact, I wasn't certain. So, rather than dive into our scene together, I invited him to take a few moments in case he needed or wanted to share.

"How you doing?"

He didn't answer. His gaze focused downward and not on me. I don't know Sam in any way other than what I've shared with you to this point, so any reason I would give to explain his silence and timidity would be purely conjecture. That he didn't have anything to say, however, although everything about his demeanor and what I could glean from his somber countenance made it patently obvious that he likely could fill a *megilleh* and then some, told me that he was in pain and didn't know how to express it. So, I delved.

"Luba?" I asked, and he just nodded. "You miss her?" I followed up, and he nodded again. "You're worried?" I continued, my words taking on a rhythm of their own now as his head moved likewise. "You feel lost?" I asked, and I could see him starting to cry, but my gut told me I wasn't offsides, so I kept going. "You don't know what's going to happen to the theatre, right?" I asked him, and his tears turned into sobs. "And you're scared because that means you don't know what will happen to you?" I probed more deeply, and he didn't answer because he couldn't.

Although everyone had their reason to mourn the loss of Luba and what it portended, for most, it was an emotional upheaval that would resolve with time. In Sam's case, however, it represented a unique and existential crisis that no one was in a position to understand, let alone fix.

"Sam, look at me," I told him, took his hand in mine, and waited until he lifted his eyes before continuing. "Do you realize that I just shared everything I'm feeling with you too?" I asked him rhetorically when we finally were looking at each other directly. "*S'vet zayn* all right," I promised, trying to assure him that all would be good, though I had no proof to offer. I then said nothing further, but the fact that I could feel him squeeze my hand with just enough vigor told me that, for the moment at least, we were okay. It then went silent for a little while between us, which was perfectly fine under the circumstances and wasn't the least bit awkward. Sam was the one who eventually broke it however, by asking a question that frankly did feel awkward.

"What did you say?" he asked, which felt like a total non-sequitur because, I'm being candid with you, there really was silence, and I don't think I said a word.

"Me?" I replied in turn with a question. "I said nothing. I was just thinking."

"You're too immersed in the *kabbalah*, Khonen. You don't even pick up a book of the Talmud anymore," Sam continued, and even though the line he'd just spoken from the play was actually quite serious in tone, he looked at me with a smile, a clear indication that his head was back in the game, confirmed by the fact that that he dived right into our scene together without my needing to prompt him.

"The Talmud is cold and dry, but the *kabbalah* burns with fiery sparks!" I replied to him enthusiastically, and smiled in return, happy that we'd reached the place we needed to be. Although I knew little of Sam, as mentioned, what I'd gleaned from our time together was that despite the upheaval in his life, he remained steadfast in his religiosity and spirituality. Where that's concerned, and I don't mean this in any way to insult him, I kind of got a kick out of seeing the look on his face as I delivered Khonen's monologue about the yay's in favor of the *kabbalah* vs the nay's against the Talmud, while he sat there riveted, lapping it all up like it was the real deal.

I'll share it with you like I did with him, so you get the picture of what made him giddy: "In the *kabbalah*, it says that beneath the earth, there is a world exactly like the one on earth. It has fields and forests, oceans and deserts, cities and villages. But something is missing. There's no lofty sky beneath the earth from which bolts of lightning can descend! From which the blinding sun can shine with a thousand flames! The same is true of the Talmud; it's deep, vast, and glorious, but chains you to the earth. It doesn't allow you to soar to the highest heights. But the *kabbalah*, Henekh? It tears the soul away from the earth. It opens the heavens to you. It leads you directly to Paradise, to the vineyard of wisdom and knowledge. It draws you to infinity. To the edge of the Great Curtain itself!"

"But the Talmud..." Sam began Henekh's retort, gesturing at me emphatically, "...the Talmud lifts the soul to the heights too! Slowly, yes. But it guards you like a faithful watchman who neither sleeps nor dreams. It surrounds you with steel armor and doesn't allow you to stray from the true path!"

I don't blame Sam for being surprised that I took a ninety-degree turn at this point in the conversation. Rather than offer Khonen's reply, I brought up something out of left field that had nothing to do with the scene we had begun rehearsing. Actually, it wasn't totally unrelated because, while passionately speaking my lines about the *kabbalah* and the world underneath the earth, my mind returned to the miracle-working rabbi Faygen's character spoke of a little earlier. That is, the *rebbe* who could raise the dead, call forth evil spirits, even the Devil himself. Sam wasn't just surprised by my bringing it up. In fact, the concept of holiness and sin being two sides of the same coin was one he still couldn't wrap his head around.

"I know, Sam," I told him when he brought up that he still has sleepless nights thinking about it. "But what did I tell you when we had this discussion the first time?"

"That *hashem* created sin," he answered me, and although he'd hit the nail maybe a little too hard on the head about the ways of God in the world, I didn't want to quibble. "And the Devil too!" he answered again with the same look of terror on his face he had the first time around, proving the point that, for Sam at least, where the lines of the play ended and real life began was a massive blur.

"Right, but what else did I say to you?" I asked him, and honestly wasn't expecting his reply.

"That me *shtupping* men and you being *nisht mit alemen*[183] are the highest form of godliness!"he exclaimed, a little too loudly, mind you. Still, other than the folks watching the clock at the stage manager's table, we were alone in the theatre, so, all in all, an outburst that was *nisht geferlekh.*[184]

"Uh, yeah," I said to him in utter bewilderment because, at that moment, I honestly couldn't recall if that's how I synthesized the play's message to him the first time 'round. Still, again he just had this way of hitting that nail right where it needed to be smacked, and if that's what I said, I guess I did.

"And you know what happens then?' he asked me, excited like he was turning the tables on me that I had to gird myself for the *khokhmes*[185] that were coming next.

"Do tell," I said sarcastically, and held my breath.

"They become *Shir Hashirim*!" he shouted aloud again as he jumped from his seat, and the youthful, playful, innocent Sam we'd all come to know and love was back.

"*Getrofn!*"[186] I said to him encouragingly, and tried a high-five, which he couldn't comprehend. "That's exactly what happens, Sam, the Song of Songs," I said, settling for a sigh of relief instead.

"Are you going to sing it?" he asked me excitedly, though it was totally out of context with the discussion we were having.

---

183. Nuts.
184. Not a big deal.
185. Wisdom.
186. Bingo!

"Fuck, man, no!" I snapped at him as my mind was fixated on a topic I needed to get to, and his bouncing from side to side like a kid in a candy store was driving me bonkers. "Sit back down," I said, waving my hand for him to bring things in close. "I need to ask you something important."

"I didn't mean now," he said softly after joining me again. "I meant to Sue-Ann."

"What do you mean?" I asked him sheepishly because, well, talk about something coming out of left field.

"*Shir Hashirim*," he said.

"And what about it?"

"It could help, you know," he added with a glance, and in the whole time we'd known each other, it occurred to me that, for a split second, he was the brighter one of the two of us.

"Okay, that's not what I want to talk about," I said, shifting gears and coming back to a topic that was now front of mind, though admittedly, it was now sharing space with Sue-Ann. Thank you very much, Sam. "Do you remember the first day of rehearsal," I began, "when Faygen said that line about the miracle-working *rebbe* and I told you that it was a bunch of bullshit, just stuff An-sky made up from superstitious *narishkeit* he recorded people telling him about holy Hasidic rabbis and their supposed miracle-working hooey?"

He looked at me dumbfounded.

"Seriously?" I asked him, though I should have guessed that some of the English he was still unfamiliar with.

"I don't understand," he asked and confirmed.

"You said it's very real," I told him, hoping to jog his memory.

"What's real?"

I groaned, shaking my head, as this wasn't supposed to turn into a sketch. "That miracle-working rabbis aren't made up fairies, that they exist!"

"Yes, of course, they're real. Very real," he finally answered me. "I know of one myself."

"Atta boy, *ot do ligt der hunt bagromen!*" I exclaimed, congratulating him for finally getting to the point. Speaking of which: "Who is it, and where can I find him?" I asked with equal vigor.

Unfortunately, I didn't get an answer, because as soon as I asked, his head dropped immediately, and his gaze likewise. Then his shoulders were hunched, followed quickly by his whole body slouching back into a position suggesting he was back to being lost and forlorn. I kicked myself, because although I should have known all along, all of the above, taken together, told me everything I needed to know about who it was and where I needed to look.

———————

No disrespect to any believers who might be reading, those of you for whom an audience at 770 Ocean Parkway and similar venues was and still is akin to a holy pilgrimage, one could prepare a lifetime for and remember equally as long. Trust me, I get it; a big deal, these things. It's just that I hadn't the faintest as to how people get to meet with *rebbeim,* and considering how fast the clock was ticking, I didn't have the time to delve into the matter to properly prepare. For obvious reasons, Sam was out of play where the topic was concerned. So I turned to Faygen, who I just assumed Luba had confided in when Sam first walked into her office, if only to see what kind of help Sam could get, fresh from being excommunicated. Unfortunately, he didn't have much to give in the way of specifics, which was very unlike Faygen. Then again, I kept my cards close to my chest, so the best I got out of him was breadcrumbs. They were enough however, to point me in the right direction, a destination, it so happens, that wasn't far at all.

Forgive me, I just assumed Sam came from one of those secluded ultra-black *shtetlekh*[187] in the mountains *nisht vayt*[188] from New York, and I never bothered asking. Wrong. Turns out he actually got booted out of the community of Hasidim, who lived not a few miles from my place. Go know. Ah! But I already hear you asking how it was that I came to find the house that the *Rebbe* of the community lived in specifically? A question! To the uninitiated, it's very simple: It's the one with the lights on 24/7 and an army of *schnorers* camped outside from morning 'till night, hoping to get in to have their lives changed. The irony, of course, is that most never do, because that costs money. What? You thought they were just doing God's work *b'khinem?*[189] Please, it's *groyse*[190] business and apparently, depending on the sect, business is very good.

———————

187. Small towns.
188. Nor far from.
189. For free.
190. Big.

"*Antshuldikt*, excuse me," I said aloud repeatedly as I began making my way through the throng of men gathered in front of the house late into the night that I chose to pay the *Rebbe* a visit. "Sorry, *zayt moykhl*, coming through," I kept apologizing as I bobbed and weaved through the mass of black-clad Hasidim to whose snickering I paid no heed, even though they were right to look aghast at the thing that was clearly not like the others. It was actually a *fayn shtikl arbet*,[191] working my way to the front of the line of their displeasure, but that's where I was stopped dead in my tracks by a phalanx of burly, well-fed *bokhers*[192] who, from appearances alone, I'd gladly take with me into a back-alley brawl, should I ever have the misfortune. "Hey boys, *vus hert zikh?*"[193] I introduced myself all cool and casual in Yiddish, which elicited blank stares in return that had me wondering if words weren't the way to get in, but rather some sign I needed to flash. Like I said, I hadn't had the time to do my homework, so if I wasn't aware of any secret society stuff, it was perfectly innocent on my part. Regardless, I was there for a reason, and when I followed up by telling them that I needed to see the *Rebbe* urgently, it wasn't blank stares that I got in return, but laughter. Lots of it.

"Guys, this is important, I need to get in," I told them earnestly, if only for the fact that the mob behind me wasn't at all pleased and was starting to close in. "Can you at least get the *gabbai?*" I pleaded, then took a piece of paper from my pocket and waved it in their faces. "I have a *kvitl*, see? I'm totally legit! Please get him!" Right, the *kvitl*. So, if it wasn't a secret sign they needed me to flash for them to part and make a path into the hallowed house, then I knew for certain that I needed the *kvitl*, which to the uninitiated is a piece of paper that lays out for the *Rebbe* the reason for seeking an audience with him, or the case he's being asked to solve.

For those who believe, apparently, *rebbeim* are empowered by God with a supernatural ability to use the *kvitl* as a jumping-off point to stare deep into the soul of the individual who presents it and scare the living shit out of them by knowing things that the *kvitl* itself doesn't reveal. I dunno, it all sounds kinda Popey to me, but if that's the hoop I needed to jump through, I had the ticket, literally. Soon enough, the *gabbai* showed up.

---

191. Nice piece of work.
192. Dudes.
193. How's it hanging?

Depending on who you ask, the *gabbai* can be described as anything from a *rebbe*'s gopher, personal assistant, *consigliere*, chief of staff, even. In the case of the stocky fellow who greeted me, if the spiffy suit and perfectly-manicured nails were anything to go by, I assumed that as far as being *gabbai* in this particular community, he was one of the higher rungs on the ladder.

Upon arriving on the scene, the men handed the *gabbai* my *kvitl*. After reading it, he said nothing at first, but chose instead to look me over carefully, which I'll admit was fair, as I hadn't given any thought to the appropriate attire. I likely wasn't acquitting myself well by showing up for a meeting in a Hasidic community in torn sweats, a t-shirt, and shoes with no socks. Eventually, a conversation did ensue in Yiddish. Still, I took no part in it as the *gabbai* started into the security detail for not doing their jobs, saying that there was no place for a crazed gentile to be in line to see the *Rebbe*, let alone all the way at the front.

"But he has a *kvitl*," one of the men quite rightly said to the *gabbai*, who nevertheless looked at him like he had a pea for a brain before replying by asking rhetorically, "how can a *goy* have a *kvitl*?!" And that's when I piped in. "I can understand every word you're saying, you imbeciles!" I yelled at them. "*Ikh bin a* fucking *yid!*" Well, to say that all hell broke loose at that point would be an apt description, if not particularly respectful, in light of my environment.

Nevertheless, the crowd surged, and as nastier words than what I spoke started flying in my direction in Yiddish, and I could feel like maybe this was gonna be the end of me; a *deus ex machina* appeared in the form of the *Rebbe*, who came out of his office to see what all the commotion was about.

"Khatzkl?" I said aloud when the imposing, larger-than-life figure of the *Rebbe* came to the door, and I could swear they were one and the same individual. He didn't answer or notice me at all, as my voice was drowned out at this point by the rabble behind me, who now had lost its collective shit at the sight of the holy man. All began shouting in the *Rebbe's* direction, pleading for him to call upon them to join him inside. The *Rebbe* paid them no heed other than acknowledging the collective with a wave of his hand and making them temper things, if only to respect the neighbors. It didn't help, and it was still bedlam when he huddled momentarily with the security detail and the *gabbai*, who handed him my *kvitl* that he looked at briefly. "A *fremder*,"[194] I could make out the *gabbai* telling the *Rebbe* with a look of concern on his face, suggesting that I was an outsider, an unknown quantity, and therefore a risk.

"*Nisht emes!*" I shouted to them over the din, calling BS on the *gabbai*. "I'm a friend of Shmuly's!" I added, hoping the name drop would catch the *Rebbe's* attention, which it did, because he actually looked in my direction. "*S'iz im shlekht!*" I yelled again, lying to him that Sam was in a bad place, hoping that would elicit some kind of sympathetic gesture despite excommunication. Time seemed to stand still for a while as the *Rebbe*, ignoring the *gabbai's* insistent entreaties that he call for the security detail to haul me away, chose instead to look at the *kvitl* once more and then to me, where he held his stern gaze for quite a while before finally speaking. "The Levi Yitzhok eulogy, I know," he said while still looking at me, turning the phrase in an eerily familiar way. "Leave us alone," he then said to the *gabbai* as he turned back towards the house, waving for me to follow, and I swiftly obliged.

"Please," the *Rebbe* said to me softly soon after we'd entered his office and, while motioning with his hand, invited me to sit opposite him. Hmm, his office: A tiny, minimalist workspace that wasn't at all what I had pictured in my mind when I decided to pay a visit. You think when you enter the inner sanctum of one of these secretive communities, it's gonna have the look and feel of something fantastical, right? You know what I mean, like holy tomes strewn all over the place, candles flickering, the air smokey from unfiltered cigarettes rolled with newspaper, all of it warping your mind back in time, which seems to stand still while you're there. Nope, I instead walked into a very professional workspace, replete with comfy leather upholstery, an air purifier, and if my eyes didn't deceive, on the little table next to the *Rebbe's* high-backed, a stack of yellow legal pads that put the cherry on top of the whole picture, which it turns out wasn't all that different from my fucking shrink's place.

Lovely.

Not a word was uttered for what felt like forever as he sat regal in his chair, holding my *kvitl* in his hands that rested gently in his lap, and waited patiently while I fidgeted, squirmed, and took my time never

---

194. Stranger.

getting comfortable in the space that felt claustrophobic from the moment we walked in and he shut the door behind us.

"That was some eulogy," he eventually said, opening up our conversation with something I hadn't expected, but in a soft and gentle tone that immediately disarmed me.

"It was hardly a eulogy," I replied, and immediately I was bothered by the fact that it reminded me that my conversation with Sue-Ann's dad opened the same way. But unlike the douchebag, the *Rebbe, l'havdl*,[195] took a genuine interest.

"You do yourself a disservice," he added, "it was beautiful." Although I wanted to thank him, I was only a tad freaked out by the fact that he spoke like he was there and heard every word, which of course, he wasn't. I think. "Why Levi Yitzhok? he then asked me, genuinely curious, before purposefully placing the *kvitl* on the table. He then took one of the pads of paper in his hand and pulled a felt-tipped pen from the breast pocket of his bespoke black wool suit, with the other. I have to tell you that despite his sharing a likeness to Khatzkl, he looked totally snazzy.

"Honestly, *Rebbe*?" I began to say to him while my mind raced for something deep and meaningful to give him, but of course, I came up empty. "I don't know. It just came to me." He nodded, said nothing, but began writing, and I don't know why, but I continued talking. "I'm no maven, *Rebbe*," I said, and for some reason, like in my sessions with my doc, I kicked my feet up on my chair and folded them one atop the other. "I really know nothing, but my *zaide, zol er hobn a likthn gan eydn*,[196] had this maxim..."

"*A yid darf visn*," I heard the *Rebbe* say as I spoke the same words and...I shuddered.

"A Jew mustn't only know," the *Rebbe* continued without missing a beat, and it didn't take long for the *khasidus*[197] to enter the conversation when he added, "a Jew must also feel, with all his heart and soul." I know what you're thinking: Any two-bit holy-roller can quote the *shemah*. You're right. But I'd be doing him a disservice if I gave you the impression that's how it came across. "And you do," the *Rebbe* said with

---

195. By comparison.
196. May he rest in peace.
197. Hasidic teachings.

a knowing glance before changing topics. "Tell me about Shmuly," he said to me, and leaned into it a little when he did.

"What do you want to know?" I asked, shocked that he heard my blurting out the reference to Sam minutes earlier amid the bedlam outside his house.

"You said *s'iz im shlekht*," he accurately repeated the lie I concocted about Sam not being well, if just to get his attention. Although, was I really lying? "You're a friend?" he asked with great curiosity, and let's just get to the point; he was looking at me like maybe I was Sam's lover.

"God, no!" I exclaimed in an embarrassingly knee-jerk response to the thought of Sam and me. "Shit, sorry," I fumbled, because what idiot takes His name in vain in front of someone supposedly blessed with His powers? But I got to the point eventually: "I mean, yeah, sure, we're friends." I then looked directly at the *Rebbe* and was seriously gobsmacked at how intently he listened to me, hanging on my every word as if truly waiting for a report about Sam's well-being. "He's fine, *Rebbe*," I said to him, "but I thought..." I didn't finish, because I didn't know how to say what was on the tip of my tongue for fear of, well, I don't know what. It's just that I'd never been in this situation before with people who supposedly have otherworldly powers. So when the *Rebbe* raised his eyebrow, giving the impression that he was reading my mind, I felt like shitting my pants because I think he drew it out of me anyway. "I thought you excommunicated him," I whispered, and held my breath in anticipation of the fire and brimstone about to rain down.

I was wrong. The *Rebbe* said nothing. In fact, his demeanor didn't change even the slightest bit as he just smiled at me and once again guided the conversation in another direction that I couldn't have anticipated. "*Herem?*" he said, using the Hebrew equivalent for excommunication. "*Herem* is a fearsome thing for the living," he continued, quoting the lines directly from *The Dybbuk*. "How much more so for the dead!"

"*Rebbe?!*" I asked him, completely stunned by the words he'd just uttered.

"From your play, no?" he asked me playfully. "If I'm not mistaken," he added with a wink.

"*Vi geshribn,*" I said to him, confirming that he'd gotten them perfectly. "But how did you...," I began to ask, but my mind stopped amid the train because it suddenly got pulled by a force that wasn't my own.

"What did you just say to me a few moments ago?" he asked me, and his voice sounded all too familiar.

"*A yid darf visn*," I said.

He smiled knowingly.

"Besides," the *Rebbe* continued on like worlds hadn't just collided, "there was no excommunication." He went on to describe that the topic of banishing Sam from the community never even came up because after all, Sam was family, his own flesh and blood. Apparently, as difficult and dramatic as it all went down, it was determined that the best thing for Sam's well-being, for the life he needed to live that could in no way find its fulfillment in the community the *Rebbe* led, was for him to leave. "But we keep an eye out," the *Rebbe* added cryptically.

I should tell you that as soon as he said it, my mind immediately went to something Sam had shared with me that, gosh, forgive me if I've told you this already, only resonated with me now, at this moment when the *Rebbe* was laying bare the truth about what happened with Sam. On that *shabbes* morning, when I took Sam up on his offer to *davn*[198] with him at his new *shul*, he shared with me the fact that one day he found a letter at his door, telling him to come to a back alley of a bakery and similarly a butcher shop in the middle of the night, where he found packages of *kol tuv*[199] along with a note that said to come each week for the same. And to this day, he doesn't know who's doing it and why.

"He told me he thinks God is providing," I told the *Rebbe*.

"And who says he isn't?" he replied with another wink, and just then, there was a knock at the door.

"But *Rebbe*, my issue," I said to him with a sense of urgency as it felt like I was done, and we hadn't even gotten to my reason for visiting.

"Yes, the *kvitl*," he said calmly as the *gabbai* popped his head in the door and told the *Rebbe* that my time was up. But the *Rebbe* would hear nothing of it. Instead, he just waved his assistant off with a brush of his hand and told him that we were not to be disturbed so long as the door remained closed. With that, the *gabbai* left, closed the door behind him, and when we were alone again in the room together, the *Rebbe* sat back

---

198. Pray.
199. All the best.

in his chair, took the *kvitl* in his hands that he again rested softly in his lap and looked at me with great intent. "Please, go ahead," he said earnestly, and I began to lay out the reason for my visit.

15

"What's the matter?" my mother called out to me somewhere not near the beginning of our latest online session, a point at which I guess I should make clear that I wasn't visible on the screen anymore.

"Fuck, Ma, nothing!" I shouted back to her while pacing around my living room, as I'd had enough of hearing how much time had passed since our last session, and that it was only through Faygen that she had any inkling as to what was going on with me. Considering the time-lapse however, I suppose she was right on the moot of the argument. Yes, she was getting *bubkes* out of me because, quite frankly, the topic of the cemetery visit was a novel for another time and sharing the random late-night audience I decided I needed to have with a Hasidic *rebbe*...well, how would *you* have explained it?

But that wasn't all of it.

"You sure?" she asked me again.

"Yes, I'm sure," I lied.

"Because you seem kind of frenetic," she added without seeing me but was keenly aware.

"Jesus, how much have you and Faygen been chatting?"

"Every day, why?"

"He said the exact same thing to me at rehearsal," I told her. On this day however, my agitation got piqued when the topic of our conversation turned to the play's opening being literally days away, and my mother couldn't contain her excitement by sharing that everyone already had their tickets and were eagerly awaiting the premiere of my show. *Everyone.*

When a Jewish mother tells you "everyone," it's cause for frenetic. I'd tell you the names but *nisht vikhtik*.[200] Paint a portrait in your mind that when she said Hank and my aunt Fayge, it means everyone they know, too. When she says my cousins Jenna and Amanda and their families, Manny with the wife and the kids with the *farkakte* nature-themed names I don't remember, it likely means everyone they know, too. Likewise, and so on, until even Joseph was no longer needed for

---

200. Not important.

confirmation, as through my mother alone, it was clear that "everyone" was breaking the box office phones.

It's interesting how, ever since being designated heir apparent, I'd managed to keep my shit together. Still, the moment my mother told me that Hank and Manny were coming in a manner of days to observe my work, I couldn't find enough hair to pull out of my body while pacing, uh, frenetically around my living room. Yeah, I get it, I overstated a little, but it was just a means of fucking comparison.

And what with Faygen now having told me that with ten days to go 'till showtime, he would be absent from rehearsals because his trial had started against the douchebag, I just...I know, I know. But believe it or not, having him there along the journey was helpful in a way I can't explain, and I kind of feel like, at this point, I don't need to. And just when I had to dive into the part of the play that, based on what Faygen had told me, Luba herself didn't know how to handle.

I suppose it was some comfort that it wasn't just me on the verge.

———

"What the fuck are you doing?" I asked Sam when I arrived at the theater the next day to rehearse the trial scene between Sender and his dead childhood buddy Nisn ben Rivke, and found him standing ninety degrees to the entrance, looking directly at a wall facing east and about to take three steps backwards.

"*Davening*," he answered, mumbling for God to open his lips so that his mouth could declare His glory in prayer.

"Yeah, hold up there for a second," I said, grabbing him by the arm before he could take three steps forward and bend at the knee. "What on earth for?"

"If this is sacred space," he said while pointing toward the door to the theatre, "our sages teach us that we are to be conscious of being in the presence of *hashem* by taking three steps forward at the beginning and three steps back at the end."

"What sage told you that a theatre is a sacred space?" I asked him sarcastically.

"Luba," he answered forthrightly, and I have to admit, although I'm one hundred percent certain that she never would have used that type of terminology to underline the importance of the stage, that he interpreted it to such an extent was kind of impressive.

"You been doing this the whole time?" I asked, and when he nodded in the affirmative, I felt nothing but embarrassment for never paying attention. Sure, all kinds of messed up to my mind, but the fact that it was totally meaningful in his and that the play, the process of mounting the production and each and every entrance into the space where we did our work merited this moment of sanctification, only served to heighten for me what I already knew was at stake.

"All right, then," I said, and let go of him so he could get on with his *Amidah*[201] before rehearsal started. "But throw in *birkas bineh* before you get to stepping forward again," I told him, and went to open the door to the theatre, which is when he grabbed *me* by the arm.

"*Birkas bineh*?" he asked, and looked at me cockeyed.

"The prayer for the stage," I replied, feigning sincerity. "Surprised Luba never shared it with you," I added with a wink before opening the door and entering the theatre.

Between us, I may have been tongue in cheek with Sam, but that only belied the seriousness of his demeanor. It was palpable, he was trembling, and although I had it in mind to ask, I didn't as I genuinely didn't want to know if what he was actually praying for was a miracle. Yes, time was running out on the clock. The reality of that could be felt as much in Sam's need to reach out to a higher authority, which I'm guessing was really the truth of what he was doing, as in the atmosphere I encountered when I walked into the theatre, where I found everyone waiting for me... and it was dead quiet. The *batlonim*, who could typically be counted upon to not shut the fuck up when required, were sitting in the audience, staring at me with lips sealed as I walked down the stairs toward the stage. Wendy sat silently in her front-row seat by the stage manager's table. Khatzkl didn't even notice me as he paced the set nervously, muttering to himself.

"All right, guys, I get it," I wanted to call out to them, in recognition that we were really behind schedule, and as captain of the ship, it was all my fault. But then Joseph walked in from the wings, trailed by Francine, looking like death warmed over, and handed me a piece of paper imprinted with the letterhead of the JCC.

"Oh my god!" Francine shouted a few seconds later as both she and Joseph looked at me in horror after I'd taken a moment to read the

---

201. Literally, the standing prayer.

letter's brief message, then proceeded to shred it to pieces before throwing it up in the air.

"We're good people, you hear me?" I shouted out to everyone in the room, including Sam, who had also entered.

"But Izzy?" Joseph looked at me fecklessly. "The letter says..."

"What letter?" I cut him off and asked rhetorically while looking around the room. "I don't see a letter." I then turned to his assistant and asked the same question. "Does anybody here see a letter?" I called out to a room full of people whose mouths were agape in astonishment. "We're putting on this play and rehearsing this fucking trial scene today, you hear me?" I shouted before turning to Joseph again and telling him to call everyone to take their places on stage for the trial between Sender ben Henye and his deceased friend, Khonen's father, Nissen ben Rivke.

"Okay, Khatzkl, go," I said to my *Miropoler Rebbe* once the men had gathered on stage, where I took a few moments to describe how I saw the scene playing out before we began to hear the lines spoken aloud. I then took my position at the foot of the stage, placed one foot on the set and clasped my hands behind my back and observed as Khatzkl started the scene off by calling for his assistant Mikhoel, a part that I gave to Sam, to bring him his staff. Khatzkl then walked over to a far side of the stage where he dramatically used the staff to draw a circle symbolizing the boundary into which the deceased would be called upon to give his testimony.

"Take this and go to the cemetery," the *Miropoler Rebbe* told his assistant in a pitch-perfect tone that sent chills, while presenting him with his staff as if it was a magical instrument. "When there, close your eyes and let the staff lead you. At the first grave it touches, stop and knock three times, repeating these words: 'Blameless deceased, I have been sent by Azriel, son of the saintly Reb Itchele of Miropol, to ask your forgiveness for disturbing your rest. He also asks that you inform the blameless deceased, Nissen ben Rivke, that the just *beit din* of Miropol, summons him immediately to a trial.' Repeat these words three times, then turn right around and return here. Do not look back, no matter what sounds, screeches, or howling you may hear behind you. And do not let my staff fall from your hands, even for an instant, or you will be in great peril. Go, and God will protect you, for no harm can come to a messenger on a virtuous errand. Go...and send Sender in."

"Excellent, Khatzkl, keep going," I said, and nodded my approval as he motioned for the actor playing Sender to approach.

"Do you remember your old friend, Nissen ben Rivke?" he asked Luba's former accountant, *shoyn eyn mol*[202] an actor, but anyway.

"Nissen ben Rivke?" he replied in a tone that was too casual for the moment, but I didn't stop to fix it. "He's been dead..."

"Know then that he appeared three times last night to Reb Shimsh...." Khatzkl interrupted him before I followed suit.

"No, don't stop. Keep going," I said, as I'd forgotten to tell everyone that Faygen—aka Reb Shimson—wasn't gonna be around for a while. "I'll take care of it. Go on."

"Know then," Khatzkl began his line again but paused if only for an instant, and I could feel him looking at me for assurance, but by this point, I'd closed my eyes, lowered my head, and begun reciting something under my breath that I alone could hear. "Know then that he appeared to Reb Shimshon thrice last night in a dream. He demanded that you be summoned to a *din toyre*."

"A trial?" Reb Sender replied, flabbergasted. "What does he want from me?"

"That remains to be seen," Khatzkl answered. "But you must attend."

"Of course, *Rebbe*," Reb Sender responded, his voice trembling appropriately. "I will do as you say."

"And you will accept our verdict?"

"Yes, I will accept."

"Very well," Khatzkl said before addressing all the men on stage. "Soon, a spirit will appear before us from the True World. We must decide his case against a man from our world of illusion. A trial such as this demonstrates the power of our Holy Torah over all spheres. A trial such as this is grave and dreadful for all eyes in the Higher Spheres are turned to us. We must be steady and unbending for...for..."

His pause was legitimate. He wasn't searching for his lines, because although the moment that the terrestrial and heavenly worlds collide had

---

202. Hardly.

arrived, no one in the room had a clue as to what was about to happen. No one but me.

"I think he's here," one of the men said, and they all looked to the circle that the *Rebbe* had drawn with his staff.

"Yes, I think he's here," another responded.

"He is here!" a plangent, ominous voice that was not my own suddenly shot forth from within me, thundering throughout the theatre and causing everyone in the room to recoil in shock.

The phrase, which he could swear he heard the first jury member speak aloud, then repeated itself as, one by one, each of the others echoed it. "He is here," they said. "He is here." And soon, the courthouse where Mel Seal was standing trial in a class-action lawsuit brought against him and his company by his erstwhile employees reverberated with words seemingly only he could hear.

"Mr. Seal," the judge, a no-nonsense woman in her mid-seventies with a stout reputation for not suffering fools, began to address him as he sat in the witness box, unsettled. "Is there something wrong?"

"No, your honour," he replied unconvincingly.

"You appear distracted," she prodded him.

"I'm...," Mr. Seal began to reply while looking disconcertedly at the nameless faces set to pass judgment upon him, all of whom were silent. "I'm fine," he eventually said after turning to face the judge.

"Very well," she replied. "Councilor," she said, calling out to Faygen, who was standing halfway between the bench and the prosecution's table, "you were presenting your clients' complaints and grievances against the witness. Carry on."

Standing cautiously by the circle he had drawn with his staff, the *Miropoler Rebbe* addressed the witness from the celestial world who had arrived to give his testimony: "Blameless deceased, Nissen Ben Rivke," the *Rebbe* called to the spirit. "This *beit din* commands you not to leave the circle drawn around you. State your complaint and grievance against Sender Ben Henye."

Khatzkl then looked at me. In fact, every eye in the room looked to me as the following line was Reb Shimshon's and the uncertainty of what would emanate this time seemed to instill a palpable disquiet.

"Sender ben Henye," the voice from within me began to speak. "The blameless deceased, Nissen Ben Rivke, claims that, in your youth, you and he were friends at the *yeshiva*. Both of you were married in the same week. Later, on the High Holy Days, you made a sacred pledge to each other: 'Should your wives conceive, and one gives birth to a son and the other a daughter, their children would be betrothed.'"

"That wasn't..." the actor playing Reb Sender began to speak haltingly the lines that called for him to be appropriately scared out of his mind. "I mean..."

"Mr. Seal, you are ordered to answer the question," the judge called out to him once again in frustration.

"I'm sorry, your honor," Mr. Seal addressed her, but all the while looking at Faygen disturbingly. "There was a voice...Mankiewicz?" he said under his breath.

"Councilor," the judge called out to Faygen, rightfully annoyed. "Repeat your question for the witness."

"Yes, your honor," Faygen replied and dutifully obliged, addressing the witness forthrightly: "Mr. Mankiewicz says, Mr. Seal, that you had a deal, did you not?"

"Yes, we had a partnership agreement. That's correct."

"No, Mr. Seal. That's not what he means," Faygen corrected. "A gentlemen's agreement, a handshake, in fact...a *t'kiyes kaf*. Is this true?"

"I honestly don't remember," Seal replied dismissively.

"Let's refresh your memory then, shall we?" Faygen gave him back good and walked over to the jury box. "Mr. Mankiewicz says that he came to you at a time of dire need to save his business. You said that you could help, but that to do so, Mr. Mankiewicz would be required to settle debts that you owed. Debts that, if not paid imminently, could threaten your life and your young family."

"That's not exactly..." Seal began to interject but wasn't permitted to finish his thought.

"Mr. Mankiewicz says," Faygen kept the line of argument going as he now started pacing the floor of the courtroom confidently, "that he didn't ask you for details, for it was none of his concern. Only that the two of you shake hands on a very simple proposition: In return for each one of you helping the other and becoming partners in the business, should anything happen to either of you, God forbid, you'd take care of each other and your families. True?"

"It wasn't that simple," Seal scoffed.

"It was, in fact, that simple, Mr. Seal," Faygen pushed back, stopping dead in his tracks and looking purposefully at Seal while pointing an accusatory finger at him. "But despite Mr. Mankiewicz's wishes, it was *you* who decided to complicate matters by presenting him with a written agreement."

"Like I just said, we had a partnership agreement."

"That contained a shotgun clause," Faygen clarified.

"Standard stuff," Seal responded, shifting uncomfortably in his chair in the witness box.

"Standard in that you triggered it when Mr. Mankiewicz's wife, Helen, took ill?" Faygen pushed back and took a few steps in Seal's direction. "And just when he had to spend whatever money he had to save her life, you went after your mentor and friend who had no choice but to hand the business over, then watched as his world unraveled as he spent every last penny trying to save his wife. But to no avail, which left him destitute with a daughter he no longer had the means or support system to care for. That kind of standard, Mr. Seal?"

"It's not my fault he didn't read the agreement before signing," Seal reacted coldly to Faygen's putting out the facts plainly for the jury to hear.

"He didn't have to, Mr. Seal," Faygen now spoke in a loud, clear, and measured voice while commanding the center of the room. "Because a *t'kiyes kaf* is a holy matter, and not holding up one's end of a sacred agreement can destroy worlds. And that's what you did, Mr. Seal: You destroyed a man's world, effectively killing him for your own personal gain. Isn't that how it played out?

"That wasn't..." Mr. Seal tried to push back. "I mean..."

"The blameless deceased, Nissen Ben Rivke, further states," I began to speak again as the voice from within me grew louder, stronger, and ever more confident in delivering the lines that Faygen would eventually speak as Reb Shimson on opening night, "that his wife gave birth to a son at the same time that your wife gave birth to a daughter. Soon after, Nissen died. And when his son arrived in the town where you live, he came to your house and sat at your table. And his son's soul was bound to your daughter's. But you were rich, and Nissen's son was poor. And you went elsewhere to seek a bridegroom for your daughter among families with status and rich dowries. Nissen ben Rivke declares that with the death of his son, he is left without a name, an heir, and a mourner to recite Kaddish!"

The theatre was eerily quiet for quite a few long moments before the *Miropoler Rebbe* walked over to Reb Sender, who shook with trepidation as he approached. "You've heard the complaints of Nissen ben Rivke," the *Rebbe* said while standing tall over him. "What is your reply to the charges?"

"I can barely open my mouth, *Rebbe*," the actor playing Reb Sender said. "I have no words with which to defend myself. But I beg my old friend to forgive me."

"You should know, Mr. Seal," Faygen said to the witness after returning to his table to review some of his documents before walking back to stand between the witness and the jury, "Mr. Mankiewicz says that he knows your motive behind closing the theatre. You want to rob your daughter of her connection to her Jewish heritage because it ties her to what she had with him, something you refused to give her."

Mr. Seal didn't respond.

"Mr. Seal," the judge then admonished him. "What is your response to your dead partner?"

"I don't know that I have one, your honor" Seal said, his hands beginning to tremble. "I can't say that his claim is true."

"You lie!" Faygen thrust his arm out at the witness while speaking in a deep, profound, ominous voice that was not his own, which caused Seal to recoil in horror. "You lie,"Seal could swear he now heard the first member of the jury speak aloud, which then repeated itself as one by one, each of the others echoed it while Faygen continued: "In fact, you had your daughter spied upon, and when you learned that she had fallen in love with a young man who does not come from a family of means, does not fit the mold you had sought your whole life for your daughter, you redoubled your efforts and sought to close the theatre out of nothing but sheer spite!"

"No, Mankiewicz, you son of a bitch! You're the liar!" Seal stood up and repeatedly shouted at Faygen in response. The judge banged her gavel down not once, not twice, but over and over again in a call for order and decorum in her court that he was willfully violating. Within no time, and while he continued screaming obscenities at Faygen and then to all who were assembled in the packed courtroom that day, the judge commanded the foreman to escort Mr. Seal from the witness box out of the courtroom, and called for a recess.

―――――――――

"This *beit din* has heard both sides of the case," the *Miropoler Rebbe* said in a solemn tone as he stood alone at the front of the stage, looking upward as if to the heavens, "and delivers the following verdict: Whereas at the time when the pact was made between Nissen Ben Rivke and Sender Ben Henye, it is not known whether their wives had already conceived; and whereas, according to our Holy Torah, no agreement can be considered valid that involves something not yet in existence, we cannot, therefore, determine that Sender was compelled to fulfill the agreement. But since the Heavens accepted the agreement as valid and implanted the belief in the heart of Nissen ben Rivke's son, Khonen, that Sender ben Henye's daughter, Leah, was his intended bride, and since Sender's subsequent actions resulted in misfortune for Nissen and his son, we decree that Sender must donate half his fortune to the poor, and for the rest of his life, light the memorial candle, and recite the memorial prayer for Nissen Ben Rivke and his son, as though they were his own kin."

"In addition, Mr. Seal," the judge began to say to the defendant when the court was eventually called back into session later that afternoon, and where Seal stood at the defendant's table listening to the verdict being read out against him, "I am adding the following sentence of my own...."

The *Miropoler Rebbe* then turned and walked toward the defendant in the trial: "Sender Ben Henye," he said while standing over him. "Did you hear our verdict?"

"I have, *Rebbe*."

"Do you accept it?"

"Yes, *Rebbe*. I accept it," Reb Sender replied, lowering his gaze.

"Mr. Seal," the judge asked him: "Do you accept this complete verdict as I have explained it to you?"

"Yes, your honor, I accept it," Seal replied solemnly.

"Very well," the judge said, motioning for the foreman to escort the jury out of the courtroom. "This court stands adjourned," she said before banging her gavel down to signify that the case against Mr. Seal was now closed, at which point all rose as the right and honorable judge stepped down from her bench and exited the courtroom.

I'm curious, how many of you would have guessed that to secure the crucial piece of the puzzle that would ensure the play went up, let alone succeed, the place I'd turn to would be that *farkakte* millennial bar with the neon vagina above the entrance? I forget the name, sorry. Show of hands? Anyone? As I suspected. Yet, with only days left until opening, of all the places you would have expected to find me, and of the myriad of things I'd be busying myself with, that's where I ended up. Wait, I just remembered: The Bushy Pussy.

It was open mic night again on the evening I showed up. My luck because, as it happened, the familiar aural assault I experienced immediately upon entering was once again offered up by that twenty-something-year-old duo from the last visit with Luba, the hosts according to the flyer out front: She of the fraught relationship with the cowbell and the other, the musician of the two I suppose, delivering this time a sort of electronic sadism out of a machine whose battery wasn't running out quickly enough. Don't ask me how my ear was particularly attuned to their din coming through the P.A. system. I suppose it's in my DNA. In reality, it was mostly drowned out by the ear-splitting cacophony produced by the mass of humanity packed like sardines into the dark, dingy little bar, because apparently, open mic is like millennial religion...even if you don't pay any attention. Which, come to think of it, lends it a sort of credence. Anyway, kidding aside, I have it on good authority from Francine and her ilk at the theatre who, when I prodded, waxed annoying about the kind of communal safe-space venue that open mic offers up for exploration of all that "truthiness" I did such a bang-up job of hearing the last time I was confronted with it.

Although it took a little while to squeeze my way through the throng, I eventually managed to get to the stage only mildly soaked from spilled beverages caused by the inadvertent bumps, grinds, "excuse me's," "how dare you's," "don't touch me's," and the like *en route*. Once I arrived, the sign-up sheet on the side of the stage indicated that all the truth-tellers had already said their piece. It seemed that after the dynamic duo just killing it only a few feet away from me were done, then if I was brave enough to put pen to paper then and there, I'd be next up. Trust me, it wasn't what I wanted to do, but despite my best efforts at scouring the room, I couldn't find what I'd come looking for, so I was left with no choice. I signed and, within minutes, got called up onto the stage by the hosts. My luck was that when I did, the sea of humanity decided to collectively shut the fuck up and pay attention.

"Uh, hi," I said into the microphone to a room full of people I couldn't see due to the one spotlight shining onto the stage that blinded me. "I'm Izzy," I added, and that was about it because with my heart fully in my throat, I didn't quite know what else to say, as there was no plan, just a seed of an idea planted into my head that for some reason I felt compelled to act upon to save the play. "All right, Sam," I whispered to him under my breath then added, "this better fucking work," before beginning to sing *Shir Hashirim*.

> *Shir hashirim asher l'shloymo*
> *Yishokeyne mi nishikoys pihu*
> *Ki toyvim doydekho miyayin*
> *Sheyn bistu mayn basherte*
> *Dayne oygn vi toybn*
> *Vi di zise vilde troybn*

"Shit, sorry," I said and stopped abruptly. I couldn't tell you if the rising chatter amongst the crowd caused me to pause after singing the first few lines or that I was keenly aware that I was singing in a language with which probably no one in the room was familiar. In either case, the song was meant as a clarion call which wasn't getting answered, and it occurred to me in the moment that maybe I was missing out on the point of the exercise. So, I switched to the common tongue, but only realized when I began that with the King James version, I sucked no less:

Thy lips are like a thread of scarlet, and thy mouth is comely;
thy temples are like a pomegranate split open behind thy veil.
Thy two breasts are like two fawns that are twins of a gazelle, which feed
among the lilies.
Thou hast ravished my heart, my sister, my bride;
thou hast ravished my heart with one of thine eyes, with one bead of thy
necklace.

"God dammit," I yelled into the mic, and slammed it to the stage out of sheer embarrassment, as I could hear laughter erupting from the crowd in front of me that I was blind from seeing. But it started to grow, and the combination of the rising tide of mockery and the reality that it emanated from a faceless mob that felt larger than it probably was, I had to escape it all. "Fucking retard," I muttered to myself as I jumped off the front of the stage, to the look of horror of one of the two musical hosts who was within earshot, the one with the cowbell. "Not you, me," I said to her as I began to make haste, which should tell you my state of frazzled, that with the opportunity in hand to tell her precisely what I felt about her music...okay, nevermind.

"Where are you going?" I then heard Sue-Ann's voice call out to me and felt a hand grab my arm to hold me back from leaving. "You have such a beautiful voice," she purred. When I turned around and saw her dressed in the same hip-hugging jeans and tight-fitting black tank top that she wore on the night when, almost exactly in the same spot as we were now standing, a ball of fire with dimples that melt hearts of stone came flying into my life and changed my world forever, I was an immediate mess.

"What's wrong?" she asked me.

"Nothing," I lied without a filter. "A lot, actually," I continued. "It was Sam's idea," I added.

"Okay," she replied, scrunching her face in confusion.

"You wouldn't talk to me, so Sam thought of *Shir Hashirim*," I tried to explain.

"You're taking relationship advice from Sam?" she asked, bemused but mostly sarcastic.

"Of course not," I said defensively. "We were rehearsing, and he just guessed."

"That?"

"Dunno, that maybe it would bring us together," I replied, although she didn't hear it, as just at that moment I got drowned out by the hosts of open mic, who had now returned to the stage, and it suddenly got deafening as their noise began anew. Sue-Ann then took me by the hand and led me behind the stage, where she pushed open a door to the back alley of the Vulgar Vulva. There, we continued the conversation, with the blaring music still audible but mercifully reduced to background noise.

We didn't say anything to each other for what felt like an eternity. I couldn't tell you what was on her mind as I observed her staring at me while leaning with her leg up against the brick façade of the building, her arms folded across her chest that gleamed in the moonlight with beads of sweat, which I desperately wanted to touch with my fingers and bring to my lips. What raced through my mind was the last sequence of events in our lives together that led to the inglorious collapse of what I believed to be our budding relationship. Whether it was the rehearsal that caused her to quit the play; the untimely encounter outside her father's; the dinner, of course; I didn't know where to begin as by now it was all of a whole: Just one giant mess that I had to fix.

"I don't want to apologize," I finally told her. Of course, if one was to interpret it at face value alone, it was probably the stupidest opening line one could deliver when *beytn mekhile*[203] is precisely what you're seeking to accomplish. But there was a ton, and I struggled to let it out one piece at a time in any coherent fashion.

"That's good," she said bitingly. "So why are you here?"

"Shit, that's not what I meant."

"You want to start again?" she asked no less assertively.

"Yes," I answered, and she tilted her head to signal for me to give it another try.

"I mean, of course, I want to," I said, starting over. "Apologize, I mean, but I want to do more."

"Of what?"

"Everything," I said. "I want to reset everything."

"Okay," she said, and added nothing more, as I guess she understood me well enough to know that I needed to work my way into why I'd come in search of her.

---

203. Asking for forgiveness.

"This is where it all started," I said to her, and pointed at the door to her left, where the music was emanating from. "Luba knew, but I didn't."

"Knew what?" she asked, seemingly interested in the thoughts rolling off my tongue.

"That it wasn't only about the play," I answered. "It was actually about the future...us."

"You and me?"

"Yeah."

"I don't think she knew that."

"She did. Trust me, she did," I said, and took a step closer to her, which I have to say had me leaning on a dumpster that stank to high hell. "That was her magic. I'm sorry, Sue-Ann, I'm truly sorry."

"Wait, where are you now?" she asked me quizzically as I'd, in fact, non-sequitured, which because the topic had been Luba, was somewhat appropriate.

Nevertheless, although I truly wished my thoughts were clearer, I was grateful that she was listening, if not hanging on my every word.

"I'm at dinner," I said, although it wasn't lost on me that from the moment I fucked that night up royally, I'd been desperate to try and fix it, even though she never gave me the opportunity, that finer point was for another day. This had to be me on my knees, and I knew it. "I never got the chance to tell you that I know that I didn't just blow it all up, but I did so in front of your friends, which made it all worse for you. I'm not using Luba's passing as an excuse. I agreed to come, and you didn't deserve the repercussions of my inability to control myself. So, this is me saying that I know it, I own it, and I'm sorry."

Sue-Ann said nothing. Her gaze was focused downward, so I couldn't tell if what I'd just said was even registering. I would have liked a conversation, truth be told. In fact, what she unleashed upon me outside her father's place was something I honestly felt she could have walked back, or at least offered up a *mea culpa* for cutting me to pieces by revealing herself to be very much her father's daughter, despite every effort she was making not to be. I wouldn't have judged her for it, however, not one bit. Not after what Amber shared with me about the fundamental choice Sue-Ann had made about her life and identity when tragedy struck, which revealed her to be even more remarkable than I already knew her to be. But if this ended up being just me groveling, I was prepared for that to be the case. Yes, I'm aware I made that point already.

"I know what the money's for," I told her, which caused her to look up at me in response and throw me a quizzical look.

"Now, what are you talking about?" she asked, and by the looks of it, she was growing impatient with the meandering.

"It's for your sister," I answered, regarding Mankiewicz's daughter, who she takes care of and considers her real family. "See, you don't have to tell me that I don't know you anymore," I said with a smile, but she didn't reciprocate.

"Nobody knows about that," she said, in an accusatory tone as well as one of concern about a secret being revealed. "How do you know?"

"Amber told me," I replied innocently.

"You spoke with Amber?" she asked like the thought was inconceivable.

"I did," I answered her. "*And* I apologized!" I said somewhat lightheartedly, hoping to lift the tone of the conversation. But it didn't.

"It wasn't her place to share," Sue-Ann said plainly, looking disappointed that I knew the truth. "That's why you're here tonight? *She* told you where to find me?"

"No," I answered her. "But yes," I followed up, and she looked at me again like enough was enough, and it was about time I just got to the point, although the truth of the matter is that it wasn't so simple. I had two goals in mind in coming to see her that evening, and while they weren't necessarily tied to one another, I didn't know how I would react if I only achieved one or neither. Unfortunately, splitting the two seemed impossible, so they got lumped together in my next statement, which, you'll recall, was Amber's direct advice to me.

"I need you," I said to her, and wished right away that I hadn't, because my interpretation of the words as I heard them aloud was that they didn't express the nuance of what I was feeling; that they were nebulous, pretty weak, come to think of it.

I girded myself for the response, which I waited for anxiously. "I'm not ready," she eventually replied after a momentary silence between us, and it occurred to me that her response was on a par with my statement, and we were therefore caught at an awkward standstill that I didn't know how to navigate away from. As much as I wanted to walk away from the evening having carded a win both where our relationship was concerned and in getting her back into the play, I knew instinctively that it was the latter that I needed to secure. The former would have to wait its turn.

"We all need you," I said, landing squarely in my role as the play's director and representative of a company of people relying on her to do the right thing. "If you've really quit and walked away, then you're not just hurting yourself," I told her, quoting someone she would be very familiar with. "You know that, right?" I asked her rhetorically, offering a smile and for the first time in the conversation since we'd entered the dank, stinky alleyway behind the bar, she did too.

"I need to get back inside," she then said, and although she didn't give any kind of response, the fact that she brushed her hand against mine as she went to open the door to the bar gave me every indication that I might just be getting some wind into my sails.

"I want you to know that I'm not angry anymore," I told her just before she walked back in.

"Angry about what?" she asked and turned around to look at me.

"When we were outside your father's place, you said I was angry," I clarified. "Angry at everything and everyone."

"And?" she prodded.

"I spoke to my *zaide,* and he said I'm okay," I said bright-eyed and with a smile ear to ear that I didn't consider, not even for a second, that she might perhaps be thinking I was just flat-out *frish, gezint, meshigeh.*[204]

"You spoke with your *zaide?*" she said, looking at me sideways.

"I sure did," I said to her proudly, and you have to believe me when I tell you that regardless of the circumstance, the uncertainty, and the pressure, saying what I did unburdened a weight I didn't realize I'd been carrying. So much so that I felt confident enough to look her straight in the eye and lay it all out plainly, no matter how things turned out: "I told him that you're everything."

"And what did he say?" she asked me, shortly after I could swear that she gasped, if only just a little.

"He said that you are...that you absolutely are."

I told you earlier that I had two goals I wanted to accomplish that evening. The first one I kind of felt was still in play and working in my favor, I just needed to wait a little while longer to truly know. The second, the one that dealt with my heart, I was sure I'd failed at

---

204. Utterly...totally...wacko.

accomplishing, pretty well up to the last second, when after I told Sue-Ann what my *zaide* thought, she walked back into the bar. But not, however, before angling her head and throwing me a look with those eyes and in that way which was hers alone, then flashing the smile that showed off the dimples and blowing me a kiss, which gave me hope that I'd one day soon accomplish that goal, too.

16

The silence was like none I'd ever experienced during the many heavies with my mother throughout my life. It wasn't simply that there was a pause in our conversation. When she heard about my visit to the cemetery, breakfast immediately flipped to suck. Like most of me, I don't know the rationale that led to my random reach-out to say that I was coming over. Not that she minded, of course, and since I'm describing, the freshly brewed coffee and French toast when I arrived were heavenly...while it lasted. Shit, sorry. That's not true, regarding me.

Actually, I was hung up on Sue-Ann and not so far from beside myself that a few days had passed since I'd attempted to win her back at the Laughing Labia, and it had been radio-silent ever since. So, I turned to my mother. I couldn't avoid it, the cemetery, I mean, and I've never hidden anything from her besides. After we'd finished with chit-chat over her enthusiasm for the play's opening night, as well as Faygen's big legal win against the douchebag, I had to come clean. Truthfully, it had weighed on me, and I'd wanted to share, despite the fact that I knew it would be *tzures*.[205] It didn't start off all that badly, what with my mother almost giddy when she heard that I'd visited her parents for the first time in over two decades. It's my description of the route I took to get there, however, that led to wine replacing coffee, cigarettes instead of berries, and the deafening silence before the conversation turned to the supposed crisis state of my mental health.

"It's time," my mother said solemnly after lighting up a cigarette, then stood facing me while leaning her back against the stove, arms folded as I sat on a stool at the island in the middle of her kitchen.

"For what?" I asked, and lit one up myself.

"To stop the experiment and get back on your medication."

"No. Next," I said despondently.

"You can't do it, Izzy," she replied somberly, like she was giving up on my behalf. "You're not gonna make it," she added, which I could quickly sense was coming from a place of genuine fear.

"Says who?" I continued defiantly.

---

205. Problems.

She didn't bother dignifying with a reply but shot me a look from a similar place instead.

"I tell you a fanciful story about how I got to the cemetery," I continued, "and you just go to 'it's time?'"

"I didn't say that."

"So, then you don't trust me?"

"I didn't say that either," she said forcefully.

"Yeah, kinda," I shot back. "How about, 'wow Izzy, what a vivid imagination you have! My talented son, the writer! What an amazing story. I'm so proud of you!' But no, it right away goes to my crazy."

"Stop it, you're exaggerating."

"So are you."

"You're not listening to what I'm saying," she pleaded.

"I am listening, and *you're* not hearing that I don't agree with you."

"We don't have to talk again about why you experimented this time," she said, taking a different direction. "But it's gone far past that now."

"And what Rubicon's been crossed?" I asked, with no small amount of sarcasm that didn't go over well. "Please, enlighten me."

"Watch it," she admonished me. "We share openly, but I'm still your mother."

"Sorry," I said, wincing because she was right. "You said it's gone far past my sexual dysfunction."

"Izzy, honestly!"

"You didn't say it, but that's what you said."

Again, she didn't bother dignifying with a reply, but shot me a look of immense displeasure instead.

"Faygen and I have watched and said nothing because we love you and want to support you. But with each episode, you're getting worse, and now you're..."

"I'm what?"

"You said it yourself just a few days ago on the computer," she said, pouring herself another glass and lighting up another cigarette. "You told me that you were losing control of your mind."

"Uh, yeah! That's because I'm stressed out of my mind with this fucking play that's gonna be a fucking disaster!"

"That's not what happened, and you know it," she said, inhaling deeply before blowing a cloud of frustration toward the ceiling.

"And Faygen telling me that I'm exactly where I need to be isn't what happened either?" I replied defensively.

"He was trying to be supportive," she countered.

"Fuck, no! You can't have it both ways, Ma!" I shouted at her. "You can't tell me I'm fine one day, and the next tell me I'm crazy."

"Stop saying that!" she shot back at equal volume. "You're scaring me."

"I swear all the fucking time," I replied, ratcheting things up even more. "That might make me an asshole, but it doesn't make me crazy."

"You're not crazy, Izzy!" she scolded me. "You have a legitimate, genetically predisposed health problem. *We* have a problem," she added, and moved her hand violently back and forth between us like it was at all necessary to emphasize in whose womb it all got inherited. "And our medications keep us safe and protected," she added.

"From what, our true selves?" I scoffed, and thought it well not to get into the weeds as to why I fundamentally disagreed with her use of the negative descriptor of our supposed inherited mental, shall we say, condition.

"No, Izzy, from dying!" she said, landing one punch. "From killing ourselves!" she added, landing another. "From hurting the ones we love!" she continued, completing the flurry. "We've discussed this over and over again. If you can't see it anymore, that's reason enough to return to the medication." It was stark, and it naturally caused the two of us to stop for a few moments to take a breath before she continued. "I take my medication not just for me, Izzy," she said calmly. "I take it for you, and I'm begging you to start doing the same again."

But what about my journey, Ma? That's what I wanted to say, but it seemed pointless, given where she'd taken the conversation. Don't think that it didn't have an impact. She's my mother after all, and by the end of it, I honestly didn't know if everything she was saying wasn't, in fact, the truth. Was I so far gone that I couldn't see what she saw anymore? Was I so dangerously close to losing my mind that I was on the edge of doing something dreadful to myself and others? I thought about telling her what I said to Sue-Ann, that my *zaide* told me that I was okay. But given what had just transpired, I feared she would find nothing to be proud of in that statement.

I began to worry that maybe Sue-Ann was only humoring me, and that once we'd left each other in the alley of the Bushy Pussy, she actually thought to herself precisely the same things my mother was now verbalizing out loud, which Sue-Ann herself said to me outside her dad's place when she indelicately told me that I needed help. I didn't know what was true anymore, and I didn't want to start into that with my mother because it would just strengthen her argument that my not knowing was a clear sign. Between you and me, I hoped that if maybe Sue-Ann would come back and the play happened, things would work themselves out, and this conversation my mother and I were now having, if it could take place then, it might be totally different. This topic might not even have come up!

That's the thing with the condition we have, right? You just don't know what you don't know, and it comes down to who you trust more: Is it your gut, which could lead you off the deep end, or the whitecoats who can very easily scribble something on a pad of paper to take to your pharmacy, but do they really know what's in your gut, if you know what I mean? Anyway, I needed my mother's advice on what else to do about Sue-Ann. I didn't know how to segue to the topic, as I was worried that the first thing she'd say to me would be something patronizing, along the lines of "maybe if you were on your medication, you'd be in a much better position to secure her return." Nope, instead, she quoted lines from the play.

"What must be done, will be done," she said.

"What did you just say?" I asked her, gobsmacked that she spoke the exact lines that the *Miropoler Rebbe* speaks after the trial.

"*Que sera, sera,*" she said and looked at me askance like it wasn't the biggest deal and began to channel Doris Day while approaching before giving her fucked-up son a hug and kissing me all over.

It isn't what she said. I swear it isn't.

―――――――

"Sender," Khatzkl began to address the actor playing Reb Sender at the next rehearsal, picking things up from where we'd left off at the end of the trial scene. "The time we have given to the *dybbuk* has nearly expired," he continued while towering above Sender, who sat motionless in his chair, still reeling from what had just transpired between himself and the spirit of his erstwhile friend from the better world. "As soon as he abandons the body of your daughter, you must immediately lead her beneath the canopy. That which must be done, will be done."

"I will do as you command," Sender replied, and exited the stage with Sam, who was playing the part of the *Rebbe*'s assistant, Mikhoel.

"Did you notice the deceased did not accept the verdict?"Joseph read aloud in English the next line spoken by Reb Shimshon because Faygen was still absent, despite his trial having ended; something about "just because it's over doesn't mean it's over" or an excuse thereabouts was what he gave, Anyway, it was meaningless to me, as we were in the last few days before opening, he was still stuck in the office and my stage manager was calling out lines into a microphone that was feeding back something awful.

"Thank you!" I shouted back at him from my perch at the foot of the stage and made with my hand across my throat that the confounding noise could stop at any time.

"We did," two of the actors on stage said in response to Reb Shimshon's line about the *Rebbe*, who was now removing his *tallis*[206] and *tefillin*[207] and rightfully not looking so good.

"I got this one!" I yelled over my shoulder to Joseph, and said Reb Shimshon's next line aloud in Yiddish to the men on stage: "That's a very bad omen. Look at how disturbed the *Rebbe* is. His hands are trembling." Although Khatzkl was doing a bang-up job acting the part of someone reacting with trepidation to the perilousness of the moment, when worlds were colliding as the play reached its denouement, I was only slightly less jittery. Apparently, there's a concept in the theatre known as "giving it up." Forgive me, I don't know its etymology, and I never really studied its history, so it could be *bobe mayses*. I remember during my time with Luba learning that after all the hard work we've put into a play, fate is out of our control. A presenting artist can only give it up, literally handing it to the audience — maybe even the gods.

As the hours ticked away in our final week before curtain, this concept came to the forefront of my mind as I began to reconcile myself to the reality that time was up, the fate of play was out of my hands, and we were just fucked. I know what you're thinking, like my mother with the "enough already with the fucking," but I'm not exaggerating. Among the myriad, the *batlonim* were shit and weren't gonna get better; the Beggar's Dance showcasing the *nokhshelppers* was definitely not going to

206. Prayer shawl.
207. Phylacteries.

go down in the annals of the play's history as one of its more remarkable interpretations. It was "tech week," another theatre term that, suffice to say, means you literally give it up to the technical team so that they can take whatever mess you've made and put it together into something presentable to an audience. The point is, the cake you've baked is effectively made, so we'd just run out of time in our case. And yes, the not-so-small matter of Sue-Ann still not having returned wasn't a good omen either.

"Lord of the universe," Khatzkl continued, eyes gazing heavenward, "may that which must be done, be done!" He then turned to Sam, who'd returned to the stage and told him to "bring in the maiden!"

Right, so the idea of giving it up is all good in theory. In practice, however, *you* try telling that to a company full of anxious amateur actors, who knew how much time was left on the clock until the opening, if not the complete shut-down of the theatre. Moreover, the person they were used to seeing pull rabbits out of hats repeatedly at this point in the proceedings had gone to live in the better world. To say nothing of the fact, by the way, that on this day, I had to tell the actors on stage to stop dead in their tracks because there was no maiden to be brought in, which meant that, once again, we were not going to be rehearsing the excommunication scene. Need I remind you that it had only been done once, on that day Sue-Ann was magnificent but left and never returned? "*Que sera, sera,*" my mother said to me over breakfast. Although she really had in mind Sue-Ann and me on a personal level, she nevertheless encouraged me to embrace the idea that if it's meant to be, on a broader level, it'll all work itself out. She added the Yiddish equivalent, which, if I translated for you, literally means that the slacks would be pressed flat, but you get the gist. It's all I could hold onto, as I couldn't rightfully keep telling the company that Sue-Ann was gonna show when, with each passing day, she just didn't.

That is, until she did, when on the eve of opening night, she walked into the theatre just at the point when we were about to start the cue to cue from the top of Act One—that's theatre tech talk, *nisht vikhtik*[208]—and a collective gasp went up in the room in response to the *deus ex machina* that was the return of Leah.

---

208. Not important.

"I needed to learn the ending," Sue-Ann said to me just slightly tongue-in-cheek when, after everyone and their mother ran to welcome her back, I finally got my moment to do the same and asked her, kinda similarly, if it was really necessary to take years off everyone's lives by waiting 'till the eleventh hour to make her comeback.

"We've never done it," I told her, then asked if she was game to jump right in and have us do it together alone.

"Sure," she answered sprightly and, as much as I was delighted to hear the cheerfulness in her voice, if not to see the spring in her step as she walked in, for the life of me I couldn't place where the confidence was coming from, given the circumstances. Nevertheless, if it would serve all of us well as we took advantage of the precious few hours we had left before people would see our work, the delving was for another time.

"All right, then," I said to her happily, then turned to Joseph to give him my instruction. "Give us the room for a little while," I told him, saying the company could take a break. "When we're done, we'll run it from the top," I added, and indeed, after Sue-Ann and I had spent some time together alone on stage working out the final scene of the play, when the company returned a short time later, we ran it from the top over and over again through until the wee hours of the morning, just as Luba would have done.

―――――――――――

"Nice of you to finally show up," I said to Faygen a few hours later when he walked into the theatre and found me asleep in the front row, where I guess I must have collapsed from whenever it was that Joseph looked at me and said that we were done with rehearsing.

"I have something to show you," he said excitedly after helping me up from my slumber, and attempted to hand me an envelope.

"Not now," I replied to him curtly and, after a yawn and a stretch, gladly took the cup of coffee he had in his other hand, which I just supposed Joseph knew to give him when he walked in to get caught up on all that he'd missed out on.

"But you really need to see what's inside," he said enthusiastically.

"I know what it says," I told him, and proceeded to get onto the set.

"How can you know when you won't even read it?" he asked, dumbfounded.

"Trust me," I said. "Now, would you get your ass up here so I can walk through what I'm hoping will be *you* not making a fool out of me in a few hours?"

"All right, all right," he replied, and joined me.

"Don't do it!" I said to him when we were standing together, and he looked at me like he always does just before he inquires about my well-being.

"What?" he asked, feigning innocence.

"You're gonna ask me if I'm okay."

"Why would I do that?"

"Because that's what you always do"

"Are you okay?"

"Fuck, Faygen, we have an audience in a few hours. What do you think?" I snapped at him.

"Well, maybe if you read what's inside the envelope, it'll make you feel a whole lot better," he said.

"You can read it aloud for the entire cast later," I told him, and insisted that we needed to take the time to get him up to speed.

"Whatever you say, Mr. Director," he said in a way that was tinged with pride.

"Good, let's just walk it through from the top," I said, and started toward the position our two characters take up at the beginning of the play. "Oh, congrats, by the way," I added, and offered him a high-five before we dove in, and rather than reciprocate, he chose to hug me instead.

In case you're wondering, I didn't go home that day. Not to rest, change clothes, or find something nice for the opening night reception, none of it. I knew the nerves wouldn't be kept at bay, and I'd likely spend the whole time on the toilet. So, I chose to stay in the theatre. Literally, I didn't leave for a second, and it occurred to me that Luba might have done the same, a thought that gave me solace. I don't know for sure, of course, but I say it with some level of confidence because if she was aware that someone was still working in the theatre to perfect the work of art that would have her name on it, she would be by their side. So, whether anything poetic ought to be ascribed, I leave it for others to determine. Still, after Faygen left, I remained in the theatre, where I sat in the front row and watched as the set designer, Mack, dressed in a jumpsuit riddled with paint, worked furiously to add some finishing touches to his work of art.

It was a tradition he began with Luba a lifetime prior, a fact that he shared with me as we sat together only minutes from the theatre needing to be vacated so that it could be cleaned in time to let the audience in. As nervous as he was, he told me that what really gave him goosebumps was that no director ever sat with him while he did the last-minute work that he himself described as insane. No one, that is but Luba, which meant the world to him. He didn't ask why I decided to do likewise, but it moved him to the point of describing how poetic the moment was; that he didn't know for sure but was pretty sure that Luba would have been so proud to know that I did what she would have and led, even in the quietest moments when no one was watching. With that in my ear, I had the inspiration for the words I would speak to the cast when we gathered a short while later, just before Joseph called for us to take our places for the top of the show.

"I'm not the one who should be standing here," I said to the company of actors, as we assembled outside our dressing rooms, everyone costumed-up, only minutes away from premiering the play of all plays in the Yiddish theatre canon. "It's Luba who should be making a speech. I just wanted to say thank you," I told them, and then added that, having thought about it all day while sitting in the theatre, rather than do the curtain call bows as we rehearsed them the previous night, it would be more fitting that as a repertory company, where there were no stars and in this case in particular the star was the play, we'd all just form a line when the lights came up, take a bow off my cue, and that would be that. As it turns out, Faygen was standing next to me and knew better, as always, than to let me get away with the perfunctory, because for some strange reason he just knows what's swimming in my head and could divine that there was more I wasn't saying.

To that end, when I said thank you one more time to a smattering of applause and tried to take a step backward, he brought everything full circle and just like he did at the meet-and-greet, when he pushed me into the spotlight to introduce myself to Luba's family and tell them what I knew about the play, I once again felt his hand against my back, gently pushing me forward so that I would be standing in the center of the circle formed by Luba's company of actors.

Fucking Faygen.

"I'm sorry," I whispered, and then the words didn't come so swiftly because as I looked around the room at the faces of the ensemble staring back at me, the men and women who as professionals by day and amateur actors by night formed the bedrock upon which Luba built her *sui generis* theatrical company, all of whom seemed eager to hear what I was going to say, I began to well up. As I found myself again staring down at my feet, I could feel my lips quivering and the tears rolling down my cheeks as the impact of where we had arrived began to take hold. Not just concerning the short journey that was our production timeline, itself a minor miracle, of course. But rather in the arc of Jewish history in general and Yiddish civilization in particular, where the mere fact that in the twenty-first century, a Yiddish theatre company was presenting *The Dybbuk...in Yiddish*, was a victory against all of the odds saying that it was an impossibility.

"When I first met you all," I eventually began to whisper, "I told you that *The Dybbuk* isn't just a play. It's a mission statement." Heads nodded in agreement. "But I also told you that it was more than a mission statement," I continued, and I could hear some voices confirming that that's what I said. "It's our *yerushe*," I said. As I thought about what it means not only to bear the weight of legacy on one's shoulders but to take on the responsibility to act, regardless of the consequences, to ensure its survival, I cried even more, and had to stop because there was something else bubbling up apropos that was about to come out.

"You also said that it was *hadras koydesh*," I could hear Nokhem's voice call out, and the company all repeated his words. "*Hadras koydesh!*" they shouted in unison, "*Hadras koydesh!*" they kept repeating, cheering enthusiastically that the play was the embodiment of "the splendor of holiness."

"There was something else you said that day," Faygen added as he came up to me, and once again, put his arm around my waist and motioned for everyone to quiet down again. "You told us that when Ansky died, the Vilna Troupe pledged to present the premiere of his play on the *shloyshim*," he said, about the end of the period, literally the thirtieth day, following the burial of an individual other than a parent, when in Judaism one is considered to be in mourning.

A collective gasp suddenly went up in the room.

317

"Today marks Luba's *shloyshim*," he added with a smile. I could hear people starting to whisper to one another that, in fact, it was at Luba's *shiva*, the ceremony in her honor, when formally or otherwise, a communal pledge was made to deliver for Luba what the Vilna Troupe actors did for An-sky and I was leading them in doing it.

"You did it, *yingele*," Faygen whispered in my ear, and kissed me on the forehead.

"We all did," I replied to him softly. "You have the letter?" I whispered back to him.

"Right here," he said, pulling the envelope from the breast pocket of his coat.

"Read it to them," I said to him, but instead, he handed it to me and insisted that it was my voice that needed to announce the news.

"I know we've all been nervous," I said to them as I took the letter out of the envelope and scanned it briefly just to make sure what I knew in my head and my heart was, in fact, written on the page. It was. "Not only about the play, but also anxious and fearful about the fate of our theatre," I added. Then, as I looked at Sue-Ann, who had been standing opposite me the whole time and was herself being held around the waist by one of the actresses while wiping tears from her eyes, I held the paper up high. "We have nothing to be afraid of anymore," I said to them in full voice, projecting it so that the world could hear: "I have in my hand a letter written by the chairman of the board of the JCC..."—the douchebag, for those keeping score—"... promising to not only keep Luba's theatre open but to personally endow it in perpetuity!"

There was, of course, more to it, but that's all they needed to hear. You can imagine the decibel level reached in the room a half second after the collective gasp, as everyone began embracing one another, and I was a lucky beneficiary of quite a few. "For Luba, *khevre*! Let's do it for Luba!" I shouted out, and my words echoed throughout the company. "For Luba!" they shouted. "For Luba!"

"Places, everybody!" Joseph then ran into the room and yelled out excitedly as the audience had settled into the theatre, and the time had arrived for us to march backstage.

"How did you know?" Faygen asked me about the letter as we all began to disperse, and he and I made our way upstairs to the theatre.

"Call it a hunch," I said to him with a wink.

"Right," he said, disbelieving. "We'll talk."

"Yup," I said as we continued up the stairs and into the darkness of the backstage area, where the sound of the waiting audience seemingly grew louder with each step we took, bringing us closer to the stage. Backstage darkness, which, if you've ever done this kind of thing in your life, you'll believe me when I say, is legit *khoyshekh*,[209] so much so that it's kind of hard to see the feet in front of you, let alone anybody else, which explains how I unwittingly smashed into Sam who rather than moving forward, was busy taking three steps backward.

"What the fuck are you doing?" he said after I grabbed him by the arm and joined him.

"Gonna pray for a miracle, you?" I answered him, and then stopped myself. "Wait a second, did you just say fuck?"

"Yes, you say it all the time. It's an important word to know, yes?" he asked me, and in the darkness, I couldn't make out what his facial expression was like, but I could guess what mine looked like.

"Yeah, we'll talk. Don't forget, *birkas bineh,*" I said, leaving the praying to Sam, and despite the darkness, moved forward a little more quickly toward the wings because as the sound of the audience now began to dissipate, eventually being replaced by a plangent, haunting drone, which is the first audio cue that sets the somber mood of the play, there was one more thing I needed to do before the lights went up.

"Hey, you," I whispered to Sue-Ann after making my way through the wall of actors gathered in the darkness, waiting to go on stage. "I didn't get a chance to say break a leg. I'm sorry," I added, and when I took her hand in mine and felt it cold and trembling, I instinctively pressed it to my heart. "You're gonna be great, we're gonna be great," I said to her, and despite the darkness I chose to believe that she was smiling. All we could do was share a quick hug because Nokhem had by now walked onto the stage and the lights were up. Although the play now began with him delivering the monologue Luba never wanted him to have in the first place—the prologue that sets the stage for the story of *The Dybbuk*—for the first time that I could recall throughout the whole process, he was right on the money.

I'll spare you the blow-by-blow of how it all went down, other than to say that it was dark again the next time Sue-Ann and I found ourselves alone together, we were acting out the play's last scene. I say alone, but it

---

209. Darkness.

was actually in the company of a few hundred other people, who I'm guessing we're just as curious as I was to see how it was all gonna work out. Between you and me, in the lead-up to that moment, although I could recount for you every beat of the play as I observed it unfolding all around me in real time, I'd be lying if I didn't tell you that my heart was in my throat from the moment I walked on stage. That's not only because I had no idea if the play would come off, but my mind also never wavered from the thought that, despite what Sue-Ann and I had worked on the night before, I didn't know how the whole thing was going to end. I mean, of course, I *knew*. I just didn't know if what we'd concocted would actually come off as theatre. Bookends, right? If you ain't got 'em...Anyway, the thought of it all as it washed over me while I stood alone backstage almost caused me to miss my cue, when from the middle of the spotlight shining down on her at the center of the stage, Sue-Ann called out to me: "Who's sighing like that?"

"It is I," I soon replied, my voice resonating over the P.A. system and throughout the theatre.

"I hear your voice," she called out, "but I don't see you."

"You are fenced off from me by an invincible wall, an enchanted circle," I responded. I walked to the stage through the darkness and, within ten steps, emerged in the spotlight facing Sue-Ann, but just far enough away to accurately represent Khonen's words.

"Your voice sounds sweet as a violin moaning on a silent night. Tell me. Who are you?" she asked me, and as she did, I took a step to my left and slowly began to circle her.

"I have forgotten," I replied, and as I started moving around her, although my focus was on the words that needed to be spoken, my heart was pounding against my chest. But it wasn't the nerves that were right for the moment. And, for a change, it wasn't something I felt fearful of because I recognized that it was raw and pure emotion. A reflection, perhaps, not only of my profound appreciation of what she was delivering, but what she had done on stage up to this moment that proved what Luba instinctively knew about this incredible young woman from the moment she met her. No, it was...Fuck, I can't write it. I just did, and it was juvenile. Sorry, but you know what I'm talking about. Meanwhile, I continued my reply: "Only through your thoughts can I remember who I am."

"I'm beginning to remember," she said."My heart was drawn toward a radiant star. On silent nights, I shed sweet tears, and there was always a blurred figure in my dreams. Was that you?"

"Yes," I said to her as I completed my first pass around, and looked her dead in the eyes before uttering my following line breathlessly. "I."

"I remember you," she continued, and I began to circle again, this time a little closer to her. "You had soft hair," she said, the tone of her voice beginning to mirror that of mine, "as though touched by dew, and gentle, melancholy eyes. You had long, slender fingers," she added, and when she did, although it hadn't been something we rehearsed, she extended her hand towards mine but precisely so that they wouldn't touch. "Awake or asleep, I thought only of you."

"But you abandoned me..." she continued. At that point, I stopped, and we were now back-to-back, distanced only by a space meant to represent the mystical barrier separating the two characters in the play who are predestined for one another. "...And the light in me was dimmed," she went on, "and my soul was overcast. Like a forsaken widow was I, so that an unfamiliar man approached me. And then you returned, and in my heart, there blossomed a life formed of death and joy formed of mourning. Why did you forsake me again?"

"I demolished all barriers and rose above death," I said, and as I began moving again, I purposely approached closely, and in doing so, I could feel the heat emanating from her body, through the sheer wedding gown she was wearing. "I defied the laws of time and ages," I whispered into her ear, then completed my circle before immediately starting my next. "I struggled with the powerful," I said, my voice rising now, "with the mighty and merciless," and it rose even higher. But then, as I approached her opposite side, I brought the volume down so that the following words I spoke were whispered softly into her other ear: "And when the last spark of my strength was drained..." I said as I turned behind her, wrapping my arm around her waist and bringing my body up against hers, "... I left your body to return to your soul."

"Come back to me, my bridegroom, my husband," she said as she pressed my arm into her body while letting her head fall back gently, and rested it against my shoulder as her other arm wrapped itself gently around my neck. "I will carry you, in death, in my heart. And in the dreams of night, we will both rock our unborn children. We will sew them little shirts to wear. We will sing them lullabies." And as she began to speak her next lines, we both started to sway back and forth in unison:

Hush, hush little ones...
Without cradle, without clothes.
Dead you are and still unborn
Timeless and forever lost.

When she finished, the next audio cue was heard, the sound of a wedding marching band. It was also the cue for me to disappear, which I did.

"They are coming to take me to my wedding to a stranger!" Sue-Ann yelled out in desperation as she turned around and saw that I was gone. "Come to me, my bridegroom!"

"I have left your body but will come to your soul!" I shouted from backstage, and my voice could again be heard over the P.A. system, reverberating throughout the theatre.

"The barriers of the circle are broken!" Sue-Ann then exclaimed ecstatically after she looked up to the back of the stage, where she could see a large shadow meant to represent Khonen being projected on the wall. "I see you again, my bridegroom. Come to me!"

"I am coming to you!" I replied.

"A great light is streaming all around me," Sue Ann exclaimed in ecstasy while twirling around in the spotlight on stage as it began to shrink quickly around her. "I am bound to you forever, my destiny. Together we will soar higher, higher, and higher," she finished saying before falling to the floor, the spotlight closing on her to symbolize the expiration of a life.

The plangent, haunting sound that presaged the beginning of the play could now be heard again as the company returned to the stage, led by the *Miropoler Rebbe*, where they found Leah lying dead on the floor.

"We're too late," Khatzkl said, before the *meshulakh* speaks the final lines of the play: "*Borukh dayan ha'emes.*" Blessed be the true judge.

The deep, resonant sound now grew so much louder that it felt like the walls of the theatre were beginning to shake from an otherworldly force that had occupied the space and was on the verge of departing. It was then, in the complete and utter darkness that had now overtaken the stage, that the theme of the play, the *makhmes vos*, could be heard:

> Wherefore, Oh Wherefore
> Has the soul fallen
> From exalted heights,
> To profoundest depths.
> Within itself, the fall
> Contains the ascension

It was eerily silent as I then quickly walked back onto the stage through the darkness, to where I knew Sue-Ann was lying on the ground, arms extended like we rehearsed, waiting for me to lift her up.

As the lights went on again for the curtain call, it was still silent, as if the audience was processing what had just transpired. And I don't know how we got it right, but as a company, we were standing in a dead straight line on stage. Only once we started to bow, off my cue as planned, the audience erupted in applause. It continued as we bowed again. It grew louder as we did another time, then another until we stopped and stood as the sound grew and grew. It was at that moment when I could feel my hand being squeezed, and when I turned to my right, I could see Sue-Ann smiling, crying, and laughing all at once. I was probably doing the same. She then released herself from my grasp to take my face in both her hands and after staring at me for a moment, she closed her eyes, pressed her lips to mine, and kissed me deeply. "You're my everything," she sighed before opening her eyes. She looked at me longingly and repeated the words: "You're *my* everything."

It was awkward, to be sure. Not the kiss, I mean. That was fantastic. I'm referring to the fact that the audience didn't let up, and the company didn't know what to do. I guess at this point in the proceedings, you just wing it and soak in the moment for what it is. With that in mind, I retook Sue-Ann's hand in my right one, Khatzkl's, who was standing to the other side of me, in my left and led the company in more bows. This time, however, unlike the first time around, Joseph called for the house lights to be brought up, which allowed us to join the audience in a communal moment that truly is the magic of live theatre. What he did wasn't planned. I guess he just knew to do it.

By doing so, I could now see my mother before me in the first row, who was crying while leading the standing ovation. In the row behind her, my Uncle Hank, my cousin Manny, and their broods. In the row behind them were the douchebag and the woman I guess was Sue-Ann's mom, though who knows.

And behind them, what seemingly stretched out before me, were six million rows of people, a blur of faces I didn't recognize, but who I felt I knew intimately and whose presence meant the world to me. And believe it or not, behind all of them, I could clearly make out Luba, who was standing, applauding, and yelling out, "Bravo!" Next to her, An-sky was doing the same. Next to him were my *bubbe* and *zaide*. And for some reason, next to them sat the Golden Peacock, who was finally fucking silent.

THE END

ACKNOWLEDGEMENTS

This novel couldn't have come to fruition without family, friends and colleagues who reviewed drafts of the manuscript in its various stages, offered support in a myriad of ways and whose generosity, wisdom, experience, knowledge and encouragement sustained me along the way.

Numerous books and other material were consulted in advance of writing this manuscript. I would specifically like to mention "The Faith of Secular Jews", edited with an introduction by Saul L. Goodman; as well as "Wandering Soul-The Dybbuk's Creator, S. An-sky", by Gabriela Safran and "The Worlds of S. An-sky: A Russian Jewish Intellectual at the Turn of the Century", edited by Gabriella Safran and Steven J. Zipperstein, for their in-depth dealings with S. An-sky, his life and surroundings, as well as his play, *The Dybbuk*.

Finally, my sincere gratitude for the following permissions: *The Dybbuk* production scripts (1998 & 2014), courtesy of The Dora Wasserman Yiddish Theatre Archives of the Segal Centre Performing Arts, Montreal, Canada; translations of poems by Itzik Manger (*Di goldene pave*, "The Golden Peacock") and Avrom Sutskever (*Ver vet blaybn*, "Who will remain"), courtesy of Anna Fishman Gonshor